Earth Fire

LEGACIES *of the* DRAGON
BOOK 1

ALLYN RANSOM

outskirts
press

*This book is dedicated
to the people without whom it could never have been written:*

*Allen Keil, who gave me the time
Jerry Jenkins, who challenged me
Martin Luther King, Jr. and Shelby Steele, whose books inspired me
And to the friends, Fantasy Tribe, Rogues, Realmies,
55 Plus Writers, and sundry others who gave me their encouragement*

*This book is dedicated
to the people without whom it could never have been written:*

*Allen Keil, who gave me the time
Jerry Jenkins, who challenged me
Martin Luther King, Jr. and Shelby Steele, whose books inspired me
And to the friends, Fantasy Tribe, Rogues, Realmies,
55 Plus Writers, and sundry others who gave me their encouragement*

Chapter One

Divhad, 18 Troleng 153, Jitherick

*S*o many houses and people steal all the good air. Zheann hugged her basket and filled her lungs with the aromas of lemon balm, fennel, faram, mint, and rue that rose from it. She inhaled again and resisted the urge to sigh. *Cool air and herbs. Warm air and herbs. Any air and herbs. How do people live without them?*

She couldn't bring herself to smother her grin. *It's a lovely day. If the shop isn't busy this afternoon, we can plant some winter crops. Even if it is, we can bake apples. Dren and I can take some to the neighbors, and the smell will put others in a mood to buy. But first, the lesson. Mistress Jenem's demonstration of carminatives and bitters is legendary. No, Mistress Jenem is legendary. I hope I make as good an impression.*

She walked through gates flanked with blue-white dragons that peeked through chalk and paint, and turned away from the counterfeit carnage on the armory's torch-lit field and the dark-haired Med who stood dreaming of the glories of war and watching men practice killing one another. Torches also lit the first market street cast in shadows for most of the day by walls and buildings.

A cart stopped partway into the street squeezed traffic in both directions. The driver looked half-asleep as he waited for people to give him room to maneuver. Zheann raised her basket over her head to pass between the wagon and the corner of the canopied amulet booth. The scent of baked goods from a little further along the road made her mouth water. *It's worth braving the market maze. Fennel and dill bread, yum.* The scent lifted her spirits as she lowered her basket.

"Rys!" A black cloak billowed, knocking the basket from her hands as the Med wearing it wheeled his arms with wild drama. Zheann tried to catch the tumbling punnet and missed. She covered her mouth with both hands as the man toppled at the feet of two Med soldiers. Cheesecloth pouches of herbs littered the ground and the man. Laughter rolled out from the Med while Rys disappeared like smoke in a storm. A Rys woman at the door of a leather goods shop gave her a sympathetic look and closed the door. She stood watching with her hand on the bolt. The gathering Med smiled like wolves. One soldier lacked both front teeth, making his smile less menacing.

The fallen Med's warm brown hair and the puff of beard covering his trembling chin were neatly trimmed. She suspected his cloak and pants had been clean before he fell. A flash of orange showed at his throat. The basket landed on his soft belly and rolled to the dirt. For the blink of an eye, everything stopped.

I never touched you. You're more than twice my weight, and you expect us to believe I knocked you off your feet yet stayed on mine? Of course, you do. You're a mud. Congratulations, Zheann. You're providing this morning's entertainment. You walked right into it. Her cheeks blazed beneath her hands and the frozen moment melted.

"I'm sorry. I should have paid more attention to where I was going." She scooped up the basket, collected bags of herbs from his trouser legs and the ground, and dropped them in it. *Good thing I tied them in sacks. How would Papa have gotten out of this mess?*

He pointed at her as he looked at the soldiers. "She's trying to hex me."

I am not! And you know it. You all know it, but that's not what you'll tell a magistrate. She glanced at the soldiers. *Are you part of the game? Or are you stuck in your roles, too?*

"Hex you?" She heard herself say. "No sir, I would never try to hex you. It was the insect on your shoulder."

Zheann, her wiser self warned.

She collected a packet of herbs that had landed on his chest and plucked at the offending insect. "My mistake, it's a pill of wool."

Stop it.

"If you'd like, I know where you can buy an herb soap that will take the scent of manure out of your clothes."

"Give me that!" He sat up and snatched the basket, spilling packets anew. "I'll have you tried for assault. They hang witches for hexing honest folk." Chuckles rippled through the crowd.

"That may explain why no Rys has been hung in my lifetime."

Zheann, Stop it! Get the herbs and go!

"I'm sorry, sir. Are you flatulent or constipated? These herbs have little value otherwise. May I know your name? That way I can send a doctor to aid you. Or would you like to teach my students the magic associated with them?"

The fallen man shoved the basket away, his nose wrinkled, and his lip curled. The soldier with the missing teeth caught the handle and held it out to her. "Here, and tell Headmaster Turisba, I hope he's well."

Zheann forced a smile. "I will. Thank you, sir. I'm afraid my touch will cause this kind gentleman further distress. Will you help him? I don't want to have to explain to Headmaster Turisba why I'm late." She scooped bundles from the ground and swept around the man. The crowd parted, amusement and disappointment in contests on their faces.

She hurried into an alley between a cobbler's shop and a smithy. *You told the man you teach. Now he knows where to find you. Could you make things any worse? Papa would never have been caught like that. Was the guard warning me that he knows where I work, or was he warning the mud whose pet I am?*

"Zheann, you are your father's daughter." An old woman with white hair wrapped like a crown pushed herself from the wall. A moss green skirt peeked out beneath her brown cloak. She smiled as she walked to where Zheann had stopped.

Face flushing again, Zheann hugged her basket and willed herself to stop trembling. "Doesn't anyone ever get tired of telling me that? No, Mistress Jenem. When my father did things like that, I thought he being brave or even having fun. When I do them, I'm afraid, and I feel like a fool. Do you think he'll have me arrested?"

"And risk Headmaster Turisba's wrath?" Jenem's voice held a nibble of sarcasm. "I doubt Lord Roll-in-the-Dirt will want to humiliate himself further. If he had done it right, the soldiers would have arrested you on the spot. The fact that they didn't means he was too obvious, even for them." She pulled Zheann's basket toward herself and sniffed. "You're doing the flatulence lesson today?"

"I didn't have time to think of anything cleverer than the truth. It will intrigue the boys." *It did when you taught it to my class. How did you tolerate me?*

Jenem smirked. "And a few girls. You were quite adept, as I recall."

"I had the unfair advantage of being both my father's and my mother's daughter."

They waited at the end of the alley to let a group of Med women in garish dresses past. *Does she have any idea how ugly that dress is, or how ridiculous a woman her age looks in it? She looks like she's wearing fish scales! Don't stare, Zheann, you already have one Med angry with you.*

Jenem tucked her arm through Zheann's and pulled her closer

as they turned onto the street. Her voice became contemplative. "People tolerated your father's antics in part because he was clever, and because of your mother's social grace and skill with herbs. You own a good measure of his quick wit and magical tongue, and your mother's skill with herbs. It would be useful if someone in your household developed some of her social grace. Not that it, or much else would have saved you this morning."

Zheann sighed. *Not a very subtle transition, Mistress. So, you've heard about Fiwal's doorstep kisses.* She felt his lips against hers again, the weight of disapproval from her neighbors, and the heat of embarrassment as Med sniggered and whistled at them. *Is there anyone within a day's walk of Jitherick who hasn't heard about them? Troubles travel in troops.* They walked to the next street and crossed. "He says he wants to show everyone how proud he is of his wife."

The old woman chuckled. "Do you suppose he believes the rumors about you and the Little General?"

"What? Mistress Jenem, don't be ridiculous. I spoke to the Little General twice. Both times more than ten years ago. Fiwal has never mentioned Captain Moln. I think Fiwal just likes attention. If he's jealous of anyone, he's jealous of my father." Zheann fished in a pocket and pulled out a large pouch. "I need to drop this off at Leed's. Let's find out what tea he brewed this morning." She strode across the street and pushed on the heavy oak door. She pushed on it a second time before stepping back to check the windows and survey the road.

Next door, a man with sandy brown curls paid Tahke as he stood next to his carpentry table. The man's wife tilted her head one way, then another, admiring a maple cupboard. A Med woman wearing a burgundy dress with black lace overlay walked along shelves displaying his wares. She examined a decorative lamp. A few steps later, she put it on the shelf and picked up a small chest with intricate carving.

The broad-shouldered Rys kept his tone neutral. "My lady, ..."

"It is recompense." She swished past Zheann.

The man dropped more coins into Tahke's hand. He and his wife hurried away with their cabinet while Tahke watched the box disappear and pushed his fingers through dark beige blond waves.

After a moment, he noticed Zheann and smiled sadly. "Where's your cousin? I could use some tea."

"I wondered the same thing. Maybe he's delivering something. When he gets here, will you give him this?" She handed him the pouch and returned to Jenem's side. Darkness filled the windows both in and above the shop. *That's odd.*

Mistress Jenem retook her arm, and they continued toward the jideker. "Zheann, did your parents teach you 'Ye fen dernai efoim?'"

No one around them seemed to notice the old woman discussing magic on the streets. *Such audacity.* "The hex for courage? Yes, I use it often." *Though strangely, not this morning.*

"Do you know the other piece of it?"

"I didn't know there was another piece."

Jenem smirked. "There is always another piece. 'Ye fen dernai haloim.' It's for wisdom."

━━━━◉━━━━

She left Mistress Jenem at her classroom and backtracked to the Headmaster's office. She found him hanging his black cloak on a hook.

He gestured for her to enter and took his seat behind a massive table that seemed smaller with him sitting there. "What's wrong?"

Is it obvious? I suppose so, why would I come to see you if there was nothing wrong?

As she related the experience, his stern face reddened all the way to his steel-gray hair, and his eyes smoldered. She sat straighter, longing to shrink and hide behind her basket. "I'm sorry, Headmaster Turisba."

He waved her apology aside. "I will look into this further, Mistress Zheann. This isn't the first time a Rys teacher has blundered into a misunderstanding. Unfortunately, there are some who feel so oppressed they think their sole recourse is..." He peered at her from under dark, bushy eyebrows, "what you Rys call *muddy* behavior. I don't suppose you had the presence of mind to get his name."

Wincing, she shook her head. "I'm sorry, Headmaster Turisba, I didn't. Oh! But there was a Med soldier there, missing his front teeth. I suspect he may know the man's name. He said to tell you he hoped you are well."

The headmaster rose. "Yes, I know who you mean. I'll talk to him this morning if I can find him. Did the man who claims you hexed him mention anyone's name? A Medenva's? A Moln's? Mine?" His brown eyes held no amusement, but she'd never known him to smile.

"He was too busy reminding me that hexing honest citizens is a capital offense." She gripped her basket tighter and pulled her elbows closer in.

He stroked his dark gray beard, and an odd light appeared in his eyes. "As it should be. As it should be. I'll look into it. If I can find him, I'm sure we can resolve the situation with a reasoned discussion. Go burp your students."

"Yes, sir."

As she left the headmaster's office, footsteps echoed through the hall. She and a Med mistress passed and granted one another a grave nod. She slipped through the door to the old wing and sighed as it worked its proportional magic. The world once again shrank to a scale more to Rys needs. Here, she was an adult, albeit a short one. She took a deep breath. She stopped and looked at the door with wide eyes. *"Go burp..." Master Turisba told a joke. A joke! I didn't laugh.*

Can anything not go wrong today? She hurried along the hall. *If he can't talk Lord Roll-in-the-Dirt out of taking me to court, the magistrate will rule in his favor. It's that, or the soldiers will have to quell a riot. If it comes to that, what choice will Headmaster Turisba have but to dismiss me to avoid the scandal? Will the soldiers speak for me? Could they convince the judge to reduce the sentence to a fine or a beating? That will depend on who he is.*

<hr>

She entered her classroom and set the basket on her table. Setting aside all thoughts about the world outside, she distributed the bags of herbs around the U of tables. The children and the herbs were all that mattered. *Who shall I pick for my victim?* She sat at her table and waited as they filed in.

Nine eager darlings took their seats and watched her. Five less interested children fidgeted with the bags or chatted. One of three bored troublemakers nudged another and pointed out the window. Of the fourteen, three showed promise with herbal magic, including the lead troublemaker. *It's too soon to tell. Wait, you'll see. And remember, you were a troublemaker.* When the bell rang, she rose.

"Let's review. Why do we use magic on herbs?"

The class responded together. "To make them do more or less of what they do."

She moved to the front of her table and leaned against it. "What does that mean?" She let the silence drag.

After ten breaths, the lead troublemaker leaned back. She frowned at a lock of her straw-like hair. "It means making the herb do whatever it does more or less than it would without the magic."

"Can you give me an example?"

"My Mama gives us ginger when we're sick," a darling offered.

"Papa uses bright weed on our hair." The lead troublemaker turned her attention to whatever the other two were watching.

"And the danger of making something more or something less?"

"Making them too much or too little."

Not as many voices on that one. "So why do we study herbs as part of learning magic?"

A boy with light brown curls grinned. "Because it's easier to make something more than to make nothing more!"

"And herbs are everywhere," another darling added.

"Good, you've been listening. Today we are going to look at two kinds of herbs: bitters and carminatives. Can anyone tell me what they do?" *If you can, you can come work at the shop.*

One hand rose. "Do bitters make things taste bad?"

Don't smile. She pointed at the student. "Often, but that's not their purpose. Any more guesses?" *One, two, three, four, five.* "The purpose of bitters is to make what you've eaten go through your body more easily. Bitters unbind bowels."

Most of the boys and several girls giggled. One girl in front blushed like a ripening tomato.

I'm sorry, it's going to get worse. "Would anyone care to guess what carminatives do?"

"Make you pee more?" a troublemaker suggested, inspiring another round of giggles.

Zheann put a small cup before him, added water and a few leaves, and murmured over them. *Mothers and fathers of Jitherick, I apologize in advance for what is once again going to be loosed.* "Drink this."

He obeyed. After a few breaths, he gave an impressive belch, and he and his classmates burst out laughing.

Two soldiers ducked through the door with the crimson-faced Headmaster trailing after them. The laughter stopped. The taller soldier looked like the Med of her childhood imagination, tall and muscular with black hair and beard cropped short to better display his sneer. The shorter soldier seemed soft and friendly by comparison, but something in his eyes made her want to hide.

Here it comes. It doesn't look like he even had a chance to look for the soldier with the missing teeth. She placed herself between the soldiers and the children and lowered her voice. "Good morning, gentlemen."

The tall guard lifted his chin. "Mistress Zheann, Captain Moln wants to see you."

Lord Roll-in-the-Dirt involved the Little General? She suppressed a groan. "I've just begun class; can it wait until —"

"Now." His hand moved toward the truncheon on his belt.

Her cheeks burned. "Of course, let me get my cloak." Her students sat staring, confused and frightened as they watched her cross the room. "Use the time to study your notes." Her voice quavered, and her fingers developed a mind of their own. She swallowed. "Before you leave, please put the herbs back in my basket." Her stomach knotted. *You couldn't let bad-enough alone, could you? You had to humiliate him in front of guards.*

"Yes, Mistress," the students squeaked.

"Please," the tall soldier spoke through clenched teeth. His eyes challenged her to defy him further.

Please? Why are you pretending to be polite? "I'm sorry, Headmaster Turisba. I'll return as soon as I can." She tied the ribbons on her cloak as she walked toward the door. *This is...lunacy. He wasn't old or fat enough to be the King, or young enough to be one of his sons, and the guards would have attacked if he had been. He wasn't military. Who did I offend?*

Behind her, the troublemaker belched again.

⸺ ◦《◉》◦ ⸺

The tall soldier helped her mount a pony and threw her cloak's hood over her head. "Keep your hood up. The captain wants you to get there in one piece." He led the pony onto the shadowed dirt street that led to Leed's shop. Eight Med traveled the usually busy road for the first block.

A wagon and twice as many Med were in the next block. Two Rys rolled a cask out of a building next to the wagon. They looked at her with wide eyes. The Med standing on the cart slapped his leg. "Come on now, get the last one in. Stop wasting time." He pushed long, brown hair out of his face as he squinted at her. "Hey, Foden, what's going on?"

The tall soldier spat. "You'll have to ask Captain Moln. He's at the palace."

At the palace? Who did I offend?

"Is it going to interfere with dinner tomorrow night? She's been looking forward to it."

Foden kept the bay pony moving. "That's up to the captain."

When he saw her watching, he snapped at her. "Mind your own business."

She raised her hands, palms up. "That's all I've been trying to do since I woke this morning. My business is at the jideker."

"Your business is with Captain Moln." He tugged harder on the reins and clucked. The pony moved forward again.

Tahke watched them pass his shop. She pushed her hood back. He peered at her and his face hardened. He put his tools on the worktable and glanced at the dark windows next door before striding away.

Tell Mama and Fiwal. Where is Leed? Where is everyone? You'd think they would want to see the...oh. In the third block, where the road met the main street, a mob waited. Her heart pounded in her ears. *Don't they have work to do? Why are they in such a hurry? Is the prospect of hanging a Rys so exciting?* She shrank into her cloak. *I suppose so.*

The tall soldier hit her head, pushing the hood forward again. "Let it be. Don't make this more difficult."

More difficult for whom? Why should I take pity on you?

As they approached the crowd, Zheann focused on the pony's ears, so she wouldn't see fingers pointing or vindictive faces doling out judgment. Her cheeks flamed, cooled, and flamed higher. Beyond the crowd, the garrison's white stone wall loomed. They turned east onto the broad main avenue.

Someone behind her shouted, "What'd the Athenque-spawn do?"

Nothing! Zheann met the gaze of a woman with wide red eyes that narrowed as she watched. *She's afraid! Why would she be afraid?* Some Med craned their necks, trying to see in all directions. Others grimaced at her or spat. Some stared.

A blaze of anger swept over her. At the same time, a chill of fear ate at her, giving her the sense that the temperature was both rising and falling. *What is going on? The only time I ever see them like this is at the Victory of Herick celebration. Is a governor or something, visiting from somewhere? Is Lord Roll-in-the-Dirt a governor?*

The soldier, Foden, glowered as the pony tossed its head, white showing in its eye. He stroked its neck and made quiet noises but kept them moving forward.

"Why'd they close the gates?"

He lowered his head for several breaths. As he brought his head up, he rolled his shoulders. "You mean the king didn't take you into his confidence? Me, neither. When he wants us to know, he'll send someone to tell us. Right now, he wants to talk to this Rys. So, when he asks me what took me so long to get there, you want me to mention your name?" He tried to move forward, but the Med were everywhere. He bared his teeth.

What do you want me to do, hex them? What hex would let me ride away? Or hide? Even if I got out of Jitherick, how could I escape with Dren, Mama, Fiwal, and one pony?

Foden gave two shrill whistles. A moment later, soldiers ran toward them from the Armory, shoving those who didn't move quickly enough out of the way. "We're going to the palace," he shouted. They passed the pony and continued pushing the protesting Med aside.

Dreams of escape vanished. She stared ahead, no longer listening or looking. They pushed their way through the crowds, turning south for a block, then east again. A short distance away, an iron gate stretched across the broad avenue. The guard who opened the palace gate for them shoved a Med back and closed the gate.

The clang of metal on metal brought her mind awake. *Who is Lord Roll-in-the-Dirt?*

⸺⊶◉⊷⸺

Foden ushered her through the white halls of the palace and shoved her through a door, announcing, "Mistress Zheann."

As she moved from the lamp lit hall into the shadowed room, a pattern on the door caught her attention. Years of use had worn the carving, but enough remained to give the impression of a dragon. *Think about it later.*

Zheann took several steps into a room thick with stale air and a hint of ginger. *This is ridiculous. No one deserves this.* The only sources of light were lamps at the corners of a massive desk. Captain Moln leaned on the desk, his face hidden as he looked at two pieces of paper between his hands. A small tray with a teapot and mug waited within easy reach. The wall of shelves behind him hosted only a handful of books and a few knick-knacks. Heavy drapes hung over two windows that were twice her height. A cold fireplace nestled between them. Shrouds draped most of the furniture. The room had died a long, painful death some time ago. *Why is he here, in the dark?*

She took two more steps toward him on a thick rug. *Be calm,*

⸺ 13 ⸺

assured, casual. You've just stopped by for a visit. "Captain, the man is lying." *That sounded desperate, guilty, and strangled.* Her cheeks grew warm again and she waited, expecting him to look at her with his twisted smile.

His shoulders rose and fell at the measured pace of iron will. He inhaled noisily but exhaled without a sound.

"Captain Moln, are you all right?"

When he spoke, his voice was much lower and more ragged than she remembered it. Each word came out as a sentence. "King. Eswok. Has. Been. Assassinated."

Is this a sick joke? No, I've never heard of the Molns playing sick jokes. They kill Rys without a second thought but not as a game. This is all about killing Rys.

His hands on the desktop tightened into fists, and his shoulders tensed. "The general," his voice rasped, "was also poisoned."

Her heart plummeted as he raised his face toward hers. She searched the room, seeking anything to look at that was not him, willing his next words away. Her gaze returned to his. "I'm sorry," she told eyes filled with fury and fire. The twisted smile she had seen as a child had grown darker, more feral.

Here it comes. And now, we die.

"The assassin used magic."

"Are you... sure?" *Dumb question, but who would be stupid enough to kill the king using recognizable magic? When the Mud find out, they'll riot and slaughter us all. Why haven't they announced it? Why did they close the gate and try to hide it? Why are they waiting to light our funeral pyre?*

"Yes, I'm sure." He took a drink of tea, straightened, squared his shoulders. His eyes sang with ferocity. "Doctor Metris has confirmed it."

Troubles travel in troops, and this army leaves no survivors. She hugged her cloak in close. "Captain, why did you call me here? You can't think I did this horrible thing. Can you?"

"The doctor said it was an unidentified purgative."

Barberry or buckthorn bark, elderflower, goldenseal, mayapple, poke root, geperra, or soapwort. What does it matter?

He pointed at the papers. "There are nine herbal shops in Jitherick and the outer city. The family deals with three, including yours. We have four Rys doctors and two Med. The king's regular physician and his two pets are in Tup Odriet tending a matriarch as a favor to the king. I know you all steal plants from land that belongs to the king and the people."

Am I not one of the people to whom the land belongs? No, I'm a Rys, and one of us killed your king and hurt your father.

"Anyone with knowledge could do the same. I'm sure a fair number of Rys know basic purgative hexes. How many have enough expertise to use such a hex to kill?" He waited.

How am I supposed to know? Anyone who found a hex in some book no one has looked at since before Mistress Jenem was born. Anyone who made a mistake in a hex a year ago and is angry enough to use it. "What does it matter? We're all going to face execution."

He made a note. "Could you hex an object to poison someone by touch or inhalation, or would they have to consume it?"

"Captain, why are we playing this game?"

"Answer me!"

Zheann jumped and hugged her ribs. "I've never heard of a hex that would produce purgation in a person using an object. An elementalist could tell you better than I can. The assassin could also have put metals or metal salts in their food but that would still involve consumption. Inhalation is also possible but not likely."

He swallowed and glanced toward the teapot. "Eating metals? How?"

"One way involves suspending very fine metal particles in what's called a colloidal solution. Colloidal gold purifies the body, improves health, and eases the pain of aged joints." *How many could do that?*

Just pick a number. "There are at least forty elementalists in Jitherick who can do something like that." She took several steps toward the desk. "Captain, please. You know most Rys would not do this. Fewer than a hundred could. Is there something I can do to keep the Med from massacring the Rys?"

The feral look returned to his eyes. "You are going to help me find the Rys responsible."

Chapter Two

Divhad, 18 Troleng 153, Jitherick

Captain Moln punctuated his statements with knuckle-strikes on the desktop. "You will testify at his trial." Tap. "I want no claims of muddy justice when I punish him." Tap. "The sooner you find him; the fewer Rys will have to die." Tap.

Zheann trembled. *Does he think he can save any of us? Does he believe I am gullible?* "S-surely Doctor Metris —"

"He doesn't seem to have much imagination or inclination to look for the truth." He spat the words as if they were as bitter as hexed rue. "If he saves the general's life, that's good enough, but you're different. You once asked, 'What's this letter?' I told you to never speak to me again, and a year later, you thanked me for saving your mother."

He remembers? She sank into a shrouded chair. Dust swirled around her and with it, a faint scent of vinegar and something else. "You did."

His twisted grin flashed. "You became a mistress at the jideker. This morning, you made a fool of my neighbor. Those all took guts, brains, or luck. You'll dig, climb, and claw your way to the truth because it's what you do, and because you have incentives."

He knows? Her cheeks grew warm as her heart turned cold. "Incentives?"

"You have your parents' reputation and yours. You have students, and they have parents. You have your people, your shop, your mother, your husband, and your little girl, Dren. The faster we find the assassin or assassins, the more of them may survive."

Survive? What else can I say? "How are you going to save anyone, Captain? Lock us all in the palace for the rest of our lives? Do you think your family or the Medenvas can stop the Med from slaughtering every Rys? Or that they will even try? Do you think the Med will ever forgive, or forget?"

His eyes met hers. "You find the assassin and I'll do what I can."

"You know as well as I do that won't be enough."

He slapped the desktop with both hands. "Do you have a better idea?"

She stroked her already smooth skirt. Instead of a better idea, she remembered the warmth of a crackling fire and the chill cobblestone floor. She'd looked at her parents through her tears. "I think the Little General killed them!"

"Don't let them teach you to hate, Little Hedgehog, you promised." Papa had looked angry, as if she were betraying him.

Later, she'd stamped her foot. "They have to be stopped."

Mama had leaned forward "That's what the Sendres said and why the Med punished them."

"They didn't punish them, they killed them, and you helped them!"

Mama had looked hurt. "You're wrong, Zheann, I did not help them. I helped you."

She'd cringed. A cry had risen in her throat. She had forced it down and curled her hands into fists. *Useless, weak Rys fists, then and now.* "No." Her voice squeaked. "Neither of us can save my people. That's why it doesn't matter whether I help you or not. Unless the assassin is a Med, the Med will kill him because he's a Rys."

"You will do what you're told!" He leaned hard on the desk.

I'm sorry, Mama. I was wrong. I understand now, at least a little. Her shoulders drooped. "It won't be enough, but I'll do what I *can*."

A bed dominated the room to which he led her, and dwarfed the man lying in it. His dark mahogany hair was cut short and looked plastered to his head. Unlike his son, he was clean-shaven. His pale hand twitched on a faded blanket that had once boasted shocking colors in a pattern that would have made her eyes ache. Doctor Metris rose from a shrouded chair and hurried over with his arms outstretched. His watery blue eyes moved from the captain to her and back. "He's resting. We can talk in the hallway."

Zheann pushed past him. "What have you discovered about the magic or the medium used? Was it something he ate?"

"Not much, I'm afraid. Yes, he seems to have consumed something hexed, but he hasn't vomited since I arrived, so I can't guess what. He is responding well to my treatment. I expect a full recovery in a week or two. The king was older, less robust."

The captain's gaze was hard and along the bridge of his nose. "The king tended to eat two or three times what the general did. He often insisted the general eat something when they conferred. Food is a topic on which they rarely agreed."

She bent close to the general's face, wrinkling her nose at the cocktail of scents in his breath. She examined his hair, lips, tongue, and teeth, and opened each eye and peered into dilated pupils. She checked both hands, including his nails. *It doesn't look like it accumulated over time. No surprise there. The assassin wasn't trying to make it look like anything other than what it was. The general may have been a welcome bonus.* She pulled the blanket from the unconscious

Med and pressed his distended belly. As he groaned, she straightened. She walked around the bed to examine the herbs on a table next to the doctor's chair. She collected a handful of winter mint and two slivers of ginger root.

The doctor stared at her and frowned. "Whatever he ate put tremendous stress on his body, not only his stomach."

The captain leaned against the doorframe. "It also attacked their minds. They saw things that weren't there."

"You saw what happened?" *Poor man.*

"I was giving my morning's report." A spark lit in his eyes as his mouth twitched.

What's amusing about that?

"The king groaned, belched several times, rubbed his gut, and puked. His bowels loosened about the same time. The general rocked back and forth a few times, rose, drew his dagger, and cried, 'Magic!' He staggered sideways into a table and puked as he fell to his knees. They screamed in pain, raved at people who weren't there, had shaking fits, and retched."

"Any specific people?"

"The king mentioned his dead sister and Taelfa. The general either called his father or me. He swore at several people he thought he was fighting, but the names didn't sound Rys."

It wasn't enough for them to die. They had to die in agony and madness. Why didn't the killer strike in public, or during the festival? That would have ignited a firestorm of slaughter. Did he think this would not have the same ultimate result? "It looks like Doctor Metris is doing what General Moln needs. Where is the king?"

"Across the hall."

The shroud covering the corpse looked like a well-traveled patch-work hill. Five chairs circled the bed. *Which family members sat with him as he died? Was it an honor or a duty?* Zheann drew back the quilt and examined the cold body. She frowned. *Someone cleaned him. How am I supposed to learn anything?* She bent over him, repeating her examination. *Of course, they cleaned him. It would be cruel to ask him to marinate in his juices, even if he was dying, and cruel to the family to ask them to sit with him that way.* At some point in his suffering, he had bitten his tongue hard enough to leave a bloody trail across it. "Seeing it must have been terrible."

"Save your pity for the assassin. He'll need it far more than the king did. It was a masterful attack. Had it been on the Chornivian king, I would have admired it. There aren't many Rys I think capable of such bold hatred, daring, and powerful magic."

Oh? And now I list the valiant Rys capable of those qualities to prove we aren't as pathetic as you claim? I don't know any Rys stupid enough to use obvious magic to kill a Med but skilled enough to do it. How? Trickery? Bribery? Threats? "What makes you think the bold hatred or daring belonged to a Rys?"

"No Med would kill the king." His tone turned mocking, "And Med can't do magic."

"Really? None of your people is capable of such bold hatred or daring? No sons who believe they'll gain the throne? None of his women, even Queen Kenora? People hide hatred, but both you and your father are known for daring, and what's more daring than endangering himself to convince others of his innocence?"

"My father did not!" His face seemed to freeze rather than burn.

"I'm not saying he did. I'm saying a Med could have. What would happen to a Rys who refused to give a Med whatever he says claims as recompense?" Anger snapped in her voice. *Did he notice? Is he proud of that form of muddy justice?*

His smile was so cold it cracked. "Did someone?"

"Not of me, and neither Mama nor Fiwal mentioned it, but it's possible. There are eight other shops and four doctors. If you don't want to hear charges of muddy justice, you can't ignore the possibility of Med involvement. Depending on the medium used to carry the hex, the magic may have been simple." She pulled the quilt over the corpse.

"Would you tell me if someone had?"

The edge of the bed gave under the pressure of her hands. *Feathers? In a room no one uses.* She raised her gaze to meet his. "If I believed you were seeking justice and my death would prevent the massacre of my people, yes."

His tone turned mocking. "I believe you. Most of you would confess to save the rest, even if the confession were a lie."

"While you Med will kill for one another, even for a lie, but not die?" She walked out the door. "Take me to the room where it happened. It won't get less foul."

<hr />

When they left the room, the captain whistled several quick notes. "I hope you have a strong stomach."

She pushed her braid over her shoulder. "If I don't, I have magic."

"Captain!"

They turned as Foden jogged to join them. Behind him, a group of Rys hurried into the room they'd left. Foden glared at her and turned to his commander. "I have reports of five fights. They don't know what happened, but they're calling for reparations." As he reported, his fists bounced against the sides of his legs. When he finished, he glared at Zheann again.

"Is her family in custody?" The captain's professional mask looked pinched.

"They didn't do anything!" Her hands shook, and she pulled

them inside her cloak, wrapping them around her ribs. She brought them out to swat at tears. *I can't do this.*

"We haven't found her husband."

Captain Moln took her by the arm and tightened his grip. "It's to keep them safe, and you focused." Hard eyes searched her face. "So focus. Where's Fiwal?"

She fought the impulse to cry out. *Don't give him the satisfaction.* She tried to pull away and staggered. "He's at..." She shook her head and pulled against his hand again. "What did my mother say?"

Foden licked his thin lips. "He told her he had to leave."

Leave? Why didn't he mention it to me? Or wasn't I paying attention? "Did you check with his parents, or —

"Yes." The word cracked from his tongue like a whip.

Her mental shoulders sagged. "I don't know where he is."

The captain nodded and scowled. "Find him, Foden. Go through the list. Get as many Athenque-spawn as you can locked away somewhere safe. Try Leed's shop and house."

"We already did, Captain. The shop and house are empty.

He nodded his dismissal.

Foden gave two piercing whistles and jogged the way he'd come.

Zheann clenched her fists beneath her cloak. "So much for 'No muddy justice.'"

He looked at the ceiling. "If the mob can't reach them, the mob can't hurt them." He sneered at her. "Some of us have enough sense to realize the dead don't pay debts. Magic is ...useful. It would be foolish to surrender it for blind revenge. We have to protect the best of you."

He pulled her to a door that led to a closed, winding stairwell. A faint acidic smell wafted through the shaft. By the time they got to the bottom step, her stomach was protesting. He opened the door and drew her into the corridor, where the scent struck like a wave. The walls looked like white marble, veined in blue. Halfway across the room, two chairs seemed to grow from the floor. *Not chairs, thrones.* Someone had placed what looked like a black cushion across the armrests. Beside those thrones, but pushed back a pace, a third ornate chair canted off to an angle. It looked big enough to hold a Med. *Is that the throne room? Why doesn't...didn't the king have a proper throne?*

She stumbled as the captain pulled her along. The waves of odor turned into a flood. She pulled the winter mint from her pocket and murmured at it. He let go of her arm. She held half the herbs out to him. He looked like he wanted to say something insulting, but he took the plants. "You see? Useful." He sniffed at the mint. The strain on his face eased.

She buried her nose in her half. The crisp scent drove away all others and cleared her mind. She put her herbs in her pocket. *That's better.*

He opened a door and stepped back.

—)((•))(—

Lanterns created small pools of light on the cedar-paneled walls, and on a patterned rug of sky blue, cream, and blood. As far as their light shone, the room looked as one would expect. A large desk like the one upstairs stretched across the far corner, next to a curtain of the same red as the rug. In the shadows at the room's center, one upholstered chair lay on its side, another, on its back. A small table rested on its top, and someone had reduced another to kindling.

She took a lantern from its holder on the wall and murmured. The light grew brighter, doubling the size of the illuminated circle. She worked her way past the nearest pools of vomit to the largest and put the lamp on the floor. Pulling her skirt close around her legs, she squatted by an ample puddle to get a closer look at the globs.

Half-chewed food was pushed to one side as if it were a slug leaving a slime trail. *It looks like someone slid through it. Ugh. The king ate more for breakfast than I eat all day. Meat. Blueberries. Vegetables of some kind. Fish, I think. Red Berries. Blackberries. I'm not sure what that is. Night berries?* She inhaled sharply. Redolence overwhelmed magic, and her stomach roiled. She coughed as she dug for her herbs.

"What's wrong?" Captain Moln asked from the door.

"Nothing." She tried not to wretch. *Everything.* She walked to a smaller pool, where the food was better chewed, less identifiable. *Yes, berries.* She used a broken piece of a table leg to roll the fruit into groups. *Red berries...blackberries... blueberries, and... night berries.* She went to a third pool, near the first but smaller. *Bread, blue berries, more meat and fish, red berries... blackberries... night berries.*

She rose and hurried from the room. Once in the bright hall, she leaned against the wall and sniffed the winter mint again. When the door clicked shut, she opened her eyes. "The medium, the food used to carry the magic, was night berries."

"Night berries?"

"They're a wild berry usually found in bogs. One reason they aren't cultivated is because most people find them too tart. Some people, like King Eswok, like to mix a few with other berries to make the flavor more complex. Another reason people don't use them is that they can upset the stomach, sometimes badly. That gives them some medicinal use as a purgative. Someone used them to fit the magic to the medium, which is not unusual, but they intensified it and added to it, so the king died in agony. It didn't matter that others might suffer. That sounds Med. So, besides 'bold daring, hatred, and magic,' whoever did this had to know the king's preferences and habits and had to know about and have access to night berries."

"Which herbalists and doctors have night berries?"

She pushed off from the wall and faced him. "I'm the only person

I know. My family has been providing the palace with night berries for years. That's why I know he likes them."

"You have night berries." He stared at her. "Does anyone know you have them?"

"It's not a secret. Fiwal, Ronsath, Leed, and Mistress Jenem know. The king's steward and anyone who works in the kitchens would know. I assume the herbal merchants would, too, and anyone any of them told. Others may know where to find them. Anyone could have stumbled across bushes or have found their own." *Could you sound less convincing, or convinced?*

"It sounds like we need to talk to your family. Conveniently, most of them are missing."

Chapter Three

Divhad, 18 Troleng 153, The Palace

When the captain and Zheann returned to the office, a guard opened the door to a transformed room. Light shone through opened drapes, and someone had uncovered the furniture. A man with apricot hair and dressed in blue trousers and a white shirt straightened next to the hearth, holding a poker. Her heart winced. *Do they make the stewards wear blue all the time? No, he hasn't worn it when he came to the shop. Oh, Etsitty.*

Two other Rys rose. The first was Naris, the palace steward, an older version of his son, Etsiel. The other, Hikiel, was older and taller than Naris with short hair of mixed of dark blond and pewter. His loose cream-colored shirt draped past his hips over a soft belly. He had a large brown stain on one cuff and several smaller stains across the front of his shirt and brown pants. He looked longingly at the door as he rubbed at the large stain with his thumb.

Naris stepped forward. "Garesherick, I'm sorry about the general. What can we do to aid your family?"

His name is Garesherick?

In his answering blink, the captain's control broke, revealing confusion. As quickly, he re-exerted authority with a shake of his head. "Will you all get over your pity? He's the general. I am not going to disrespect him by treating him as less. He has spent the best part of his life defending this kingdom, and once he's recovered, he will continue where he left off. If you want to help him, answer my questions." He sat at the desk. "Sit."

He sounded civil, almost casual. They call the captain by his name?

Hikiel dropped into a burgundy armchair, keeping his stained sleeve from touching the upholstery. His gaze rolled around the room and to the door.

The older steward gestured toward a chair. "Mistress Zheann?"

She passed Hikiel to get to the offered chair, sat on the edge and slid back. Her toes touched the floor.

Zheann leaned an elbow on the arm of the chair and covered her mouth. *Etsitty is his father's son. How many times has someone told him that? Is he as tired of it as I am?*

A shadow of emotion crossed Hikiel's face. "Sir, if we could... There're things I need to do."

Fear? Anxiety? Guilt? Do any of us not feel those things?

The captain waited for several breaths before asking, "Who ordered the night berries?"

The men exchanged looks. Hikiel rubbed at the spot on his sleeve.

Naris leaned forward. "No one ordered night berries, Captain. The king is the only one who requests them, and he hasn't." A pained look crossed his face. "Mistress Zheann?"

"I haven't had the chance to check but I —"

"I didn't order them," Hikiel said, "but they were there last night. I figured Naris ordered them. They weren't on any menus, so I had Yenai make the dish to surprise King Eswok. Is that why Yenai and the lads got sick?" A tear slipped from his eye. He rubbed harder at the stain.

Sick? Zheann rose. "You should have told me others had gotten sick."

The captain frowned. "Sit. Doctor Metris sent medicine for them before you arrived. If they're not already dead, they'll survive."

He met her gaze for a breath and turned to Naris. "Neither you nor Etsitty knew anything about there being night berries in the palace?"

Both men shook their heads and Etsitty answered for them. "We only go to the shop for or check deliveries of specific requests. Hikiel and his people handle the routine kitchen matters."

"It never crossed my mind there could be something wrong with them," Hikiel said.

"Why would it?" *And if he were responsible, why would he have his people make the dish, and eat it? To turn suspicion away?* She shook her head.

The captain frowned at her and turned to Hikiel. "Do all your people know herbal magic?"

Hikiel stood. "Most of us, and some more than others, but I swear to you, none of them would do this. We all have families."

"Were all your people there this morning?"

"Yes." Hikiel licked at his thumb.

"And your people, Naris? Where's your other son? He works at a smithy, doesn't he?"

"Yes, Captain. Torweno has not been to the palace since before the festival. He's always preferred the outdoors and doing things with more immediate, practical results. The one person missing from my staff this morning is probably giving birth."

The captain wrote. He straightened and grimaced. "When was the last time any of your people went to her shop, or they delivered anything to the palace?"

A chorus of heads wagged.

He looked at them for a long time. "Naris, I want a list of all the Rys who work in the palace and the ones who got sick this morning. Start with any kitchen workers hired because of their skill with magic."

Etsitty smirked. "I'll take care of it."

"You may go."

———— ((●)) ————

After they left, the captain sat writing.

Zheann swung her feet. *Did anyone from the palace come to get the berries? Mama or Fiwal would know. Except, he and Leed are gone. Where? Why? This does not make sense.*

"Well?" He watched her with hooded eyes.

"First, I doubt they hired kitchen workers because of magical skill. Most Rys don't put a lot of effort into learning magic anymore. I have fourteen students. Jenem has fewer, and they're older. Half may take an interest. There's not much reason to learn magic or even do decent work when the Med take most of what you make or do as recompense. Second, no one from my household came into the city, and no one from the city came to the shop last night. Our evening business was a farmer who brought us simma to sell for him."

"What do you think of their stories?"

"I doubt they have the necessary bold hatred or daring. If they do, they hide it well."

"Do you know a hex that makes people tell the truth?"

"No. If it ever existed, the records of it would have been destroyed a hundred-fifty years ago. We aren't stupid enough to give you Med a hex that will help you trap us. Naris, Etsitty, and Hikiel know neither they nor their families would escape retaliation. But they know about night berries. They know they can get them from my shop. The story that the berries appeared sounds incredible. I doubt they did it, but that doesn't mean one of their people couldn't have. Before we talk to them all, we should look at the records from the shop." She glanced toward the door. "When did Yenai and the others get sick and why did you ask about Torweno?"

"They got sick after the king died. They don't have permission to eat the king's food, but that doesn't stop them. Sometimes they make extra. I asked about Torweno because he's got a temper like Leed's. I've always thought Naris and Etsitty were loyal, but Torweno is another story. What did your shop send the palace since the festival?"

"I would have to check the logbook. We deliver a variety of herbs every week or two, depending on the time of year. We have an excellent recipe for keeping bugs away from clothing and bedding." *Stop it. He's not a customer.* She sighed and walked toward the desk. "Even with a palace full of Rys workers and Med who might benefit from the king's death, you still think Leed and Fiwal are responsible?"

He frowned at her. "Did I say they were responsible? They are missing. They had access to the night berries and the palace. I suspect they are involved, but I'm still looking. Could the stain on Hikiel's sleeve be from night berries?"

"No, they would leave a deep purple stain, almost black. He wouldn't have licked his thumb after rubbing it on something with a deadly hex on it. I'd guess it was meat or gravy." She cocked her head. "But if you wanted to make people think you were innocent; you might make a victim of yourself."

Anger flared in his eyes. "I told you, the general didn't!"

She raised both hands. "I was thinking of Yenai and the others who got sick with her. We should ask Mistress Jenem to help us. She taught every Rys who's attended the Jideker until I started teaching last year. She'd have an idea who might know the kind of hex used."

"She is near the top of the list my men are gathering either at the garrison or here. If they took her to the garrison, it might be a while before we can get her here." He went to the door and spoke with the guard.

———◦《◉》◦———

Moments later, the door opened, and Dren pushed her way into the room, her face full of determination and her voice, of reprimand. "Mama!"

Zheann lifted the protesting child to her shoulder and kissed her pale blond curls. They smelled of lavender and rosemary. "It's OK Dren, dear." *I'm sorry, Little Hedgehog. I won't let them hurt you.* Tears threatened, and she blinked them away.

Ronsath followed, rubbing at her arms and peering around the room as if she expected to be attacked. She had loosely plaited and woven her graying light golden blond hair. It was one of her favorite ways of wearing it, but it always reminded Zheann of a net.

I'm sorry. "Mama, where's Fiwal?"

A tired look crossed her face. "He called from the shop door and said he needed to leave. By the time I got to the counter, he had gone."

The captain stood. "Sit. Did you try to catch him?"

Ronsath settled onto the front third of a chair. Her eyebrows rose. "Leaving a toddler alone in a room full of herbs?"

Zheann hid a smirk in Dren's hair. *I know, Mama, but what can you expect?*

"Did you have any idea they were planning this?"

Ronsath took a deep breath. "Captain Moln, if you tell me what *this* is, perhaps I could help more."

"Fiwal and Leed used night berries to poison the king and the general. The king is dead."

So much for keeping an open mind.

Ronsath paled. "Oh, I am sorry. But Fiwal? That's ridiculous. Zheann?"

The captain took a deep breath. "Ronsath, do you know anyone else who grows or has access to night berries?"

She looked around the room as if searching for the answers, and finally back at the captain. "No, not to my knowledge."

He made a note. "Did you give or sell night berries to anyone in the past three days? Did a Med claim them as reparation?"

"No, and as far as I know, neither did Fiwal and no, all my dealings with Med this week have been mutually beneficial."

"Did you or Fiwal make any deliveries to the palace in the past day or two?" He wrote again.

"I did not." She glanced up.

Captain Moln's eyes narrowed. "You didn't, but Fiwal did."

"Fiwal left the shop for a brief time around lunchtime yesterday. I was busy with a Med customer. I didn't ask where he went."

Am I wrong? Could he have done it?

Ronsath's light gray eyes lit with hope. "Could it have been an accident?"

"No!" The captain slammed his open hand on the desk.

They all flinched. One of his papers flew off the desk. Dren whimpered, and Zheann took her to the window, shushing her.

"I can't imagine Fiwal hating anyone enough to kill, even King Eswok. He's not that kind of fool. Whoever did it must know what the Med will do."

"I tried to tell the captain that." Zheann looked into the haunted, blue eyes of her faint reflection. Smoke rose from beyond the palace wall. *Do they realize yet the doom that is over them?*

Someone knocked at the door. Etsitty entered with four Rys servants carrying trays. "I thought some refreshments might be in order. Since we weren't sure what sort of tea you'd like, I brought several, and something for the little one." He held a rod about the size of a finger out to Dren, green on one side and golden on the other. "It's a recipe my grandfather found. It's excellent for calming and occupying a toddler when the adults need to be serious."

Dren grabbed it and stuck one end in her mouth, chirping, "Koo" around it.

"You're welcome." Etsitty handed Zheann a small pouch. "Here are some other treats in case you need them for her, later." He grinned at the girl, but his gaze returned to the bag.

Captain Moln glowered at the steward but accepted a mug a servant handed him. "Thank you, Etsitty, you may go." He sipped the tea, put the mug on the desk, and added honey to it. He paused for a breath. "Do you want some tea? They brought enough food for an army."

Zheann put Dren in a chair. "Sit there and eat the treat the nice man brought you." She tucked the pouch into her pocket and joined her mother and the captain around the desk. Little pastries and crackers topped with soft cheeses surrounded four large teapots. Even without taking off the lids, she smelled winter mint, ginger, birch, and bog berry. Ronsath poured a mug of winter mint, while Zheann took the bog berry. They went to the couch and sat with the plate between them.

"Mama, Leed's shop was dark this morning. They can't find him or his family. Do you have any idea where they might have gone?"

Ronsath's eyes drifted to the desk. "He sent Rinsha and the girls to visit her parents before Victory of Herick."

Zheann raised both hands and let them fall to her knees, where her fingers took up a tattoo. "Of course. I forgot about the holiday. It seems as if I'm not thinking clearly about much. Captain, he sends his family away every year. Maybe he went to get them." She sobered, "I don't know why he didn't tell us, or at least tell the carpenter next door. Tahke asked me where he went."

She reached into her pocket. As soon as she teased open the bag, she smelled almonds. *Poison? In case?* She pulled out a golden cookie, spread with a pale-yellow frosting. She returned it to her pocket and pulled out the bag. "Here, you take Dren's treats. She'll be more comfortable staying with you." She popped a cheesy cracker into her mouth while Ronsath tucked the bag away.

"And you don't know why Fiwal would disappear at the same time, again with no warning? Ronsath, who was the Med customer?"

━━━◄(●)►━━━

Foden strode in. His red face looked like someone had screwed it into the dirt. He sucked at the blood and dirt on his lower lip as he pulled the seam of his uniform sleeve into position. It slid, revealing brown and red stains on a cream shirt sleeve. The scent of manure wafted out from him. When he stopped across the desk from his commander, he put two record books in front of him and flexed his right hand several times.

Captain Moln's nose wrinkled under furrowed brows. "Did you find them?"

"We searched both shops and home and confiscated their sales journals. We also found this on her bed." He pointed at Zheann with the note and read in a voice higher than his own. "Dearest Zheann, the opportunity we've been waiting for has come. I can't explain now. I may be gone for a couple of months, but when I return, we will have the lives we've always wanted. All my love, Fiwal."

Her face warmed as she took the note, trying not to touch the muddy spots. *Fiwal's voice is lower than yours. What do you think we are, mice? No, you think we're spoiled children who can speak over herbs and berries and make them kill. Well, we can, but we're not the spoiled children. We're not the ones who are going to kill all of you.*

Dren covered her nose with both hands. Zheann read the note while crossing to where Ronsath sat. She handed the girl over and reread it. "Yes, it looks like Fiwal's writing. It's the sort of thing he'd write."

"What opportunity is he talking about?"

"I can't imagine. We have the shop, Dren, and my teaching. He always seemed happy with them."

The captain snorted. "Those are your dreams, not his. Leed wants all Med to die. Does Fiwal want that, too?"

"What? No! He's never talked about anyone dying. Sometimes he gets enthusiastic about something harmless. Usually, he has a scheme to become wealthy. That way we can run away somewhere you Med can't find us and take it all as recompense." She rubbed at the back of her neck and read the note a third time. *I thought... assumed we had the same dreams.*

"Then what does he want?"

The memory of his lips against hers on the doorstep that morning flashed through her mind. *I thought he wanted the same things I do, that he wanted me.* "I... don't know."

Foden sneered, and blood seeped onto his lip. "How about a wife who notices he exists?" He wiped at his lip. "Leed rented three horses at about dawn's end. They rode out together, heading east. I sent a squad after them."

She rose, shaking her head. "You shouldn't have done that."

Foden's face grew redder and his hands balled into fists, but he stared at the captain.

Zheann wilted a little but stood her ground. "I'm sorry. You're used to Rys who lay aside their magic except in duty to you. If Fiwal and Leed did this, they have no reason not to use all the magic they know against you."

The captain's twisted grin appeared. "I thought you said Rys don't bother learning magic because they don't want to pay recompense."

"A lot don't learn any more magic than they need to learn for their work. That doesn't mean there aren't some of us who think it's a bad idea to lose that knowledge. Some of us agree with you that magic is useful."

Captain Moln glared at her, then at Foden, whose look of contempt faltered into one of confusion. The Med regarded one another for several breaths before the captain reviewed the papers on his desk. "Send scouts after the squad. I don't want the Rys to know we're following them. Have them send a bird as soon as they've found the Athenque-spawn. You and I will ride out to join them before high sun." He pulled the journals across the desk and opened the one on top.

———⊙———

Before the door closed, Zheann took Foden's place. "Don't pretend I'm not going with you. You told me you want me as a witness, and you need my protection." Scorn and doubt filled his dark eyes, and she gritted her teeth. "Would you like me to reduce the palace to rubble to show you what you could face?"

He looked past her. "Could she?"

"Oh, it wouldn't be too difficult," Ronsath said.

He met Zheann's gaze again. "I'm supposed to trust you?"

"Why would you change now? Do you have a map of the Med Kingdom?" *I have no idea what I'm looking for. What's east? What deal could they be after that would need such a hasty departure?*

The captain found and unrolled the map. Zheann examined it, tracing a finger east past villages and hamlets, to Jifreb, a large city along the coast. *It's more detailed than the one at jideker. Where are they going?* "I met Fiwal on my first day of jideker, when I was looking at a map like this." She let her finger slide further east. "He told me ice dragons live in the Great Ice Land." She tapped a large white area across a narrow sea to the east. "Mama, did he ever mention them to you?"

"Never."

The captain frowned. "A journey to the Great Ice Land doesn't take a couple months unless they get trapped there for the winter."

"It might if you had to find something." She pointed far to the east. "I can't think of anything else he would consider such an exciting opportunity that he couldn't wait to discuss it with me. If Leed offered him a chance to go, he might have gone. He can be... impulsive."

"The word is foolish. There's nothing there but ice and reindeer. He believes in ice dragons?" Scorn seeped through the captain's words. He found the page in the journal with the most recent sales and ran his finger down the list.

"Ice dragons, Captain, like the ones you Med have been painting over on the walls for three generations. Like the ones he looks at every time he stands at our door and looks toward the city. Like the one carved on that door. The symbol of the Rys kings from Rysa to Taelfa, who enslaved the Med, and Taelferga who freed them. Ice Dragons, or to use the word from the old tongue you Med are so fond of, Athenque. It sounds mad. It may be mad, or I may be wrong, but that would be a dream big enough to cause him to run away like this."

"Does he think they're going to help him take the throne?" He flipped to the previous page.

He's not going to find any record. They aren't that stupid. "None of this makes sense. Why kill the king if he's going to bring the dragons back? Why put his people and his family at risk? Did something go wrong? Why would he abandon his family? Why leave a note that makes it sound like he's learned of a chance to buy three barrels of jewels for a jar of beans? These aren't things I would have thought Fiwal would do. And for all Leed's anger, I can't imagine him believing in ice dragons or going along with such a wild adventure."

The captain closed the ledger. "If you're right about Fiwal, the night berries may have been the price he paid to get Leed to go along with it. They may hope to throw the kingdom into chaos, with several sons vying for the throne. They probably hope to launch a revolution while the Guard is away from Jitherick chasing them. Not surprisingly, I don't find any record of a sale."

"But Fiwal left *us* here. They left the Rys behind to die. Leed hid his family, but I never thought he would leave us all to die." Zheann blinked back tears.

"Or to finally fight back," Ronsath said.

Zheann raised her hands and let them fall. "And instead, we're doing as we have done ever since Taelferga surrendered to Herick." *Are they right?*

"No, Zheann. We're doing what is right. If they are guilty, joining them in their crimes would make us no different from the Med or King Taelfa." She raised a hand, without looking away from Zheann. "Captain, don't be as big a fool as they are. This is not a Rys crime against the Med. It is a crime against us all. That's why we must work together." Her hand trembled as she placed it on Zheann's shoulder. "See to it you come back, for Dren's sake and mine. If he's guilty, see to it he does not."

Chapter Four

Divhad, 18 Troleng 153, Jitherick

Both Captain Moln and Foden seemed to think they'd dressed like merchants. They still wore black trousers, but the captain's shirt was charcoal and Foden's tunic was mustard with rust stitching around the collar. They donned heavy, black cloaks and they both carried their bows with them. *They still look like soldiers.* At least with their hoods up, they might not be recognized. The dark green riding trousers and shirt they gave her hung on her, but the dun cloak hid the poor fit. They rented mounts from a nearby stable, big bays for the Med, and a little, dappled-gray mare for her. Two soldiers escorted them through streets riddled with debris from surrounding buildings. Med crowds cursed and threatened but made way before them, their faces masks of exhausted rage.

As they got to Main Street and turned toward the gate, one escort charged his horse into a group. The Med he challenged raised his hand, showing a fist-sized rock. He turned his hand over, dropping the rock and spit at the horse as he backed away. Zheann jumped at the sound of a crash. A shutter on a third story window swung loose. A Rys man with sandy hair flew through the window, pleading as he fell. Zheann froze. A screaming blond woman struggled but followed him. Zheann closed her eyes but opened them when more cries assailed her. Two children tumbled to the waiting Med. "No!" A hand grabbed her arm and she screamed as she struggled to pull away from the captain.

He tightened his grip. A long, shrill whistle drowned out their screams. Zheann winced and tried to put a hand to her ear. The people around her stopped. The captain bellowed over the mob noise. "You've done enough. Go home!"

"What have the Athenque-spawn done, Captain?" someone called.

The captain pushed his hood back. His lips curled in a snarl. "The Rys haven't done anything!"

You know they won't listen, and why do you care?

"Is she the one?"

Zheann gasped. *Ye fen...no*

"Retribution!" The word floated among the Med. Someone threw a stool through the already shattered window of a home. A Med leaped on a wagon and echoed the call. As soldiers struggled with him, the smoldering riot reignited. The mob moved like a swarm of locusts, attacking anything at hand. It seemed to flow away before splitting into two, one part doubling back and trampling those who didn't turn fast enough. The other part streamed toward the gates and divided again, the center rushing through into the outer city while the sides fought to close the gates.

The captain whistled again, this time more shrilly. He and his men surrounded Zheann as the living flood surged toward them. She muttered magic. Pain exploded first in her shoulder, and a breath later in her leg as the stone fell. Whistles swirled around her like leaves on the wind. Horses reared and kicked. Med screamed as they fell and rolled, trying to escape hooves and weapons. The captain whistled two notes and pointed. An arrow arced from somewhere and hit a thatched roof that burst into flame. More arrows followed, igniting the roofs of several houses. Those inside and a few from the mob rushed to put out the fires. Soldiers clubbed their way toward the gates, pulling men off of them and flinging them into the chaos or bludgeoning them.

Zheann finished her magic and tossed a handful of dust into the air as the Med around her beat at the edges of the mob. More cries filled the air. Those between the captain and the gate writhed and twisted. They fell and dug at their clothing and heads with their fingers. Some pulled off shirts and tore at their skin. A few chewed at their arms. More rocks flew. One hit a soldier's face. He fell from his horse. The mob converged on him.

"Come on!" Foden's horse plunged forward. Zheann kicked her horse, and they drove toward the gates. A Med slipped between the horses and grabbed at Zheann. His eyes widened as her horse hit him. It stumbled as the man fell beneath its hooves. Cracks sounded like echoes. Zheann held onto the saddle. *Don't fall off!* The gates were breaths away but only part way open. More people lay on the ground between them and freedom. They threw themselves out of the way and continued writhing and scratching.

The horses galloped through the gates and raced along the west wall. The painted blue eye of an ice dragon peered through layers of paint and chalk. *It seems angry. I never thought it looked angry before.* Bells tolled. Some rioters turned from their mayhem to chase the horses. Two got near enough that the captain and Foden swung their truncheons. Foden's victim spun clear. The captain's screamed and clutched his shoulder. "Come on," the captain shouted. They turned east with the wall. Captain Moln signaled to the soldier who had come with them. He disappeared among the burning houses to their left.

They wove around abandoned carts, broken furniture, and corpses. A few Med moved aside. Most seemed to be watching the city and nursing their injuries. A few stared, unmoving. The father of one of her students sat leaning against a doorway. She glanced over her shoulder. *Is he alive?*

"Keep going!" The captain swung his arm forward. Only when the horses raced out from the buildings onto the wide road to the east did he slowed them to a trot.

———⊶⦿⊷———

Foden stood in his stirrups and looked toward Jitherick. "Not your smartest move."

The captain gave a rueful smile. "No, it wasn't. I lost my temper." His face turned hard again. "But no one comes out of a riot the better for it. I knew enough about that family to know they didn't deserve that."

Foden cocked his head. After a breath, he shook it and glared at her. "What did you to them?"

"I made them itch."

"Itch? Is that all?" He gave her a condescending smirk.

I can imagine giving Dren a look like that. "You have never itched as much as they do. They may not have much skin left by the time they stop scratching." She tucked one shaking hand inside her cloak. With the other, she held the reins and the saddle. "It's still a hanging offense."

The captain scratched at his beard. "Under other circumstances, it would be. If you're going to hang for hexing, you might arrange something a little more impressive." He looked at his hand and grinned. "It would be embarrassing to hang because you made someone itch. Injuries?"

"A bruised shoulder."

The captain looked behind her and gave a crisp nod. His gaze returned to her. "How will Leed and Fiwal be likely to travel? Try thinking the way they do."

"What do you mean?"

The captain grimaced and spoke with exaggerated patience. "Will they stay on the road, cut off cross country, or ride to the Tocene River and hire a boat? Will they care for their horses or run them to death and rent new ones every time they find a stable?"

Perversity sharpened her tone. "I didn't think it was necessary to supervise Fiwal's business travels. I left that to him. I left the business to Fiwal and my mother. I had a daughter, my classes, and my herbs. I trusted them. I thought it was working well. I didn't pay attention. There seemed no reason to be more involved. Maybe if I had..." *Maybe I didn't care to know.*

Foden snorted. "If you had, he'd have lied. That's what I do when one of my women asks questions I don't want to answer."

"Don't they suspect, or don't they care?"

His look darkened. "If they know, they realize it's not their business."

Fires flared in her cheeks and rose to her forehead. *I'm glad I'm not a Med woman. Do all Med feel that way?* She bit her lip. *My ideal life. His Med travesty. Twins.*

"Can you find them with magic?" the captain said.

"There are people who can, but I don't know how. Far Sight would let me see where they are, but that doesn't mean I'd know where that is. How many landmarks are there along the road? It would take time, I'm not sure I could do it while riding, and they may sense the magic."

"Then what's your best guess? How will they travel? By river or by road? I'd prefer they not know a Rys is helping hunt them. Even more, which Rys."

She chewed her lip, considering. "They'll stay on the road when they can. Taking the river needs someone else's cooperation. Cutting through the wilderness is likely to result in too many delays and detours. I imagine they'll run as hard as they can, at least for a few days. I don't recall either Fiwal or Leed ever being cruel to an animal, but they never seemed fond of them either. They'll rent new horses. Isn't that what you assumed they'd do?"

Captain Moln plucked something from his cloak. "And you said earlier they're more likely to hex than to hide." He dropped the offending object.

"No, I said if they decide to hex someone, they have no reason not to use something nastier than itching."

———«()»———

When they slowed to a walk to rest the horses again, the captain took a drink from his canteen. "Tell me about Fiwal and Leed."

They passed a small meadow. *Blood weed. That wouldn't be good. No signs of disturbance. Good. What do you want to know?* "Leed has been angry for as long as I've known him. He did well in jideker, but for him, magic both makes us Rys and gives us power. Since we can't wield it freely, he sells it."

"He's a Rys."

"Is that how you see us? All like Leed?"

He considered. "No, most Rys are sheep. Some are rams. Others are kids. A few are sheepdogs. Leed's a ram that wants to be a sheepdog. I always thought we needed to keep you both on leashes."

"What does that make you, Med?"

Both men answered. "Wolves."

"Then why are you afraid of us, sheep?" She waved away their answers. "You're right though; Leed wants to be a sheepdog. He takes every Med slight against any Rys as a personal insult. It's been worse since his sister's murder. That's why he sends his family away during the festival. His daughter, Liesin is almost as old as Oret was."

"As I recall, Oret fell out of a tree. It was an accident."

A breeze rustled leaves of yellow, orange and red. They danced like fire. A hotter kind of fire lit inside her and her voice snapped with it. "Why was she in the tree? I suppose you think that family this morning also died in an accident."

"Your people killed the king!" Foden shouted behind her.

The tinder in her soul blazed. "When were they told that lie? "

"They haven't been yet, but they suspect the truth." The captain gave her a cold look.

"No, they don't. They're blaming all Rys for something one, or two Rys did, or for something a Med made a Rys do. That family didn't die because they killed the king or broke some other law. They died because a pack of wolves saw some lambs and decided a closed palace gate is enough of a cause to be malicious. It's not the first time Med, even Med soldiers, have killed because they could."

The captain peered at the road east for a long time, working his jaw. "You were telling us about Fiwal and Leed."

She unclenched her fists. "I never thought Fiwal and Leed liked each other. I thought they traveled together for convenience. I don't mean that they hated each other, but they didn't seem to spend time together except when they were traveling. Of course, when they took trips together, they would have talked. What else does one do on a trip but think and talk? Leed's anger keeps him focused. He needs it like air. Fiwal rarely seems angry. He accepts Med oppression the same way my family does. The way most Rys do. It's part of how things are."

"We aren't the oppressors," the captain said.

Zheann opened her eyes wide. "Really? Are we sheep oppressing you?"

"Given a chance, you would."

She spread her hands, palms up. "We rejected that option one hundred fifty-three years ago."

"Because we defeated you."

"Oh, Captain, don't talk nonsense. If King Taelferga had fought, your people would still be slaves. He surrendered because he believed what the Rys had been doing was wrong. You didn't defeat us. We defeated ourselves."

"And that proves you still think you're better than we are."

"I've proven I'm realistic." She ran fingers through the nearest locks of the pony's mane. "What would it take to convince the Med the Rys don't think we're better than you?"

"Stop thinking it."

"What if it's the Med who need to stop thinking it?"

His jaw clenched. "Leed and Fiwal?"

Don't smile. "When Fiwal is angry, he doesn't kill people. He embarrasses them. He isn't as clever as Leed, but he has more love for magic and more imagination. He keeps pushing for more. He wanted to learn more magic and to do more with it. Mama is right, he's not skilled with herbs, but he is better with elemental magic than she realizes. After we wed, I noticed he pays attention to people around him. He...performs for their benefit. Did he perform for me, and I didn't notice? Was that all it was? Am I such a bad judge of character?" *Is that why he kisses me on the doorstep, as a punishment for disappointing him somehow?*

"You sauntered up to a Med and asked for help." The captain's crooked smile lacked its usual anger and faded. "I didn't consider Fiwal a particular threat, either. We watched the two of you because of your skill and position, not his."

"You watched us?" She swallowed and lowered her voice. "Yes, I guess you would, and that may be what Fiwal wanted."

"We watched Leed more closely because he has a big mouth." He glanced at her and a smile flashed across his face again. "He shared his anger."

"Yes, Leed is like a straight line. Fiwal, more like Dren's scribbles." *Simma?* She stood in her stirrups to look around and pointed. "Do you smell simma?" She dismounted, dropping the last hand-span. Foden grabbed her mare's reins as she hurried to a pile of ashes along the roadside. Squatting, she tapped the ashes, then dug her hands into them. She put her hands near her nose. The drying mud smelled of sharp simma and woodsy mibehen. She rose and wiped her hands on her trousers.

The captain seemed to be losing the battle with a smile.

He almost looks like a person when he smiles. "What?"

"What did you divine, Mistress Zheann?"

"You mean besides the fact you're mocking me?" She walked to her horse. "You have your answer to how they're traveling. The herbs I smelled are stimulants. They may have used a hex that will keep them going with little food or sleep for several days."

The captain cursed as he helped her mount.

She frowned at the fire's remains. "Fiwal told me they had experimented with stimulants but had given it up." *Why would he lie about it?* "The effect tended to be whimsical and unkind to the body and mind. They may suffer insomnia. They may be high-strung, aggressive, or impulsive. It could drive them mad if they did it wrong. I doubt they would give it to the horses unless they were already stimulated themselves. I'd think it would make them uncontrollable. What I don't understand is why they would have wasted any of it to drown the fire." She wiped at the ash mud on her trousers. Smudges covered her hands. *Keep them away from your face. Where's a stream when you need one?*

"Someone coming along the road could have interrupted them. They could have made more than they could take with them in a hurry." The captain turned his horse in a tight circle.

Foden grimaced. "So, if we're lucky, they'll have taken it and will kill each other along the road."

His commander scratched at his beard. "This would have taken time, but it doesn't look like my men found it. Did they miss it, or was it made after my men passed?"

Foden frowned. "Why would they pay attention to a fire pit? They could have seen it and rode on. Only a Rys would stop to play in ashes."

"Let's hope so. Otherwise, they may be behind our men." The captain urged his horse to canter.

Chapter Five

Divhad, 18 Troleng 153, east of Jitherick

Over the canopy of autumn color, a column of smoke rose black against the evening sky. The captain reined in his horse and nodded toward the trees. "Foden."

The soldier glared at her as he dismounted and handed his horse's reins to the captain. He jogged to the trees and crept out of sight.

Zheann watched where he disappeared. A breeze carried a scent that suggested cooking. *Why is there so much smoke? And what are they cooking that smells like sulfur and copper?* Her stomach tightened.

The captain stared, his face still as he pulled his bow from his shoulder and nocked an arrow.

I suppose he expects trouble all the time. What else can he expect? He's spent his life killing and destroying, taking and being afraid people are going to take from him.

"Mistress Zheann, can I trust you?" His quiet voice held none of his usual authority. It sounded hurt. "If Fiwal or Leed attack us, can I trust you to help us? To use magic to defend us?" He searched her face.

She let her gaze drop to her hands. She held the reins as if they could save her from something. *That's what I came to do, isn't it? If they're around the corner, Foden can shoot the from the trees. That would be the end of it. But what are they cooking?*

The captain turned to the road; his face hidden.

She spoke to his back in hushed tones. "I can't promise anything. I will help you and protect you as long as I believe I'm doing what's right."

"The road turns ahead. It's an ideal place for an ambush. Since we're not hearing fighting, the battle is over. That's not a smell you forget."

Her stomach roiled.

Foden reappeared in a few breaths and jogged back. His usually stern look had turned clouded, grim, and a little green and his voice was hoarse. "It looks like at least six of the patrol are dead, both men and horses. Rys are burning the corpses."

"How many Rys?"

"A handful. I didn't see Leed or Fiwal. It looks like a disposal detail." He spat.

"Then we should join them." The captain dismounted.

Foden grimaced. "She should stay here."

"No, you need a Rys witness and knowing what they've done may help me prepare." *Especially since I have no idea how to go beyond "sticky thorns and biting insect" hexes. Making the mob itch seemed a terrible way to let us escape. Into what madness are you leading us, Fiwal? How can your hatred be worth this, Leed?*

"You don't want to see what they did."

"No, I don't, but I don't have any choice. There's a limit to the herbs they can carry. If I can figure out what they used and how they used it, I can protect us or even fight back." *Just like I could have reduced the palace to rubble. What am I going to do when they figure out the truth? Who am I kidding?*

The captain put out his hand, blocking Foden. "Keep your head. I want her to see what they did." He turned and helped her dismount. "If you need to use names for us, use Gares and Bin."

They took a reluctant stroll around the bend in the road. Ahead, a lump of red, white, and dusty brown with a horse's head at one end, and a tail at the other lay in the road. The bloated lump looked too big for the head. Beyond it, another mound, wearing black pants that seemed ready to burst, oozed something clear. *My people did this. Not the mad, muddy Med, not the southerners. My people. My cousin. Maybe my husband. Leed would say he was repaying a debt we've long owed. What would Fiwal say? Something about being a hero striking a blow for Rys freedom.* Her hands trembled.

Their horses snorted and scuttled sideways, the whites of their eyes showing. Reins burned Zheann's hand as her horse spun and cantered away. Both soldiers swung into their saddles and chased after the horse as Zheann rubbed her hand and stared after them.

A gangly boy with big green eyes and sandy hair joined her. "Your horse is right. You don't want to come any closer. There's bad magic here."

She pulled her hands into her cloak. "I see that. I'm sorry. What are you using for shields?" Behind him, an older man clapped the shoulder of a man who stood next to a farm horse. Someone had put cloths over its nose and eyes. The man holding its bridle walked backward, talking in smooth, hushed tones. The horse towed a horse carcass toward the roadside, leaving fluid and slough in its wake.

Her eyes watered, and bile rose in her throat. She searched her bag and found some winter mint. Holding the leaves to her nose, she murmured her magic and inhaled.

"Yeah," the boy said, "it's pretty rank."

The soldiers returned, stopping when the mare balked. They dismounted and tethered the horses to tree limbs.

Zheann and the boy joined them, and she handed them some mint. "Put it to your noses and inhale."

"Will it work on the horses?" Foden pressed his lips together.

"It should."

The captain pointed past the boy. "What happened?" He held the leaves out to the mare, and she sniffed and blew at them.

"Don't know. Someone heard screaming." He looked at the captain with a raised face that reflected the horror around them.

The captain held the leaves for his horse, who sniffed once, and bit them. He pulled his hand back, surprise flashing across his face, followed by anger and amusement. As he watched the old man approach, both those gave way to repulsion.

The older man kept his gaze lowered. "I'm sorry, sir, as you can see, something terrible has happened. If you want to stay on the road, you're going to need some magic. Or, you might ride out into the woods aways. Orn can take you out far enough."

One smaller lump was brown at one end, mottled red and white at the other, and capped with a mop of dark sandy hair. *Rys? Do not faint. Do not throw up.* "I need to take a closer look. What are you using for a shield?"

The man squinted at her and his nose wrinkled. "There's a swimming hole over there." *Orn's mother is there. She has the magic. Why do you need to take a closer look?*

She gave him what she hoped was a hard stare. *You figure it out.*

The Captain gave the dapple's neck a few final pats. "We'll get the magic and help."

The old man's eyes widened, but he quickly recovered. "There's no need, sir."

Through clenched teeth, he said, "We'll help."

The old man rubbed his hands together. "You should have her hex the horses, too. It'll be safer."

Orn loped ahead as the captain and Foden led the horses to the stream through a thicket of trees and a meadow.

Zheann followed, plucking leaves, and tucking them in her pockets.

Foden angled closer. "Got any ideas?"

"Yes, it looks like the damage caused by some oils, probably plant oils. The magic intensifies the effect and spreads it out over the victims, or in their way. I saw someone's arm erupt in blisters once when some plant oils were splashed on it. It wasn't as grotesque as that, but his arm is still a scarred mess ten years later." She gestured toward the road. "They probably prepared it beforehand and spread it on the breeze as the soldiers came around the bend. If they were upwind or shielded, it wouldn't have mattered." She bit a leaf, wrinkled her nose, and dropped it. "Gentlemen, when we get to the pond, do whatever Orn's mother says unless I tell you otherwise. When we finish, give them some money; as much as you'd give a Med who took care of your dead."

The captain sneered "Those men were on the king's business."

"So are these Rys and it's a particularly nasty business. Aren't your men worth it? Isn't your own life worth it?"

•◦•

He tromped to the pond, and Zheann had to trot to keep up. Orn waded in to where a wisp of a woman with sandy hair stood thigh-deep in the water and explained who they were.

She waved them in. "Bring your horses with you and wet them."

The men hesitated. Zheann waded until her horse balked. She pulled on the reins, but the mare refused. The captain handed his horse to Foden and walked to where Zheann stood, humming, and stroking the small horse as he walked by. He stroked her nose a few times, then grasped her cheek-piece. "Come on." The horse tossed her head. He repeated the strokes and coaxes, she took one small step. And another.

Zheann waded after them. "We'll need to get the horse into the water and make sure she's wet."

"Not going to happen. Splash, gently." The captain nodded at Orn's mother. "While we're doing that, tell us what happened."

"We heard the screaming. About the time some of us ran to see, three horses came galloping through town like mad things. The screaming stopped, but we ran to see anyway, and found that." She waved toward the road.

"Three horses?"

"Two riders," Orn said. "Rys."

When the horse and they were dripping, Orn's mother handed Zheann two small pouches, and the captain one. Zheann tied one to the noseband and the other to a clasp on her cloak. The captain glared but fastened the bag to his belt. Orn's mother murmured magic.

Zheann pushed her braid over her shoulder. "Do you have any idea what they used? Have you ever seen anything like it?"

"Nah, but I suppose some witch could do something with mint oils and lirgen sap or even pitch." She handed them some cloths. "Tie these on over their muzzles, and over your noses and mouths."

What would they think of being called a witch by a Rys?

"What about our eyes?" The captain's filled with concern.

Orn's mother smiled. "The magic will protect you, even once the water is dry. I know it doesn't make sense, but it works."

In response to the captain's squint, Zheann shrugged. "She's right. Magic isn't always rational. It worked on the men back there."

As soon as they turned toward the shore, the mare lunged, pulling Zheann off her feet. Foden grabbed the reins and held them while

Zheann struggled to get her footing. She sloshed onto the bank and took them back.

The captain lost his balance as he trudged after her, throwing his arms wide to keep from falling. He took the reins of his horse and returned to the pond's center. Foden followed and they went to work splashing the bays.

Zheann tied the filly to a tree and wandered in the meadow, keeping an eye on their progress while plucking leaves with trembling hands. She let her thoughts drift back to an afternoon in an apple tree. "Have you ever seen a witch, Papa?"

"Yes, of course, Little Hedgehog, I've seen both Rys and Med witches."

Her mind filled with her little girl laughter. "Med witches? Med can't be witches."

"There's more than one kind of magic; some even the Med can use. Magic is a form of power. All power is subject to misuse, and it's tempting to use our magic because it's a power the Med cannot answer. Magic born of hatred is the handmaiden of cowardice. Using magic to harm the Med is like using a spade to chop the head off a snake. Sometimes it's necessary, but the snake has no defense against the spade."

"Why would you chop the head off a snake?"

"Because if you don't chop them into pieces and bury them separately, they return to eat the chickens' eggs."

Two years later, when she'd objected to something Leed had said, he'd looked disgusted. "Magic is the only weapon we have against the Med, and hatred gives us the courage to use it."

"You promised."

Yes, Papa, I promised. Her skin crawled. *"But now I have to go to the road and examine to what the handmaid gave birth, and I can't stop shaking. Ye fen dernai efoim.*

The captain walked over with both their horses, looking grim. "After a while, you get better control, or you get used to it."

"I don't want to get used to it."

"Get over that. Getting used to it lets you pay attention to more important things, things that may save your life."

"May I remind you of that later when you're angry?"

———⊶⦉◉⦊⊷———

When they got to the road, Zheann tied her horse to a tree and walked to the nearest lump. White and red dripped from angry pink and white tatters that dangled from brown cloth like a cascade of flowers in the rain. *A hand.* She shuddered. The fabric above the tumbling flowers of flesh stretched like an overfilled wineskin. Beyond the shirt, brown hair poked out through and encircled other masses of erupted tissue. At their core, something white shone. A pale artesian spring erupted as the white surface tore.

She fell and crabbed backward gulping air. *Ye fen dernai efoim! Don't vomit! Don't breathe!* She sat hard and examined her hands. She wiped her face and examined her hands again.

"You all right?"

She nodded without looking at whoever spoke, wringing her hands in a pantomime of cleansing. After two deep breaths, she got to her feet. *Fiwal would never consent to this, and it wasn't done in a hurry or out of fear. Leed can't even claim it was the stimulant hex because he can't have done this without practice. Had a hex gone wrong?* She wrapped her arms around herself and wandered to the next corpse while the captain and Foden helped drag a horse to the pyre.

The second corpse had something stuck in its oozing, blistered torso.

A Rys walked over, rubbing at his lower back. "You may as well go to the inn. It's down the road a piece. They're not going to share any secrets."

The voice from before. They already have. "Take a step to your left, please."

He glanced over his shoulder, gave her a conspiratorial frown, and stepped left.

The dagger came out bloody, and she wiped it on the corpse's shirt. "Whoever killed him was doing him a favor, but I doubt the Med will see it that way. Do you see the sheath?"

"It'll be on another corpse. Check his belt or his leg."

Using the blade's point, she pushed at the shirt until she found his belt and the sheath with a dagger still in it. *Even better.*

"Here," the Rys said impatiently. He unfastened the belt, pulled the sheath loose, handed it to her, and wiped his hands on his pants. He looked from his hands to her. "After a while, you get careless. I hope we get done before the magic gives out."

She coughed a laugh. "Me, too. You might want to go see Orn's mother again." She walked to the far side of her horse and pulled her canteen from the saddle. Murmuring, she rinsed both daggers and the sheath and slipped them into her bag.

Across the road, Captain Moln shook his head and turned away. *No? No, don't take the daggers? No, I can't believe how obvious, or how useless you're being? No, what?*

She walked to where the Rys lifted the corpse by the shoulders. She bit her lip, grabbed the corpse's ankles, and pulled. The body barely cleared the ground, but they moved it sideways several paces.

"Those Med seem like pretty good fellows," the light blond Rys said.

"Better than I expected, but don't tell them. I have a better grip, let's try again." After five more lifts, they made it to the pile of bodies. They put him beside a corpse whose face looked as if it had melted.

The sun's glow faded behind the mountains. The moon climbed over the trees to the east, orange and flattened along its bottom edge. *The shielding might last late as midnight. Belgan is almost full and will give us some light. If Leed and Fiwal wait for us or hear us coming, we'll die like the soldiers. Even with shields, if they use different magic, it may not help. If we wait until dawn, they may be a half a day ahead of us. We already lost a third, but it will be harder to see them after dark. This is undoubtedly the most foolish thing you've ever done.*

"Don't compete with yourself, Little Hedgehog. Eventually, you always lose." Papa had told her, "Do better next time."

Captain Moln stopped next to her, his profile grim. "We will eat and sleep for a few hours at the inn, then leave before dawn. The moon will let us see without torches. Maybe we won't make as easy a target as...those men." For a heartbeat, fear shivered in his eyes.

Chapter Six

Tarewo, 20 Troleng 153, east of Jitherick

Dim light and deep shadow danced along the rough wood beams. A gentle mix of lavender, mint, and hiaba whispered sweet nothings in her nose. They told her stories of home, laughter, and contentment. Of Mama, Papa, Fiwal, and Dren. Her heart moaned its need to hold them again. *Don't think about them. Go to sleep.* She took deep breaths, whispering magic into the scents, sights, and sounds around her. She whispered magic even into the discordant sawing of Foden and two other sleepers. She whispered magic into anything that promised oblivion. Asleep, she dreamed of Med corpses. Awake, she dreamed of Rys corpses like a pox on the ground, and of two blond heads next to a blood-spattered doorway. Between, they flowed together in a confluence of horror and misery.

Are they dead already? Her heart ached. *The Little General said his men will protect them, but the king is dead, the general is ill, or worse. If one or more of the king's sons, or his wife, wants the Rys slaughtered, who is going to stand against them? Or against a city full of enraged mud? I should have brought them with us, at least a little way, then sent them off into the forest.*

Foden snorted and sat up and she closed her eyes. The bed creaked as he rose. In her mind's eye, she followed him as he walked by, turned, and walked between the rows of beds.

Is there any other possibility? Did someone else kill the king? All the evidence seems to point to Fiwal and Leed. Are they taking a simple trip to make a legitimate deal, and someone else killed the soldiers? Is Fiwal innocent? So far, the magic has been herbal. Did Leed trick him? Could I be wrong about it all?

"Wake up."

Her eyes snapped open.

The captain straightened, towering over her like an oak. "It's time to go."

She dragged herself out of bed, rushed through a trip to the privy, and hurried to the inn's door. The Med had already mounted, and a Rys waited by her mare's shoulder with a box at his feet. On her second try, she pulled herself into the saddle.

The innkeeper waddled over, rubbing at the small of her back, and handed the soldiers sacks. The captain gave her something large that flashed gold in the torchlight. "Use what's left after your expense for the village, in memory of the soldiers."

Wide-eyed, she put the coin in a pocket. "Thank you, sir. We will. Please stop by on your return trip." She gave Zheann a smaller bundle.

"Thank you." Zheann's voice cracked. She leaned close to the innkeeper as tears fell. "Retribution is coming," she whispered. "Flee to the wilderness beyond the mountains or into Coilea if they will let you."

The woman pulled back. She put a hand over her belly. "Red berries. Thank you, I'll keep them in mind."

The captain watched her with hard eyes. "No torches. Let's not give them an easy target." He clucked at his horse, but after it took a step, he tugged on the reins. The bay tossed his head. "She's right. Red berries. Especially the ones from west beyond the mountains. Keep the money to use for them. The ones around Jitherick aren't good this year."

Zheann dug into her bundle, taking longer than needed to pull out a warm biscuit. The captain rode by her on one side, and Foden on the other. As he passed, Foden said, "Are you going to warn every village we ride through?"

Captain Moln glared across at his soldier. "They honored our men. And, if one of your women is ever willing to admit her child is yours, you might not see things quite the same way."

"They know better." Foden pulled his bow from his shoulder and rode with it across his saddle.

"If we're lucky, we'll kill Fiwal and Leed today." The captain scanned the road. Moonlight turned the black night gray, creating shadows of shadows.

Zheann shoved half a warm biscuit into her mouth. *That's why they left when they did, to take advantage of the full moon. That sounds like Leed, too. Fiwal would have killed the king during the festival. Who thought of the night berries? Leed wants to punish the Med. Fiwal wants to look good, to be the hero. Leed's the herbalist. Using the night berries makes us conspirators. Unwitting ones, but conspirators all-the-same. It gave Leed control. He's the planner. He sent his family away to protect them. Fiwal undoubtedly dreams of swooping in on a dragon to save us.*

The captain rode a few paces ahead, jaw grinding a biscuit into submission. His gaze took his head sharply right. Shadows shifted. His shoulders tensed and released.

Her lips pressed together. *You're afraid! You finally believe what I told you. Have you decided you need to be frightened of me, yet? And what happens if we don't kill them today, or tomorrow? What happens if they find the dragons? What will Fiwal do when he returns to Jitherick in victory, and we are all dead?*

After dawn, the captain broke the silence, his breath, cloud puffs. "Where are they finding these hexes?"

"What do you mean, 'finding them?' We teach them at the jideker. Captain, the magic used to kill your men isn't much different from the magic I used to make the mob itch. They used a different medium, but the idea is the same. It's the first lesson I teach my students, and we review it at least once a week. When dealing with herbs, magic makes the herbs do either more, or less. The oils from some common herbs can burn and blister skin. Leed made the oil do more and either spread it with dust or mist on a magical breeze. I did the same thing with a different herb. He could have done it while hiding in the trees." *Leed would have wanted to see it.*

"So how do we avoid the same fate?"

Do I lie? If I do, will they get reckless because they think themselves protected?

"You don't know."

"These are things the Med have forbidden us to think about for three generations. I've never heard of any shield that protects from everything. Different shields work for different things, but none of them last indefinitely. I'm thinking about it, but I don't have an answer, yet."

"What about the Rys Council? I'm sure they think about things they aren't supposed to."

He knows about those? How much? Who am I kidding? He probably knows more than I do. "As far as I know, the Rys Council hasn't met since before you were born. The stories are exaggerated. They aren't magical battles, with Rys flinging hexes at each other across a field. They're more like you going before a magistrate. In the worst cases, I suppose the council may silence the Rys." She raised her hood to shield her eyes from the early morning sunlight.

"The general told me about his men finding a Rys bound to the armory's door about six years ago. Someone had cut out his tongue and healed the wound. Do you know how to silence a Rys?"

I forgot about him. The soldiers killed him, as I recall. "Yes, of course. Most of the time it doesn't involve cutting out tongues, but if it does, that comes after the silencing. Silencing doesn't have to be permanent. I've silenced students twice. A teacher must know how in case a hex turns dangerous. That's the first thing I plan to do to Fiwal and Leed, but I can't do it if they aren't present."

"Pretty convenient that they won't be able to answer questions." Foden scratched behind his ear and squinted at her.

"I can let them continue to use magic."

The captain gave her a baleful look. "If you can't shield us, or stop them from hexing us, how about making us invisible?"

"If I did that, we couldn't see each other or any of our belongings. You could shoot an arrow at an enemy and hit one of us. Telling us to stay behind you would be a waste of time. You'd have to remember exactly where you put everything and hope you aren't sitting or sleeping where someone else wants to walk. It wouldn't protect you from a hex like the one they used back there."

"But if they didn't see us, they wouldn't know to use the hex." He gave her a twisted grin. It became a twisted frown. "So, our only hope is that they are riding east, celebrating their triumph and not looking back. Any time you want to return to Jitherick, you're free to do so. Or if you want to go back to the town and join them on their trip past the mountains. That might be the better idea. I'll write a note to the general to have your family released."

He thinks I'm useless. He may be right. What made me think I could protect us? Thinking? What thinking? There was no one else. My husband. My cousin. My responsibility. Her shoulders sagged. "If you order me to return, I'll follow anyway. I became the Rys Council the moment we left the palace."

"Your mother sent you. She's on *your* council even if she's not on *the* council."

"We can use her as a hostage," Foden said. "Fiwal *might* love her."

"Never reach into a wolf's mouth to help a Med rat, Little Hedgehog," Papa had told her. "They will both bite you."

Too late, Papa. Peevishly, she said, "They have both had time to plan. Rys haven't used magic as a weapon for three generations. How am I supposed to have learned to fight?" *I sound like a student whining because I don't have my homework done. People have died. People will die. Our only hope is to surprise them and for me to figure it out how to keep them from doing any more harm.*

The captain's gaze moved past her, roving across the road. The fear she'd seen before still burned in his eyes, but something else smoldered there, too. "We knew we were hunting when we left Jitherick. You told us it would be dangerous. You were right. The general and I discuss Rys rebellion on a regular basis. In the few rebellions the Med have faced, we won by overwhelming force or cunning. We knew someday we'd have to get the Rys to help us stop a coup. The problem is we can't train Rys to help us without giving you the tools to defeat us. What we feared has come upon us. If we fail, it's our fault."

So now you're making excuses for me? It was more comfortable when you mocked me. "Foden's idea of using me as a hostage might work with Fiwal. Even if he doesn't love me, sacrificing himself to be a hero is a dramatic gesture he'd like. It might be enough to let me get close enough to silence them or respond to what they're doing on. Leed won't be as gullible."

He scratched at his beard. "Close enough? How close is close enough? Do they have to hear you muttering or something?"

When she chuckled, his eyes sparked, so she hurried to answer. "No, the hex works against their voices; against the sound, and sound can't hear. But there's a limited range. It's like hunting with a bow. You can shoot an arrow without seeing your target, but you're not likely to hit it."

Foden snorted.

What? You can? No, don't let him make a fool of you.

"So how close is close enough?"

"I'll need to see them. Closer than twenty paces would be best. I think I can silence both at the same time if they're within five paces of each other. They will still be dangerous. When I made the rioters itch, I hexed the dust right there, but I could have hexed it before we left the palace. Leed isn't likely to believe I'm a hostage or want to play hero. He's more focused. I suggest you make Leed your first target."

The captain frowned. "Let me guess, he thinks you and I are friends or lovers."

Her face burned. "I asked you what a letter was! I was six years old! They need to grow up." She glared into the autumn leaves and fumed. As her anger cooled, a thought trickled into her consciousness. *How does he know people remember? Do Med pick on him about it? But he's the Little General. Wouldn't he just beat them up?* Her mental jaw dropped. *Like he beat up those boys who were harassing Mama, and then claimed it was revenge for disrespecting him. That would have just made it worse. So would my thanking him for it. This trip will make it worse, too* Her face heated again.

———— ›«()»‹ ————

Clouds piled on each other like boys at play as they rode through the day. They darkened to the hard metal of soldiers arrayed for battle as they traveled. They skirted a thicket under the lowering sky, and the walls of a city and its castle appeared in the distance. The keep's southern edge had crumbled. When they drew closer, thatched and tile roofs of a village came into view to the north. The road curved around the city walls to the village.

"We can reach Jitamyas before sunset," the captain said.

Foden grimaced. "We'll get wet."

"We shouldn't even stop at Jitamyas. I hope the rain slows them more than it does us."

"What's this village?" Zheann stood in her stirrups to get a better look.

"Jitdornoi." Foden used his head to point toward the walls and warmed to his subject. "A couple hundred years ago, it was a Rys stronghold. Besides the castle, they had a big jideker. It started to crumble even before Taelfa enslaved the Med. By the time Taelferga surrendered to Herrick, the Rys had abandoned the castle. I suppose if something threatened them, they might still go into the city." He glared at her. "What?"

"Nothing. I'm impressed."

"You thought I was a dumb mud."

And clearly, I was wrong. "No, I didn't. I didn't expect you to be interested in history unconnected with the Med."

"It does connect to us. It's supposed to be the oldest castle in the kingdom. Some say Medenva built it to protect himself from the Athenque, and Donezan took it from him. Others say one of her brood conquered it. Some say Donezan built it herself. Those folks can't decide what she was afraid of, us or something else. Herrick lived in Jitdornoi. Only Rys live there now."

The captain looked over his shoulder, amusement lighting his eyes. "I forgot about that. The general told me Donezan built it."

Queen Donezan built it? Before she built the palace at Jitrysais? She stared at the ruin. "It doesn't seem to have the same feel as the palace at Jitherick."

"It was a fortress, not a palace." Foden looked from her to the ruins. "But that's one of the arguments against her having built it."

"Which theory do you believe?"

He smiled. "I think it was around before the Athenque queen came from wherever she came from, but I'm a soldier, so what do I know?"

More than I suspected.

Besides the inn, the village had a stable, at least a score of houses, and what looked like a small jideker. Wary Rys watched them approach. One, wearing a dark blue cloak, wiped at his face, and looked up. *Blue? Is he the mayor or something?* Something landed on Zheann's hood, and on her hand. She brushed away the clear liquid as several more drops splattered against her. *Why are they standing in the rain?* Thunder rumbled. Her pulse quickened.

The captain pointed at a tree in the distance. "Zheann, when I tell you, run. Don't look back and don't stop until we tell you. We'll catch up. Don't ask questions and don't argue."

The man in the blue cloak took hold of the shovel leaning against the building beside him.

"Go!"

Zheann kicked and her mare bolted. Several men raced into the road with their tools. She held the saddle with one hand. With the other, she gestured and murmured. Light flashed in the nearest pursuers' faces. Her horse shied. Zheann swayed and tightened her grip. Something hit her back. Gasping, she murmured again. Her horse galloped past men as they tried to stop her. Rain pelted her, but the road cleared. She leaned forward and stopped murmuring. The rain beat against her back. *Where's their magic? Where are the Med?*

She straightened in the saddle and moaned as pain lanced through her ribs. Light and heat flared before her. Her horse veered and kept running as lightning flashed. She saw lights in two windows before they raced across a field. Thunder rumbled. They slowed to a trot as they approached a stone wall, following the barrier to the left. Zheann clung to the saddle. Something made her cloak flare out at an odd angle. With great care, she moved the cloth. Something dark and hard stuck out of her shirt. *Arrow!*

"Find them!"

Who's lost? She shook her head. *I am. They're looking for me. Why can't I think? Ye fen dernai...what was the word? Haloim. What damage did the arrow do?* She coughed. Her hand came away from her mouth dark. *Blood?*

Her horse turned to the right following the wall. She whinnied and cantered. Zheann let the horse go where she chose. *Injured. Think, Zheann.*

I can't... Something is wrong. She reached under her cloak and gripped the arrow shaft near where it entered her back. She murmured. The arrow shaft snapped, and the fletching fell away. Fire snaked through her. She pulled her feet free, trying to curl around herself and clinging to the saddle. *Magic. Hexed arrow. What magic? How do I counter it?*

The mare spun, lurched, and landed hard. Zheann lost her grip on the saddle and hit the ground. She screamed and grabbed at the arrow. Explosions of light cascaded through her mind, as thunder rolled again. Darkness enveloped everything for a breath. She pushed to her knees. Her bowels spasmed. She fought the urge to vomit and failed. With trembling fingers, she pulled a pouch from a pocket. Her fingers slid along the wet, leather cord. She tugged at the lip of the bag, poured a small pile of herbs into her hand. *Wrong herb. Nothing to do for it.* She murmured and licked them out of her hand.

Biting the pouch, she grasped the arrow shaft and keened as she pulled. Her fingers slipped. She let go. *Some thing's not right. Not just shock... what kind of magic?* She bit the pouch harder and pulled on the arrow with all her strength. She murmured through clenched teeth and tried again. She sobbed, dropping the bag into the mud.

Voices she didn't recognize came from somewhere to her right. Ahead of her, a door hung at an angle, one hinge torn free. She raised her head, the raindrops cooling her burning face. She wanted to open her mouth and let the rain pour in. *Not the castle. It's too low.* The voices came again, closer this time. She staggered toward the stone building. A spasm in her lower abdomen dropped her to her knees, and she crawled the last four paces. She collapsed on the smooth stones of a floor and wretched again, too weak to push herself away.

"Check the ruins!"

She opened her eyes, pushed away from the stench of vomit, muttering. She crawled until her head found a stone wall. Her body twisted inside. *Don't scream! Breathe, slow and deep. Is this how the king felt?* She crept along the floor, found another wall, and crawled more.

At last, she found an opening. She slipped through it, sat in the mud, wrapped her arms around her ribs, and rocked until the pain eased. She crawled again until her strength failed. She crept to escape the voices, and the smells of blood, vomit, and excrement following her.

When she found no more holes in which to crawl, she dropped to the floor and curled on her side. Cramps twisted her stomach. She wretched but nothing came. She closed her eyes, letting the tears drip from her nose and her cheek.

She sensed someone standing over her. Thunder rumbled. As she drifted into unconsciousness, Fiwal bent over her and touched her side. "Tsk-tsk, now we cannot have that."

Chapter Seven

Igsole, 21 Troleng, 153, Jitdornoi

"Halfling..." the voice sounded like Papa's.

Who's halfling? The darkness was replaced by a foggy twilight that revealed nothing.

"Tainted." The second voice sounded disappointed.

Who are you? She tried to push herself onto an elbow. Her arms would not cooperate.

"Giving us its life..."

"We don't want it..."

"...Don't need it."

Where are you?

"Dying..."

Do you even know I'm here? Where am I? What happened to the castle?

"Not our way..."

"Let the dying one die."

I don't want to die.

"Not the law."

Help me!

She tried to force her eyes to focus, but everything seemed to blur and shimmer, and the voices prattled.

The Rys are going to be slaughtered.

As softly as a ghost of a whisper, a voice said, "Go."

"Thank you," a voice chirped. A vague shape coalesced out of fog and glow.

She closed her eyes. Fire blossomed in her side and cooled to warmth. *A dream. Nothing more than madness, but at least in madness there is less pain.*

⸺◦((◦))◦⸺

She woke to twilight in a stone room that lacked one wall. It opened into a magnificent garden in a forest. A voice, like a cloud in her thoughts, said, "Do not fear. If you must move, move slowly."

The dead king's bloated body floated in her memory. Her voice, saying, "Captain, the man is lying." Dren sleeping on a couch that wasn't hers. Fiwal's face in the morning light. Grotesque red, white, and brown lumps in the road. A surprised pregnant woman. Exquisite pain. Shimmering lights like sky fire. *But less, and more.* Panic rose, but it seemed as far away as the western ocean. There, but not touching her. *Magic.*

"Yes, halfling, that is what you would call it."

The same voice as before? "Who are you?" Her voice came out a whispered croak. Something between her and a dark wall shimmered. "Where are you?"

The shimmer took the shape of a woman who looked like her mother, but younger. It sparked. For a moment, it looked like an enormous bull...a child...a frog the size of a man's face sitting in the air...a falcon... fire...

Wait, that was me! Am I dead? Is that why I can't feel?

"No, dying one. You gave your life to us. We are returning it to you. It is the law. You cannot die here." Other fires seemed to join the first.

She sat quickly, gasping. *Arrow.* She touched her ribs. *No blood. Like it's been healing. Even my shirt looks new.*

"Yes, halfling."

"The law," another voice said.

The fire separated into flames and winked out or shimmered into the twilight, leaving one. The remaining flame became a man with a shimmering sword...a school of tiny fish swimming in the air before her... a tree. She rubbed her eyes. The shimmering thing looked vaguely like a Rys child. "Who are you?" *What are you?*

"I will seem who and what you choose." The child disappeared in a burst of shooting stars. They faded, replaced by a boar followed by butterflies. A moment later, the butterflies became a mirror that became a tree.

You can hear my thoughts?

"*Thoughts?*" a deeper voice joined the conversation.

The halfling is bound to the earth that shares its other nature. It speaks from both natures. The glowing tree became a child again and looked at her. "Yes."

Ah, yes. That's right.

"What's a halfling?" *Are the Med right?*

Yes. There have been some who left us, who lived among worldlings. It is against the law, but magic and matter together made what is both and neither: a halfling.

The twilight shimmer faded for a breath as thunder rumbled. Darkness appeared, and someone shouted, "Tell Kaff there's no one here!"

"Did you check the jideker?" A few breaths later, "Well?"

The place where the darkness had been filled with luminescent swirling mists. Zheann's hands shook. *The people who hexed me...tried to kill me, they're still trying to find me.*

"Do not fear, halfling," one voice said. "You are safe. The villagers cannot find you here."

"The men who were with me."

"Men? You came here alone."

Riddles. Games.

"Riddles? What are riddles? Games are fun, but now is not the time for games. You were dying. You must heal."

"There were two Med on horses who came here with me. The townspeople attacked us."

"Yes, the worldlings." The child became a horse. "They are riding east. When you are well, I will take you to them." The child returned.

"I need to find them now. They're in danger."

The child disappeared. For a moment, her solitude burned. A bird of prey stretched and folded its wings. The child reappeared. "They are safe. You will find them when you are well."

"I can't wait." She pushed herself to her feet and wobbled, but the pull and pain in her ribs were tolerable. The child took hold of her arm. He steadied her. *Strong.*

"You can wait." the child said.

Boy or girl?

"Neither, I will seem what you choose."

"My name is Zheann," she said. "What's yours?"

"I have no name that is not me, Zheann. You may call me what you wish."

Athenque. Trickster. The word ambushed her from the stories her father told her hidden behind years of schooling. *Ye fen dernai efoim.* She backed against something hard and jerked away. It didn't move. She put a hand against it. *A rock. Am I still where I hid?*

"That is a word worldlings use for us. He does, and yes."

What? Who does what? What is he talking about? Fear remained, but out of reach. "I didn't believe you were real."

"We are more real than you."

Think. There's no time for stupid questions. Why am I not afraid?

The child released something into the air. "You are right. There is no time. You do not fear because I have told you that you need not, and you know I am telling you the truth."

"That's the dumbest thing I've ever heard."

"I find that implausible, but it does not mean I am wrong."

She threw her hands in the air. "You're an Athenque. You're a trickster. You hexed me."

He bowed. "Of course, we hexed you. We have kept you alive and caused your injury to heal. But fear is foreign to this place, and I assure you, there is no reason for it. I will not harm you."

She imagined the ice dragons portrayed on the walls of Jitherick.

"They were of us. They chose to be otherwise."

What? "I think my husband and cousin are going to find them. That's why I must find the...worldlings. We have to stop them."

"I will go with you."

"The law!" a chorus of voices said.

"You can't. The Med will never accept you."

It thundered, and the chorus grew silent.

How do I explain an Athenque to Med?

Where the child had been, a Rys man stood, dressed for travel in brown trousers and cloak. His hair was the same light blond as Dren's, but straight where hers was curly.

That helps.

His silver eyes shimmered.

Her pulse quickened. "Wait, you said there's no time. Does that mean when we leave here, we will be when I arrived?"

"We could be."

"Can we go back before—"

He frowned. "No. What was must be. To go before would kill your body."

"Can you find Fiwal and Leed? Or the ice dragons? Can we get the worldlings and all step into the world where they are?"

"You are here because you gave of your life to this place. It is the law that we receive you. The halflings from the town cannot come here. The worldlings cannot come here. When we leave here, you will not return."

She sighed. "The Med aren't going to like you. They think you're a monster."

"Those who are, are. Those who choose to become, become. Sometimes, even the Med know some truth."

"Can't you ever answer a question with a simple answer?"

"You are a halfling asking worldling questions of what you call an Athenque. These are the simple answers."

She groaned.

"Some questions will have answers. Some will not. You worry about your world. You should. If the ones you call dragons come there, your world will become a battleground. There are things you will need to learn before then." He smiled. "The worldlings are looking for you. It would be an appropriate time to join them."

"I'll need my horse."

"She is waiting for you at the door."

"Do you know how to ride?"

"It's more fun to be the horse, but I can ride." He guided her through the building. Her horse waited there, flicking her ears, and twitching her tail. An Athenque stood next to her. It shook like a dog, splattering drops of light. The figure gave her an impish grin.

"Will you call me, *Athenque*?" The first Athenque said.

"No!" Zheann considered. "I'll call you...Estaen. He's my favorite poet."

Estaen shimmered as he smiled at the other Athenque. "She gave me the name of a poet."

The Athenque laughed.

"Is there something wrong?"

"No, Estaen is a good name."

She walked to her horse and put out her hand. The rain pelted her skin. The Athenque laced fingers together and helped her mount. When she turned toward the path, Estaen had mounted a sleek, deep silver charger. She pointed toward the horse. "Is the horse you, too, or another Athenque?"

"Another."

It looks like they're getting rained on. Don't be rude. "Do you want a name, too?"

"I like the rain." Estaen turned his face toward the sky, closed his eyes and grinned.

At the same time, the horse said, *A name does not change me. I want to run.* The horse grew a horn. It turned black with eyes of fire and grew wings before regaining its quicksilver coat. Her mount tossed her head once but didn't seem alarmed by the changes. Together, they turned and galloped through the ruins. A drenched sentry party scrambled out of their way. Estaen laughed. The horse whinnied.

———— «◊» ————

Estaen led Zheann out of the bailey and around the castle walls. Light shone through windows across the field. *This road is well-traveled by both Rys and Med. At least they're not likely to be out in this rain.* "Why did they attack us?"

"The people of Jitdornoi turned their backs on their heritage long ago. They do not remember us, and we do not interfere with them. Shall we ask them?"

Ask them? "Excuse me. I'm the woman you tried to kill, and I have to say, you piqued my curiosity. Why did you do it?" She resisted the urge to snort. *That's the sort of thing only Papa would do.*

Lightning flashed as Zheann's dappled mare reached the road. In its wake, the night deepened suddenly, curling around her like smoke. Her horse skidded to a stop without a sound and stood trembling. *Magic!*

Zheann's heart raced. She blinked, willing her eyes to adjust, but the dark remained and the thunder she expected did not roll. "Estaen!" she said, but while her mouth moved, she didn't hear the word. *Silence! Ye fen dernai haloim.*

Hands dragged her from her mount. Before her feet hit the ground, she kicked. Her foot hit something solid that moved away. Arms wound around her waist from behind. She screamed in silence, kicking and thrashing. Someone shoved something into her mouth. Stinging rivulets dripped in her throat. She struggled harder, freeing one leg, and kicking toward where the person holding her other leg had to be. Pain exploded in her temple.

⸺ ⟪◍⟫ ⸺

Pain snapped like sparks. Someone whispered, "Don't try to speak."

She groaned, and fire raged through her throat. *Estaen?*

".. rest," the voice said.

She lay on her stomach, draped like a sack of wheat across a saddle bumping her ribs with each step. Water streamed across her back, arms, legs, and neck. Something made of a rough material covered her face. Pins of light stabbed her eyes while her throat and mouth burned.

"She's comin' round."

"Good, I have some questions for them both." Another voice. It sounded farther away.

Estaen?

Yes? The whisper came again.

Are you hurt?

No. They are...village...seem to... there...chance...ask.

Why don't you do something? The horse stopped, and hands pulled her to the ground. Her knees buckled. Wetness flooded, and mud oozed along her legs and back. Her hands, tied behind her, sank into the clay.

We are learning.

Learning what?

"They won't do much answerin' 'til the ohema wears off," the first voice said.

Ohema? Good. It will wear off in about a sixth.

Whatever we care to from whatever they teach us. If you do not want them to suspect anything is amiss, do not look at me when you think.

Estaen, do you know if they've caught the Med, the worldlings?"

I have not seen them.

Someone pulled the cloth from her head. She blinked through the rain at her horse and three blond Rys holding torches. They looked alike enough to be related. Water streamed from their hair and clothes. Mud splatters and smears on their chests gave way to smears from waist to knees and merged to a coating the rain didn't seem to touch around their knees. One was mud-soaked from shoulder to foot on the right side. *Couldn't they have stopped under the trees? Out of the rain?*

Why?

Never mind.

A villager leaned toward her. His breath smelled of greasy meat and garlic. "I saw you with the Med. You from Jitherick?"

She nodded.

Two more Rys dragged Estaen through the mud and dropped him beside her. His demeanor remained calm. A smile flickered in his eyes. *Do not fear, Zheann.*

You're enjoying this.

Of course.

"I didn't see you with the Med. Where did you come from?"

Estaen looked at him with wide, calm eyes.

The interrogator shifted his glare to Zheann. "Are you after the generals?" He and his four neighbors glowered as they waited.

Generals? I hope they think I'm confused, not guilty.

The interrogator's lips pressed into a line. "Amdiri and Sevem."

At least they weren't claiming kingship yet. She mouthed, "Who?"

"She's lying." The man nearest her stepped closer and slapped her.

She yelped. The pain roared through her, bringing sobs that further fueled the inferno in her throat. She tried to roll onto her side, but he pulled her to her feet. He and the interrogator dragged her into the woods on a narrow trail.

━━━━━◦()◦━━━━━

They arrived at an area beneath a canopy of leaves with little underbrush. Rain beat a calming tattoo in the foliage, but none touched her. *Someone did an excellent job of roofing. Why didn't we go to the inn?* A pot warming on the fire spread a faint apple scent through the camp and made her mouth water. *Chamomile.* She smiled.

The interrogator sat on a log beside a tawny-haired woman and poured a mug that steamed as he cupped it in both hands. "She says they're from Jitherick, but they're not after the Generals."

The woman slid along the log, avoiding the puddle forming around him.

"I say she's lyin'," the other voice said behind her.

I'm gettin' tired of hearin' I'm lyin'. Zheann let her head hang and whispered in quick phrases.

"And where did the Rys with the fine stallion come from? I didn't see them go through town." The woman wore her tawny hair pulled tightly away from her face. She dressed in a heavy but faded shirt and pants that were splattered with dried mud.

"Don't know. They came ridin' into the trap Kaff set. It worked real good, like General Amdiri said it would. Didn't see him before. Maybe he was ridin' scout or something."'

"On a horse like that?"

"Come on, Luhaxa, they're city folk." He pulled a knife out from behind his back and pointed it toward Zheann. "She had this on her. What's a Rys doing with a soldier's knife?" He handed it to Luhaxa, who put it on the log beside her.

I had two, where is the other?

A Rys in a blue cloak stalked into the camp, throwing back the hood. He faced the pair at the fire for several breaths, hands on his hips, before turning to stare at her. "I thought you said you killed her."

"I did," someone behind her answered. "General Amdiri said to kill any mud who rode through. She rode through with the mud. I hit her in the back. She should be dead, Kaff."

That sounds like something Leed would order.

His brow furrowed as he looked past her. "So General Amdiri told you to kill any Med who rode through, and you shot a Rys pet, who had no choice about ridin' with them. You claim she's dead and then she gets dragged into camp lookin' lively for a corpse." She flinched as he pulled her to her feet. He jerked her shirt above her trousers and examined her back and ribs.

"General Amdiri gave me geperra. It should've killed her."

Someone behind Zheann groaned.

Kaff glared at her. "Well, one's a healer. I'm thinkin' she couldn't have healed herself with her guts coming out both ways and her limbs turning to ladies' ribbons." He dropped her and pulled Estaen to his feet. "So, I'm figurin' you're the healer. Am I right?"

Estaen tilted his head a little and smiled. *Since they seem to think we should not talk, remind me what the gestures are for "yes" and "no."*

For "Yes," your head nods up and down. For "No," your head turns back and forth.

With Kaff's attention turned to Estaen, Zheann bowed her head. She mouthed the words of a hex with clenched teeth. Her throat and mouth burned like she was swallowing a torch.

"You from Jitherick, too?"

Estaen frowned. His head moved left, then right in a mechanical manner.

Good thing it's a short hex.

Kaff studied him for a several breaths. "You're trying to stop the generals?"

The mechanical twitch repeated.

"Will the mud return to rescue you? Are you of any use to them?"

How do I tell them that would be for the Med to judge?

Zheann bit her lip, choking on laughter.

"Kill them now," another said.

Try raising your shoulders and letting them drop again.

Estaen shrugged.

The cloaked man looked from Estaen's calm face to hers and back. He shoved Estaen down beside her. "If he knows how to heal geperra poisonin' we'll keep them around until he can tell me his magic. After that, I'll decide whether to keep them until the generals get back. Keep an eye on them both." He strode past her.

"I don't like it, Kaff," Luhaxa said.

He turned around. "I'll bet you don't. I don't recall askin' your opinion."

"It won't bring Lil back."

"No, but it'll keep it from happenin' again," Kaff said, and turned to the fire. "So how many of you are supposed to be keepin' a lookout? Anyone know where the Mud are? It's only a third's ride to Jitamyas, and they can send birds to Jitherick and Jifreb. I figure you either kill those Mud before they get to Jitamyas, or you disobeyed the generals' orders. We'll have maybe four days to escape before they bring several thousand soldiers here."

If they're not too busy elsewhere.

Someone behind her said, "We have sentries keepin' watch."

"And yet the report I got said two mud, one Rys, and three horses and we have no mud, two Rys, and two horses. Find the mud and kill them!"

———— ((●)) ————

After a few breaths, the sound of movement behind Zheann died away. The interrogator left the log next to the fire and strode past Kaff with a yawn. As he passed her, something hit the side of her head, sending another jolt of pain through her.

Luhaxa dipped a mug into the pot, fished a few pieces of plants from the surface, and handed it to Kaff. He sat where he could see both her and his prisoners. "I hope whatever they did doesn't have mud coming through town for long. There's harvest to bring in."

"This is more important." Luhaxa sipped from her mug.

"I know what the generals said, but more important than havin' food for the winter? Gran says it's going to be a tough winter."

"Your gran isn't always right."

"Maybe not, but the generals are Rys, too." Kaff tipped his cup again. He frowned at Luhaxa. "I wish they'd waited a month, or even two."

"Then you'd be complainin' about the cold."

Get ready to leave. Horse, will you bring my mare with you, please?

Of course, but would it not be better ...lings return? Horse's deep thought-voice rumbled.

There's no knowing when that will be, and since the two of you seem to be leaving doing anything to me, I've hexed the tea. So, if you're coming with me, get ready to go. I'm beginning to wonder why everyone is afraid of you.

Luhaxa yawned.

... part ... you need to learn. Estaen's eyes shimmered.

Luhaxa watched Kaff's chin dropped to his chest. She glared at them. "What're you doin'?" She tried to stand but sat again hard enough to make her teeth crack against each other. She tipped toward the flames.

Not into the fire!

Luhaxa's eyes opened a little, and she tilted to the side and slid beside the log with her mouth moving.

Zheann gritted her teeth in a grin, stood, and wobbled. "Come on."

Estaen took her by the elbow. "Would it not be easier to escape if you freed your hands first?"

"How did you...?" The ropes fell from her hands. Something shoved against her other shoulder. She turned toward the touch and nearly kissed her horse's nose. "Never mind." She took the horse to the logs around the fire. There, she collected her knife before using the log as a step to mount her horse. "Come on, let's find the Med before they get hexed."

Estaen grinned and pointed. "The road is that way."

They rode into the rain along a narrow trail at a trot. They had slipped from the firelight when someone behind them shouted, "Hey! They're gone!"

Someone else shouted, "Kaff? Lu?"

A third, "Their horses are gone."

Zheann leaned closer to her horse's neck and clucked. *Maybe I should have asked for an Athenque horse.* The little horse snorted and continued splashing her way through the mud and puddles. She followed the trail around a bend and came to where the path met the road. As she turned her back on the lights of Jitdornoi, a shadow detached itself from the trees and raised a bow. "Captain!" she croaked, and her jaw dropped as she turned in her saddle.

Horse continued onto the road. Estaen held the arrow, considering it with the same bland look he'd given the villagers.

"No, Captain! Friend!" she wheezed. *Estaen, remember, you're supposed to be a Rys!*

She jumped and turned the other way as a whistle pierced the night. Foden rode from the woods behind them, one hand raised. "Riders, coming fast," he shouted. "We'll sort you out later. Go!"

Her horse cantered, following the captain's mount. With one hand locked onto her saddle, she checked behind them. Four horses appeared from the woods. Zheann spun forward again. *Can we outrun them?*

More riders appeared from the woods ahead and ranged across the road.

The captain raised his bow, nocked an arrow, and released it in half a breath. A horse squealed.

They'll have magic! If they silence us again... Not if I get there first. Her pulse raced as she murmured the first few words of a hex.

A howl sounded over the storm. Zheann gasped, expecting fangs to sink into her leg. *Where?*

Estaen lowered his head and looked at her, his lips still pursed. He grinned as howls echoed all around them. Lightning flashed again. In the instant before the light blinded her, wolves streamed through the trees. When her eyes adjusted to the dark again, a wolf leaped at a rider, knocking him from his saddle as she raced by. Other wolves loped on either side of her tongues lolling.

Athenque?

Friends. They are better judges of people than either the Rys or the Med.

Two lightning flashes later, she watched the last wolf disappear into the forest.

Chapter Eight

Tarewo, 20 Troleng 153, east of Jitdornoi

Zheann had trembled until her muscles had given up. She worked one hand free of wet reins and pulled it inside her cloak, flexing her fingers and trying to ignore the ache the motion produced in her arm and shoulder. The fire in her throat had long since died. All that existed was the cold, the dark, the wet, and the ceaseless bounce of her dappled mare's slow trot. White plumes floated away with each breath. *How can the air inside of me be warmer than the air outside? She shifted carefully in the saddle. If I move, the weight of the water in my cloak will pull me off. Instead of hitting the ground with a thud and breaking a bone, I'll land with a splash and drown. I'm too tired to cry, and too cold to think thoughts too dark to consider anyway.*

The captain, little more than a dark cloak against the backdrop of trees and rain turned in his saddle. "Let's stop long enough to tend wounds and eat something." His voice sounded like gravel. He dismounted and toddled over like a doll whose knees don't bend.

She loosened the hand still holding the reins and accepted his help to dismount. As he took her weight, he sucked in a breath and tucked his elbow closer to his side. He clenched his teeth and grumbled in her ear. "Who is he?"

Who is who? Didn't we do introductions? No, I practiced them.
"You're injured."

"Zheann." The gravel turned to a low rumble.

"His name is Estaen. He healed me from geperra poisoning and risked his life to help me escape from the villagers. I trust him." *That wasn't the answer I practiced.*

"You trusted me. You trusted Leed and Fiwal."

"I can't be wrong all the time. Can I?" *Don't answer that.*

He pushed back his hood and glowered at her. A gash in his cheek stretched back to his ear. It had scabbed over, but he looked bloodless and his lips, blue.

Estaen walked over, drew a dagger from his belt, and offered it hilt first to the captain. "I will aid you as I can, or if you wish, I will leave you to your quest."

"And ride back and tell the traitors where to find us?" Foden spat into the mud.

"The traitors he helped us escape?" Zheann glared at him.

"For his own reasons."

The captain looked at Estaen's dagger. "I have a dagger. Save yours for when you want to butter bread. I don't trust you, but Foden's right, I want you where we can watch you. Foden, he's your pet for now." Foden grumbled but the captain continued. "You two can make us somewhere dry to rest and build a fire. Once we get dry you can hex our clothes, so they don't get wet again."

"Why?" Estaen asked.

The captain looked at Zheann. "Oh, and speaking of daggers, I suppose you can keep the one you stole from Venn's corpse."

<hr />

Zheann fumbled through her bag, pulled out a small lamp and

filled it with oil. She murmured, and it glimmered. "Estaen, help me get some branches." She trudged into the undergrowth, pushing blackthorn and redberry aside. *We need to make a shelter like the one in Jitdornoi.* Following some rising ground, she found an area free of puddles in a stand of evergreens and put the lamp on a stone.

Estaen followed. He dropped an armload of branches and watched her. She selected a stout piece of wood from the pile and walked to a tree. Murmuring magic, she stretched until her ribs complained, and tipped the branch onto the tree's limbs.

Estaen cocked his head. "What are you doing?"

She longed to stop, put her hands on her hips and say, "What did I tell you?" *Didn't he hear what I thought? Be patient.* Despite her self-admonition, her voice came out clipped and condescending. "Making a shelter. Get some ... you have no idea."

"You have much to learn." He patted her shoulder. The pain in her throat and muscles eased and her clothes dried. He selected a branch, paced off ten steps and balanced it on tree limbs as she had. Rain stopped falling between them. His lips remained in a smile the whole time. His gray eyes were soft, with nothing in them that hinted at smugness.

His lips aren't moving! He's not hexing, but he is. How? He makes it look easy.

"It *is* easy." He lifted an armful of wet leaves and tossed them. They landed on the invisible roof with a splat as lightning flashed and thunder cracked. He found another large branch and dragged it to the shelter's east side. The wind ceased to blow. "Add a branch at that end." He walked to the other end and put his branch on the ground while she hurried to do as he said. *Theatrics are amusing, but they serve best as the crown and not the head.*

What? Irritation flared. *Show-off. Stop it, Zheann, he's trying to help.* "Thank you, Estaen. Someday, you can show me how you do it."

"You are welcome. It is one reason I came with you. Our friends are coming. We'll discuss it further another time." He threw two more collections of leaves onto the roof.

Zheann gathered and arranged some wood and murmured at it. Flames crackled through the kindling. *Our...friends.*

The Little General had expressed his opinion on that idea long ago, more than once. "We are not friends."

━━━━━━⊕━━━━━━

As Captain Moln and Foden arrived, Zheann pointed. "Come in from the west."

Foden ducked under the leaf roof. "A little low."

"Next time, you make it." Zheann took a saddlebag from him.

"Children." The captain ducked as well.

Zheann rolled her eyes. *It's not my fault you're giants.* She took off her cloak. "Let's treat your injuries, Gentlemen."

Foden seemed to puff, as if inviting her to look at him. The pose disappeared. *Mockery? Vanity? Habit? Med!* He removed cloak and shirt and knelt near the fire. He remained still as she examined, cleaned, and murmured. *No wonder he is careless about his women.* Except for four punctures in his forearm, most of his injuries were bruises and looked at least a day old. *This would work better if I had blood balm or quick heal.* "What did they do? Hit you with a pitchfork?"

"Yeah."

Estaen stopped before him. "May I help?"

Foden flinched and looked at Zheann.

She nodded. "He does excellent work. He healed me from an arrow wound and geperra poison. His jideker teaches magic without the tools we use. I'd appreciate your letting him work so I can learn."

Foden looked at the captain and took a deep breath. "You missed your calling. You should've been a merchant."

She gave the back of his head a withering glare.

As Estaen lifted Foden's arm and passed his hand over the punctures, they closed and faded as if they had never been. "Use your words. You learned them, and without them you bar the door to your magic. It does not matter if they are nonsense. Commit yourself to them."

"Nonsense?" She straightened. Doing so didn't make her much taller than the Med kneeling in front of her and only allowed her to see Estaen's face.

"You spoke your magic when we built this." He gestured around them. "I don't know what most of what you said meant, but part of it included fish flying through rocks. Whatever it means in your mind controls your magic. Without words, your magic lacks direction. We can work on it later."

From the corner of her eye, she caught the captain smirking, and she nodded curtly. *Nonsense? It's not nonsense. Mistress Jenem uses words, and she's the best we have. She taught us to use words.* She murmured. Heat rose through her face when the bruise failed to heal. *Focus.* She repeated the hex on a deep bruise on his shoulder. It faded but didn't disappear. She glanced at Estaen, but he didn't seem to notice. They finished work on Foden. He stood.

The captain's narrowed gaze moved from Estaen to her. He stood for several breaths before removing his shirt and kneeling by the fire. He was more battered than Foden. Besides the gash on his cheek, an angry bruise blossomed around his ribs, and a puncture went all the way through his shoulder. *He's slighter than Foden, and even than his father. Why am I surprised?* "Estaen, will you take care of his ribs?" She murmured over the gash on his cheek. "Some Med like scars on their faces. Would you like one?"

"No."

"Good, it would have made you look like a boar." *He's the Little General. I expected him to be the epitome of mudness. It's almost disappointing. Sort of like the Athenque. And the Rys.*

When they finished, the captain stood. "How many more towns have joined the rebellion? We can't fight our way to Jifreb. Zheann says the only way to make us invisible would mean we couldn't see each other or our things. Does your ... jideker have a hex that will make us invisible to others but let us see what we do?"

Did he hesitate when he said 'jideker'?

Estaen's smile broadened to a grin. "What an interesting idea. Would you want your horses to leave no tracks? Would you also wish to be silent only to their ears?"

The Captain's eyes widened. "You can do it?"

Estaen looked toward the horses and considered. "Three possibilities come to mind. First, we change our bodies. You might say we get rid of them. I suspect it would be uncomfortable and I am not sure how it would affect such items as clothing or weapons. I doubt you could take much with you. The second way would be by changing light or our relationship to it." He moved his hands through varying angles as if trying to illustrate. "The people of Jitdornoi tried something like that when they attacked us. It took them considerable time to set it up, they had the benefit of being stationary, and they only needed the magic to work for a brief time."

Zheann snickered. *You lost them at 'first.'*

"Ah, and the third way would be by clouding their minds, so they do not see what they see. That would be the easiest way, but we would have to hex every person we meet. But what happens if we don't know we've met them? It would have limited usefulness." He retrieved the captain's shirt and cloak, shook them gently and handed them to their owner. He did the same with Foden's clothes. While they dressed, he said, "Some rest will do you all good. I'll keep watch. It will let me give further thought to your quest for invisibility."

The Med looked at each other.

He smiled. "Do not be afraid. My knife is only good enough for buttering bread. If I meant to harm you, I would not have healed you or dried your clothes first."

Foden sneered at the captain. "If all Rys were as helpful and obedient as he is..."

Estaen's face hardened as he turned to face Foden. His voice gained an edge Zheann had never heard from him before. "You should thank the dernai the Rys are not all like me. My obedience is to the dernai, and to you only as long as he permits."

Dernai?

"Who or what's 'the dernai'?" Foden asked. His sneer turned to confusion.

"The master, my lord."

Estaen.

His eyes danced. *...at ease, halfling. They are not as weak or unobservant as you believe. The look on your face is more apt to stimulate curiosity than my words.*

The captain handed a bedroll to Zheann. "If we survive this, maybe you should study at his jideker. You might learn something, and it will get you away from Jitherick, at least for a time. It will be a loss to the jideker, but it will be a chance for you to live in peace." He unrolled his bedding, sat on it, pulled his bow into his lap, and examined the string.

A chance to live. An opportunity for Dren and Mama to live. If they're even alive when — if — we get back. "It might be a clever idea if his dernai allows it."

Estaen beamed. "We could arrange something. The dernai turns away no lost sheep who seek to learn his ways."

Not long after, she nestled in her warm, dry bedroll and snuggled in warm, dry clothes. Rain pattered its tattoo on the leaves. *Estaen, thank you for helping with the injuries, and with drying everything out.*

It is my delight, halfling.

She curled further into her blanket as thunder rumbled. *Tell me about your dernai.*

After a moment, he answered. *What would you like to know? The dernai is the master of the magical realm, Zheann. All magic comes from him and is his.*

"Ye fen dernai efoim." It's in the Athenque language.

No, it is the language of a people who live far from here. Your people were taught it as a key to power.

I thought you said I spoke nonsense.

Not all of what you said was nonsense. I recognized the words fish, flying, and rock. You have replaced forgotten words with new ones that mean nothing to me but mean what you need them to. All the words in "ye fen dernai efoim" come from the old language.

But you said 'dernai.'

The word got your attention, and it does mean master or lord in a way that your words do not. It also means more than either of those. There is a great deal your people have forgotten.

My people. It poured over her again. She bit her lip as tears fell. *Estaen, it doesn't matter what my people have forgotten. The Med are slaughtering them because of what Fiwal and Leed did. My family may already be dead. Can you or your dernai do something to stop that? Could you and Horse go to Jitherick and rescue any Rys who are still alive?* She turned and peered at him across the fire.

Another silence. *We are here to help you, if you need it, against the Athenque you call dragons.*

The captain shifted on his bedroll. "Mistress Zheann, why are you crying?" His voice sounded both impatient and almost gentle.

She wiped at the tears. "You know why. The Rys are being slaughtered."

Foden glared at her from his bedroll. "Because —"

"Binra! Enough."

Foden's eyes widened. He opened his mouth, shut it again, rolled onto his back, and closed his eyes.

The captain scratched at his beard and smoothed it. "The general will protect as many as he can. I told you, the Rys are useful. "

Will he? Or will he agree with the mob? "Can he over-rule the princes or the new king? Can he stop all the Med in the kingdom?"

He pressed his lips into a thin line. "The princes respect him. Queen Kenora does, too, and she'll keep the other women in line or send them packing. He is used to getting his way, even with King Eswok. It's too soon for the new king to be crowned but the general commands the troops. He can't protect them all, but he'll do what he can. You need to focus on what you can do and not what you can't. You can't do anything about what's happening in Jitherick. You can do everything in your power to stop Fiwal and Leed."

"I am." She glared at him, then at Foden, who appeared to have fallen asleep.

"Don't get distracted." He settled into his bedroll. "Estaen, I want to be on our way in two thirds."

"Of course!" Estaen winked at her. *They depend on you for their lives, halfling, as you depend on the general for your family's lives. I did not join your party merely for the fun of it, though it has been fun. I joined it to give you some of what you lost, perhaps more than what you lost, and to give you hope."*

More than we lost?

The Athenque who left the magical realm had their reasons for giving you what they did. They may have wanted you to be like them, but not to be their equal. You may learn more than they wanted you to. We will discuss this more soon. For now, rest. Your way is not likely to get easier.

They mounted their horses in the dark. When the captain looked at her, she shifted her gaze to the rain splashing in puddles. "Estaen and I need to ride together so we can discuss how to kill Fiwal and Leed."

"I thought you had it worked out: silence them and hand them over to me." The captain shook his head. "Foden, take the lead until sunrise." His tone sounded as dismal as the patter of rain as he circled to the rear and glared at her.

"Why do we need to discuss killing Fiwal and Leed?" Estaen gazed at her with a sad half-smile and clear silvery eyes.

Why? Because they've already killed the squad sent after them, and they seem to be building an army, and... "I suppose it's not the killing we need to discuss as much as what comes before it. Fiwal and Leed have had time to plan. They seem to have developed some deadly traps and tricks. They've recruited followers, at least in Jitdornoi. As the captain said, we can't fight our way to Jifreb but what if we must? I told the captain I had to come with him because he needed someone to protect him and his men from Rys magic. Right now, I'm not sure an army of Rys would be enough. They've had time to practice. I haven't. Leed and I are herbalists. Fiwal is an elemental. All we can do is follow and respond to what they've done, and I doubt it will be enough." *That may make no sense to you.* Along the road, the leaves danced and dripped.

Estaen's look turned pensive, but eagerness hid in his eyes. "Pursuit and response are always the greater challenges. Begin again. Your goal is to prevent Fiwal and Leed from doing anything else harmful and to hold them responsible for the harm already done?"

She pressed her lips together. *Isn't that what I said?*

Estaen continued. "And when they do something that does not make your task easy, you feel like a failure. Failure, in this case, not only means

Fiwal and Leed do more harm and aren't held responsible. It also increases the number of Rys the Med killed in retaliation. You think yourself caught between two monsters and responsible for the actions of both."

The captain's eyes turned to brown fire. "There's one monster. Fiwal and Leed bear the responsibility for what happened and for what is happening. And they are hoping to find at least one monster greater than they are to help them."

"So, your goal is to stop one monster before it can find another, thus placating a third?" He tilted his head and gazed at the captain.

Zheann rolled her eyes and pulled her cloak closer.

He looked amused. "So far, you have been successful in limiting the damage they have tried to cause. Because you are pursuing, you can do little more until you catch them. Again, what is the problem? Why do you seek my help with it?"

She took in a sharp breath and bit it.

He looked as if the sky were clear and they were enjoying a stroll.

She sighed and fidgeted with the reins. "Your dernai seems to have a different approach. I wanted to know... I hoped you would have a better idea of how to stop them." *You sound like a tongue-tied boy trying to invite a girl to dance.*

The captain pulled out his flask and uncorked it. "What happened to the woman who was going to destroy the palace to show me what we could face?" He closed his eyes and took a sip.

"It would have shown you what you could face. You are the defenseless castle." In a small voice, she added, "I didn't think I'd be the defenseless castle, too."

Estaen's light voice turned ominous. "If you believe that, you are already in their power, in the grip of their deceptions. You are no more a defenseless castle than they are. Why do you do their work in their absence? Why are you helping them by hexing yourself? You said Fiwal is an elemental, and you and Leed are herbalist. All three of you have magic. You think they have more magic because they combine what you differentiate, and they have the advantage of advanced planning. What do you, Fiwal and Leed do with your magic?"

"We are all merchants. I'm also a teacher. They kill people."

"And you are trying to figure out how to do the same. Are they as tied to words as you are?"

Words, again. What is his problem with words? "All the Rys I know use words, even Mistress Jenem. So, I expect they do. But they set traps in advance and leave them for us to trip. We don't have that luxury." She pulled out her flask and took a sip.

"Why not? Why can you not respond in advance?"

"I don't know what they're going to do."

As he raised his hand, fire flared at his fingertips. He tossed it skyward. It rose for a pace then disappeared.

"What're you doing?" The captain put the cork in his flask and wiped at his mouth with a fist.

"Trying to get Zheann's attention." Estaen patted her knee. "I think you are getting distracted. Let's try again. What must you do?"

She sighed like a student tired of repeating her lesson. "We have to kill Fiwal and Leed before they find the ice dragons."

"How would you kill any other Rys?"

The captain snorted. "For what they've done? Slowly and with relish."

She shuddered. "But most other Rys don't use their magic to fight back."

"But they are still Rys. They can die just as any other Rys or Med. Killing them, then, is not a problem. Being convinced that it is a problem is a problem."

She snorted. *It's like I'm in a bog and every step means carrying more mud!*

Her father grinned at her from the past. "When you walk in a bog, Little Hedgehog, always carry a stout stick and check the ground before you step. Trying to lift yourself out of mud is like trying to walk on air, only stickier and stinkier."

"What have they done? What kind of magic?"

"They used herbal magic to kill the soldiers. They used herbal magic to poison me. They used elemental magic to catch us, and herbal magic to keep us quiet."

"Were any of those hexes beyond your skill?"

"No, but that doesn't mean I could prevent ..." Her cheeks burned.

He gave her a coy grin. "To prevent them from capturing us? Did I? Your magic let us escape. And yet, you are looking to me to do what is before you for you. Why?"

The heat in her cheeks grew. *But you're an Athenque. The captain's arrow didn't hurt you. The ohema didn't hurt you either, did it? You could have —*

What would you have learned? Zheann, it is wise to fear what can injure you only when it can harm you. There is little need to fear a shark when you're sitting on a mountain. You know much of what they can do, which means you can prepare for it the same way they did for you.

What's a shark?

A large fish with sharp teeth.

"Next problem," Foden said over his shoulder. "What do you know about the ice dragons?"

Estaen's eyes shimmered. Zheann watched in silence. Neither Med reacted.

"They are Athenque," Estaen said. When both Med cursed, he looked at them with something like pity. "They are not from this world. You would call them magical beings. They do not use magic like the Rys. They are magical. They left their natural home. They are...traitors."

"So Fiwal and Leed could bargain with them." The captain fingered the nock of his bow.

Estaen laughed. "I doubt they have anything the ice dragons want. Fiwal and Leed are seeking beings as lawless as they, but far more powerful. This does not bode well for their relationship, or for us if the dragons decide to use them."

"Wait, you said the ice dragons are traitors?" The captain sounded confused. "But the Athenque are evil."

"Captain, if the Athenque your people know are the traitors, then all the Athenque you know are evil. Does that mean you know all the Athenque or that all are like they?"

The captain glared at Estaen, at Zheann, and back at Estaen. With a twisted smile and exaggerated slowness, he said, "How do we defeat the ice dragons?"

"You don't. You're right. We must try to find your traitors before they find the Athenque."

The sky changed from black to murky gray, and the forest around them dwindled to scrub and meadow. A river slithered through weeds in the distance. The rain, unhampered by trees, fell in sheets and blew in their faces. Able to see farther ahead, the captain pushed them faster.

How do I work silence from a distance, so it only works on Fiwal and Leed? Either quickly so they can't stop me, or cleverly. At Jitdornoi... Estaen, are you listening to me?

I am now. Before, it would have been rude.

Jit-dornoi?

Yes, the people who founded the village were aware of what you would call the magical realm. They respected the dernai until Donezan taught them otherwise.

What do you call the magical realm?

Home.

No, really, Estaen, what's its name?

It has no name that is not it, Zheann, any more than I do. If "home" is not enough, then the only other possibility is Jitdernai, or as they put it, Jitdornoi.

But they don't know now?

It would seem not.

"If I didn't thank you for hexing our clothes last night, Estaen, thank you." The captain stood in his stirrups, shielding his eyes with his hand, and scanning the sea of yellow and green. "I don't see them."

"No surprise there, given the weather." Foden appeared to be inspecting their surroundings, too.

What would it be like to live where there was nothing but grass? Empty. Lonely. With no trees to climb. And the odor. It reminds me of the bogs. "How far is Jifreb?"

"All day." Foden pointed. "Between here and there we'll go through one more village. We'll be within an arrow shot of another. Depending on the weather, we'll catch sight of another ruined castle or two. The gray break in the grass is the Tocene River or one of its branches. The Jifreb fleet can come this far upriver, at least. The Chornivians have tried to split the kingdom several times. The castles and the fleet have been what protected the land. The castles have been neglected because the Chornivians and Dattuckers haven't been as active for the past couple generations. The fleet is threat enough. Each ship is a floating fortress. We'll see some when we get to Jifreb."

"I'd like to read some of those books."

"If we get through this, I'll lend them to you, one at a time."

Zheann blushed when she realized she was pouting. *It doesn't matter. I won't have the chance to read them.*

Foden continued to look toward the river. "That might be a fleet ship." He pointed. "If it is, I doubt it's a big one."

Zheann followed his finger to a dark shape rising above the grass.

The Captain pointed north. "Riders. Med. No Rys from the looks of it."

Zheann stood in her stirrups. Six Med on horseback splashed through the weeds. She edged her horse away from the riders. *The forest is too far behind us. We'll never make it.* She pulled a packet of herbs from her saddlebag and mouthed a hex.

Estaen watched, one eyebrow raised. When she finished, he nodded.

What? I did something right? She gave him a sardonic smile as she rode to the captain's side and the Med slowed their horses to a trot, then a walk. *Yes. I prepared for their attack. But they're just Med.*

The principle is the same.

"Captain Moln," the lead rider called.

"Yes."

The rider pushed his hood back. His short, dark hair and trimmed beard were mostly gray. A scar traced his beard along the left side of his face. He squinted. "The general sent word you're looking for two renegades. These seem a little docile."

"These are pets," the Captain said. "We think the renegades plan to go to the Great Ice Land. They followed the road from Jitherick. They should have come right to you."

"We came upriver in *The Arrow* last night," the scarred man said "and sent out three teams of scouts. I haven't gotten word from the others, but I doubt they could've slipped by all three."

The captain frowned. "They might not slip by. They killed a squad within a few thirds ride out of Jitherick. You should put together a force to go west to Jitdornoi. There's a group of renegades there under the leadership of Rys named Kaff and Luhaxa. They attacked us using magic. You should take the best Rys you can with you."

Scar glared at him. Little-by-little, caution crept into his disdain. His gaze strayed to the road west and back to the captain. "How far do you think it's spread?"

"The other villages along the way didn't attacked us. Two others know something is going on. I'm assuming the general sent pigeons to all the garrisons. When we get to Jifreb, you can send a pigeon and a rider with a report."

"And you think you can trust your Athenque-spawn here?"

"I told you, they're pets."

"One of your pets has a better horse than you do and they're still Rys."

"It belongs to the jideker master," Zheann said. *Estaen, Horse, if they try to take Horse, what will you do?*

Ride his horse.

Be ridden to their town and then return to the Dernai.

Scar's glared focused on her. "And the other one needs to learn her place."

The captain backed his horse. "I don't have the time to train a horse right now. If you want him, take him. For all his beauty, I'll bet your horse is a better worker. He would make a good parade horse for a prince or Queen Kenora, unless being around magic all his life did something to him. As for her, she's not your pet, not your problem."

Scar seemed to peer at the ground to the captain's right, apprehension and anger debating on his face. He spat and turned his horse toward town. "They'll all be dead soon enough. Let's find your renegades before they cause any more trouble. Do you want to ride to Jifreb, or take the ship to the Jifreb Delta?"

"Ride. We're still hunting."

———— ((O)) ————

They followed Scar and his men, but the captain fell back far enough to talk. "What hex did you have ready for Captain Libvas? More itching?"

"No. I reversed the effect of something used to calm a child's skin. It would have made every touch feel like a punch or stab. I think the horses would have felt it, too. I didn't know if they were soldiers or bandits."

"And those are about equal." He smirked at her. "I don't blame Rys for being afraid of us. We've given you reasons. I don't suppose you think there's much reason not to hex a Med, but I need you. So, do me the favor of not getting yourself killed when I'm trying to keep you alive."

She leaned back. *Don't get silly, Zheann. You're useful. He's not your friend. How many times did he tell you that?* "It's an idea I'm considering for Leed and Fiwal. If talking makes their tongues hurt enough, they can't hex." *If it works.* Her mouth stretched into a smile. "It would be nice to test the hex a time or two. Know anyone convenient?"

The captain rubbed at his jaw. "Not convenient, no."

Around her, the grass bent under the blows of the rain and the whip of the wind, and thunder rumbled. *Mama always says to do the right thing even when they don't.* "Thank you for protecting Estaen's horse. I'm sure his master will appreciate it."

The Captain snorted. "Why would I protect the horse? Or Estaen? Pretty doesn't get the job done."

"Thank you, anyway."

Chapter Nine

Myot, 22 Troleng 153, Jifreb

By high sun the rain had slackened to a drizzle. Scar found the other search parties and sent them to *The Arrow*, while he and his men continued as their escort. He growled his refusal to leave them and grumbled his displeasure at staying. By after-high-sun, he pointed out the tall hills of Jifreb.

Hasn't he ever seen the mountains west of Jitherick? It takes days to get to them and they're still visible from the city. I guess that's not fair. I haven't seen Jifreb before, either. It never seemed important. Papa traveled. Fiwal traveled. It let me do what mattered to me: build my little, imaginary castle. That would have been Fiwal's problem with it. It was little. He didn't fit into it.

Behind her, Foden sat tall, like the trees to which she often compared the Med. He scanned ahead, over to the river, and when his survey included her, his gaze narrowed. "What?"

"Can you tell me something interesting about Jifreb?" Beside her, the captain rolled his eyes and winked at her.

"I saw that, Captain." After a breath, Foden grinned. "It was a Chornivian city in the time of Rysa and Medenva. Either Rysa's children or grandchildren conquered it when it was a normal, walled city. Over the centuries, people built on the old city, and outside of the walls. Those hills are the outside. There's more inside, but it's not likely we'll have any reason to go there. It's mostly Med at this point. The Rys also made the fleet and felt safe enough with it and their magic they spread out across the delta. There have been four battles fought over the city since Herick took the throne but none under King Eswok."

Zheann shuddered. *People live inside the hills? No sunlight? No air? What are they, ants? The Med live there? Why? Maybe for the same reason they live inside the walls at Jitherick. Fool's status.* "Thank you." Her voice sounded choked and small.

He frowned.

She cringed inside. *I'll bet that's how I look when I answer a question and get a "Yes, thank you" in response.* "I mean it, thank you. I never knew how different things were away from Jitherick. It's interesting, but a little overwhelming. I do want to borrow one of those books." *That's right. Flatter him. Make yourself sound as stupid as you are. Why didn't we learn these things?*

He gave her a tight-lipped smile.

She returned it. *Yes, I know. I keep pretending.*

Two thirds later, they followed Scar's squad by a bridge that rose above their heads and returned to earth on an island. Zheann stared. Beyond it, another bridge rose and fell on another island. To cross the river, one used four bridges. Jifreb stretched along rock escarpments on both sides of the broad delta. Each structure afforded its owner the best possible view of the adjacent waters. Many buildings had poles mounted on their roofs with what looked like large lanterns on them, and railings along each flat roof edge.

They rode past the western edge of the southern mountain. Behind the buildings and decorations, the rock was smooth. *Outer walls.*

Estaen frowned. *To think that they did only this when they could have had palaces for each family. Halflings lack imagination.*

The Med are worse.

"The Med aren't stupid, Little Hedgehog," her father had said. "They are efficient and clever. Taking requires less effort than making, especially from those who do not act in their defense."

Each layer rose like a step above the last, with buildings, walkways, and roads. They rode the ramp to the first level and passed a green carpenter's shop with a beige tile roof that hung over an open area filled with wares. Next to it, someone had painted a tailor's shop blue. *Blue! In Jitherick it would be burned down in hours.*

A Med woman with bright violet hair came out the door with a large package. She waved at them. Scar and one of his men waved back, and the man hurried over to her and dismounted. She touched his arm, turned, and strolled on her way.

Zheann looked over her shoulder. *Blue. Are Rys that bold here? Why didn't Fiwal, or Papa tell us? We could have moved here. Is there a chance a place like this might escape Jitherick's madness? Not if Scar has his way.*

They arrived at a squat building of faded yellow that shared a courtyard with a bright green stable. The Captain thanked Scar and watched as the soldiers rode away. "Bin and I will see to the horses, then see if we can find anyone who knows about our friends' departure. And remember, we're Gare and Bin."

"That will give us a chance to find the local herb shops and the jideker." *And talk.*

The captain scratched his beard. "I figured you might want a bath. If the merchant belongs to them, he might kill you."

Zheann sighed. "If the Rys crewmember on the wharves belongs to them, he might kill you. I'll bet every ship has at least one Rys sailor. Any Rys you walk past might belong to them. A bath would be wonderful, but not at the risk of our not finding out as much as we can."

"Be careful." The captain turned away.

Estaen held out a hand. "Will we take the horses?"

The captain snorted. "On a ship? Let me guess, you leave your jideker less often than Mistress Zheann leaves Jitherick. No, but you can pay to board your pretty horse here."

"Thank you. That is not necessary." Estaen stepped aside. The horse tossed his head, dodged to the right, and galloped away. Some people scrambled out of his way; others tried to catch him. He dashed between two buildings with a whinny as the Med stared.

Zheann put both hands over her mouth and leaned against her horse. She shook with stifled laughter. *Horse, you're a show-off.*

A laugh whinnied through her mind.

"Are you crazy?" Foden waved his arm after the horse.

Estaen cocked an eyebrow. "I suppose that depends on your definition. He will either go home or find some other way to be useful. Better that than for him to stay here and tempt your friends to be foolish."

The captain's eyes narrowed. "He's hexed, right?"

Estaen looked at him for a breath. "You could say that."

Zheann handed her mare over to a stable hand and asked about the town's herb shops and jidekers. He gave her directions to three herb shops. "There's only one jideker here, and it's near an herb shop. You can get directions from there."

———— ·《◎》· ————

They divided at the road along the lowest tier, the Med turning east, and Zheann and Estaen, west. As she walked along the waterfront, Zheann ogled. *A year wouldn't be enough to learn all I could here, but I'd go blind or mad with all this color.* The building dominating the next level had been painted brilliant yellow, with burgundy and blue striped shutters and blue trim. She squeezed her eyes shut, opening them again as she lowered her gaze to Estaen. "You're coming with us?" Behind him, islands of green and gold dotted the gray water.

His eyes shimmered. "Yes, there is much you need to learn, but you may prefer that I do not."

"Why?"

"Worldlings tend to want more than we can give. I am the dernai's servant, not yours." He walked to the roadside and leaned on the wall as if he were enjoying the sea air. The breeze teased at his light, beige-blond hair, blowing bangs into his silver eyes. "You said we are magical. It is not as simple as that, but it is what you can understand right now. You teach magic. You know it does not direct itself. It must obey the laws set for it, or magic meant to bring fire would cause floods."

She smirked. "It sometimes does."

He held her gaze for a long time. "What a good imitation of the captain. You may understand magic better than most people around you, but you understand only a little. Sometimes, you forget or misunderstand what I am. When you ask me to do what I cannot, you will hate me for refusing."

She gritted her teeth as she slammed a mental door on her thoughts. "Like what?"

"Telling you the future. Changing the past. Causing things to happen as you wish. Giving you victory."

A thunder of feet raced toward them. A hand gripped her wrist and pulled her against the wall. Her free hand ached and stung as it struck the stones. One boy stumbled past her, pushed off the wall, glared, and ran off with his friends.

Estaen released her and looked after the boys.

Don't hex them. She leaned against the wall next to him. "If you didn't come with us to help me stop Fiwal and Leed, why did you come? For fun?"

He grinned. "No, Zheann, though it has been fun. I came because of the dragons."

"If you came to keep Fiwal and Leed from reaching the dragons, why are you telling me this?" She rubbed at her forehead. "What are you trying to tell me? In plain words, please."

"You see? You are already angry because I do not make you understand. So, I will tell you in plain words. I did not come with you to stop Fiwal and Leed. I came to help you face the Athenque if you cannot stop Fiwal and Leed. I also came to help you understand magic better, to help you help your people. I told you before. If they bring the dragons here, your world will become a battleground. I came with you to help you face that battle."

We're going to lose? What am I saying? We're going to die anyway. Either the Med will kill us or the dragons. What does it matter which?

"I do not know whether you will win or lose. I do not believe you will all die. That would be a great tragedy. I told you, magic must do what it is sent to do. But it will not be easy."

"Isn't the best way to prevent the war to prevent Fiwal and Leed from finding the dragons?"

"I am not here to prevent the war." He watched her.

"But you said—"

"I do not want you to lose, Zheann." Estaen took a step toward her. "I will help you as the law requires and permits, but my presence or absence changes nothing in what you must do. This is what I am saying: I will not fight your battle for you. You must face your battle and win your victory, or all you have done will be for nothing."

She walked to what looked like two massive, wooden disks fastened to the wall. Boards connected the disks at regular intervals. *Like the spokes on a wheel.* A wave struck a connecting board, spinning the wheel. More wheels decorated the wall for as far as she could see. *Pushed back and forth, and around in circles by waves. That's how I feel.*

"Zheann, when the Athenque you call Queen Donezan came to

the Rys, she gave your people magic. She taught them as you teach now. You did learn some things on your own. But, once she left, you replaced the understanding of magic with skill with magic. The time of King Taelfa was the greatest era for magic skill among the Rys, but the understanding had already departed. By the time King Taelferga surrendered to Herrick, the decline of skill had begun. The Med hastened the loss. If the dragons return, you will need to understand the nature of magic and to think creatively."

"I understand magic. Wait, how do you know King Taelfa's time was the greatest era for magic?"

"You know a little magic, and you have adapted your use to your needs. You are doing well, but if you understood magic, you would not use words, especially not words in a language you do not understand. You have a great deal to learn and little time in which to do so. You need to discover more now than you have learned. For instance, I have told you before that we are magic, and we cannot die. Why does it surprise you that I am acquainted with the history of your world?

"Well... because..." She raised her hand. "We're chasing fish. What are you trying to tell me without telling me this time?"

"There is reason to hope but not to hope for that on which you have set your heart." He pointed toward a green and brown building. "There is the first of the herb shops you wanted to visit."

<hr />

She pushed through the door into the shop and quickly sidestepped a Rys man with a crying boy. He nodded at her as she held the door. A Med woman in a crimson cloak glanced her way but went back to dickering across the counter with a plump Rys woman with sandy hair braided down either side of her head.

"How can I help you?"

Zheann turned with a smile and looked up at the tallest Rys she could remember meeting. She pointed toward the other end of the shop. "I would like a small pouch of mustard, and another of faram. I'd also like a bottle of peppermint oil." She followed him to the shelves and lowered her voice. "There are some other things we may need, but part of my group came ahead of the rest of us, perhaps you know them. Fiwal Sevem and Leed Amdiri, from Jitherick?"

He looked over her head. "Hey, when were Fiwal and Leed last here?"

Zheann cringed.

The woman hummed. "Maybe last Tevarn? A couple months ago, anyway."

He finished packing the mustard and faram. "Let me go get you the peppermint oil."

Zheann put out a hand. "If you have any camphor oil, I'll take some of that, too."

———

Estaen leaned against a half wall, smiling with his face turned toward the gray and white sky. She dodged through streams of people as she crossed to him.

"From the look on your face, they did not come here."

"You already know they didn't. You knew before I went in."

His silver eyes searched hers. "I did not know until you told me. I do not know everything, and I have no reason to eavesdrop on you. I was watching a bird fly and thinking of other things."

Watching... He looks... she sighed. "They haven't seen them in a couple months." In a dejected tone she added, "Come on."

When she entered the second shop, her heart sank. She picked up an empty basket and put it on the shelf, then rubbed her hand on her cloak. Something crunched under her boot, and she took a step back. Whatever it had been, she had ground it to powder. She righted a basket and shook the contents to the bottom. *At least they're fresh.* A man came through the door wielding a broom like a staff. His head shone, but long white hair streamed from below his ears like a cascade over rocks. He straightened and put the broom against the wall. "I'm sorry about the mess. Some students came in for supplies for jideker. Some Med came in after them like fish after bait. You know how it is. Is there something I can get for you?"

"I'm sorry, I'm sure you want to get this all cleaned. My husband, Fiwal and—"

"Get out. Take your business elsewhere."

"What did they do?"

Red-faced now, the man leaned on the counter and pointed in her face. "They came in right after I opened. They acted like the Med hooligans from this afternoon. They wanted all kinds of stuff. Some I'd never heard of. They went a little crazy; made a mess. If you're with them, get out."

"Sir, I am sorry. We came here to stop them, but we don't know what they're trying to do. Knowing what they were looking for may help me find them." She met his pale green eyes. *I'm telling as much of the truth as I can.*

He sighed. "They wanted firethorn and ice flowers, and something called yasaga. I sold what I had but told them they'd have to check with the shop across the river for the rest. I suggested they not come back. For some reason, Fiwal thought that funny." He wiped the counter with a yellow rag.

"What are ice flowers used for?"

"They grow in ice and snow in the Great Ice Land. Mostly, we use them to break ice flows on the river."

"Did they say anything about the jideker?"

"No, they were in a hurry. They talked about the Great Ice Land. If they've gone there, good riddance and I hope they get trampled by reindeer."

She pushed two coins on the counter. "My name is Jenem. If they return today, silence and bind them and send for me at the inn."

The clink of metal against metal ushered her out the door. She pushed her back against the wood and heard a small tearing noise as a nail head pressed against her shoulder. Soldiers mounted on horses the colors of light and dark leather trotted past. The nearest soldier eyed her, and both her heart and mind raced. *General Moln sent me here. Captain Moln is at the wharves. I'm here on the king's business. I'm not the Rys you're looking for.* When they were gone, she counted to ten as she exhaled. *Can you act any guiltier? Can you draw any more attention to yourself? Get a grip, Zheann! Where's Estaen?* "Estaen?" Her voice sounded shrill.

Walk back along the building to the next street. There is a small tavern.

We don't have time.

You'll find it as valuable as visiting the jideker.

What? How? ...Estaen?

After four breaths, she sighed. *I'm coming.*

She walked between the two buildings sideways to keep from snagging her cloak again. A little boy holding his mother's hand grinned at her and waved. She waved but retreated several steps as a cart full of fish passed within a hand's breadth. Her eyes watered. "Excuse me." She ducked behind the Rys pushing the cart and wove her way across the street. *Poor man. Give me herbs any day.*

<hr />

Estaen sat at a table across from a Rys with moonlight for hair. She wore a plum top with a lace inset that rose around her neck like a collar, and a soft gray cloak. On her right shoulder and left wrist, she wore black and white birds, like crows but smaller. Their wings and tails shone iridescent blue. They seemed to chat together until the one on her wrist looked at Zheann and said, "Hello." The voice sounded like two, both high but not quite in unison, with a buzzing quality. The bird cocked its black head, blinked, and said, "Hello there! I'm Danden."

Birds that talk?

The other bird clicked and cackled.

Estaen rose and pulled the third chair out for her. "Ah, Zheann, please join us." As he spoke, the woman turned toward her.

Lavender eyes! Oh, how beautiful. Wait! I've seen her before!

"Eunaela, this is Zheann Sevem. Zheann, this is Eunaela Mothea." His hand pressed on her shoulder and she sat. "You've met Danden. His lady bird is Naori."

"I heard you sing in Jitherick." *Stop staring. Everyone in the world has heard her sing.*

Eunaela laughed. The low, comfortable sound drew Zheann into their circle. "Estaen tells me you're a teacher at the jideker there. Is Mistress Jenem well?"

"When I last saw her, she was." *Is she still? Say something.* "You know her, then?" Her mind groaned.

"We've talked. I would like to get to know her better." She stroked Naori's black head. "He also tells me you're looking for information about dragons."

Why would you tell her?

Estaen's gaze grew stern. *You have much to learn. She knows some of it.*

Eunaela leaned on the table, her eyes shining. "Are you talking magically?"

"I'm sorry? What?"

"How do you hear him?" She turned to Estaen. "How does she hear you?"

"I shout at her." He waved a hand absently.

Zheann glared and quickly scanned the people around them. "You mean she knows? Estaen!"

He gave her a steely look. "Soul singers notice what others do not and remember what others forget. More to the point, Zheann, as I have noted before, I do not serve you."

Eunaela put her hand over Zheann's. "Don't worry so. I'm good at keeping secrets that need keeping."

"You're discussing them here."

"And except for Danden's, your voice is the loudest."

Zheann's face burned.

Eunaela squeezed her hand. "I don't know what's happening, but I know you're overwhelmed. I think we can help each other. You have an interest in dragons and the Great Ice Land. Why?" Small lines gathered at the corners of Eunaela's eyes and lips.

She seems honest, but I trusted Leed, Fiwal, and Estaen, and look where it's gotten me. "I am looking for some people who are looking for them."

She nodded; her eyes full of excitement. "Dragons are central to the stories of how the Great Ice Land became a land of ice and snow. You are looking for something called the Awasain Jeingsi."

"Ah-wa..."

"Ah-wah-say-in Jay-ing-see. It means 'high place of the cursed ones,' or 'cursed mountain.' According to Kotich legends, they trapped the dragons in a ring under the ice and snow on the peak."

"A ring?" Zheann's jaw dropped.

Both birds squawked and buzzed.

She lowered her voice. "How are we supposed to find a ring under ice and snow on a mountain?" *For that matter, how do dragons fit in a ring? Her pulse quickened again, but her mind refused to move.*

"That, I suspect, is where you will have an advantage." Eunaela winked at Estaen. "He may not be allowed to tell you where it is, but once you're near, he can find it. The other thing you need to know is that according the stories and legends, Athenque are always tricksters. Even the good ones." Her eyes twinkled.

Danden looked at Zheann with one eye and talked.

Wait. That's a hex!

"Oh, Danny boy." Eunaela squeezed his beak shut. "That's naughty. No telling secrets. Don't worry. He hasn't any magic. The other thing Estaen told me is that you want to go to the jideker."

"They may have information about the dragons or the magic they hope to use, which may help us — me find them and stop them. I may also find a book on the nature of magic."

"I'm told it is an impressive collection and that the master may part with some, for a price." She winked. "My price for the information I've given you is that you take me to the jideker with you. I'll contribute a thousand mips, when you're done with the books you want, I will buy them from you."

"A thousand mips!" Her mind raced. *The shop has never made that much in a year. I only hoped to borrow the books.*

"I don't want my name or face associated with the sale so I will wear a disguise." Eunaela leaned with her elbows on the table, her chin on her fist. "There is one more thing."

Spoken like a merchant.

"When your adventure is over, assuming you survive, you tell me the whole story. Is my information worth the price?"

Chapter Ten

Myot, 22 Troleng 153, Jifreb

Eunaela left them at the table. A fleeting time later, a woman with sandy blond hair and hazel eyes, wearing a deep chocolate cloak over tan shirt and trousers joined them. "Do I look sufficiently unlike myself?"

"I would recognize you anywhere," Estaen answered and Eunaela laughed but turned to Zheann.

Zheann longed to ogle but settled for observing. "The color change is dramatic, of course. I can't tell what you did or how you did the rest, but I wouldn't have recognized you. You may be overdoing the voice a little."

Eunaela gave her a tight-lipped smile. "Shall we go?"

They rose and walked to the next level, past buildings that would make a rainbow envious. Zheann touched Eunaela's arm. "Do you know why?" She gestured toward a group of buildings. One, painted gray and red, stood next to another of ivory and blue. Next to it towered a three-story building painted chocolate and pale blue. A nearby cottage was painted something between orange and pink, green, and creamy white.

Eunaela seemed to forget her disguise. She grinned and spread her arms. "Don't you love it? It is visual poetry. Not the kind of poetry that makes sense, not the kind Estaen Parklaw wrote, but it serves the same purpose. It makes the coast more visible from the sea. More importantly, it lifts the sailor's spirits after they've spent months with the blue, gray, and white ocean and sky. If I ever stop traveling, I will paint my home with bright colors." She considered for a moment. "Perhaps like my wagon."

A knife drove into Zheann's heart. She pulled her cloak in tighter and moved closer to the singer. "Eunaela, King Eswok was murdered. We think the men looking for the dragons killed him. Retribution has begun in Jitherick. I doubt you will settle safely anywhere, but here would not be the place. If you can make it to Coilea, you might escape."

"Ah." She hummed a slow tune.

Ahead, a rosy brown wall blocked the road. Tall stone pillars inscribed with scrollwork stood on either side of the gate. The smell of home filled the air. Thyme lined the cobblestone paths that fanned out from the entrance. To their left stood a rosy brown building the park's length. The door, six windows on the first floor and seven on the second were all painted white. Soft light shone from lamps suspended over each window. *How many books will the Master sell?*

"Of course, trying to save Rys will only make things worse. We must save as many books as we can."

A Rys came out, grimaced at the clouds, and turned to lock the door. Zheann ran to catch him. "Master?"

"How can I help you?" His deep voice flowed like honey from the comb. His face was the wrinkled blond leather of a farmer. His green eyes darted from her to behind her and back.

"Master, my name is Zheann. I teach at the jideker in Jitherick. I realize it's late, but I can't wait until tomorrow. I need to do some research. May I use your jideker, even for a third?"

Suspicion squeezed his eyes. "What research can't wait until morning?"

Estaen opened a pouch and tipped three creamy balls as big as the tip of Zheann's thumb into his hand. The master's eyes widened as Estaen said, "These will pay for any books we find useful."

With his gaze focused on Estaen's hand, he mused. "I was on my way to dinner, but I suppose I will lock you in and return after I eat to let you out and re-lock the door." Estaen put the smaller two balls into the master's hand. He shoved them in a pocket and unlocked the heavy oak door carved with the same scrollwork as the pillars. "Do you think you'll need more than a third?"

"No, a third will be sufficient," Estaen said. "We appreciate your graciousness. You will not miss the books we seek."

The headmaster appeared unconvinced. He looked at Estaen's hand again. "The library is straight down the hall. It has a standard magical lock."

Zheann took a lamp from its wall hook and murmured the magic to light it as he locked the door.

⸻ ⋘◉⋙ ⸻

From the door, the hallway ended in darkness. "The jideker must be cut into the rock under the next level. How big is it?"

"Magic plays a bigger role in life here than it does in Jitherick." Eunaela shivered as she walked. "Isn't this exciting? I'll pay you for the books I take."

"Give your mips to Zheann if you wish, she may need money for the journey."

Someone had painted the first doors to look like herb gardens. Next came doors with murals of a pond reflecting a mountain, a river, a waterfall, and several stormy seas and after those came several rooms whose doors were unadorned wood. *Herbal magic, water-elemental magic, administration?* "What did you give him?"

"Pearls."

"What are they?"

"The easy answer is they are stones found in the shells of some sea creatures. Worldlings who live along the shore often consider them valuable." He handed one to her.

She held it near the lamp and watched the play of iridescence across its glossy surface. "It's beautiful."

He held it in the light. "Yes, it is. With the other two I paid him; he can buy a new library. Collect any books you want. Eunaela can take as many as she wishes with her. You can arrange to have the rest taken to Jitherick while we continue with your quest."

"He'll never agree." She stopped as a pair of carved doors loomed.

Estaen swing his arm in a dramatic arc. "Allow me." The doors squeaked as they swung wide.

The lamps glowed. *It's as big as the main hall of a palace!* Books not only lined the walls but filled shelves in rows that went on forever. Eunaela chortled and disappeared into an aisle.

"How are we ever going to find what we need in a third? They must have some way to organize it." Zheann went to a cluttered desk. She opened a thin volume on the top of a stack of books. "Good, they keep an index in their lazy man's stack." Following her finger along the page, she said, "Nature of magic, east wall, unit twenty-two. Pick out whatever book you think is best." She continued through the list. "Dragons, east wall, unit twenty-nine." She carried the index with her to the east wall and examined the carved numerals at the top of each shelving unit. Estaen took a two-sided ladder from between sections eighteen and nineteen. When he got to unit twenty-two, he climbed and ran a finger across the spines.

Zheann found another ladder at unit forty, returned to twenty-nine, and climbed. The word *Dragons* caught her attention three shelves from the top. She pulled that book and the next two from the shelf, wiped the dust off, and flipped through them quickly. The next book described insects. She moved left and found a thin volume inscribed *Athenque*. She added it to her pile and took them to a table near the door.

She rechecked the index. *Water wheels, row twenty-six, unit one.* She ran across the room and selected two of the fourteen books on the subject.

Estaen called to her as he walked across the room. "Where are the books on Rys history? Perhaps they will have something about Queen Donezan there."

She checked the list. "South wall, unit four." Estaen put several books on the table. He shimmered and disappeared. "Let's see. Dragons, Athenque, water wheels, Queen Donezan, Rys history, the nature of magic... What else? Magic combat or defense or warfare?" None of those terms appeared, but *Compendia* did. "South Wall, unit one."

The books she wanted would be on the lower shelves. One was a hand's breadth thick. Some titles were in foreign languages. She selected *Compendium Taelfa* and wished the captain had come with them so he could carry it. Another had no title on the spine, but *Compendium Donezan* and a flying dragon were embossed on the blue leather cover. She put it with the others and lugged them to the table. Estaen joined her and added four books.

Eunaela carried an armload of books from the stacks. Dust smudged her nose, but her grin could have lit the room. "Music. Poetry, including one of Estaen Parklaw's that I've never read. History, including copies of Keherth's *Ageless Queen* and *After the Queen*, and four books of ancient stories." She put them with the others and hugged herself. "Do we have time to get some more?"

Zheann shook her head. "The headmaster is never going to agree to this. Some of these must be priceless."

"Or they are nothing more than dusty old books no one had requested in a lifetime." Estaen fingered the books about the queen. "Or six."

Eunaela looked as if someone had eaten Danden and Naori. She met Zheann's gaze. "Pessimist." She turned to Estaen. "Barbarian."

Estaen raised an eyebrow. "Select the ones you want to take with us. Send the rest to someone who can protect them until you arrive. Eunaela, you have time for one more quick excursion. I will make a list of the titles we have chosen so we can make sure to take them with us."

"I can fit them in my wagon." She jogged into the stacks.

Zheann scanned the list. *Herbs, aisle two, units thirteen through sixteen.* She ran and selected an armful. They met at the table, and Zheann traded one of the eight for an herb book.

The door to the hall opened. The headmaster leaned against the door. "I was early. You must have had good luck."

"We will take these with us." Estaen pointed to the books that already made Zheann's arm ache. He also gestured at Eunaela. "And our friend will bring a cart in which to transport the rest if you will put them in a crate."

The leather-faced headmaster regarded the books and frowned. "I'm not sure. I had thought you were doing research that couldn't wait. These cover a wide range of subjects. I thought we were discussing a *few* books."

Eunaela hummed.

She's hexing him! Zheann looked away. *That's...*

Necessary. Estaen drew another pearl out of his pouch, and the master's focus of longing shifted. "This pearl alone would pay for three times as many books as we've chosen, and I have already given you two." He placed it in the headmaster's hand.

He held it as if it were a bubble. "I will get them packed as quickly as possible tomorrow morning."

⸺⟨◉⟩⸺

When they got outside, Eunaela hugged them. She danced several steps, but stopped, glancing pink-cheeked across the courtyard. She grinned and shrugged. "I'll bring the cart by early and help load the crate. I'll try to coax a few more books out of him. That's why I'm keeping five hundred mips. You cannot imagine how indebted I am to you, or how excited I am. If I can, I'll wait for you in Jitherick. If not, I'll see you in Tup Odriet. I'll be careful." She handed Zheann a clinking pouch and took the list of titles from Estaen before she hurried toward the tavern.

They followed Eunaela's directions to the third herb shop. *Jifreb is huge. I thought Jitherick the kingdom's hub. It may be in the center, but there must be ten times as many people here at the periphery and the jideker is better. From what Eunaela said, there is more freedom here. Or, there has been.* She saw the longing in the headmaster's eyes again. *I wouldn't want to teach at a jideker with anyone who is willing to sell books. The hex only tipped the scales.* A lantern lit as they walked by. "Did you and Eunaela both use magic to get him to agree?"

"There is more than one kind of magic," Estaen said. "I am not permitted to bend him to my will, but I can entice him to bend to his own."

⸺◦《◊》◦⸺

When they arrived at the third shop, Zheann handed all but an herb book to Estaen and went inside. It was as big as the other two put together, but the scent stopped her. "Bog berry!"

"Would you like one?" The shopkeeper in a deep green dress with tiny yellow flowers embroidered at the hems placed a plate of scones on the counter. "When things are uneasy, I take solace in cooking." She laughed and held her arms out to better display her ample waist. "As you can see, things are uneasy often."

"Thank you." Zheann's mouth tingled in anticipation. The bog berries' tartness balanced perfectly with the honey's sweetness. "Oh, thank you. This is delicious! If I made scones this good, I would make things uneasy often."

The shopkeeper grinned as she took the plate to the door. "Why don't you come in and have a scone or two?"

A good cook and a good merchant.

Estaen followed the plate through the door. He put the books on the counter and took two scones.

"You visited the jideker, and they let you leave with books?"

"The headmaster made sure the jideker benefited from the exchange. I teach in Jitherick. I came here hoping to find new books. He agreed to part with these to supplement our jideker. What inspired your cooking? Did it happen to be disagreeable traders from Jitherick? They are the primary reason for our journey."

"A Rys council?" She wove her way back behind the counter.

Is she going to ask for the scones back? Zheann put hers in her cloak pocket. "Yes."

"Oh dear. Do you know they've stimulated themselves?" She bit a tiny piece from a scone.

"Yes. What were they looking for? What did you sell to them?"

"They were looking for firethorn, ice flowers, yasaga, and tireshet. I don't have any tireshet, and I didn't have much firethorn or ice flowers. I sold them half of my yasaga. Leed said something about getting on land by sunset. Chances are good they've left Jifreb."

"How long does it take to reach the Great Ice Land?" Estaen asked from the window.

"It depends on the weather and the port. On a good day, Swisao takes all day. Guelph is closer but there's nothing in the Great Ice Land except snow, ice, and reindeer." She put a small flask on the counter. "If you plan to go after them, you'll want some Sea Calm. It will keep you from vomiting everything you've eaten for the past month." Her belly shook as she laughed. "I didn't think to suggest it to them. They might have to take some time to recover once they reach shore again."

"I'll take a small bag of rye and another of spelt. If you'll part with a small bag of yasaga, I'll take that, too. Is there anything else you can suggest?"

The merchant considered as she filled the bags. "From what I've heard, the reindeer herders like sweets. Would you like some honeycomb?"

"Yes, please." Zheann put coins in her hand. "Have you ever considered moving there?"

"The Great Ice Land? Are you kidding? It's cold enough here, but it's not *always* cold here."

"True enough, but there you might be safe from retribution."

The shopkeeper stared at her. "That much trouble?"

Zheann added a scone to the sack. "Yes." As she and Estaen left the shop, the woman bit a scone and waved.

<hr />

Darkness fell as they walked to the inn. They found the captain and Foden at a table near a bright yellow wall. Lanterns seemed to glow from everywhere. Estaen deposited the books on the table. He pulled the *Compendium Donezan* from the stack and opened it as he sat.

Keep the lies simple. Zheann reported the little they'd learned. "The master at the jideker said Leed and Fiwal might be going somewhere called Awasain Jeingsi. Kotich legends say they trapped the dragons in a ring under the snow and ice on the Cursed Mountain.

Both Med grimaced and squinted at her.

"I know. I'm hoping these books give us something more helpful."

The captain watched her for a breath and shrugged. "We didn't have much better luck. We know which ship they sailed on, but it's not due back until at least tomorrow night. We found a captain who will take us to Swisao or Guelph. He says the best times to leave are the midnight tonight or after high sun tomorrow, as the tide is going out."

"Tide?"

"The water gets deeper twice a day and shallower twice a day. I made arrangements with both the innkeeper and the ship's captain."

A young man brought bowls of steaming soup and a platter of bread and cheeses to the table.

Glancing at him, Zheann turned to the captain. "Why didn't the Med make Jifreb their capital?"

He searched her face. "Why would we do that?"

"It has access to the sea and the river. It's not stuck in the middle of nowhere. It's beautiful, and the people who live here are making advances."

He waited. "In magic? Jifreb might infatuate you, but it's less central to the kingdom. That would make ruling the west more difficult. The river divides it into several pieces, and it's on the sea. The land around it is gentle. It's close to the Ice Land. I have never heard whether the shutters protect the people from weather or invasion, but they are exposed to both. I would have thought you'd notice how poor the land is for crops. I suspect they ship in more than they grow, which makes it dependent on other areas."

He dipped bread into his soup and chewed it, gesturing with what remained. "Don't forget, King Eswok didn't choose Jitherick as the capital. Neither did Herick. The Rys made it the capital as long ago as the time of Rysa, but at least by the time of Taelfa, the Tyrant. He built it on Med backs. When we took what belonged to us by right, Herick ordered us to keep it as we'd built it. We've done so, even though it means ducking through doors built for children and sleeping in rooms with space for little more than the bed. Haven't you ever wondered why no one demands the jideker find a way to remove the dragons from the walls? Every time we paint the walls, we celebrate the defeat of your tyranny. If we had destroyed it and forced you to rebuild, there would be no reminder of your shameful acts. The victory would be complete, but it would be over."

Estaen leaned back. "So, Jitherick keeps the war alive for both the Rys and the Med?"

"We've sworn to slaughter the Rys rather than submit to them again." The captain glowered at her, seemed to dare her to answer.

"Then I'd better start reading because it seems Fiwal and Leed want to follow Med strategy." Zheann grabbed the top book.

⁓⁓⦿⁓⁓

She had just opened *Athenque* when Foden said, "I think I've found where the place you were talking about is. He put his book on the table, opened to a map of the Great Ice Land. He pointed to a spot along the west coast, about halfway between the narrow stretch of water that separated the Med Kingdom from it and the picture's top. "Awasain Jeingsi. It's an island."

Zheann reached across the table. "Let me see your book."

Foden put his hands across it. "I want to see if it says anything else. You can have it when I'm done."

Despite herself, she smirked. "Fair enough." She opened her book. "*Athenque are magical beings native to Kathen, a realm into which the living cannot enter. Donezan described it as a place of death, a place in which she, as a deathless one, could not remain.*"

That doesn't make sense. Does it mean she's not native to Kathen? Not an Athenque? Did I enter Kathen in Jitdornoi, or—

"That's about all it says. The Kotich don't go there." Foden pushed the book across the table.

She found the page. Putting a piece of paper against the picture, she murmured, watching as the image appeared on it.

Foden wrinkled his nose as if he suddenly smelled manure. He stalked away.

The captain chuckled. "Why do you mutter when you hex? We don't know what the words mean. Even if we did, they don't work for us."

She swallowed her annoyance, but her cheeks warmed. "As a child, I tried yelling my hex. My parents always said magic is quiet and responds better to quiet, the same way people do. They teach quietness at the jideker. Can you imagine ten or twenty children all yelling their hexes at the same time? I always believed the words are the language of the universe. It seems I'm wrong."

Estaen smiled. "Part of what she says comes from a language the Athenque taught her ancestors. Part is nonsense."

Zheann glared at him. "I think the words mean what I mean them to mean."

"Even though you have no idea what that is." The captain smirked.

Her cheeks grew warmer. She put a spoonful of soup into her mouth. *Too much salt.*

He tapped one finger on the table.

The heat in her neck and face grew. She put her spoon down. "There may be a little arrogance in it, too. The words make it clear we can work magic and you can't. Our murmuring reminds you, but it also reduces the chance that Med will notice us and take offense at our hexing than if we did it more loudly. Why don't you and Foden get some sleep? The rest of these are about magic. They won't make much sense to you. We'll go through them and join you."

He closed his book and stretched. "Good idea." He rose, with something unreadable in his dark eyes. "We don't hate you, Rys."

"No, no more or less than Fiwal and Leed hate the Med."

He glared and walked away.

That wasn't fair. He's not the one you're mad at.

Estaen took the thin volume on the Athenque from the table. He paged through it and held it out to her. "The Rys who wrote it never encountered us. He based his claims on stories he found in ancient sources he mistranslated. You will find it both speculative and disappointing. Your book will be far more authoritative and both more and less amusing. He is correct that we cannot die. Whenever he quotes Donezan, bear in mind that she left what she called Kathen because she hated it. The Med hate the Rys. Does that mean the Rys are as the Med describe?"

She pursed her lips. *Good point.* She grasped the book.

Estaen kept his hold. "Zheann, I warned you that you would be angry, and you will be again. I have told you that I will do what I can. I will not abandon you when you need me." He leaned closer. "You gave of your life to us, and I have a responsibility to you, but it is neither my only responsibility nor my greatest. There is another —"

"Yes, I know, your *dernai.*" The word sounded bitter to her. "You even took that magic from me."

He cocked his head. "How?"

"'Ye fen dernai efoim."

He gazed at her.

She sighed. "It isn't about courage; it's about your master or some master."

He released the book. "You're right. It is not about courage; it is about need. You have believed an error. It means 'may the lord protect,' or 'may my lord protect.' That makes it more honest. I have not taken magic from you; I have revealed its power to you."

"I don't think I like your master." She put the thin volume on the table.

"That does not matter. What matters is whether he has protected you. I assure you; he has."

"Nonsense."

"Am I?" His eyes burned.

"Are you what?" she snapped. *Is he angry? Amused? Confused? Or is he playing some stupid little game?*

"Nonsense."

A game. "I didn't say... I didn't mean you."

"I know. But the dernai did. He sent me to protect you."

⸻ ◉ ⸻

She rolled her eyes and opened a book on the nature of magic. When the words blurred, and she closed her book, Estaen also closed his. She yawned. "I'm sorry, Estaen. I didn't mean to hurt your feelings. Your dernai doesn't make sense. None of this makes sense."

"Did the magic you know make sense to you when you were a child?"

"No, of course not, but I'm not a child now."

"When it comes to magic, you all are. As you learn, your journey will become easier. Let me give you something to consider. Is magic alive?"

"No, it's a force."

He gazed at her. "Now do you see why I must do as the dernai commands?"

"But..." She lowered her voice. "You seem alive." An idea came to mind. She collected the books. "Are you saying that when you talk to me, it's your dernai speaking?" *That would be terrible, embarrassing, humiliating.*

"Appearances can be deceiving. Is the man you see before you physical?"

"No?" The word dragged from her mouth. The books didn't provide any answers. "No," she said again.

He continued watching her for several breaths. "Be comforted. You are not speaking with my dernai. I exist at his choice, but I am not enough to be an extension of him."

What does that mean?

"Get some sleep."

As they climbed the stairs on their way to the room they were to share with the Med, she said, "Don't you sleep?"

His eyes shimmered. "Only to maintain appearances."

Chapter Eleven

Uxio, 23 Troleng 153, Jifreb

As they hurried from the inn to the ship, Zheann yawned, wrapped her cloak more closely around herself, and cradled half the books. She'd thrown the other four, and the purchases from the herb shops into her bag. The strap dug into her shoulder. Fog drifted into pools of light from the pole lamp that punctuated their winding path. *At least it's not raining.* More pole lights lined the wharf. Two moored ships glowed. A Med stood at the gangplank to the nearer. Men unloaded the more distant. Beyond the pier, darkness waited.

"That's the ship we should be taking," Foden said.

"It's hard to sneak up on anyone on a fleet ship." The captain pushed back his hood.

That's a ship? Peering, she made out the outlines of something at least four times the size of those with lights. She saw no details in the shadows, but she felt something that made her want to squirm.

Estaen caught her eye and looked toward the darkness. *They have used twisted magic on that ship. I am glad we will sail on another.*

I am, too. Zheann followed his gaze. *Twisted magic. That's a good way to describe what Fiwal and Leed are doing.*

No, Fiwal and Leed are misusing magic. They are not twisting it. You do not yet have the knowledge to understand more than that.

Foden folded his arms across his chest. "Maybe, but she'd be hard to sink, and she could send their ship to the bottom."

Captain Moln stopped at the gangplank. "We want to be underway as soon as possible."

The ship's captain, looking like the rest of his crew in white trousers and shirt wrinkled his nose as he grinned. He was as tall as Foden, and his hair seemed to have migrated from his head, past his wide eyes, to his narrow chin, making him look like a bald goat. "We will once we get things straight. They call me Dorlew. As soon as you're on my ship, my word is law. My men are my men, not yours. They do not answer to you, they answer to myself. That includes my Rys. You and your men are my men, and that includes your Rys. If someone disobeys me, both you and the one who disobeys will go for a swim. It's not likely I'll decide to have mercy until it's too late to save you from freezing to death. You'll stay where I tell you, do what I tell you, eat what and when I tell you. You want to give the orders? Buy *The Chaser*, and we'll obey you until we mutiny to save ourselves from your incompetence at sea." He stepped back and gave a welcoming bow. "As long as you keep that in mind, hurry aboard because the tide is on the way out."

Captain Moln's shoulders relaxed. "You heard the man." Foden took long strides up the gangplank, but the captain wheeled on Zheann and Estaen. He spoke in hushed tones through clenched teeth. "You will both stay in my sight or Foden's. Captain Dorlew's not the only one who can put someone overboard. Am I understood?"

"Yes, of course." Estaen scratched at his hairless chin.

When the captain didn't move, Zheann lowered her gaze. "Yes, sir."

"And keep your vile opinions to yourself." He stepped back and swept his arm toward the gangplank with a courtly bow.

Show-off.

⟫⟨●⟩⟨

The water had looked calm from the pier. The deck looked level and stable, but each step tipped to a different angle. She grabbed the railing and tried to follow Estaen.

He walked as if he were crossing a room. A square hole yawned before him, and he stepped into it sinking a short distance.

Stairs? We travel in the hold? She hurried after him down the stairs. Her stomach sank. *It looks like a cottage without windows and smells like a root cellar that serves as a prison for...what are they called? Good thing we're only spending one night.*

A Rys sat at a large table that filled half the area between the stairs and the galley beyond it. His hair looked almost colorless and as if someone had cut it with a knife. "Your berths are there." He pointed to her left with a mug. Along the wall were long pieces of canvas tied by rope to beams at either end, stacked in three columns of two berths. On the opposite wall, two of nine berths were occupied. He finished drinking and put his mug on a tray beside another mug and a pitcher. "I'm Tinjier. Did you happen to bring Sea Calm?"

"Yes, do you need some?" Zheann produced the flask.

He laughed, but his long-suffering look said she'd failed some test. "Let me guess, your first sail? No, I wanted to know if I needed to fetch more buckets." He gestured to the tray. "Three drops in a cup of water." He administered the first round and handed it to the captain. "I'll leave the bucket under the table there in case someone needs it."

On deck, Dorlew interrupted his unending series of commands with a bellow. "Tinjier! Stop your dawdling! Get your useless carcass on deck and do your job. Do you expect me to climb the rigging?"

"Ah, my captain's voice." Tinjier dashed to the deck.

Zheann added the elixir to two more mugs of water. She and

Estaen drank as the captain eased himself into an upper berth. "Now that's the way you lot should act."

"You lot," we Rys? Or "You lot," including Foden? She separated the hems of the hammock below his and tried to sit. The material pushed her chest toward her knees. She twisted sideways, and her berth constricted around her. *Ye fen...* She rolled her eyes. *More meaningless jabber. I guess if we're wrapped like sausages, we won't fall out every time the ship rides a wave.* She tensed and relaxed muscles and inhaled deeply in her battle for calm. *How do I breathe in these things? I will not make a fool of myself.* The shouting over their heads decreased as the ship's motion increased. *It's like being in a tree on a windy day. I can get used to this. Think about something else... like magic. Estaen asked if magic is alive and physical. It's a force. He seems to be living. But if the Athenque aren't...*

That's right, Zheann.

Something hit her shoulder. "Ow!" Her eyes snapped open. She struggled with the hammock for a breath before separating the hems and peeking out.

The captain stood with his back to her. "Come on. Time for a mandatory ship tour."

The captain. Ship. Right. Before Zheann could extricate herself from her cocoon, the captain's boots crossed the floor. She heard other quiet movements, muffled voices. By pushing both hems apart and shoving her legs out, she managed to escape the hammock. *There must be a better way to do this.* She blinked and raised her hand to block light streaming through the hatch. The captain handed her a mug, and she emptied it before recognizing Sea Calm's bitter taste and pleasant effect. She followed the captain. *How long has everyone else been awake?*

Weight lifted from her when she stepped into the sunshine, but a breeze from the water raised goosebumps. She snugged her cloak in tight. Besides Dorlew and Tinjier, there were three Med sailors. One looked around Dorlew's age, and enough like him to be his relative. Another looked like he hadn't been away from a jideker for long, and the third as if he should still be in one. *Shouldn't there be more?* Behind the ship stretched blue water. She turned. Nothing but water.

Maybe it's a good thing I drank the Sea Calm. Ye fen... a strange longing and fearful ache filled her heart, and a sense of déjà vu. She'd been collecting herbs in a clearing when fog had rolled in. It seemed as if the world vanished in two breaths. *It's the same here. The sky is clear, but the world has disappeared. It's the sort of pain Estaen Parklaw would have written about in one of his poems.*

Captain Moln looked like a student waiting for a teacher. Foden stood behind him, watching him. Estaen leaned over the railing and stuck his hand out.

What are you doing?

Checking to see if the water is wet.

What?

Dorlew took his place before his class. "Now listen. The front of the ship is the bow, and when you move toward it, you're going forward. The back is the stern, and when you go toward it, you're moving aft." His voice sounded bored as he pointed the way he'd mentioned.

How many times has he given this lecture?

"That side is always starboard, no matter which direction you face, and the other side is port. Keep it straight and go where I, or one of my men tell you."

"If you find a leak or a fire, scream your fool heads off. We've never had either, but *The Chaser* is wood, we're a long way from land, and the water's a mite chilly. Don't move the stuff you find on the deck because you think it looks cluttered. Everything is where it is for reasons you don't need to know. Now, Tinjier tells me you've all had Sea Calm, so you can have a few minutes to look around before I send you below again."

Tinjier caught her attention. She walked over to where he stood, weaving around the piles Dorlew told them not to touch. *No land in any direction. I know they can use the sun and stars to guide them, but it's like the world went away.*

"How are you holding up?"

Lie. "Well enough. The Sea Calm has helped. I haven't felt sick yet. Why? Is there something wrong?"

"No, the sea makes some people a little mad. I don't get to talk to many Rys. I hoped you were a sane one, especially since your friend over there looks like a crazy one."

She smiled. "He may be, but I'll bet the horse he left in port knows more about magic than both of us put together could learn in a lifetime."

"You should have brought the horse instead."

Laughter danced from her. It threatened to dance away with her. *He's going to think I'm a crazy one.* "I doubt he's crazy, just curious."

"There's a difference?" Tinjier glanced over his shoulder to where Estaen stood looking at the sky.

"Well, yes. Crazy is individual. Curiosity spreads to others." She pulled her hood up.

Tinjier blinked. "That might explain Dorlew sometimes." His smile looked forced. "Looks like your curious friend wants to spread some crazy. I have some ropes to straighten and coil."

⸺ ⸺《◉》⸺ ⸺

Estaen arrived as Tinjier hastily retreated. "It is time we work on your problem of speaking your magic. Would you prefer to work here or below?"

Problem? "Below. Captain Dorlew is going to send us there anyway." He followed her into the cabin.

When she sat at the table, he continued into the galley and scavenged miscellaneous items, putting them into a pot. He put a candle on the table. "Light this, please."

She held the candle, murmured, and the wick caught fire. She raised an eyebrow at him.

Estaen tilted his head. "Why do you speak your magic?"

"I told you, that's what they taught us."

"Yes, but why did they teach you? Why were they taught?"

She blew the flame out with a sigh. "It helps us focus, and it lets the teacher know we are working the magic right." *Ha! Good reason.*

"Since I can hear what you say with your mind, the second reason doesn't apply here. You're right. It is a valid reason for students of Rys teachers. Your first reason: focus, is foolish. Would you not also focus if you said the magic in your head?"

She held the candle and thought the magic.

"Why don't you believe it will work, Zheann?"

"Who said I don't believe?"

"The candle."

She snorted. "Candles can't speak."

"Neither can they hear."

"If they can't hear..." *Of course, they can't hear.* She tried again. She put the candle on the table. "It's not working."

"And does magic work the first time your students try to focus it by speaking?"

"No, it takes practice."

His pale eyes shimmered.

She held the candle again. The second time she rehearsed the words, the wick caught fire. *I did it!* She blew out the flame and relit the candle. "I still don't see how this is going to help against Fiwal, Leed, or the dragons."

"It won't help you against the dragons. When you do not need words, you can work more magic more quickly, without warning your victim about what you intend." He took the candle away from her as the captain walked down the steps. Estaen put the flame out with his fingers, handed the candle to him, and gestured toward the tallow.

The Captain held his breath as she lit it again.

Estaen nodded. "It will help you break the hold the errors you've believed have over you. For instance, you claim you learned herbal magic, while Fiwal learned elemental, but you lit the candle."

She pointed at it, "That's elemental, but it's easy elemental. Everyone learns it."

"What makes the hard-elemental magic hard?"

"It takes learning about the elements: water, air, earth, and fire, and how they work. I don't suppose it's any harder than learning about herbs, but people tend to choose one or the other."

Estaen took the candle and held it. "Understanding the nature of things is helpful. Understanding magic is more so. By understanding it, one is free to work with whatever is at hand. If you understood magic, you would be better at elemental magic than Fiwal. His greater understanding of the elements would mean nothing. The candle disappeared in a ball of light from which Zheann shielded her eyes. The light winked out as Estaen put the candle on the table. "And the nature of magic is not found in your words." He took an onion from the pot and walked across the cabin. When he got to the space behind the stairs, he threw it.

The captain raised a hand to catch the odoriferous missile. Less than a hand's breadth from him, it veered sharply right and crunched against the hull.

Zheann leaped up, grabbed at the onion, but closed her hand on air. "Estaen!"

It ricocheted across the cabin to Estaen's waiting hand. Onion juice dribbled on the dark boards.

Captain Moln glowered. "In Jitherick, we hang Rys for less than that."

"They hang Rys for less than nothing?" Estaen tossed the onion into the air and caught it again. "No wonder they seek the dragons' aid."

The captain took a step toward him. His right hand drifted toward his dagger. "Are you this insolent to your master?"

"That would be for my master to judge but thank you for helping with my demonstration." He turned to Zheann. "You will not understand magic as long as your attention is on what is not magic."

When the captain continued to glare, Zheann rested her fingertips on the table. "Gares, did you want something, other than to beat a Rys?"

"I didn't..." He closed his eyes for two breaths. "Dorlew suggested I make lunch." He took the onion from Estaen on his way to the galley. "I'd better do it before he throws me overboard."

"Did you have to bait him?" Zheann said.

Estaen met her gaze. "If I had thrown the onion at the wall, would you have paid as much attention?"

She considered for a breath. "Probably not."

The captain filled a pot with water. "Zheann, since you're lighting things on fire, light the stove."

On her fourth try flames appeared. Her smile made her face hurt.

<hr />

Estaen returned to the table and emptied his pot. Twine, a fork, two more onions, a wooden cup, several pieces of charcoal, and a piece of faded cloth fell out. He put the pot aside. "Spend the morning working magic you know with these or anything else you can find to play with. No words." He ascended into the sunlight.

"I may have to reconsider the idea of you going to learn from his master." The captain chopped root vegetables and tossed them into a pot. "But knowing how to throw and knock onions aside will be useful in battle."

Zheann examined the candle. "What does he want me to understand?" She lit the wick, blew it out. She held an onion in her other hand. She worked magic to make it stronger. She weakened it again.

"Whatever you did, undo it," the Captain said.

"What?"

"The onion." He rubbed at his face with the back of his wrist.

"Oh, Sorry. I did."

She lit the candle again. *Ye fen dernai haloim. What's that asking some lord to give? Wisdom? The Athenque are magical. The Rys are halflings, both physical and magical. The Med are physical. He said magic can only do what it's sent to do. If the words don't control it, how do I send it? I think.* She blew out the candle and put it and the onion on the table. She closed her eyes. *No, I do more than think. I will. Where is the magic? Nowhere.* She lit the candle again. *There.*

A memory flashed through her mind of holding a piece of resin and wanting it to glow. She had scolded it. Mama had said, "Hush, Zheann, magic is quiet." *Was that the first time I heard someone say that?*

Papa said not to be angry. The magic wouldn't want to come if I was mad any more than I would want to go to Papa if he were mad at me. I've told my students the same thing. What does he want me to figure out? What is the mistake children make? They try to force the magic. They try to be the magic or make the magic. The magic is not within us. It's not ours. We use it. We use it to make things more, or less. Why can't I apply what I teach to what I do?

She pushed the onion into a wobbly roll. She stood and tried it again using magic. *When I made the Med itch, I used magic to throw the dust. Is that all he did with the onion? No, he threw the onion.* She worked through the hex she'd used. The onion hit the galley wall, missing the captain by an exhaled breath. *I did it!*

"Zheann!"

"I'm sorry, I forgot you were there. I was trying to figure out how Estaen did it."

"And did you? Or do I get to be the target of more food?"

"It didn't hit you. You weren't the target." She leaned on the table and her face burned. "I didn't have a target. Now step back. Let me see if I can bring it back."

He glared, then quickly moved to stand beside the onion.

She pulled on the onion. The second time it flew and struck her shoulder, and she yelped.

The captain doubled over in laughter while she wiped away tears. She turned at the sound of footsteps on the stairs.

Foden was half-way to the floor with his dagger in his hand. His eyes narrowed from alarm to suspicion.

"She...can't...catch," the captain said, gasping.

The furrow in Foden's brow deepened and his nose wrinkled. He put his dagger in its sheath. "Gares, how many onions are you putting in the soup?"

His question brought new waves of laughter from the captain. Foden watched her rubbing her shoulder. "What happened to you?"

"I hit it with an onion," she said.

"How?" He settled into his hammock. "Don't tell me. I'll stay over here to watch."

Onion juice leaked onto the table. She considered the other items Estaen had left her. "Is there any more twine around?" After a quick search, she wound it into a ball and practiced with it until the crew came below for lunch.

Chapter Twelve

Divhad, 24 Troleng 153, at sea

Zheann considered the table, large enough for four Med on each side. *If it weren't bolted to the floor, and I pushed it into the hull, we might sink. What else can I use?* She threw the ball of twine. It bounced off the wall and rolled across the floor before she could use magic on it. She picked it up and threw it again. "What does this teach me?" she said as she crossed to retrieve it.

Another battle raged behind the captain's eyes. This time, it seemed to be between anxiety and amusement. "Basic battle skills. Attack and defend."

She crossed the cabin three more times, chasing the twine. The sixth time, it dropped next to the table.

The captain applauded with exaggerated lethargy.

She rolled her eyes. "I was trying to throw it toward the bunks."

"At least you managed to stop it."

After hitting the twine twice more in ten attempts, she gave it to the captain. "Once I get ready, throw it at me." She hurried to the other end of the table and leaned against it as the ship's bow rose. *This would be easier on land.* She held on to the table as *the Chaser* crested the wave. *Remember, it can't hurt. It's only twine.* She worked her magic. "Ready."

He threw the twine.

She rubbed her breastbone. "Ow, not so hard!"

He caught the twine she threw.

"Ready." This time the ball stopped a pace away and fell. She threw it back. When the captain grew bored with the game, she practiced throwing it and pulling it back.

Tinjier descended the steps and caught the twine. He tossed it to her and continued to the galley. "They'll be coming for dinner soon."

Estaen followed him but sat next to Zheann. "How is your shoulder?"

"Sore, I managed to hit the twine ball three times and to shield against it eight."

The captain sat opposite him. "She takes too much time on her shield. I could release three arrows before she gets ready."

Estaen cupped his chin in his hand. "Now that you are not saying the words, try not thinking them. Instead, simply mean them."

"Simply mean them?"

"Yes. When you try to throw twine, are you confused about what you are trying to throw?"

"No. I'm confused about what you're trying to teach me."

"Then why do you need to say or think *twine?* When you are throwing it, do you not know what the target is? Why think anything more than 'Go'?" His knife lodged itself into a cross beam above their heads.

"Hey!" The captain glowered.

"Don't worry, Captain, it's only good enough to butter bread."

Go, she told the twine ball. *Go!*

The twine arched toward the same beam but missed and dropped on Estaen's head. He caught it before it hit the table. "You see?"

"Maybe"

"Now, does it matter whether you are throwing twine or the table?"

"I'm sure it matters to Dorlew."

Estaen pursed his lips. "You have a point. Something smaller than the table would be wise. Perhaps the captain would volunteer."

The captain rose and leaned on the table. "You want me to give her permission to hex me?"

"Not hex, merely move."

He glowered at Estaen. When he seemed ready to explode, his squint changed. What had seemed like lightning building to strike became a deep, dark pool. "That might be useful, practiced slowly and with precision."

Zheann chuckled. "You'll be lucky if I don't throw you through the hull or out the hatch and into the water. You can't be seriously considering ... You are." She rubbed her face. "I'll try, but only after you, Foden, and *The Chaser*'s crew all sign a paper saying you have granted permission. I don't want to be killed for hexing a Med who asked me to."

Chapter Thirteen

Divhad, 24 Troleng 153, at sea

Zheann took a bite of thick slice of rye bread. "How far ahead of us do you think they are?"

"The better part of a day, if they kept moving." The captain sipped at his mug of tea and wrinkled his nose at it. "If we're lucky, they don't know about Awasain Jeingsi, and they're wandering around. If they asked a Kotich storyteller, they'll have learned."

Zheann tried her tea, and almost spit it into the cup. She swallowed and coughed. "Wow! Strong." She took another, smaller sip. "I think I can get used to it."

A shadow fell over the hatchway. "Come on deck." Dorlew walked away again. They put their food down and hurried to the deck. He swung his right hand in a long horizontal arc starboard, "The Great Ice Land."

A ribbon of white lay on the water and she walked to the railing to drink in the sight. The sense of foreboding and lostness receded like a wave. *We're going there. That's where we'll find Leed and Fiwal, and where all this will end, I hope. We are no longer in a fogless fog.*

"I figure well reach Guelph in a third or two. It's the largest town you'll find along the coast this far north, and it's an active trading center. Once we leave there, it'll be another day before you'll see Awasain Jeingsi, if we don't stop in any ports."

"Have you seen any ships heading west?" The captain said.

"Two. One wasn't the *Tern*. The other was too far away to tell, but I doubt it."

"Take us in close enough to Guelph to see what ships are in port. I want to stay on deck with your crew, to help keep watch. I'd prefer they didn't surprise us. Once we know who is there, we can go to the docks."

Zheann turned toward the conversation. "I thought we were going to Swisao."

Dorlew shook his head. "If they're headed to Awasain Jeingsi, they wouldn't head south to Swisao. If they did, they'll have to come north along the coast. Guelph is a more likely destination, or at least it's on the way."

"Is there a jideker in Guelph? I mean, do any Rys live there?"

Dorlew sneered. "Yeah, of course, plenty of Rys and Med live there. It's not a Southern Kingdom. There are about as many deer-herders. They call themselves Kotich. Don't know that you'd think much of their jideker, but the Kotich tell stories. If you plan to ask about the mountain, you'll want to ask Nuagte and Kwin. Kwin's one of your kind. They don't run the town, but folks say even the ice appeases Nu. Of course, I can't say she won't invent most of what she tells you." He looked at the deck, moving his fingers as if he were counting. "You have about a third to decide if you want to visit."

Captain Moln joined her at the railing. "It makes sense that they would come here. Their movements have been straightforward. Only you and I will visit Nuagte and Kwin. Dorlew's men can find out if the ship they hired came to port. We'll spare the people of Guelph a visit from Estaen."

Zheann sniffed as she leaned on the railing. "I hope they went to Guelph, but I hope they've already left."

He frowned at her.

She turned to look at the white ribbon floating on blue water. "I don't want other people to suffer when we're killing them."

⸺⸺◈⸺⸺

He's got to be kidding. How are we supposed to get up there? Zheann and the captain had left Dorlew to find out if the *Arctic Tern* had been in port. Pebbles crunched as they crossed a narrow beach. She peered at white and blue ice that stretched to the sky. Rags fluttered, zig zagging from the beach to the top of the cliff. Fat people in brown moved along the rags with amazing dexterity. One person stood about halfway to the top, holding something up. A white bird flew near and plucked it from the hand. In a few places, brown rectangles marked the ice. *A path? Stairs? Doors? Do they live in the ice like the people of Jifreb do in their mountains?* "Have you ever been here before?"

The captain tilted his head to regard the cliff. "About eleven years ago. The general and I spent about a week hunting reindeer." He pointed to their left. "They use a platform over there to move cargo between the pier and the town. Unless they've changed, I doubt they would take us even if we paid. If you can't make it to town by the stairs, you have no business in Guelph. One of my men told me there are some villages along the coast where you must climb a rope. They pull cargo up by hand. Not neighborly, but safe. Ready?"

She stepped onto the black stones that lined the first tread. "The Kotich must be tall."

"They're shorter than Med but about the same height as the people of all the other kingdoms. And they may look as fat as King Eswok, but it's their clothes. It's not that everyone else is tall, it's that you Rys are Athenque-spawn. When you got magic, you shrank.

Some Med think that dragons are about half your height, and the paintings at the gate are exaggerations meant to frighten raiders."

"You're joking, right?"

He smirked as she took two steps to get from one tread to the next.

She turned her focus to the steps. *Don't tell him how ludicrous that sounds. What would Fiwal think if he freed the dragons, and found they were Dren's size?* She stopped.

"Need a rest?"

She tilted her head and glared at him. "The stories say that the dragons are trapped in a ring under the snow and ice on a mountain."

"Which supports the idea that they're tiny."

"No, it supports the idea that Athenque are magical beings who can be any size they want to, or any size a hex compels them to be." *Ha!* She strode past him, head held high. *But how will we find something that would fit around my finger, or even his finger?*

When they reached the top, they both stopped to catch their breaths. An icy road lined with light poles like the ones in Jifreb ran between brown buildings. Smoke rose from the center of many domed roofs. Other buildings' roofs were sharply peaked and had many chimneys. The nearest, a domed type, looked like it had a crack running along the side, and several more breaks in front. *Not cracks, seams. A building made of leather. That's got to be cold.*

Several shaggy deer wandered over to them and didn't run away when the captain waved at them. He pushed one and chirped. "Any idea...where...the jideker... is?" He swallowed, inhaled deeply, and coughed.

"I... don't even know...where the doors are. I thought you've... been here."

"They're flaps, and they move Kotich buildings around to suit changing needs."

"Oh. I suppose... the jideker will be ...a big round building.

Or a group of big round buildings, in a town full of round leather buildings."

A Med in ornamented deer hide walked out of a brick structure. "What're you looking for?"

"Nu and Kwin," the captain said.

"They'll bae at the jideker." The Med gestured at the road east. After considering them for two breaths, her shoulders slumped. In a resigned tone, she said, "I'll take you."

They followed her trudging form to a side road where she made the vague gesture again. "Try in there." She walked back the way they'd come.

———

The captain smirked and waved his hand as their guide had. Seven round, domed buildings lined the street. All had smoke rising from the center of the domes. He led Zheann to the largest structure and tugged the flap to the side.

Underneath, she found a more conventional door. She tapped on it and, hearing a voice, fumbled with a latch that turned instead of slid. Inside, she discovered that the animal skins wrapped a framework of wood, deer antlers, and bones. The leather's inner side still had a long, chestnut brown fur attached. Overhead, seven bones curved along the dome, with the narrowest part at the apex. *What creature has hair or bones like those?* In a square around the central fire, there were low bookshelves and a circle of seven tables. Ten people read at four. At each place where someone read, a carved piece of wood extended above the tabletop.

Warm and cozy. Zheann skirted the bookcases. She stopped at the table where a woman sat. She wore leather nearly the same color as her skin. Gray hair hung to her shoulders. "Mistress Nuagte?"

"That bae me." A stocky woman at another table and with more gray in her hair gestured to a chair a lanky Med was vacating. "Come. Sit. What do you want?"

"Mistress, I want...I need to know about the dragons, and about Awasain Jeingsi. Do the dragons truly exist?"

She stared at Zheann with heavy-lidded, sleepy eyes.

"Did two Rys already ask you about them? Please, it's imperative that we know." *Please, say something.*

"How bae you going to Awasain Jeingsi?"

"By ship. Is there a better way?"

"Better? Yes. Faster? Mm, doubtful."

"Mistress Nuagte, will you help us? Did the two men talk to you? What did you tell them?"

"What d'ye want with the jeingsi?"

I hope jeingsi means dragon. "Nothing. We want to stop the men before they get there. Before they do something foolish."

"Too late for that, but maybe we stop them before they do something more foolish." She closed her book with a slap and stood. Like the *Compendium Donezan,* an embossed dragon decorated the cover. She collected it and two other volumes. "Ship, eh?" She huffed. "We go now. We find Kwin, and we find your two jeingsi before they find the jeingsi." She tapped the dragon on the book. She pulled the piece of wood out of the the corner of the table. She held it as a short staff as she examined Zheann from head to toe. "You call me Nu. Everyone does."

Nu turned toward the other readers, and they nodded. She stopped and looked up at Captain Moln. Her eyes narrowed further. "I remember you. You bae the Med boy who called the deer."

His face reddened. His mouth twitched.

"You still call deer?"

"No, but I still whistle."

"Hm. Calling deer bae more useful."

His mouth twitched again, a little harder.

Was that twitch a smile? A real smile?

She considered Zheann. "Do you have more Rys with you?"

Zheann grimaced "One, and one more Med."

Nu snorted. "You bring Medsi to a battle with Ryssi and jeingsi."

The captain snorted. "Dead Rys can't work magic, and we haven't found the jeingsi yet."

"True, true." Nu's eyes twinkled. "But the Ryssi bae not so easy to kill except by Medsi, because it is only against Medsi they do not use magic."

——◇——

The captain followed Zheann, who was hurrying to stay with the leathery woman. They stopped at a path to another building, and Nu shouted, "Kwin, come out! You bae right."

A Rys boy pushed aside the leather flap. "He asks where to meet you."

"The water. Quick. We go now!" Nu snapped her fingers several times. She walked to the corner but turned north. They followed her into a small building that reminded Zheann of her home behind the shop. A bag full of equipment sat on a table that looked ready to fall apart. Nu added the books and a few more items and closed the flap. She hefted the bag to her shoulder. "We stop at the trading post. You get what I tell them. You pay, or you do not get what you need, and you likely die." She watched the captain's face darken, then pushed past him. "Medsi we jeing baniksi."

"Meds" maybe "are" ... cursed somethings.

At the main road, she turned toward the sea. "What bae your ship?"

He glared at her. "*The Chaser*"

She grimaced, showing yellowed teeth. "How many of you climb mountains? How many bae archers?"

"Foden is a mountaineer. We're both archers."

"How many know ice?"

"Foden might, but Zheann and Estaen don't know those things either." He turned toward her, "Do you?"

Zheann pointed at the largest building in sight. "If I shot an arrow at that building, everything but the building would be in danger, unless I use magic."

"You're not much better with magic."

Do not throw something at him. Wait until practice. "Estaen can hit what he aims at, but I doubt he'd use a bow."

They turned toward a large building with a pitched roof. Smoke rose from three chimneys. Instead of skins, there were glass windows with shutters thrown wide. "You have money?" Nu asked.

They nodded.

As they entered, Nu repeated her finger snapping. "Come, now, these bae buying to go on the glaciers. Two Medsi, three Ryssi, and me. Two heavy bows. Two light."

The captain squinted at Nu and gave her one of his twisted smiles.

Zheann stepped closer. "Estaen and I won't need bows."

"Two heavy, two light," Nu said.

The shop had only one set of shelves stocked with herbs. Weapons, clothes, food, tools, and even toys cluttered every surface. *Fiwal would love this place.*

The shopkeeper scuttled in beaming his best merchant smile. He was Rys, but his skin had the same leathery texture as Nu's. His tousled hair and small teeth were brilliantly white. One bright blue eye shone in greeting, but the other looked milky.

As Nu continued listing items, Zheann wandered to the wall and examined the baskets of herbs. She filled pouches, recording the contents on tags sewn into the seam. *I'll have to try ...* Her heart sank. She pulled out her purse, but the captain shook his head. He counted out the charge. "And when we come back, we'll be returning what we don't use. I expect a refund."

What? No "King's business?" No "recompense?" Zheann put all but one herb pouch on the counter. She murmured at it, working magic for long enough that the captain glared. "I noticed your eye," she said to the old man. "Make a tea with these. Let them steep for a third, then strain out the herbs and put three drops in your eye, every third during the day. Keep using it until your eye clears."

"When you return from the glaciers, stop in. If it's working, I'll give you refund for all this." He grinned at her.

An honest grin?

Nu stared at her for a breath before turning to the shopkeeper. "We use your sled."

The old man winked. "If Kwin bae going with you, tell him to send the deer home. If not, I send Higor to fetch it. You bae going to sea?"

Nu growled an answer in Kotichite, and he answered with a boisterous laugh.

⸺⸺•(◦)•⸺⸺

By the time they finished loading the sled, another Rys man arrived. His nearly white hair contrasted sharply with his sun darkened skin.

Does the cold turn Rys hair white? Or are they all related?

"About time, Kwin."

"You aren't at the shore yet." He added his pack to the sled and walked to the corral next to the shop murmuring at the deer with fat antlers. Two came close. He put leads on their harnesses and made quick business of hitching them to the sled. He chirped to coax them into motion. Nu led them north, past the stairs, to an area of ice with ropes strung on light poles at her waist level.

Kwin waved a hand with high drama. "Going down."

"Jeing Rys yanayen" Nu's tone seemed derisive, but she smiled at Kwin, and he returned it. The ground lurched. They sank toward the beach.

It will take as long to ride to the beach down as it did to walk to the town.

Kwin stepped closer. "So, what brought you on the hunt to find these fools?"

"One is my cousin, the other my husband, and I am a mistress at the jideker in Jitherick. I didn't give the Captain a choice."

"You know Mistress Jenem."

Zheann smiled. "Yes, she was one of my teachers."

"She and I have been epistolary lovers for... oh well, it feels like centuries. I was one of her students, too, until I caught the wanderlust." He gave her a coy smile.

"She has decided it was time to step back from teaching a little. I agreed to help with the herb craft. She's teaching elemental magic now." The ocean, though never still, seemed languid in its roll. Gulls dipped and glided, scolding the ships. "You and Nu both make it sound like you knew it wasn't wise to give Fiwal and Leed information. What did you tell them? Why did you tell them anything?"

He turned toward the sea as well and sighed. "Nu is a Kotich, and a tribal shaman or teacher."

"Shaman?"

Kwin scratched his ear. "The Kotich who follow the old ways are a superstitious lot."

The floor stopped sinking. Nu snorted. "Hoon." She lengthened her stride, joining the captain as he crossed the pebble beach.

Kwin turned a little pink under his tan but he waved at her back and called, "Mish." He looked at Zheann. "Don't ask. Now, the

Kotich believe there is a magical being out there somewhere they call the Father of Skies. The shamans are, well, sort of intermediaries between him and us. Their main tasks are to preserve stories about him and teach Kotich ways. I came here for the stories and haven't run out yet. Sharing information is natural to them, especially if it deals with travels. She had second thoughts after they left and told me about them. I told her they were cursed fools. We were planning to leave when my class ended, but we were going across the ice. Nu's brother went to sea and the ship sank. He survived and came home, but the stories he tells leave a person reluctant to trust the deep. Were it not for the Jeingsi, I doubt she would." He glanced her way. "So now that they are out of earshot, how bad is it likely to get?"

Do I play dumb? Lie? That's not fair. "The worst. Since this isn't the Medenva kingdom, it might not come here."

"But best to be prepared." He acted as if she'd commented on the weather. "I'm glad you arrived when you did. The trip across the ice would have taken at least six days, even with two sleds and eight deer. Even if we had sakwa, it would take five days."

"What's a sakwa?"

He walked for several steps in silence. "It's a long-haired beast as tall as a house. They have a nose that hangs off their faces like an arm. They can move them and even carry things with them. The bones the Kotich use to make their domes are either tusks or sometimes ribs. They have legs like tree trunks and can carry three or four people, going faster than a reindeer over long distances. The ship will still be faster. Chances are we'll still be too late. I'm hoping the dragons will need time to stretch and yawn, eat your family, regain strength, and figure out where to find more food." When she winced, he added, "Sorry."

"How many jeingsi are there?"

"Ask Nu. It will take her mind off her being in a leaky box that attracts objects on which to wreck itself. I have heard as few as one and as many as six." His eyebrows rose, and he turned toward her. "You're Zheann."

"Yes."

"That's right. Jenem wrote about you. You are Ronsath and Poyen's daughter. She said you were going to take over the jideker."

Her face grew warm. "She was generous."

"Clearly, she didn't mention me in a way that made my name stick in your mind."

"She doesn't tend to talk to me about much but magic and teaching. What can you tell me about the dragons?"

"Nothing Nu can't tell better. Have her tell you. I'll warn you, though, she can't summarize a story. It's not in her blood."

————)((◊)) ————

Captain Dorlew met them on the dock. "As nice as it is to have you and Nu aboard, Kwin, next time slit my throat, will you? She's below, and my crew is going to mutiny before we leave the port. Go make her stop. I'll have my men unload your cart."

Before they got to the hatch, a stream of Kotichite spewed out. Kwin looked at her with an expression of long-suffering. "Did I mention Kotich can be expressive?"

"Is she saying anything that makes sense?"

"She's looking for the things that will sink the ship."

"How is she likely to respond if I hex her?" *Estaen, where are you? Can you help?*

She hurried into the cabin. The captain, Foden, and Estaen sat in their berths, watching as Nu continued removing things from a cupboard onto the table and scrubbing the shelves. Tinjier rearranged things in another cupboard. A Med stood at the galley entrance, truncheon in hand.

How will cleaning keep us from sinking? What will he do when she challenges him?

Kwin walked over to Nu, pushing down on air with both hands. "Nu, this bae Dorlew's ship. Tinjier wouldn't allow a leak. Let him put everything away."

Nu glared at him.

He moved closer. "Nuagte, you can go back to the jideker if you wish. I have seen you face a bear and a sakwa. Your great ancestor was Nuyoo who faced the jeingsi. The sea is more fearsome, but I have faced it, and I bae a jeing Rys. I'll tell you what: I'll take full responsibility if we sink."

She threw the rag she'd been using on the table. "That bae too late and the sea bae much bigger than a Sakwa." She strode to a berth on the crew's side and inched her way into it.

Zheann pulled Sea Calm from her bag and added three drops to a mug of water. She walked to where Nu huddled. "Here, drink this. It will keep your stomach calm."

She took the cup and drained it. "I do not know the sea can make the stomach sick, too." She glared at Kwin.

"Now it won't." Kwin raised his hand when Zheann offered him the cup. "Sea Calm bothers my stomach more than the sea does."

As Zheann scanned the cabin, Captain Moln met her look and rolled his eyes. She walked over and handed things to Tinjier: cloth, candles, two empty flasks. He packed them away without a word. The sailor guarding the galley put his weapon away and ascended out of the cabin.

"Gares!" Captain Dorlew shouted.

Captain Moln took the stairs at a run. A moment later, his shout had Foden following him. By the time Zheann reached the stairs, Foden was halfway back. He handed her several short staffs like Nu's. She put them on the table and turned around in time to have four quivers of arrows, and two heavy bows swing at her face. She leaned back and brought her hands up, first to ward off the blow, then to grab them as they fell. Kwin and Estaen joined her, loading the table with Nu's commanded supplies.

The captain added the last load to the table, and they divided the pile among themselves. The floor beneath their feet shifted as *The Chaser* slipped away to the freedom of the ocean once again.

I don't need a bow.

I know, Estaen. Take it anyway. Maintain appearances. After Zheann put her things in her berth, she sat next to Nu. "Are you feeling better? Can you tell us about the Jeingsi?"

Nu looked around the cabin, eyes wild but face composed. She tapped her staff against the floor. "Hear the story of the Jeingsi. Once, the Kotich do not live on the ice. We live in warmth and sun. We grow into seven tribes. One day, a jeing hunts our deer, then two, and they grow bold, attacking tribal camps. Nuthov, our chieftain says, 'Kinsmen, these who come to rob us must bae cursed, for they are a curse to us. Seek the wisdom from the Father of the Sky. Learn how we must do this.'

"The Shaman bae Ocojee, Nuyoo..." She glared as Kwin made a circle with his finger, then she sighed. "They seek wisdom from the dark moon to the dark moon, and they return to the council fire. Ocojee stands before Nuthov and says, 'Kind Father, you send us to seek the wisdom from the Father of the Sky. We return now with what we find. To the north and west, there bae an awasain that bae a ring rising from the sea.'"

The mountain is a ring? How? As she listened, Zheann pulled out three bowls and spread herbs around them. She poured water into the containers and used magic to heat it before adding herbs to each. She nodded at Nu.

"The shaman of each tribe goes there and brings sacrifices from each tribe. The jeingsi come to take the gifts and we speak the magic to trap them there. But if we imprison them, the magic of that prison will cover our land.

"And so, the shaman make gold bowls, and gold torches, and they take many deer and gifts. They walk for many days to where the land ends. They cut trees to make boats to take them to the awasain. There, they find a man who baen't Kotich. 'Who bae ye?' Solviya asks.

"'The Father of the Sky tells me to come to help you curse the jeingsi.' His face is like a child's, but his eyes like a shaman's.

"The shaman sense this bae good, and they welcome him as they climb the awasain. They stand on the ring of the awasain and herd the deer into the center. They put the gifts into the ring as well. They wait for many days. They fast, and the deer cry for food. And the jeingsi come, flying east across the sea, the sun shines on their skin as on water. The shaman hide among the rocks, and the jeingsi come to feed and to claim their prize. When all six are feeding, the shaman rise, and chant their magic. The jeingsi roar and try to break the hex, but they cannot leave the inside of the ring."

A ball of twine bounced off Zheann's shoulder. She looked up to find the captain glaring at her, his finger across his lips. Her face burned, and she looked at Nu. The shaman didn't seem to notice. Zheann tried again with her lips pressed into a thin line. The water in the first bowl turned a deep crimson.

Estaen seemed to be listening with as much rapt attention as the Med.

"And, one jeing climbs the side of the ring beneath where Solviya stands. He does not see the jeing. The man who is not Kotich pulls a long knife from his belt and enters the circle. 'Do not stop your magic,' he cries, and joins his voice to theirs as he fights to keep the jeingsi in the ring. Snow falls, and they chant. For four more days, they sing, and the snow falls so they cannot see the next one. The man who is not Kotich disappears with the jeingsi."

The water in the second bowl turned brown.

"At the end of four days, Ebbiui says, 'We do magic for four days, as the Father of the Sky tells us. Let us do magic three more days. That way we bae sure the jeingsi do not escape.' For three more days they do magic. When they turn from the awasain, they find that ice covers the awasain, and it grows along the shore. They return home, and the ice follows them.

'Jeingsi!' Nuthov said. 'I send you to rid our land of jeingsi, and you bring a curse with you.'"

The water in the third bowl turned blue. Zheann pointed to the captain's arrows but he sat staring at Nu. Foden tapped the captain's arm with his knuckles. He glared at Foden, who pointed at her. He glared at her but brought the quiver to her. She dipped the arrowheads in each bowl. When they dried, she returned them to the quiver.

"'It baen't a curse,' Ebbiui says. 'It bae proof the jeingsi bae trapped. If the ice melts, the jeingsi escape again. So, my tribe celebrates, and I teach no more magic to the shamans, so they do not melt the snow.'"

Captain Moln stood, slapping his thighs. "You mean you don't know the magic to trap the dragons again?"

"No, we do no more magic, to keep the jeingsi trapped beneath the ice."

"Great," he turned to Zheann. "Is this the story you think Fiwal knew?"

"He said the dragons live in the Great Ice Land. He never mentioned any traps. He thought they were our allies. He may have thought they didn't know we needed help, but I doubt he thought they needed ours. They were our symbol and the emblem of our kings. Most of us don't think they are connected to our wickedness.

Our crime began with King Taelfa." She stared at the hull for a few breaths. "I guess that doesn't make sense. We were raised believing Athenque are evil, but the dragons also remind us of a time when we thought we were free."

Nu sighed. "They ask about the jeingsi. Say they hear stories and want the true story. I bae a shaman, I tell them. They bae happy to hear my stories, too happy maybe. After they leave, I tell Kwin. We ask others. They leave on their ship soon after they talk to me, but they don't buy supplies for ice, except for clothes. So, maybe they fall and die. Maybe they freeze and die."

Zheann waved two arrows gently. "If they don't, these will kill them, even if it doesn't work against the dragons."

Foden rubbed his face with both hands. "What do you mean it won't work against them?"

Her face and shoulders relaxed. *Stick to what you decided to tell them.* "A book we got in Jifreb is about the Athenque. It says they are magical, not physical like we are. The books on the subject teach that magic is not alive, and it's not physical. If the dragons are magical, they aren't alive. That means they can't die."

Nu grunted. "Yes, that bae why the Father of the Sky tells the shamans to trap them."

Chapter Fourteen

Solim, 25 Troleng 153, Off the coast of the Great Ice Land

"Come up here," Dorlew called. Captain Moln and Foden bounded up the stairs. Zheann followed, squinting in the sunlight. Dorlew pointed at Estaen as he stood at the bow. "That's Awasain Jeingsi," he said. "We will arrive by tomorrow morning. If we run dark, they won't know we're coming."

Zheann joined Estaen at the bow. *Where?* The Great Ice Land filled the starboard horizon like a ribbon, and at its northern tip, a bump rose like a wrinkle. *No, more like an "A" written on a string.*

Estaen, are they there? The dragons? Your ...friend? The man who was not Kotich?

I can find them nowhere else.

Kwin leaned on the railing beside her. "If the dragons escape, how angry are they going to be that the Kotich thwarted them?"

"Very," Nu said.

She came on deck? I suppose we can sink as easily if she's here as we can with her in the cabin.

A voice rang out from above them. "Ship ahead!"

Dorlew pointed at the hatch. "The show's over! Get below!"

"We can help fight," Captain Moln offered.

"Ye can swim! We don't know there's a fight to be had. Do as you're told!"

———◈———

Foden met the captain halfway down the stairs and handed him his bow and quiver. The captain nocked an arrow and headed toward the deck again. "The rest of you say in your berths until we know what's going on."

Zheann climbed into her hammock with her books. "Kwin, what sort of magic do you know best?"

Color rose through his tan cheeks. "The Kotich don't use magic. They worry it will release the dragons. The Rys who live there don't use much. I teach basic elemental. It's been years since I was what you would consider good."

Nu said, "He understands animals and ice."

And that settles that! She held a book out to him. "Here. See if you can find anything useful."

"I'm sorry, Zheann." He took the book.

"You have no reason to be sorry. Papa told me making assumptions was like walking on ice. Sometimes it holds you. More often, it doesn't, and you end up wet, cold, and in need of rescue. I assumed because you're Jenem's friend and a teacher that you must be at least as skilled as she." She smiled. "Splash." She opened another book. *Find something useful, like a chapter entitled, "How to Trap an Athenque." Athenque are magic. Magic is power. Does Jenem or Fiwal know how to make a power trap? There might be something in the book on water wheels.* She found it and skimmed the contents.

"I doubt anyone is as skilled as Jenem." Kwin grimaced as he sat at the table. "We are both passionate, but about different things.

She loves magic. I love exploring and collecting stories. So, let's see where this takes us."

Estaen picked up the book Zheann had discarded. "*Compendium of Queen Donezan*. That should be interesting." He sat in his hammock.

⫸⫷◉⫸⫷

Sometime later, the captain clomped down the stairs. "I hoped they'd be dead or gagged and bound to the ship's mast. Their captain decided the money wasn't worth any more of their madness. He left them on the island. The good news is they don't seem to have any idea we're following them, and none of the crew saw any dragons. Dorlew traded banners with the other ship. If they see us, and we're lucky, they'll think the captain reconsidered."

"It sounds to me," Estaen said, "as if Dorlew has performed a clever bit of magic."

"What?" The captain squinted at him.

Estaen filled a mug with water and handed it to the captain. "To make it seem there is one when there are two produces the effect of magic without the power thereof. Things are not always as they seem."

The captain's eyes widened as the contents of the mug steamed. "So, it seems like we Med are good for something." He sniffed at the mug and took a sip, and then a slurp. When he caught her watching him, he said, "Shouldn't you be practicing your battle skills?"

Ginger tea. That would be nice but how did he do it? Zheann held up her book. "I am. I'm trying to find a hex that can trap magic." She put the book aside and found her ball of twine. Before long, Kwin asked her to teach him. It was dinner time before he knocked the string aside. Zheann had hit a dozen.

"We're not very effective," Kwin said as he sat.

"It is progress," Estaen said. "You might spend the evening considering how to make your magic larger. Treat it like a shield instead of a club."

They ate and spent the evening experimenting before crawling into their berths.

———— ((O)) ————

Tracks in the snow guided her. To the left, the ground fell away through clouds a long way below her. With the certainty found in dreams she knew the drop never ended. The icy ground expanded around her feet. She stood before a stone ring set in the ice and put out her hand. *Can I take it from the ice?* A fierce wind blew stinging snow into her face but did nothing to the fog rising around her.

Fiwal stood a short distance away, his navy cloak blowing, looking at her, his face twisted with hatred. She drew a bowstring and sighted along the arrow's shaft. Something moved through the fog and snow. A massive blue-white head rose and jaws closed around Fiwal. His muffled scream ended abruptly. A large blue eye opened in the mist and gazed at her.

She woke with a cry and tried to sit up. Her head hit something. When she forced the hems of her berth apart, the captain, Foden, Kwin, and Nu were watching her. "I'm sorry." Her face heated. "It was a dream." *Wasn't it?*

Yes, halfling.

Tinjier leaned over the hatch's side, peering at her along the ceiling. "Everything OK down there?"

"Yes," Foden said. "She had a nightmare."

Tinjier fell silent for a breath before saying, "Well, since you're awake, come see this. It will drive the nightmare away."

They all hurried to the deck and looked beyond the bow. High in the sky, a ribbon of green light undulated.

"Sky fire." Kwin clapped Nu's arm.

Nu grinned. "This bae a good sign. The Father of the Sky will protect us."

The ribbon writhed and coiled. Other ribbons of green and white slithered by. Zheann leaned on the railing, trying to get closer. "We see them at Jitherick, but never like this."

A dim red light appeared beneath the green ribbons. It seemed to grow, and to fall in on itself like a starving fire. Zheann gasped. *Magic!* She worked her own, directing with her hand. The red glow arched westward into the sea. Several breaths later, a clap of thunder split the air.

"What was that?" Captain Moln asked.

"I assumed Leed designed it to free the dragons. I knocked it into the sea. I almost can't believe I did it, but I'm afraid I made a mistake."

Estaen peered north. "A small one."

"Mistake?" Foden said. "You stopped them."

"I doubt it."

"Wave!" the youngest sailor shouted from overhead.

"Get below, batten the hatch!" Dorlew ordered as he and his men scrambled. Moln wrapped his arm around Zheann's shoulders and shoved her onto the stairs. She missed the first several steps and landed in a heap at the bottom. Estaen leaped over her and pulled her toward the hammocks as the others raced after them.

As Kwin hurried down the stairs, he shouted, "Nuagte, hiyu ani!"

Nu struggled with Captain Moln at the hatch. She lunged when she reached the top of the stairs but managed to keep her feet under her as she landed. Captain Moln followed her and Foden slid the hatch closed behind him.

Down shifted from under her feet to somewhere behind the stairs.

Zheann grabbed the steps to brace herself but lost her grip when the bow plummeted. She slid forward, found another timber and held on. Captain Moln squeezed the breath out of her as he wrapped his arms around both her and the wood. She hung suspended for a moment before they crashed into another trough. The ship leveled out. The captain released her, and a third wave pitched him into the stairs.

When the fourth wave passed under them, Kwin, sounding weak and far away, said, "They seem to be getting smaller."

Like when you throw a rock in a pond. The 'rock' must have been tremendous. She dragged herself to her berth and dove in headfirst as the next wave hit. The cocoon of fabric closed around her, rubbing her side along the wall to the limits of its straps. She parted the material and put her face in the gap.

Nu spewed Kotichite words like a geyser as she hugged a beam. Kwin held on from the other side. He looked ready to vomit, but he gave Zheann a tight-lipped smile and rolled his eyes at the wood between himself and Nu.

Foden cursed as another wave hit. He lurched to his berth stepping on a bag that broke open under his weight. Grain spilled out and slid aft. He tumbled in, letting out another curse as his head hit the wall.

"Estaen?"

"I am under the table." He lay under the table with his hands beyond his head. As the ship's bow rose, he seemed to be standing with his hands up. When the bow plunged, he stood on his hands. The clutter sliding aft and forward slid around the table, which had clearly been bolted in place. A maniacal grin filled his face.

You could have stood there and made fools of us all.

Would it have made fools of you? I could have, but it was more fun and more useful to make a fool of myself in the eyes of our Med friends.

More fun I can understand, but more useful?

It is sometimes useful to be under-valued. It is easier to meet low expectations, especially when one is trying to seem other than what one is.

The captain stumbled across the room and took hold of an empty berth. He stretched a hand across the room. "Nu, give me your hand."

More Kotichite streamed out, but she held out her hand. More than a hand's breadth separated them.

"Come on, Nu," he coaxed.

Kwin patted the hand still wrapped around the beam. "If you believe in your sky father, ask his help and let go."

The unending words turned fiery, but she stepped toward the captain and took the offered hand.

He pulled her to the berth, helped her into it. He shoved his arm between the narrow end and the wall as another wave sent debris sliding aft. In the lull between up and down, he and Kwin lunged for their berths.

When something struck the hatch cover, they all jumped. The thump turned into a series of blows followed by shouts and curses. The captain and Foden clambered to the hatch and unbuttoned it.

Tinjier descended the steps with Dorlew and another sailor behind him. "The Captain's arm is broken." He made his way to a cupboard. Standing back, he opened it, letting the contents spill onto the counter and floor.

Dorlew held one arm close to his ribs with the other. "Move!" He kicked at Estaen as he slid onto a bench.

"Would you like to take my place?"

Tinjier finished collecting supplies. "Good idea, Dorlew."

Dorlew bit back a comment. With the sailor's aid, he lowered himself to the floor and settled himself under the table. He wrapped his good arm around one table leg. Tinjier slid under one bench, and the sailor under the other. "Hold him still." He took a deep breath and murmured. He took hold of Dorlew's arm and punctuated his words with the crunch of the bones realigning. Dorlew yowled, accompanied by the chatter and hiss of debris sliding past them.

Why didn't you heal him, Estaen?
Why didn't you, Zheann?

———— ◉ ————

As she rode out the waves and watched things slide, ideas came together. *Oh, no.* "Captain, let's go on deck." She sprang from her berth and clambered up the steps. She slid several paces toward the stern. Heart beating faster, she scrambled sideways and held onto the railing. She pulled herself toward the bow as the ship rode the swell. She clung to whatever she could to slow her descent as it slid to level again. A red light sank like the setting sun over Awasain Jeingsi. She waited.

The captain held the railing next to her. "Should we go below?"

"Not yet. Have you ever thrown a rock into a pond, or stepped in a puddle and seen the ripples move out?"

"Yes, of course."

"I think that's what I did, what Estaen called my 'little mistake.' Mistress Jenem teaches students what happens when you mix things you shouldn't. She uses a tub of water, so everyone can safely watch small explosions. That's what happened tonight. Whatever I threw into the sea exploded. Now, imagine what would happen if that explosion took place inside a mountain."

His eyes narrowed. "Wouldn't the mountain act like the tub?"

"If the thing that explodes is small enough and the mountain is big enough or strong enough. I have also seen what happens when an explosion is bigger or stronger than the container. I've seen pieces of tub buried so deep in a rock wall all you see is the hole. I've heard stories of debris killing people a block away. I thought them cautionary tales, but what will happen if the mountain explodes and crashes into the sea?"

Something scraped on the deck behind her. She turned. The youngest sailor pulled a bird from a cage, pushed a note into the holder on its leg. "We're sending word to warn Jifreb. If she gets there in time, Jifreb can send warnings to other towns." He tossed the bird into the sky and she flew southwest.

"Warning?"

"Pa says waves like that may wreck some boats if they stay small. They may get bigger as they get closer to land. He's heard of waves drowning whole towns."

Why couldn't I have been wrong?

The captain stood watching the mountain for a long time. "We'd better make sure it doesn't explode."

She looked toward the mountain. "I'm afraid we're too late."

Chapter Fifteen

Tarewo, 25 Troleng 153, Awasain Jeingsi

Maybe I was wrong. Awasain Jeingsi, cloaked in white, towered majestic and alone in the bright dawn. *'Cloaked' is the right word.* The mountain's sides sloped in gentle curves from a collar instead of a rocky peak. As if someone had decapitated the summit and left the cloak behind, its hood thrown back. They beached the skiffs on a narrow beach of black and gray stones.

"Strap on the ice shoes as I tell you," Nu said. As they obeyed, she went down the line, testing and adjusting the straps and muttering in Kotichite. Next, she handed out long scarves and pairs of leather mittens. "Tie the cloth over your faces. You see through Rys leather glass. Without it, you go blind."

Zheann held her scarf up. After experimenting a little, she got it tied so the leather remained over her eyes. "Why would we go blind?"

Kwin grinned and covered his face. "Two reasons. First, the sun bounces off the snow. It burns the eyes. Second, the air gets bitterly cold."

Nu held her short staff in mittened hands. "Take hold of it so." A metal spike snapped out from the bottom. "Use it to check for thin ice or loose snow. She climbed onto a ledge, testing the ice before her, and from it onto the main ice pack. "Like so. It bae faster than pulling you out of holes." She climbed onto the ice. If you walk where Kwin or I walk, you bae safe. Walk this way." She poked at the snow with the staff before raising her knee high and lowering it to the snow where she'd poked. "Step only if the staff does not sink far. A little way up, we tie ourselves with rope."

Zheann stepped onto the ice. She put her second foot in Kwin's boot print. When she tried to take her third step, her foot didn't come free. Sighing, she copied Nu's march. *Are we supposed to go all the way to the top of the mountain like this? I'll never make it!*

Ahead, a trail turned up the slope for a short distance before it continued around the mountain. Nu chuckled. "Jeingsi. They learn ice bae hard." She followed the trail.

Foden jabbed his stick into the snow. "This isn't like the mountains west of Jitherick,"

"No," Estaen said, "The world bleeds here. The mountain is like the skin around a scab."

"Bleeds?" Zheann asked.

"The stones on the beach are dried world blood," Estaen said. "Poetically speaking."

Zheann coughed a laugh.

The captain asked, "Do you ever make sense?"

"Hush," Nu said in an exaggerated whisper. "Voices go far on ice."

Kwin spoke in hushed tones. "He's right. I've read of mountains that are like forges, a fire in them burns hot enough inside that rocks melt and flow like ore."

"I've never heard of them," Zheann said.

At the same time, the Captain said, "Then how is there ice on it?" He considered the slope. "No, wait. Don't tell me... magic." He sounded disgusted.

Kwin chuckled. "And the fire may have gone out."

"But Fiwal and Leed are using something hot, something explosive to free the dragons. They may not know about them, either." Zheann searched the collar. Sunlight nibbled at the eastern slope.

"Do you think they'd stop if they knew?" Foden scoffed.

"No, they won't believe us. Even if they do, they'll assume the dragons can fix what they've broken." She continued marching. The spikes on her boots kept her from slipping, but she worried about tripping or getting stuck. Sunlight seemed to gallop down the mountain's eastern side while they plodded along. *How long before they free the dragons? How long before they notice us? How long before my legs fall off?*

After a third, Nu stopped them at a place where the snow leveled enough for them to stand as a group. "Rest. Drink water. It will get harder."

Zheann's legs trembled and ached. She eyed the snowbank, longing to sit for a little while. *You won't want to get up and keep going.*

Kwin pulled a coil of rope off over his head. He tied it around Nu's waist and stopped in front of the captain. "May I?"

The captain nodded. Kwin tied the rope around his waist. "Don't fall. You'll take the rest of us with you."

The sun glinted off the sea and the snow. Zheann adjusted her mask, appreciating its protection. No people stood on the collar as Kwin added her to the line. Nothing appeared or moved. "Do you think they can see us?"

"If they look." The captain tipped his head back. His black cloak hood almost seemed empty with the scarf tied over his face.

It's enough to give one nightmares, as if Med don't do that even without the mask.

Kwin waved a hand, dismissing the issue. "The sun reflecting off the snow may blind them unless they have leather glass over their eyes. I keep hoping to find them huddled in the snow and blind. If they do see us, we will be tiny."

No. Somehow, they made it. They're at the collar, waiting to see if their hex has worked. As she gazed at it, her heart sank. *The collar is the ring from the Kotich stories.*

Foden took the rope from Kwin. He tied the rope around himself with deft hands, returning the tail to Kwin.

"Very good." Kwin's voice, though quiet and muffled by the mask, expressed appreciation.

The ground quivered. Nu looked back the line, her hood looking as empty as the Meds'. Captain Moln looked her way as well. Through the black fabric, Estaen's eyes still shimmered. *In my imagination? Are we too late?*

Estaen held his hands out from his sides, allowing Kwin to bind him. *They have not escaped yet. I still have hope.*

≈·《◎》·≈

As she turned a corner, Nu muttered, "To migansi kalieran barasav."

Kwin translated. "Wall."

Foden loosened the knot, let the rope fall around his feet, and worked his way past Nu. He peered up at a wall of ice that rose to more than twice his height as he pulled off his mittens and tucked them into his belt. He ran his bare hands over the icy surface. "I wish I had my gear. No one told me we were going to be mountain climbing." He pressed his fingers, curved like talons, against the ice and pulled his body up. His left knee bent, and his left hand shot up at the same time. His foot found no purchase, but his fingers did.

Next, his right foot found something that held his weight and he pushed himself up. He found another handhold and another. In the space of ten breaths, he was lying on the ledge with his hands held toward them.

He caught the rope the captain tossed, stood, and pulled Estaen up. "Keep watch. If you see any Rys or any dragons, hex them." He pulled Zheann up next, followed by Kwin. He braced himself and wrapped the rope around his shoulders. "Ready, Captain."

The captain stood looking up, his face black within the hood. "Funny." He put his gloves in his belt and with Foden pulling, climbed the wall, slipping twice. "Next summer, if we aren't at war, we need to brush up on my rock climbing." He put his mittens on, and they pulled Nu onto the ledge.

Nu pulled a bag out of her pack. "Here. Eat this, then drink." She handed them something that looked like overdone bacon. She pushed her scarf over her mouth and chewed on it.

It smelled like leather and smoke. Zheann bit off a piece. It tasted like smoke and leather and chewed like an old pouch. *It needs everything.*

Nu grinned, chewed with enthusiasm, and swallowed.

Kwin held his. "Sakwa jerky. You don't want to know more than that."

Zheann kept chewing. She remembered Papa saying, "Don't do magic with your mouth full, Little Hedgehog." She swallowed.

———————

When they rounded the south slope again, the sun shone overhead. *The Chaser* looked like a tiny child's toy on the vast blue water. As Zheann turned to follow Nu and Foden something in the ice moved, a pale shadow in glistening white. She recoiled, stepped off the path and slid down the steep hill, yelping. The rope around her waist pulled tight, turning her scream into a gasp. Kwin and Foden hauled her onto the path. Foden put his mouth to her ear, "What is wrong with you?"

She pointed at the mountainside. "I saw..." Five black clothed faces followed her gesture, then returned to her. "I swear."

Estaen covered where his mouth should have been.

Nu gave her a small flask, and she pushed up her mask and swallowed something too sweet. She took a second before handing it back. Her racing heart slowed to what felt like twice its normal rhythm. The ice beneath them thrummed, and her heartbeat accelerated again.

They cannot...the ice. Estaen's thought whispered.

"I'm all right. Let's go." As they resumed their march, she focused on the captain's boots. *They can't escape the ice. Otherwise, they already would have. That means Leed and Fiwal haven't broken the hex.*

A soft murmur answered.

Do not speak! Estaen roared in her mind.

Daughter, has he told you we are evil? The voice in her head sounded muffled but gentle.

No, not exactly. We already knew that.

Zheann, do not listen to them. Do not talk to them.

How do I do that?

He is lying to you, the new voice and Estaen said together.

Free us, and we will give you your heart's desire. The voice purred. It sounded masculine but felt feminine.

Dren playing in a field near home came to mind. She shoved it away. *They can't free us from the Med. The price is too high.*

We can protect your daughter and your people.

Zheann, Estaen said.

Shut up! I know.

He would have you serve his dernai. We can give you power. Your people can take your rightful place. What proof do you have that he tells you the truth? The voice paused. *Do you see he has nothing to say to defend himself?*

Silence. *Estaen?*

Yes, halfling?

Aren't you going to tell me they're lying?

I have already told you everything you need to know, halfling. Repeating it would not make it more, or less, true. You must choose to trust me or to trust them.

That's not fair! You're putting this all on me.

I cannot make your choice for you. Estaen's mental voice sounded as calm as the dragon's.

You said you would deal with the dragons.

I will.

He is lying. He will leave the work to you and take the credit. More than one chuckle effervesced in her mind. *Your only hope for freedom is with us. Your daughter's only hope for freedom is with us. We can take you to her and protect her.*

Estaen's full-bodied laughter exploded in her mind. *With whom would I take credit? Her friends are here. Have you deceived yourselves into thinking the dernai does not know?*

If he knows, why didn't he tell you where to find us? Doesn't he trust you with knowledge? I can understand why, after your failure in Amarg. What was that boy's name? After several breaths, the voice continued. *Wasn't it... Ti'ilar? I remember how his mother wept when you handed him to her, burned, bloody, and broken by his own hand.*

His hand did not take his life. Estaen's voice sounded bottomless.

No, yours did. Your meddling. Your trickery. Your obedience to the Dernai. Just as you are doing now. Will you give Dren to her as you gave Ti'ilar to his mother? Ask him, Zheann. Ask him about Ti'ilar. Ask him how far he will go in obedience to his dernai. Will he sacrifice you? Your daughter? Your entire world?

Zheann concentrated on putting her little feet into the captain's boot prints. *Estaen said he is magic, and he must do what he was sent to do. What were you sent to do?*

We are no less magic, but we do as we please. He does too, for all he claims to obey his dernai.

Zheann put her hand to her mouth to keep from laughing. *Before, you said he obeyed the dernai too much. Now you're saying he doesn't obey? You ought to make up your mind before you speak it.* She rolled her eyes. *Your Papa's daughter! Sassing dragons!*

Estaen's laughter echoed through her mind again. *Touché.*

———•《◉》•———

"Zheann!" The Captain's tone told her he'd called her at least once before. His face was less than a hand's breadth from hers.

"What?" The word came out sharply, and she winced.

"What are you doing?"

What? I'm listening to dragons. Can they free the Rys? Only by killing or enslaving the Med. The Med are killing us already. Would it be wrong to give us a weapon, to let us defend ourselves? "Thinking."

"Nu, hold," he said over his shoulder and looked back at her. "About what?"

Zheann closed her eyes. *I don't want to debate with any of you.* Not being able to see the path's edge made her anxious. She opened her eyes again.

The feminine voice sounded syrupy. *That is the way of slaves. Don't you see how much they fear us...how much he fears us? Even his dernai is afraid of us. Why else would he send another in his stead?*

Estaen's thought voice sounded amused. *If he fears you, why would he send a failure like me? Zheann was right.*

The emptiness of the captain's scarf-hidden face unnerved her.

She steeled herself for a storm. "About how everyone seems to want to use me."

After a long moment, he shrugged. "That's the way it is for heroes and leaders. It's the only life I have ever known, the only life the general has ever known... the only life the Med have ever known. You can resent it all you want, and you can sit in a corner and whine about it when this is over. Take a deep breath, Zheann. Keep focused on what will let you look Dren, your mother, and me in the eye. Now, who is everyone?"

Her face burned, and she was thankful for the scarf covering it. Somewhere, two dragons laughed. She glared. Realizing the uselessness of the gesture, she rolled her eyes and chuckled.

"Zheann?"

No time for something cleverer than the truth. "I'm sorry, Captain. A dragon is offering me enticements. She wants to use me, too."

Nu and Foden both grumbled.

The captain inched closer. "Then they've escaped?"

"Not yet."

"Zheann?"

"Captain, if you had heard her arguments, you'd still be laughing."

He unwrapped his scarf. "Take off your scarf and look at me."

She did. The bitter brightness and cold stung her cheeks. Brown eyes, squinting against the brilliance, searched her eyes and her face. His gaze moved past her and returned to her eyes. "Nu, let's get going."

Moments later their path snaked out around a boulder. Thunder rumbled.

Zheann gazed at the summit and at the cloud that seemed to form in an otherwise blue sky. She stood, watching the cloud approach.

"Avalanche!" Nu shouted. "Run!" She pulled on the rope.

The rumble grew into a roar. The ground sent tremors through her legs and spine, all the way to her teeth. The captain grabbed Zheann's arm and dragged her along as she tried to get her feet under her and march.

Push up and out! Estaen's voice boomed in her mind, and she obeyed instinctively. White enveloped them, gliding over their heads, and flowing around them like water, creating a white twilight around them.

It's burying us!

Keep pushing.

Something black about the size of a wagon hurtled past Nu. She screamed and backpedaled into the captain.

He released Zheann's arm but stood his ground, pushing against the large woman. The motion all around them stopped. Sunlight shone brightly as the snow cascaded toward the beach. *Will it destroy the boats?*

The Captain swore. Snow that rose over his head blocked the path. He put his hand against the mountain. "Nu, can we climb over it?"

Nu shook her head. "Dangerous."

Foden pointed over his shoulder at the snow-covered path behind them. "We don't have many choices. We either dig our way one way or dig our way the other."

"It likely baen't stable." Nu poked at the snow with her staff. It sank in easily.

"Digging will take too long. Rys? Any better ideas?"

Kwin inched toward Nu. "I'll go across. If I'm tied, and you don't let go, you can pull me back if the snow slides. When I get to the other side, I'll anchor my end of the rope."

"Why not push the snow off the path?" Estaen asked.

Zheann rolled her eyes and felt her face warm again. "How do we do that without burying us under another avalanche? We don't have time to play guessing games. Leed and Fiwal won't wait before they either attack or free the dragons, and the dragons won't wait."

Zheann glanced toward the summit again, expecting to find a dragon staring back. Instead, a hooded figure stretched his arm out. Something spread from his hand. Countless tiny rainbows floated like snowflakes on the breeze.

"Shield!" Estaen raised a hand. The cloaked person yelped, recoiling as though something had hit him. He disappeared.

Zheann gasped and raised her hand. *Fiwal!* The prisms burst into vibrant flames over their heads. Each flare died within a breath of igniting.

Estaen continued as if nothing had happened. "You are right. Push the snow down the mountain. Use the path you can see."

"Estaen—"

"Must you argue your inability to do everything?"

No, but it would be nice not to have to.

Ah, you now understand the wisdom of my refusal?

No! Yes. But you're an Athenque.

So, because you think these things are easier for me than for you, you think I should do what you do not wish to, and without cost?

That's not fair!

You are right. It is not.

Her face burned. She worked her way forward holding on to the captain's arm. He pulled her hand free, took her by the waist, and put her next to Nu. His hands remained around her waist, holding her in place. She raised one foot and stomped against the ice, keeping it level. *Don't step on your own foot, or the captain's. It's a capital offense, no doubt.* She raised the other foot and brought it down hard against the ice.

She took Nu's staff and placed it beside hers in the loose snow against the mountain. She worked the magic to make two shields, then pushed Nu's staff toward the precipice. A second avalanche roared into the sea, but the snow above the path remained, held by an invisible dam. *That was easier than I thought it'd be.* "Hurry. I don't know how long it will last."

You had help, a deep male voice grumbled.

Nu took her staff and hurried along the path. As she approached another area blocked by snow, it broke free. The way to the summit cleared.

Through the mask, Estaen's eyes shimmered.

Or is it in my mind?

And we can teach you much more than he will.

The sky along the collar turned rosy. As the blush gained intensity and its color deepened to berry, she stretched her hand toward it, tried to throw it into the sea. *Estaen, do something!* The glow faded, and a cheer rang from the summit. *Fiwal again. If we weren't too late before, we are now.*

⸺ «(◉)» ⸺

In a dance of knives and bodies, the Captain and Foden freed themselves, pushed past the others and ran along the path. They pulled their bows from their shoulders and nocked arrows while she struggled to untie the knot at her waist but couldn't loosen it. She sent magic into it. The rope crumbled.

A hand touched her shoulder, and she jumped. Kwin pointed toward the summit in the opposite direction. Estaen had climbed to the top. He waved at her, glimmered, and disappeared.

"What was that?" Kwin said.

Zheann scrambled after Estaen. Her right foot stopped midstride. She tumbled, tried to catch herself, found nothing under her left hand. *No!* Images of Dren that would never be paraded through her mind as she grabbed at the ice with her right. The solid surface slid through fingers padded by mitten. Dren, on her first day of jideker. Dren as a young woman, smiling at a nice, young man.

The straps of her pack yanked against her shoulder. An arm snaked around her waist. "You're all right. You're safe."

Be careful, Zheann. The dragon's voice rumbled like a contented cat. *Don't worry. We'll meet soon enough. Your little girl looks sweet. There's much we can teach her once the children of Rysa are free from the children of Medenva.*

She pushed his hand away. "We have to get up there." She hurried after Estaen.

Kwin followed. "Estaen's a Kwusejeinsye, isn't he? An Athenque."

———————

Together, they followed Estaen's path onto a jagged circle of ice and rock. *The collar. The ring.* The wind threatened to push them off. She stood, bent over, gasping for air. Kwin pulled her behind a rock large enough to hide three Med. The ledge, made of ice and shiny black rock, was broad enough to hold her shop, and littered with boulders. Jitherick would have fit into the concave area where the mountain peak should have been. A ruby glow filled the bowl.

We failed. Where are the Med?

Fiwal and Leed stood with their backs to her. One walked a short way, kicked a small boulder, and laughed.

Leed, but what is he doing?

He bent and put his hand against the rock. As he turned toward Fiwal, his eyes widened. He gave her one of his best merchant's smiles. "Whose side are you on? The Med have been defeated."

Wait, the rock moved when he kicked it. Ye fen dernai haloim, the Med and Nu!

Hands firmly grasped her shoulders. She tried to turn, but Kwin tightened his grip and said, "Did you...kill them?" Eagerness filled his deep voice.

Leed glared down at the black lump and back at Kwin. "No, I want them to see our victory made complete. I am going to give them to the dragon when it emerges. And you, too, unless you convince me that you are on our side. Start by removing those masks."

One hand released her, the other slid down her arm and tightened again. There was rustling then a scarf fell at her feet.

She felt him tug at her scarf. "Are you tricking them?" she whispered.

He pulled the scarf from her head and murmured in her ear. "What do you think?"

The cold bit at her skin and she found it hard to breathe. *Silence them! Silence them and tell them all they've done to their people then let the Med slit their throats.*

"Zheann?" Fiwal looked happier than the day Dren was born.

How dare you smile at me?

"Oh great, and I suppose one of these mud is the Little General. I should have known that you'd betray us." Leed looked beyond her. "What's your name, and why should I believe you aren't with her?"

"My name is Kwin Jeron, and I came to the Great Ice Land to get away from the mud."

"I know some –"

She cut him off. "Why are you doing this?" Hatred raced through her gut like a fire through dry grass. *How dare you smile at me? I don't want to know. Don't tell me.* "Why?"

"To prove we were right." Fiwal opened his arms as if to hug her.

"To free the Rys. To punish the mud for their crimes." Leed sneered. "I should have known you'd betray us."

He looks like a mud.

Her father pleaded in her memory. "Don't let them make you like them."

"To give you the throne you deserve, and to make you proud of me." Fiwal squinted at her and cocked his head, his joy melting to confusion.

Fury rose in her and gave her words. "You killed the king. The Med are slaughtering our people for it. They pushed children out of windows. They've burned Jitherick and Jitdornoi by now, or soon will. I don't know where your family is, Leed, but it's likely Mama and Dren are dead. You've hexed the mountain to free the dragons, and when it explodes because you did it wrong, it's going to kill thousands. You left your family behind to die for your crimes. Tell me again who betrayed whom."

One of the Med pushed himself to hands and knees and shook himself slowly.

"Give me a throne? Who am I going to rule, the dead? Fine. My first command is that you both die for your crimes. Your names will be considered too horrible..."

Leed shook his head. "Don't you ever stop?" He grunted as the captain slammed a shoulder into his back. They landed together with the captain's dark cloak covering them.

The captain rose to his knees, rolled Leed onto his back, and drew a dagger from his belt. His face swung toward the pit. He dove sideways, kicking at Leed as ice and snow sprayed around them. An icy blue form erupted from the crater. Something constricted around her like belts of iron and jerked her skyward.

Fiwal reached out toward her, his voice a howl. "No!"

Reality narrowed to the sun, the sky, the roar of wind in her ears, and the dragon. She shivered as the wind buffeted her.

A throaty laugh rumbled through her mind. *I am your dernai now, Zheann,* a familiar deep feminine voice rumbled. *I told you we would meet soon.*

Chapter Sixteen

Tarewo, 26 Troleng 153, near Awasain Jeingsi

B lue and white filled Zheann's vision. The wind whipped her hood from her head and bit at her face. Her body trembled though she couldn't tell whether more from fright or cold. As she squirmed, the talons wrapped around her torso tightened. A moment later, her chest ached. *I can't breathe. Please, I can't breathe!* The claws holding her loosened and she slipped. She wrapped her arms around the first finger and screamed.

It sounds as though you can... fragile.

Rys, not Athenque. Unlike you, I can die.

Fragile and untrained. The dragon's wings swept over her, deepening the shadow. They swept up and stretched out as the dragon soared. Light filtered through the skin, creating a subtle play of colors ranging from a purpled blue to a white that looked clearer than snow.

Beautiful, like the pearls Estaen showed me, only with blues and whites.

Thank you. The bitter cold faded to mere cold.

Why do you bother flying? She answered herself with mockery. *Because it's fun.*

No, the dragon rumbled. *It suits my purposes.*

Take me back to the mountain...please.

Her rumble turned into a chuckle. *It pleases me for you to ask, but, no.*

Zheann's sense of up shifted from the dragon to somewhere closer to her feet. Blood flooded her head. Over her shoulder, white rushed at her. Zheann gasped in preparation for a scream and collision. With a snap, up soared over her head again. The universe got caught in a whirlpool of blood draining back into her body through a neck too narrow for the purpose. The dragon released her, and she fell several handbreadths. Her knees gave way and she fell in the snow. On hands and knees, she gulped air, willing the dizziness and cold away. Her trembling turned to shudders, and her teeth chattered. She swallowed and swallowed again between wheezed inhalations. She pulled the flask of Sea Calm from her bag and took a sip. After seventeen breaths, the frozen world around her stopped spinning.

A Rys woman gave her an amused smile. Her dark blue cloak and gown embroidered with pale blue dragons were out of place, and out of fashion. So was her long blond hair, worn loose to her waist.

Don't be petty, Zheann, especially when she can hear you. That sounds like something Papa would have said.

"Then your father was a wise man." She flicked her skirt with one hand, spreading its material to its best advantage. "We have not been properly introduced. I am Donezan. Are stories still told of me?"

Zheann bit her lip. "Of course, ... Queen Donezan." *That's not possible. Or, even if it is, who else would an Athenque claim to be? Then again, if Athenque can't die, she could be Donezan. Does it matter if she's lying? Be careful, Zheann.* "The story told most often is that you corrupted Rysa. Our magic is your useful, but tainted legacy."

Donezan tilted her head. "I suppose — what did you call him? Estaen? I suppose he told you that."

Awasain Jeingsi rose far to her left. Blue separated her from it.

Even if I could get away, how would I get there before I freeze? What is happening there? Are there more dragons, and are they attacking the Med? "No, I learned it in the jideker. After you disappeared, the Rys became a great power. Your descendant, King Taelfa enslaved the Med, the descendants of Medenva. His grandson, King Taelferga, led the Rys to free them. We have been repaying our debt to them for the last three generations."

Donezan gave a hurt little pout. It fell apart as she chuckled. "Medenva never forgave me for choosing his brother over him."

A dragon-shaped shadow passed over them, and a dragon with ebony scales landed nearby. The muscles in his legs and back rippled.

He's posing like Foden. The dragons on the gates of Jitherick look noble, dignified, regal. Like Donezan. This one seems murderous. Zheann's face grew warm, and she inched closer to Donezan.

Donezan laughed, a light, bell-like sound. "Venkis is less fond of my children than I am. Do they, at least, remember and respect me?"

Zheann said, "A few may. Most have forgotten. Many of us accept the Med's story. They think you're a monster. I always thought that you were, well, someone who lived a long time ago, nothing else." *If you are her.*

"Did you distrust the one you call Estaen this much?" She waved her hand. "It doesn't matter. You're right, of course. I will lie to you just as you will try to lie to me. Sadly, for you, I can hear the struggle your thoughts have with saying what your mind does not think."

Pull yourself together, Zheann. You don't have time to play these games. She stepped closer. "Queen Donezan, the way Leed and Fiwal freed you may cause the mountain to explode. If it does, it may push the sea over a place you once called home and destroy ... your children. The people you left on the mountain are trying to help me. We tried to stop them because we fear you, but also because they magic they used is dangerous. Can you tell if the mountain is going to explode? Can you stop it? Estaen didn't seem to think he could."

Donezan turned toward the mountain. "No, I don't suppose the Dernai would let him. He's like that. You're right, though. The mountain does seem to be less stable.

Let it. The he-dragon's deep voice ground through her mind.

She took another step toward Donezan. "If you care about *your children*, you have a chance to prove it, but we must go now. Can you tell how long we have until it explodes?"

"Mountains like it sometimes leak and sometimes explode. You could be right. I don't know if it will explode, or when, but I suspect it will not be long. A month, perhaps. It would be exciting to see."

Exciting? Athenque. "I need to return to my friends on the mountain, and we must warn everyone to flee over the mountains in the west. When we get there, I will need some time to convince Captain Moln you will help us."

Donezan gazed out across the snow. Her profile was a balance of Rys refinement and Med strength. "Yes, you might be right and if so, of course, we must do what we can to help." Donezan stepped back and shimmered as she became a dragon again. She was longer and taller than the other but seemed more gracile. Her neck arched as she looked at Zheann. *I will carry you.* Zheann backed away, but the talons closed around her again, reaching from chest to ankle.

————))•((————

Stop squirming, Child. You will harm yourself. As your dernai, I will protect you.

Venkis' gruff thought struck her mind. *Get used to it unless you intend to walk back to your people.*

Her hands, feet, and face grew numb. *I hope the Sea Calm works. How are you going to convince the captain to work with the dragons? He's said his people will die rather than serve the Rys again. Is there any other way? If the sea comes as far as Jitherick, will they stand at the walls and watch rather than flee to the mountains because the dragons are there? Will the dragons go live on their own and let us go? What will Estaen do? Where is he? Estaen?*

No, the answer whispered in her mind.

He's gone back to his dernai in defeat, coward that he is.

The he-dragon, what did she call him? Venkis? Her teeth chattered until she stretched her mouth open in a yawn. She squirmed again and searched her memory for a hex that would create heat without burning. *Donezan said she'd lie when it suits her purpose. Can I trust anything either says after that? What do you really want?*

Power. Revenge. The words were like breaths, and she couldn't tell who had thought them.

Donezan changed direction, and blood rushed to her head. A few breaths later, it ran back out. When Donezan released her this time, she staggered several steps before dropping to her knees. The world stayed in place. *So cold.* She yawned again. One of the boats rested on the beach. *Ah, there's the other. Where are the Med? Estaen? Estaen!* The ground trembled, as if it, too, were freezing. *Or angry, or feverish.*

Donezan became a woman again. "He's not here, Zheann. Your other friends are on their way down the far side of the mountain. I thought this would be a more comfortable place for everyone to meet. We can use those boats to build a fire so that everyone can get warm. You may be right about the mountain. It has never trembled before today."

Zheann pushed to her feet and tried to wiggle her toes. She took a step. And another. By the fifth step, her feet burned. She gritted her teeth and jogged toward the mountain. *I'm going to meet them. We need to talk before they get to the beach. Don't burn the boats. The captain may need them.*

You are to stay with me, Donezan said in an imperious thought.

Or what? Or you'll prove you're everything the Med believe? You'll abandon your children to die when the mountain explodes? You'll be even more useless than the dernai has been? Zheann climbed onto the icy path.

I do not care what the Med believe. We do not need you; you need us. Nothing the mountain does will harm us. I will not forget your insubordination.

I'm sure you won't. But you aren't queen now, and there aren't enough of your kind to control us all. I need to convince the Captain that you're here to help us, and that won't happen with you standing there. You could show you're better than Estaen and his dernai by stopping the mountain from exploding. If you can't do that, it doesn't matter whether you kill us, or the explosion does. You'll still be left with no children. Even if you go elsewhere, find another husband, and start another family, your failure will haunt you forever.

Donezan chuckled. *You are my daughter. A clever gambit. I will confer with my companions.*

By the time she reached the ice wall, she was warm again everywhere except her feet, which burned. The huge step had cracked, with the gap wider at the top. She found loose snow and pushed it with her fingers and breath, working magic to bind the sections together. She found chunks of snow and fastened them to the face.

"What are you doing?" The captain squatted on the ledge.

Zheann winced. "Don't do that!" She glared at his masked face. "I'm trying to get to you." *Can she be there and here? Can she hear me this far away? Where's Venkis?*

The captain put the sharp point of his staff against her chest. "Let's start with your proving you're you."

Her already pounding heart raced. *That problem wasn't on my list.* She squinted as daggers of light stabbed her eyes, and staves made of ice and wind battered her face. "Will the fact that I walked up to you and asked what the letter in my book was, and you said, 'the letter is ux' do? Or the fact I'm going to suggest we let the dragons help us save our people?"

"Are you out of your mind?" He pulled the staff back, sat on the ledge and dropped to the path, advancing faster than she retreated. "What does Estaen think of your stupid idea?"

"He wouldn't approve, but he's not here. I don't know what happened to him." She pointed at Fiwal and Leed, both bound, gagged, and tied between Foden and Kwin. "I thought you'd have killed him by now." *Am I glad he didn't? Or angry? Which should I be?*

"I decided I wanted answers," he said. "Don't change the subject."

"I'm not. You're taking a chance on Fiwal and Leed."

"This from the Rys who takes a chance on everyone." The captain spoke with exaggerated patience, as she sometimes did to her students. "Zheann, the dragons are the enemy. Even Estaen said so. Only your family seems to think otherwise."

"They're the most recent enemy. I've lived among my enemies all my life. You and I are enemies, but we've worked together since you called me to the palace. I came with you to save my family and my people from your people. Now both our families face destruction. Estaen said his dernai won't let him help us. These Athenque don't serve his dernai; his rules don't limit them. If they can help us save your family, are you going to say 'no'? Because I'm not." She lowered her voice. "They want something from us. If we're useful to them, they'll keep us alive like you want to keep the Rys alive. It will allow us to keep an eye on them, learn about them and figure out how to defeat them or live with them."

He groaned. "You're doing it again!"

"I'm sorry, Captain, I wish I had a better idea."

"You could have discussed this one with us before making your decision for us."

"Do you have a better idea?" she said.

"The Med have vowed to die before we ever serve the Athenque-spawn or the Athenque."

"They all vowed, including the newborns? Or is it acceptable for you to decide for everyone but not for me?"

The captain looked toward the summit. "We could try to find Estaen and his dernai. They may be Athenque, too, but they're not on the dragon's side."

"What?" she said. "How did... How long have you known?"

"Zheann, we aren't idiots. We patrol on the road to Jifreb on a regular basis. There is no jideker. You didn't exactly give me a choice. At first, we didn't have time to sort it all out. He seemed fond of you and helpful. Now, he's gone, and you're turning to his enemies. Have you considered the fact the dragons might be the reason he's gone?"

"Of course! What do you want me to do, Captain? If Estaen told the truth, then they can't kill him, so, where is he? His dernai sent him to fight the dragons, but he's not. He's not allowed to do anything about the mountain, but two dragons have offered to do what they can. I know the dragons are our enemies, but what if Estaen is, too?"

"Two dragons? We saw four escape from the mountain." His mask wrinkled as his face moved underneath.

Another twisted smile? Probably.

"Do you even know what the meaning of loyalty or friendship is?"

Four? Two more? She shook her head. *She did say she'd confer with her companions. Pay better attention.* "They are doing whatever I have to keep my friends and family, and yours, alive. I know the dragons are our enemies and I know she intends to rule both our people. I don't know if they can or will help us, but I don't have any other ideas. Again, do you?"

"We sail *The Chaser* to Jifreb and spread the word, so people can flee to the mountains and let the dragons drown. We live or die by our own hands, or at least by the hands of those we trust."

The sun reflected off the sea, creating a pathway of fire. "They won't drown. They'll still be around, and if they're not helping us, they may decide to hurt us. The wisest thing we can do is keep them where we can see them. There are two other things you deserve to know: she claims to be Queen Donezan, and they can hear my thoughts. They may hear the thoughts of any Rys. I haven't figured out how it works yet. Proximity may be a factor. I know they can hear at least some of what I think."

He swore. "That makes you the enemy, too."

"I always have been, haven't I? I'm an Athenque-spawn."

Chapter Seventeen

Tarewo, 26 Troleng 153, Awasain Jeingsi

As Zheann led the others to the beach, her father's words echoed in her mind, "Don't let them make you like them."

Hush, Papa, they'll hear you. I don't want her to touch your memory, or Mama, or Dren. It's too late, anyway. I'm a jeing, Papa, a cursed fool. I hoped to prevent this disaster, save the lives of a few Rys, fix what Fiwal and Leed did. Ye fen dernai haloim. What do I do?

Donezan stood on the black stones, the hood of her blue cloak thrown back and her hair shimmering. Behind her, the sea and the skiffs made a dramatic backdrop. Her chin lifted.

As if she's contemplating the mountain that has been her prison. Or which of us she wants to kill first and whether to serve us with herb tea or wine. She's stunning. Perfect. And it seems she's not listening.

The captain stepped close, and spoke into her ear, his voice muffled. "The deal is off, Zheann. Tell her you've been overruled."

"I can't do that. Not unless—"

"It doesn't matter, the general and the princes will never agree."

She kept her voice quiet but made sure it held an edge. "You tell her. I doubt she'll care. She'll enjoy crushing your father and the princes. Why would she care anymore if the Med die than the Med care if the Rys die? I'm trying to save both. Your pride may be in the way, but that doesn't mean mine is. The Rys haven't been allowed pride in a hundred and fifty-three years and didn't deserve it for almost as long before that. Don't waste time talking about your vow never to serve the Rys again, because you won't be. Try your way if you must, and if you have a chance when you get home, take your family, my family, and the princes somewhere far away. Don't tell me where. If I can, I'll make sure they escape."

"I'll protect them, but the battle hasn't even begun yet."

"That's the best time to start."

Cries, inarticulate and foreign, came from behind her. She spun as Leed strained against the rope tied around his wrists and screamed through his gag. Nu put her weight against the rope tied around her waist and shouted, "Torevikikoraoleostakjeingdogan!"

"I should have killed him when I had the chance." The captain strode toward Leed.

Leed lurched forward with a choked yowl. Something brown burred away from his legs, stopping against Kwin's arm as Leed fell to his knees. Kwin brought his staff around for another strike. The blow landed across Leed's shoulders and knocked him to the ground.

"Nicely done," Foden said.

"Enough!" Donezan's voice boomed. She strode across the beach, magnificent in her displeasure, with her cloak and gown flowing behind her.

She looks ready to do battle with an army. How does she do it? Is it because she's tall? Or is she using magic?

"Zheann, who are these people?"

Zheann hurried over. "Queen Donezan, may I present Captain Moln and Lieutenant Foden, of the Medenvar Army. Nu and Kwin, teachers of the Kotich. Leed, my cousin and Fiwal, my husband. They are the ones whose meddling may destroy the mountain."

The Captain pulled the scarf from around his head and dropped it on the ground as he stepped before Donezan. "This is not your business."

"I'll decide for myself, once I hear what he wants to say." The gag and bindings fell onto rough black pebbles. Leed climbed to his feet, wiping blood from his mouth. His face twisted in pain and fury. When he murmured, Donezan glared at him. "I gave you a chance to speak. Don't waste it on gibberish, and when you come to me, look presentable."

Leed's eyes widened as the swelling and bruises faded. He took several steps and tried to shove the captain. When the captain didn't move, he walked around him brushing dirt from his cloak. He ran the fingers of one hand through his blond hair before kneeling before her.

Zheann rolled her eyes. *A little obvious, Leed.*

The captain didn't seem to notice the short man in front of him. His squint relaxed into his twisted smile.

She won't like that.

Leed looked up at Donezan. "I freed you. These people all came here to stop me from freeing you."

"And what reward do you seek?"

"I want the Rys to be free, the Med to pay for usurping the Rys throne, and her punished for treason." He pointed at Zheann as he approached Donezan. "My Lady, I never imagined the great Ice Dragons could assume a Rys form."

A strangled cry came from close behind her. Fiwal stood by her, shifting from one foot to the other, his eyes pleading. Kwin held one arm, and Nu the other.

Donezan looked at him. "Do you have something to say, too?" His bonds dropped away. "I see you avoided the beating he endured."

He worked his jaw. "He never imagined anything about you. All he wants to do is hurt the Med."

And you don't?

Donezan smiled poisonously. "And what reward do you want for your part in freeing us?"

Fiwal's green eyes looked bright as he lowered his gaze. "Your majesty, I have believed in you all my life. Your kind, I mean. I didn't know where in the Great Ice Land I would find you, but I came to find you. I want you to free the Rys, yes, but even more, I wanted to prove you exist."

She gazed at him. Her brilliant blue eyes examined him and sparkled. "You are an amusing liar with your half-truths and subterfuges." She turned to Leed. "I will grant most of your request. The Rys will be free of the Med for as long as they serve me, and the Med will pay through their submission to me. But, for now, Zheann is mine."

Zheann sensed... something nudging at her mind. As quickly as the awareness came, it went again, and the expected foreboding took its place.

The Captain continued to stare at Donezan. Foden took his place a step behind him.

She'll enjoy breaking them.

Well, of course, my child. The decision is theirs, but if they choose to be broken before being made mine, I shall enjoy the challenge. Would you prefer I kill them? It seems like a waste of their potential.

<hr />

Fiwal shook free of his captors and drew Zheann several paces away. He leaned close and whispered. "Leed killed the soldiers."

"And you freed the dragons," Zheann said, "so you would have the honor of putting me on the throne, and of being king." His hair, darker and less golden than hers, stuck out from his hood. Her fingers itched to tidy it.

Green eyes filled with tears. "For us. For our people."

Zheann snorted. "You did it for yourself. Did you ever think to ask me what I wanted?"

"I knew what you wanted. You are capable of better. You are meant for better."

"Is that why you told your friends in Jitdornoi how stupid I am, how you have me bamboozled?"

"I... no..." He gaped as his face turned red. "I did it to protect you if anything went wrong. They knew you didn't know anything about what I was doing." He looked toward the others, and back. "OK, it was a stupid idea."

"So now I forgive you, and every thing's all better? No harm done? No one cares whether you took part or stood by. The king is dead. Several Med soldiers are dead. They were slaughtering Rys in Jitherick when I came after you. It may have spread to Jifreb by now for all I know. Did it never occur to you the dragons might have their own ideas?"

"Yes, but I thought we could convince them to include us in them."

Zheann laughed and covered her mouth with both hands. The laughter rolled out anyway, bitter and cleansing. "Oh, they do, and we are, more's the pity."

Pebbles rattled. Fiwal looked around, ending with a long look at the mountain.

Zheann pulled his arm, turning him toward her. "Yes, the magic you used to free the dragons damaged the mountain. It is going to explode and push the sea over the lowlands east of the mountains. The Med are killing our people because of what you and Leed did. If we don't get there and warn them, those who survive will drown because you wanted to put me on the throne."

His eyes lost their focus as he shook his head. His voice came out as a deep whisper. "It wasn't supposed to happen this way."

Zheann walked toward Donezan and the captain.

———◆———

The captain spoke in brusque tones. "He has killed the king. He has killed my men. He has endangered both Med and Rys. He is the reason we need to stop the mountain from destroying our homeland. I will see to it he stands trial for those crimes. Before you protect him, think about this. He killed the king and committed treason because he hates the Med. What will he do when he doesn't like your rule any better?"

She waved a hand. "What he might do is irrelevant. We can't die."

"It's difficult to rule without subjects."

Her smile broadened. "You are a true son of Medenva. For all his hatred and love of me and all his jealousy of Rysa, he never retreated either. Have you ever considered what it would be like for the Med to have magic? I can make that happen, make you their equal." She appraised him. "From the looks of you, I can make the Med better."

Zheann grimaced. *What's worse, the idea of magical Med, or her blatancy?*

Donezan's laughter rang through her mind. *Prudery or jealousy?*

The captain mimicked her appraising look. "What you can do is irrelevant. We can and will die before we become your pets. And after seeing what being magical had made of you, I'm not interested."

Good taste, dignity, maturity. Zheann smirked.

All over-rated. Donezan shrugged with one shoulder. "You have until we reach Jitrys to change your mind. If not you, perhaps your well-trained hound. For now, however, I am going to let Leed and Fiwal live for the same reason I am letting Zheann and you live. Treason is nothing more than the refusal to submit to someone who claims to have a right to demand it of you. I can hardly fault someone for treason unless it is against me. After all, we are traitors, too."

Leed took a step, but Donezan raised her hand. "Listen carefully, my son. Zheann is mine. These sons of Medenva are mine. You are mine. If you harm them without my permission, you will answer to me in ways you cannot imagine. I will pardon your treason against the them. I will not brook it against me, and I can keep you alive indefinitely."

For a moment, Leed looked ready to argue. His eyes widened. He retreated a step and lowered his gaze.

She smiled again. "That's better."

⸺ ⸺

Two shadows passed over them and out to sea. The black dragon with red and yellow markings on his face banked and landed beyond the skiffs. The skin of the other was leathery like Donezan's, but darker blue and with white whiskers. He landed in the sea and settled into the water shoulder deep. A light voice sounded in Zheann's mind. *"She's right about the mountain, and she's right about you. That's disgusting."*

Donezan tried to look grave. "It seems Zheann's canny guesses were correct. The magic used to free us awakens the mountain and we can do nothing to stop it." She smirked, composed herself, and smirked again.

"We must get our people over the mountains to the west," Zheann said.

Donezan crossed her arms. "That won't work unless we can block three passes. Still, damming the passes will be much easier to damming the mountain. As I recall, the land beyond the mountains is higher."

A fourth dragon landed further away. Like Venkis, he wore scales, but they swirled in a painful mix of red, yellow, blue, and white. His black horns curled like a ram's.

"First, introductions are in order." Donezan gestured toward the dragon with the black scales. "This is Venkis." She gestured toward the deeper blue dragon. "This is Sharn." She repeated the gesture toward the last dragon. "This is Genter."

I thought Athenque didn't have names.

A smooth, deep voice that Zheann didn't recognize spoke into her mind. *That's a convention of the dernai we rejected. We chose to name ourselves.*

Genter?

Very good.

"We will carry you to your homes." Donezan said.

Nu shook her head. "No, we go to the ship, return to Guelph, and warn the Kotich." She strode to the nearest rowboat, pushed it past Venkis into the sea, and scrambled aboard.

Kwin stopped beside Zheann and handed her a small sack. It was heavier than she expected, and she fumbled with it for a breath. "It's a present for Jenem. I hope she appreciates it. We'll ask Captain Dorlew to send a bird to Jifreb." He jogged to the second boat and followed Nu.

The captain glowered after them.

They are mine. The thought-voice sounded like a growl.

Yes, Venkis, one is, I know. Later.

"Well, Captain, now you have no choice. You either accept our help or sit on the beach and watch the show. I don't understand why you are being stubborn. We're trying to help you, to save the lives of your loved ones. In return, do we not deserve respect? How is that asking too much?" She passed Leed and stood before the captain.

"We learned the first time. We're not stupid enough to make the same mistake twice." He looked toward the boats for several breaths before looking at Donezan. He scanned her from head to foot, sneering, and pointed at the dragon in the water. "How are we to stay mounted? We'll need saddles, or straps, or something."

Donezan held out her hands. "I said we will carry you. One in each hand. It's safer."

It also shows who is in charge. Zheann put Kwin's pouch in her bag.

Donezan smiled. *It's a lesson you all seem reluctant to learn.*

Zheann smiled back.

Be careful, child. Impudence ceases to be amusing quickly. You would not like me to become bored and drop you, would you?

You don't understand, Queen Donezan. We are already doomed.

And as I have told you, I can change that. We will save as many of my children, and as many of your proud Med friends, as possible. Then you will learn to trust us. Donezan put her hand out toward Zheann. "I will carry Zheann. Venkis, you bring the Med. Sharn, you bring Leed and Fiwal. Genter, see if you can find our friends and convince them to help.

As the black dragon rose and sauntered toward them, Foden stepped back. "Captain?"

Captain Moln stared at Donezan. The ground shuddered. "How long will it take to get to Jitherick?"

"If Jitherick is between here and the mountains, perhaps half a day. We will arrive during the night."

"Jitherick was Jittaelfa," Zheann said. "There are dragons painted with magic on the city walls."

"Ah, then before it was Jittaelfa, it was Jitrys. We won't get there by sunset, but we should be there by midnight. That is, if your fear doesn't continue to detain us."

The captain turned his back on the dragon queen. "Foden, Leed is your prisoner. Keep him with you. I'll go with Zheann and this *lady*. Someone else can carry Fiwal."

Donezan's chin rose as she considered him. Slowly, her lascivious smile returned. "Are you changing your mind? Yours is a better idea. You can become accustomed to being near me." She took several steps back, and in a shimmering, the woman became a dragon.

Must you?

You sound like the dernai, Genter, only more petulant. How many worldlings have you loved?

"None, Donezan. I'm not that desperate for attention, and the dernai is not wrong about everything."

Donezan laughed. *I must for as long as it amuses me to do so, and your reaction is quite amusing.*

The Captain turned as if to respond to her. His eyes opened wide. He swore and took several steps back as he drew his sword halfway. He pushed it into its sheath and stood his ground, allowing Donezan's talon to close around him.

Zheann closed her eyes as Donezan grasped her. *Genter? If you find Estaen, will you tell him I said, "I'm sorry."*

If you wish, but it will do no good. The dernai does not forgive, and so, neither does he.

Please tell him anyway. Thank you.

Zheann steeled herself as Donezan spread her wings and launched herself into the sky.

Chapter Eighteen

Tarewo, 26 Troleng 153, Jitherick

I'*ll never feel warm again.* They had landed in a clearing to the south, and she and the captain had walked as far as the outer city. She coughed as smoke carrying scents of wood, thatch, food, sulfur, and things she didn't want to name swirled around her. Red embers pocked the black ruins. A thick layer of dust covered everything. She stepped on something that gave way beneath her weight. She lurched sideways, and the captain's hand tightened on her shoulder. *Please, let that have been wood.* More dust fell, like gray snow, or like ash from a hearth. Tears fell and her heart ached. "Do you think—"

His hand pushed against her shoulder, turning her toward him. "Your family is fine. Mistress Jenem is fine. I left orders to protect as many Rys as they could in the palace. It's a big building." He paused, and when he spoke again, his voice was gentler. "Do you want to stop where your home was?"

"Later. You need to talk to the general and take care of our families. Mourning the lies of my life can wait." Ahead, torches held by soldiers lit the wall. Zheann gasped. Soot blackened some sections, while others looked as if something had bitten them, sheering through the wall's bones. High over the head of one soldier, a blue eye peeked through the smut.

"Has he crowned the new king?" The captain looked past the soldier, pain creasing the corners of his eyes.

"No, sir." The guard's face relaxed. "The general will be happy to see you, sir."

Captain Moln straightened, but his shoulders relaxed.

Zheann grinned at him. *He's alive. Maybe my family is, too. At least until he finds out what's happened, what I did.*

He took her arm and strode into the city. Two buildings that looked like boxes had replaced the shops and houses along the main street. "At least there are enough Rys left to build."

They walked along the wall of windows. Light shone in two. The next block had two more massive structures, as did the third. Soldiers stood at the doors on the third block. By the time they passed it, the palace was visible beyond an expanse of rubble. Lights shone in both it and the field. Crews loaded debris onto carts, while soldiers stood by.

It looks like the city has been turned into the Armory.

"Wipe your tears, Zheann. You'll feel readier to face the general, and maybe some princes."

She wiped at them. Grit from the ash seemed to tear at tender skin below her eyes. "I'd need a bath to be ready to do that, but there's no reason for me to. There's nothing I can tell them that you can't. Go, make your report, and get our families on their way. The less I know about what the two of you discuss, the less Donezan will know. I'll go to the kitchen and get food to take to the clearing."

Gray dust streaked his face and coated his mustache and beard. On the left side, it looked like he'd rubbed it in instead of off. "How sure are you about the mountain?"

"No more than the last time you asked. What I'm sure about is if we do nothing and it happens, we'll perish. If we go beyond the mountains and it doesn't, we'll look like fools." *Donezan said she thinks I'm right. Would she lie to me about that? Yes, if it got her what she wants. For some reason, that seems to be us. Maternal affection? Power? Glory?*

"Better live fools than dead ones?"

"Exactly." She lowered her voice. "You might want to wash your face before you report to the general."

He signaled to a soldier near the palace entrance. "Take Mistress Zheann to the kitchen. Tell Hikiel or whoever's there to give her whatever she needs. After, take her wherever she wants to go. If anyone gives her trouble, arrest him. If anyone gives *you* trouble, end it."

The soldier looked from the captain to her, and back. His face was as dusty, but not smeared. He looked at the road before opening the door to a clean, bright hallway.

"Thank you, Captain." She followed the soldier into the light and warmth of the palace.

⸺⸻◈⸻⸺

The soldier glanced at her several times, but always looked away if she looked toward him. They left colorful corridors with beautiful candelabra and entered a network of wide hallways lit with utilitarian lamps. A Rys passed her pushing a cart. *Halls wide enough to let the servants pass one another in service to the king. What would it be like to live in a house with stone walls, walls crafted with magic as these must have been? Probably uncomfortable. You never get to be alone.*

When the guard glanced at her again, she smiled. "How bad has it been?"

"About what you'd expect. People are angry, they want justice."

Meaning that Med want blood. I want justice, too. The Rys want it as much as the Med. I'm afraid we all face disappointment. What will they do when they find out about the dragons? Will they wait until after the mountain explodes before they go to war? Is there any way this mess can get worse?

The kitchen reminded her of a smithy. One forge-like oven had a door as tall as Zheann. *I wonder who the elemental is that keeps the shielding going.* Maybe they all learn how to do that.

Etsitty excused himself from a conversation with two maids and hurried around the scarred wooden table to join her. His appearance was tidy, but dark circles under his eyes and the almost wild look in them told a different story. "Mistress Zheann, how may I help you?"

What happened to Hikiel? "I need simple dinners for four Rys and two Med, packed to go with us. Make that five Med. Do you know if there any herb shops left?"

He brought supplies from several shelves with far too little on them. "I doubt any Rys shops of any sort survived. The rioters destroyed more than half the inner city and most of the outer. The general took us into the palace and the soldier's barracks. More escaped into the forest and bogs. The Med destroyed without discrimination. They've threatened rebellion, but he's the general, and so far, the princes have backed him. Some refused to live in the buildings the general had us construct, but they gave in after a couple cold nights. What news have you brought? Did you find the assassins?"

"Yes, but it's complicated. I can't tell you more but tell Hikiel and your father things have gotten worse."

"How could they have gotten worse?" He raised a hand. "I'm sorry, I know, you can't tell me."

Zheann helped him pack a large basket, which the soldier took from the table. *How could they have gotten worse? I let the captain talk to the general alone. He's the general. The captain will obey his orders.* She turned to the soldier. "I want to go to the jideker and my shop."

"Mistress," Etsitty said, "the jideker was destroyed. I've heard more Rys died at the jideker than anywhere else. There is a curfew from dusk to dawn."

The jideker? The children? "I have already broken the curfew by coming here. Were the rioters under orders from the princes or the general?"

"Not that I am aware of." Etsitty kept his gaze focused on her.

"Who was their leader?"

"I couldn't say, Mistress."

Because you don't know or because saying will bring reprisals? Or because the Med standing beside me was one of them? She turned to the soldier. "Were they arrested?"

"No, Mistress."

"I see. I want to go anyway, and when I finish there, I want to go to the ruins of my shop." *Oh, don't give me that look, it's not like walking through the door of either will turn you into a Rys. You can't believe that, can you?* She slipped a knife off the worktable and collected two large sacks from a pile near the door.

Words she'd said long ago danced through her memory. "Papa, is it true Rys who go into the garrison lose their magic and come out Med?"

He had laughed, and said, "Who told you that?"

"The curfew," the guard said.

"I don't suppose they can kill me twice if I go where the captain told you to take me, now can they?"

⸻ ◆ ⸻

The soldier rolled his dark eyes. Zheann took a lantern from a hook on the wall and they left the palace through a service door. Three young Rys shoveled ashes out of firepits. A second soldier joined them with a brusque nod. They walked to the gate and picked their way through the debris. The building from which the family had been thrown no longer stood. Neither did Leed's herb shop or Tahke's carpentry shop. Only charred timbers remained. *Is Tahke helping the builders?* Her heart wept.

One of the jideker's gates hung part way closed. The other lay on the ground. Small fires burned among the ruins to her right. Neither of her feet would move. *The first time I walked through this gate, I was terrified, wondering what the giants would do. The first time I walked through them as a teacher, I could hardly contain my excitement. The last time, I was worried about Lord Roll-in-the-Dirt taking me before a magistrate. I never thought there'd be a last time.* She turned to the columns that had held the gates and examined the scrollwork she'd ignored. *Like at the jideker in Jifreb. Where is Eunaela? Does she still have the books? Does the library here still stand?* That question removed the shackles from her feet. *Go to the classrooms first, then the library.*

The ceiling and part of a wall had collapsed into her room. Dark marks smeared and formed smudges on the remaining tables. She swallowed and wiped at the tears that would not stop falling as her mind whispered the names of children she would never see again. She turned her attention to the floor. A smaller piece of rubble rocked. It rocked a second time before flying into the darkness.

A soldier grumbled.

"Calm yourself," the other said.

"She's not mumbling."

Careful, Zheann. Making progress is fine unless it gets you killed. "Yes, I am. I was doing it quietly. Would you prefer that I shouted? I'd get done faster if you helped."

The guards grumbled and moved toward the courtyard.

Another small rock followed, and another. She glanced; the soldiers were still there. She chose one of the larger rocks. When she couldn't throw it, she returned to throwing smaller ones. She stepped into the cleared area and touched the floor in several places. Pulling a square of stone from the floor, she gathered four small books from the cavity beneath it.

She went to the area that had been Jenem's room. She threw several rocks and pushed the remaining smaller ones out of her way. She collected seven more books. In the corner, she found a trinket box. She put everything in her sack and wiped tears away. *Whatever it is, it's a piece of her life she'll get to keep, if she's alive.* Anger exploded in her. *I promise I will get this piece of your life back to you.* The emotion evaporated. *If we survive. If...* An explosion rumbled. She cringed. *Will we know? Will we hear the water? Maybe it will crumble slowly, and the waves won't come. And perhaps I'll wake up, and this will all be nothing more than a nightmare.*

⸺◈⸺

The guards followed her to the main entrance. All the doors stood open or were missing. Nothing remained in Master Turisba's office. She looked at the guards. "Is Master Turisba well?"

The older guard shoved at something with his toe. "Haven't heard."

Did he get to talk to Lord Roll-In-The-Dirt? How is it that things that don't matter anymore come to mind so much? You're dead, Zheann. They can't kill you more than once. Why can't you get that through your thick skull?

Another part of her mind whispered, *because you're still alive, and have the sense to want to remain so.*

That sounds like something Estaen would say.

Before she reached the door to the library, she could see the empty shelves. She stopped at the door and whirled to face the soldier. "Where are the books?"

"How am I supposed to know? Check with Master Turisba."

The younger guard took a step back. "One night early on, there was a big fire in the courtyard."

"Did you fools at least save some Med books?"

The younger guard lowered his gaze as the older guard took a step toward her. "Mind your tongue, Mistress!"

"Why? Because Med are allowed to lose their tempers and Rys aren't? Med can destroy the city and kill anyone they want, but a Rys no bigger than your children can't even tell you what fools you are?"

His face darkened. "We aren't the traitors."

"Oh? Destroying Jitherick isn't treason? Burning the books meant to teach your children about the greatness of the Med kingdom isn't treason?" The younger guard's eyes held remorse. She knew hers held nothing gentle. "Where is Master Turisba?"

The older guard looked at the ceiling. "I don't know."

The younger shook his head. "Probably at home."

Would Master Turisba have tried to save any books? Could he have snuck any Rys books out? Would he have? Maybe. "Can you find Master Turisba and give him a message? It's critical."

"He can't unless you go to the palace. We're supposed to protect you."

"I don't need two guards."

"Yes, you do." The older guard scowled. "When we see another guard, we'll send him to find the headmaster."

"Take me to his home. I can tell him myself." She walked away. *I'm not sure why I bother. It might be better if everything associated with our learning over the past thousand years was forgotten.*

"It's the middle of the night!"

"It's important. Do you know where he lives? It will only take a moment once we get there. After that, I want to go to my shop."

"With all this food, I thought you wanted to feed some people."

"I do. Neither stop will take long."

Grumbling, they took her to the headmaster's home, in a cul-de-sac snuggled against the north wall. A light shone in a window on the ground floor, and another on the floor above it. Paving stones led from the dirt street to the door. A dark form moved across the window. As she walked toward the door, it opened. In his most authoritative voice, Master Turisba said, "Who are you and what do you want?"

"It's Zheann Sevem and a couple of Med soldiers." She kept walking.

"Mistress Zheann? Come in." He stepped back. He wore a long, charcoal gray robe almost the color of his hair. A yellowed bruise covered the left side of his face and spread across his nose.

"I can't. I'm sorry to come here this late. Are you all right?"

"You should have seen it before, and the look on his face when he recognized me. I was never a soldier, but I had nine brothers. Are *you* all right?"

Stupid question for which I don't have time to think of a smart answer. She stepped close to the door and lowered her voice. "Master Turisba, if you have any books from the library, take them into the mountains. Leave tonight. I don't have time to explain beyond saying if anywhere is safe, the mountains will be."

He stared at her. "Will you be heading there?"

"Yes. Take your family and go."

She walked to the road. "We have one more stop on the way to my destination. You won't have to carry the basket much farther."

She led the soldiers through the gates. A group of Med boys scavenged through the mess. They cheered as one held something for them to see.

Zheann bristled. *What have you won? You're out here rooting like sows in hopes of what? Finding some hidden treasure? As if your parents didn't already take half of everything we owned?* A scavenger walked toward her.

"Back off," the older guard said. "Take your spoils and go home. She's Captain Moln's pet."

Her muscles relaxed when the man obeyed but she frowned. *Coward.*

"Don't let them teach you to hate, Little Hedgehog."

The memory burned. *Papa, right now, it's about all I have left.*

They walked to the pile of rubble that had once been her shop and home. White stones lay scattered among pieces of brown wood. *They didn't burn it? Fiwal's hex worked? Why is that a surprise? He's a good elemental. I'll have to tell him. It's only fair.* A loop of leather stuck out from under broken furniture. She pushed the wood aside and retrieved a leather necklace with a dull gray, resin pendant. She held it to her chest, fighting sobs. She took a step, then another, searching the rubble until she got to the fireplace. As she turned, a lump a shade lighter gray than the stones of the hearth caught her attention. She knelt and picked up a doll. Brushing at the ash rubbed the gray into the cloth further. She hugged it as her heart tore. She closed her eyes and willed time to stop.

"Mistress, are you all right? It's time we went back."

Ye fen dernai efoim. She shoved the doll into her bag and stood. *No, I'll never be all right again. Why do you ask such foolish questions? Because you're following a Rys around after curfew and she's acting like a madwoman.* "Not yet."

"Is there something you're looking for?" he said.

My life. Freedom. Hope. Papa's apples. She strode to where the blackened orchard stood. The guards followed her through it to an area the fire missed. When she'd put six into her pack, one of them sighed. The younger one stepped forward and plucked one from over her head. "Mistress we need to leave."

She kept picking. "Soon, but we can't go back into Jitherick. I have to meet Lieutenant Foden a little way south." In the light of her lantern, both men looked dusty and miserable. "How long have you two been on duty?"

"Since morning, Mistress."

Anger ebbed away. "Come with me to where I'm meeting Foden. Then you can go." She strode south with the guards following.

———◦((◦))◦———

Once she got past the ring of ruins outside the city walls, she focused. *Queen Donezan, could you send Foden toward the city gates to meet me? I doubt the Med with me are ready to meet you, and I have more food than I can carry.*

She walked on, holding branches covered with gray dust out of the soldiers' way. *Can't she hear me, or does she want me to think she can't?* When she got halfway to the clearing, she made her request again.

How compassionate. Where is Captain Moln?

Talking with General Moln. There were things I wanted to get before we leave. The Med destroyed the jideker, the library, and my home. They stepped on Dren's doll. You're getting hysterical, Zheann. She swallowed hard. *They didn't need me, and I needed to think.*

Sh. You think too much, Zheann.

I have a lot on my mind.

If you'd like, we will build a jideker, and you can teach. Your family will live with me. There is much I can show you. Foden is on his way.

Thank you. She counted twenty paces then called his name. After another twenty she called again.

"Coming." Irritation filled the word.

She held the lantern high. "Over here." He slowed to a walk and waved to the soldiers.

"Thank you, gentlemen." She handed apples to both, and they rubbed the dust from them. "You may return to the palace. I hope they let you go to sleep soon."

Foden collected the basket and looked at the sack at her ankle. "What's that?"

"Papa's apples. We'll need the seeds."

Foden rolled his eyes but looked past her when someone behind her whistled. When she didn't see anything in the trees, she looked at him.

He whistled as he took an apple from the basket, wiped the gray from it and took a bite. "I guess the captain was right. Good thing I know better than to make a bet with him." He finished the apple as the captain and the general emerged through the underbrush.

When Zheann pointed to her head, the general nodded. "I want to meet Donezan and the others. Are the explosions and the ash from the mountain?"

"I think so." *I will never ask how things can get worse again.*

"Then let's get this over with. We have a lot to do before we leave." He and his son stepped around her and led the way to the clearing.

Fiwal and Leed sat next to a small campfire. Donezan stood with the fire behind her, wearing a black cloak over a black skirt and pale blouse. Her hair was still loose. Another Athenque stood as tall as a Med. His cream-colored hair swept back from a widow's peak. His beard and mustache circled his mouth without continuing along his jaw. He dressed in a gray brocade coat over dark pants. The third looked Rys: short, clean shaven, with long, sandy hair. He was broad shouldered and wore blue trousers and shirt, with what looked like a piece of animal skin draped over his right shoulder. *Which is Venkis and which is Sharn? I think the one in gray is Sharn. The one in blue is Venkis.*

One of them chuckled in her mind, a low, resonant sound.

The general stopped two paces from Donezan, with the captain at his right shoulder and Foden at his left. "You must be Donezan."

"My proper title is Queen Donezan. A larger delegation is appropriate when meeting your saviors and masters."

"You are not our queen, or savior, or master and I don't have time for games. I've issued orders to all garrisons to evacuate past the mountains with as many civilians as they can and block the passes. You can start killing us now, let the explosion or flood kill us, watch us survive without you, or help. Your choice."

"Zheann," Donezan said, almost purring, "explain to him how little chance he has without us."

Zheann blinked. "I—"

The general lifted his chin and pointed at Donezan. "We lived without you for generations. We will either continue to live without you or die without you, but we will not become your slaves. You can keep Fiwal and Leed, but Zheann is coming with us."

"She made an agreement with us."

"She had no right to do so. She is on the king's business. Until he releases her, she is not free to agree to serve anyone else." He held her gaze for a moment longer before walking away, with the captain and Foden on his heels. "Mistress Zheann, come with us."

I told you.

The amused-sounding thought voice was unfamiliar, and she guessed it was Sharn's.

Donezan pushed a stray lock of hair behind her ear. *He's going to make things more interesting. Zheann, go with them. Speak to my children. Bring them out to me and let them decide for themselves.*

Zheann jogged after the Med. *I should have gone to that meeting. Things just got worse.*

Chapter Nineteen

Tarewo, 26 Troleng 153, Jitherick

The general sat at a desk made of polished oak. The captain and Foden stood opposite him, waiting, and taking the place that would have let her address him as either an equal or a proper supplicant. Zheann leaned on the side of the symbol of the power denied her. "General, please. The dragons have more power and more knowledge of magic than we do. We need their help." *You sound like a spoiled child begging for a new toy.*

"What we need is a plan. If the only thing you can contribute to it is 'we need their help,' leave and let us get to work." He looked at his son. "I sent orders to the garrisons to evacuate within two days. By this time tomorrow night, I want Jitherick empty. The only personal belongings will be what their owners can carry. If a Med makes a Rys carry something, the Rys gets to keep it."

"There'll be resistance."

"They have four choices. Obey, join the Athenque, stay out of our way, or die. No one who can walk rides. We'll need the animals and carts to move food and supplies. By dawn, I want three parties on their way. Each party will need builders, military, Rys, and support. One party will go to each pass. Three garrisons will head to the northern pass, and four to the southern. The remaining seven will move people through the middle pass. Each garrison has been told to send teams ahead to build dams and camps."

She clenched her fists, knowing she had nothing against which to beat them. *It would only hurt my hands if I did. Threatening to destroy the palace will only convince him more that we don't need the dragons. What can I say?* "General, please, listen to me..."

"Not if you're going to suggest we accept the Dragons' terms." His eyes echoed his mouth's frown.

"We don't have the power or the knowledge of magic to dam the passes. They do."

He bared his teeth. "They *might*. They might *not*. Do you want to serve them? Do you want to enslave your people to them?"

"No, of course not! I don't want anyone enslaved, but I don't have the love affair you Med do with throwing your lives away in a romantic gesture of defiance. I thought the goal was to keep us alive. The captain and I already agreed to their terms. It isn't right to renege on an agreement."

"Neither of you had the authority to speak for the kingdom. If you or the dragons thought you did, that's not my problem. When we're gone, they can loot Jitherick as their payment. You have a choice. You can stay with the dragons, or you can go to the middle pass and work toward keeping us both alive and free. If we can't dam the pass, we'll have to find a way to live in the mountains until the water recedes, if it does."

"And if we survive all this, will the Rys be free? Will we owe the Med nothing more? Will we have paid our debt?" She opened her eyes wide, hoping challenge and rage would force him to capitulate.

He frowned. "I'll speak to the princes about it. First, we have to survive."

Liar. "Have my mother, Dren, Jenem, and your family left?"

"Your family rode out when I went to talk to the dragons. My family will stay with the princes. Now, can we discuss the plans?"

"You seem to have them well in hand."

The captain gave her a warning look. "Zheann."

"I need to think, Captain. You seem to have no problem breaking your word, I do."

"I warned you. One of your reasons for allying with them was to figure out how to defeat them. Your agreement with them was as much a fraud as mine, and if you believe they'll abide by any rules, you're a fool."

"I have no illusions they will keep their word any longer than they must to achieve their goals. I don't suppose we will keep our word any longer than we must to achieve ours. But my father used to tell me not to hate because when we hate, we become like the ones we hate. They might not abide by any rules, but if we follow their example, we are worse than fools. Make your plans. It's clear you don't need me or want my advice." She headed for the door, expecting a bellow or a hand on her shoulder with every step.

⸺⟪◈⟫⸺

Zheann stalked into the corridor, turned right, and continued to where it ended, past closed doors etched with dragons. She stood where a mahogany rug and a golden carpet with mahogany and green swirls met. The air smelled stale. *Where do you think you're going, anyway? You don't have a home. The people you care most about... the people you should care most about are on their way west, with the dragons or dead. Can you walk away and let the rest die? And didn't you say things got worse because you weren't at their last meeting?*

Her angry self answered her guilty self. *I don't care. I can't stand there and listen to their foolishness, and they won't listen to me.*

Guilty glared across the darkness of her mind. *That's the real problem. You're angry because they won't listen to you, but you're not saying anything. You're ...*

"Are you lost?"

She jumped. *...running away.* A guard stood two paces behind her. *Skulking in shadows?* "Yes. Where did Mistress Jenem and Ronsath stay?"

"This way." He pointed over his shoulder and led her to another office three doors from the General's. Someone had added two beds and a crib to one end.

"Thank you. If the captain comes looking for me, tell him."

"Yes, Mistress Zheann." He walked away.

Zheann, could you say something more stupid? Would he keep a secret from the captain if you asked? She lifted Dren's pillow and buried her face, inhaling her scent. *What am I supposed to do? Who do I betray?* She took the pillow to the desk and quickly made a list.

"Dren, Mama, and Jenem." *The general said they're on their way.* She murmured the magic for Far Sight. Dren's head lay against Ronsath's shoulder. A cloth hid all but her pale curls. Ronsath squinted into the night, peering where Zheann was but was not. *She senses the magic.* Jenem gestured a greeting with her fingers. Both they and the six soldiers who rode with them wore cloth tied over their noses and mouths. They rode horses, as the general had said. She waved her hand, dispelling the magic. *I don't want to know where they're going. It would do no good to demand a horse and ride after them. How would I find them? The general will tell me that if I want to join them, I'll have to run. Could I fly?* She shuddered. *After tonight, I don't care if I ever fly again. Besides, the whole idea was to keep them safe by sending them away from me.* She drew a line through their names.

"Leed and Fiwal" *They're with the dragons. Fiwal may have reconsidered, but there's nothing I can do about them right now. If I didn't betray them before, I am now. What does it say of me that I can cross their names off with no qualms? This is what they have done to me. I can't let it happen to Dren.*

"The Dragons" *Donezan has made it clear. She intends to rule us. She also said she'll lie when she chooses to. They are the enemy, but I've worked with enemies all my life. I agreed to her terms. What else could I have done? I could have gone with Kwin and Nu and sailed and ridden back. The Med could have sent reports ahead. And she might have killed us all. Now, if I don't commit treason against her, I'm committing treason against the Med and the Rys. If I do, am I condemning us all to death?*

"The captain, the general, the Med" *I don't owe them anything. They've used us and will continue to use us for as long as they can. They're using me. They'll betray me and insist I break faith with the dragons.* She worked Far Sight again, this time into the general's office. Father and son discussed something. Foden was lying on the floor, apparently asleep. She moved to the general's right side. On the desk lay maps, reports, and lists. The general moved, and for a breath, Zheann saw only blackness. The general, now on her right, lift a report from the floor and flipped through it.

She waved her hand again. *Mama, you said to do what is right. What do you do when it looks like everything is wrong?*

"The Rys." *They already serve the Med. If I cannot free them, which would make the better master? The captain would reject both. What if the dragons are the only way to keep them alive? Are they better off dead than enslaved?*

"Estaen and the Athenque." *What happened to Estaen? He said he'd deal with the dragons and they're all here. No, Genter isn't here. He was looking for Estaen...and others. Who are the others? The stranger who wasn't Kotich? Another dragon? Why isn't it with Donezan? More questions to which I don't have answers. What do I owe Estaen or his dernai? He saved my life. He can't lose his. He left his home to come with us. He helped me with magic. If he were here, he'd tell me to consider the nature of magic. He'd go with us to the mountains, and I'd do all the work, but I would still be free. I keep saying I can't, and we can't, but magic does what I can't all the time.*

She worked the magic for Far Sight a third time, this time without murmuring. Darkness surrounded her. *Am I in something again?* She walked forward, and the darkness stretched leisurely around her. Something moved. *Estaen?* Something struck her. It crushed her as it shimmered and faded. Light exploded around her, within her. A dizzying sense of hope filled her, but the deep darkness struck again, crushing it into nothing.

Chapter Twenty

Igsole, 27 Troleng 153, west of Jitherick

Whose cow is lowing outside my window? Something tickled Zheann's nose and cheeks. *Papa!* She wrinkled her nose. *But Papa got sick and died a long time ago.* She bounced against something hard and uneven. Pain jolted through her head. *Why is my bed moving?* She finally woke enough to open her eyes. Not a bed, a cart. *How did I get here? Why does my head hurt?* Something pushed against the bridge of her nose. She ran her fingers along the edge. *Dusty cloth?*

"Here." The captain climbed over the bench back and knelt next to her. He wore a piece of cloth over the lower half of his face.

He folded a tarp back and pushed her against the sideboard. She gasped and cringed at the pain. She tried to get her hands to her head, but his arm got in the way. He raised the edge of cloth on her face and gave her a sip of wine that sent warmth and comfort through her. She tried to take the flask, but he pulled it away. "It has to last until Doctor Metris can make more."

Around her, a sea of torches ebbed and flowed. Riders and horses alike had cloths tied over their mouths and noses. They blended with the ash-murkiness. Some were close enough she might have been able to touch them, were it not for the shroud of gray, dry snow descending between them. Beyond those men, torches bobbed, held by invisible hands. By the time the men were only a handful of spots away from her, their torches were nothing more than feeble red blotches. Something touched her head and face like warm snowflakes. She brushed at her face, then held her hand out and investigated the darkness. Her heart beat faster. She pulled her hand back and shrank against the boards. "What's going on?" Her voice rasped.

"We're heading for the mountains. We've heard several explosions, but no water yet. There doesn't seem to be a rhythm to them." He seemed to be watching her, waiting for something.

For what? She scanned the darkness. "Where are the dragons?"

He straightened, swaying with the cart as his dark eyes searched her. "What's the last thing you remember?"

"I was walking toward the palace, debating how to make your father see reason." She rubbed at her temples and winced.

"That was a day and a half ago. He didn't change his mind. You walked out in a huff. A third later, the guard found you unconscious. We left when it should have been dawn, but the sun never rose. Now that you're awake, we can move faster."

Your father turned his back on the best chance we had to survive, and I'm the one holding us back?

The captain took a large-mouthed jar from Foden and removed the cork. "Drink some soup."

"And we brought your father's apples," Foden said.

"Thank you." The broth smelled enticing. She took a mouthful and chewed small, tender vegetables. *Sweetroot, mushrooms, and sage.* "Who made this?"

He squinted at her. "Someone at the palace. Why?"

"It's good."

"You haven't eaten in more than two days. Dirt would taste good. Doctor Metris said the attack was magical. You aren't to do any magic until he says so."

No magic? "Captain, if I can't do magic..."

"You'll have to teach other Rys how to the same way Estaen taught you. Good thing you're a mistress at the jideker. You don't look injured, but it sounds to me like a head wound. I've had men knocked out who forgot events around the injury. Headaches can last months. You and the doctor need to find something that makes you recover faster." He pulled something from his pocket. "You were making a list when someone attacked you."

She held it toward the torchlight, willing her eyes to focus. "It looks like I've included everyone but the Kotich and the southern kingdoms. I don't remember why I made this, or why I would have crossed anyone off."

"Not surprising."

"Did my—"

"Yes, your mother, Mistress Jenem, and six soldiers took Dren toward the mountains around the time the general told Donezan we wouldn't surrender. He wanted the dragons paying attention to him and not to a couple Rys women sneaking off. By now, I imagine Dren either has all six men fighting to see who can make her smile or has them trying to escape baby duty."

Doctor Metris rode out of the gloom on an ash-colored mare. The shoulders of his cloak had pale smears. He brushed at his left shoulder, smearing it further. The scarf over his nose and mouth had a blood stain across it. "I'm glad to see my—"

A report, as loud as thunder and with an ax-sharp edge, cut off his words. She recoiled. Soup broth splashed onto her hands. The captain grabbed her jar of soup with one hand and her shoulder with the other. The wagon jerked as Foden struggled with the reins and talked to the restive horse. Echoes rumbled from the west.

The doctor's clear blue eyes filled with compassion. "How much pain do you feel? Do you feel dizzy?"

Something inside her head seemed to slosh as she shook it. "Your medicine helped. The explosion didn't."

"Get used to them." The captain turned to Dr. Metris. "Is there any reason she can't ride?"

"No. I doubt it will do more harm. The only questions deal with her comfort and concentration."

The captain gave a quick whistle and gestured. Two soldiers rode over. "Take over the wagon." They dismounted onto the cart, handing their horses' reins to the captain and Foden. "Give Mistress Zheann a hand," he ordered as he turned his mount in a circle. He moved his horse in close as a soldier put Zheann into the buff mare's saddle with all the care given a sack of wheat. "Foden, you're on her right," he said and brought his horse around to her left. He and Foden traded the soldier's packs for theirs and tied them to the saddles. "Doctor, you follow her. Zheann, you set the speed."

"Why didn't you leave me in Jitherick?"

"And miss the chance to see you pull down mountains with your magic the way you threatened to do to the palace? I'm hoping you're wrong about the water. In case you're not, by the time we get to the mountains you need to have several ideas about how to keep it from coming through the pass. The doctor needs to have you ready to implement them."

She took a slow breath. *Here we go again. Now I understand why Estaen kept refusing to help. It's not about bringing the heights down. It's about building the pass up.* "Builders would know better than I how to do what you're talking about." She clucked at her mare. The throbbing in her head didn't get worse even with the jounce of a trot.

"And they will, but I want your ideas, especially since you spent time with Estaen, and they didn't." The captain whistled three staccato notes.

Zheann winced. "If the explosions don't kill me, your whistles will." Around her, horses trotted as soldiers kept pace with them. "If we survive, you'll have to teach me to whistle. It will get my class's attention."

"Saying 'if' clouds your thinking. We will survive because our children deserve to be free. That means we use anything and everything we can, even the dragons if we can do it on our terms."

Our terms? Your terms.

"How's your head?"

"It aches, but it's not too bad except when the mountain booms or you whistle."

He grinned wickedly and repeated his triple blast as he urged his stallion to a canter.

———◆———

With nothing to tell them about passing time, it seemed days before they reached a place where dim torchlight reflected. The captain whistled twice and dismounted. He helped Zheann do so as well. He called to someone, "Check the water before anyone drinks."

The soldiers spread out along the bank and dismounted. One dipped something into the water and brought it over. Gray floated at the top, but the water below it turned a sickly shade of yellow.

Captain Moln grimaced. "Make sure everyone knows." He turned toward her when she chuckled. His eyes widened as she put her hands over her mouth and laughed.

"Om-om." Her laughter-garbled utterance brought out another wave of laughter.

Both the captain and Doctor Metris walked toward her. The doctor's face showed concern, the captain's, frustration.

The captain's voice held a tone of warning. "Zheann, what's going on?"

Doctor Metris pointed at a large rock. "Let me check you over."

She sat rocking and laughing. He approached as if he feared she'd attack him, which fueled her laughter further. After several breaths, she calmed enough to trust herself to talk. "I–I'm sorry. It's just—" She laughed again. "The water. One herb hexed to counteract it is…" She chuckled. "…onions."

The doctor stared at her.

The captain snorted. His grin was as twisted a grin as he had ever given but lacked the hostility she'd always seen in it. He turned toward the soldier. "Let everyone know, and if there are any Rys who can hex onions to make the water drinkable, have them do so."

The soldier trilled out a series of notes, stopped, then whistled a second set. In the distance, someone repeated both.

Zheann sat and rubbed at burning eyes. "Can I have another sip from the flask now?"

"How bad is your headache?"

"Bad enough for me to want relief before I try working magic." *Yes, I know, "No magic until your head doesn't hurt."*

"No magic until your head doesn't hurt. She can have some more medicine."

The captain handed her the flask. She took a generous sip and enjoyed the spread of comfort as the doctor checked her eyes and reflexes. "Now, try standing on one foot for me." She stood and balanced first on one foot, then the other.

When the doctor murmured magic, Zheann gasped and sat on the rock. The doctor held her up until the pain subsided. The voice that came from her mouth sounded like a croak. "Can you do something about that?"

His answering smile looked as weak as her voice sounded. "Whatever happened to you didn't harm your body. It harmed your connection to magic. Do you know the only real difference between a Rys body and a Medenvaris body is size? There are no special physical organs that give us the ability to do magic. It's – magical. Everything I've learned is about healing the body."

"So, you don't know how to fix what's wrong with me." *Now I know how the captain feels every time I tell him I don't have an answer to his problems.*

He hesitated. "The fact that magic causes you pain tells me whatever part of you does magic isn't dead. It's injured. That magic wouldn't have hurt you before. I can continue to use healing magic on you. It might help. For now, all I can suggest is that you treat it like you have," he glanced toward the captain, "fallen from a tree. You might want to avoid Rys who are using magic. That won't be hard. There aren't many of us."

She watched him walk into the gloom. Something splashed behind her. She squinted, watching the expanding rings in the lights from the camp. *There is something in the dark.*

It was a fish.

No, it was something in the dark.

A brief time later, as the captain handed her a steaming cup of tea, she said, "Why aren't there more Rys with us? Were that many slaughtered?"

"No, less than half the Rys in Jitherick were killed."

Less than half. Are you proud? Ashamed? Is it just the way it is? Do you think we should thank you for your generosity is sparing so many?

"We're the second wave. The first was the advance crew. They'll build camps and explore the pass. Quite a few Rys went with them. When we get there, we'll focus on your plans. The reason the third group hasn't caught up with us is that it has the most wagons and the most people. Some will have supplies we won't find in the mountains, and some have things we can't afford to lose. The Rys will come with the wagons. The fourth wave will be people from the east.

Seven districts are coming through this pass. Three each through the other passes. People will be coming all the way from Jifreb. The General will lead the fifth wave. He'll stay as long as he can to hurry stragglers along." He stared into the dark for several breaths. "Make a list of Rys and Med you want on your team. If they're alive, we'll conscript them. The general also sent word to the governors beyond the mountain. We'll see if they send help."

"What about the princes?"

"Only a few princes will be useful. They'll come with the third wave. Kathoa is with us, riding separately for security. Two or three will ride with the fourth wave. I think Esherick is staying with the general."

"And the southern kingdoms?"

His eyes widened. "They won't do anything to aid us unless we ask them to help exterminate you, Rys." He rubbed at his jaw under the cloth covering his face. "The general has sent warnings. They all have some lowlands. It will depend on how high the water rises and how hard the waves hit. Chorniv and Teftor would be no great loss. You can bet Lartile will have the Chornivian army set to invade the moment he sees a chance. Coilea, Stadum, and Dattuck? It's hard to say. How are your plans coming?"

She held up some paper. "That's what this is for. If something happens to me, at least you'll have a copy of my ideas for someone else who can work magic to try."

"While you write, I'll fish." He walked to the river and pulled an arrow from its quiver. A moment later, he stood with the shaft nocked.

Blank paper. How does one stop water? Freeze it, boil it, evaporate it, divert it, drink it. Too bad we can't find one of those places where Estaen's people are. The water couldn't kill them. No, that wouldn't work. Water is physical. It can't be contained in a place that is magical. Could we use the waterwheels to power what we use? Use the water to stop the flood? That may have to wait for Rys from Jifreb.

A series of reports from the mountain drew her attention. *How can we know when it explodes if it ever does? Far Sight, but I'm the one who knows where to look. It might take days for anyone else to find it.* She braced herself. Pain blossomed and receded. *Where's the magic? What if it never comes back? Don't think about it. Think about the flood.* With a sigh, she began writing. When the captain called her to mount, she handed folded sheets to him. "There's the start. It's not much but hold on to them. That way more than one of us has them."

—— •((○))• ——

They traveled along the riverbank. Ash flocked every surface, making it look as though gray fur covered the world. Zheann brushed at her mare's neck, and the skin crawled under the touch. *The ash is irritating her. If I could use magic — what could we use as the physical part? Maybe water.*

"Captain." Foden jerked his head back and to Zheann's right.

Torches burned. Horses trotted. Men rode. The river looked like a gray blanket. *What?*

"I see." The captain stared ahead. "Doctor, can you hex torches?"

"Hex them?"

"They have been failing for the last third. We're out of pitch. Can you relight them?"

The doctor's light blue eyes widened.

Zheann stood in the stirrups to look back. "I can teach you the magic." Two groups of torches flowed together, then spread out into a line.

"I know it!" He glowered at her. "I even know how to extract the pitch."

The captain's eyes lit with wicked amusement. "Good. We'll keep going as long as we can unless we find a pine grove.

Her father chuckled in her memory. *"Little Hedgehog, help is only helpful if both the helper and the one being helped are willing. More often, one or both trips over pride and blames the other because their hands are dirty."* She grimaced at her ash-covered fingers.

"How much further to the mountains?" Her hands shook. *Stop being ridiculous! There is no reason to fear the dark.* She clenched her fists and rotated her shoulders. The knot between her shoulder blades loosened but the trembling didn't cease. She hid her hands beneath her cloak.

"Too far," the Captain said. "The size of our party and the noise from the mountain will protect us from predators unless we get separated. In the dark, that can happen, and tying ourselves together would be a disaster if something did happen. Predators hunt near water. The other groups have more Rys, but they won't have more torches or pitch. No one could have predicted this darkness." The anger in his eyes said, "It's not my fault."

He's right.

"As it gets darker, tempers will flare. Foden, tell those who have torches to form one column. Stretch it out as far as possible and keep everyone moving at a trot. Take the doctor with you. Put him on a wagon and have the spent torches taken to him. Even if he can't rekindle them, he can collect them for when we get more pitch. We'll go until we find a stand of pines or until we have no choice but to stop."

"Come on, Doctor." Foden spun his horse, whistling and shouting orders as he rode away.

Doctor Metris met her gaze, anger smoldering in his pale blue eyes that seemed to say, "It's your fault." He mounted his horse again and rode after Foden.

A torch between her and the river sputtered and died.

Chapter Twenty-One

Igsole, 27 Troleng 153, west of Jitherick

They ate their next meal while riding. Zheann's eyes burned. She closed them and jerked awake. No one around her grinned. *Maybe they didn't notice. You're lucky you didn't fall off your horse. They'd have gotten a good laugh out of that. Why don't you try doing something useful?* Zheann focused, looking for magic. *Ye fen dernai haloim. Somewhere out there, Mama, Dren, and Jenem are facing this darkness. Are they wandering, lost without torches? Don't be silly. Jenem is an elemental. What about the first wave? They have Rys with them. They'll be keeping watch for us. Won't they? They'll send some scouts out to lead us in. Won't they? What if they don't see us?*

The Captain's torch failed, and he swore.

Zheann gasped. "There's something in the dark."

"Where?" Captain Moln rose to full height in the stirrups, searching the road ahead.

She scanned the area as well. "I'm sorry, I thought I saw...a shadow, I guess."

"A shadow... in the dark." He peered at her, sarcasm dripping from every word.

"My eyes must be playing tricks on me." Her cheeks burned.

"If you see it again, let us know."

The soldier to her right looked at her from the corner of his eye. *He thinks I'm crazy, too. He might be right.* "Since I woke up, I've ...sensed there was something in the dark."

"All the time?"

"No, only when it gets darker."

"Has anything like this ever happened before?"

"No."

After a few breaths, he looked away from her. "It can't be something stalking us. If it were, you wouldn't only sense it when *your* circumstances change. It may have something to do with what happened at the palace, or with the dragons. Don't think about it. Think about how to stop the water."

She glared at the darkness ahead. *Whose stupid idea was it to try to stop the sea? Mine. A dam won't do it. How can we plug the whole pass? Even with magic I doubt we have the time. The papers I gave the captain will be useless. Estaen would tell me to consider the nature of magic. Of course, he could make a dam of magic and have us all stand behind it to watch the sea strike. He could. Why can't I? He'd say because I don't believe. A shield large enough to stop an ocean?*

The Captain stood in his stirrups again to look back along the road. He whistled several notes. "Make camp. We can't make it to the mountains without lights. Zheann, we need torches to ignite when someone approaches them. What else is needed besides wood and pitch?"

Zheann blew out a breath. "Cloth would be good, but we don't have it. We can use bark, leaves, or even grass instead. If we had time to experiment, we might find all this ash useful. More Rys who can work the magic. Doctor Metris and I both know how to light them. We'll figure out the magic to turn them on when someone approaches."

He turned his horse in a tight circle and raised his voice. "Ges, I want twenty teams bleeding pine trees for pitch then felling them.

Another twenty teams can make torches and fires along the road heading west. Spread them out. I want as large an area as possible to have light. If necessary, we'll find a way to move the fires along the road. Have the doctor and any other Rys with us, report to Zheann. I want torches ready to be hexed before the third wave gets here."

"Sir!" Ges looked old enough to be the captain's father. "You shirkers heard the captain. What're you waiting for? A formal invitation to get yourself kicked all the way to the mountains?"

Med dismounted, collected axes from their gear and jogged into the trees.

"Keep her out of trouble." The captain whistled four descending notes and strode into the chaos of his troops.

Ges' eyes twinkled at her. "Stay out of trouble and out of the way. Is there a hex that keeps wooden carts and sleds from burning?"

She stepped out of the way of another Med. "If they can smear the wood with clay or mud it would help."

He turned to a group of soldiers. "Cramner, you and your men build low sleds. Slather them with river mud. Attach ropes to them so we can sling them between four horses or men. Once a Rys fireproofs them, build a fire." He put his hands on his hips and glared at them. "I'm not getting any younger, lads!"

——— «◉» ———

And while all of you are doing that, I'm going to stand here looking helpless...worthless... She took her canteen from her saddle and held her hand out. "Give me your canteen and the captain's. I can't work magic, and Doctor Metris doesn't want me around when it's being used, but I can fetch and carry until the Rys who are with us get here." She took them to the river and pushed the layer of ash out of the way. She put her shirt's sleeve over the canteen's mouth and filled it. She filled the second and the third as the soldiers fell into a rhythm with their axes. She hung the filled bottles on saddles and worked her way along the line of horses.

"I can't work magic, but I can fetch and carry." Pathetic. If I can't work magic, I can't teach, or sell. Without magic, I can't seek refuge among the Athenque and their dernai, even if I could find them. If I can't work magic, all my ideas to block the pass are useless. Without magic I'm a short, weak, useless ... Med. Her cheeks grew warm. *Good thing they aren't Athenque.*

"You OK?"

She spun. The canteen splashed. The older soldier grinned at her. "You're more skittish than my little Scoree."

She fished out the canteen out and held it to drain. *What is Scoree? I can't imagine a Med child being skittish. Could he have a pet mouse?* "Yes, I ...the dark must be getting to me. What's your name again?"

"Artgesy Gaumio at your service. You may call me Ges, almost everyone does."

Now what? "What do you do?"

His charcoal eyes twinkled. "I train the recruits. It's the main reason I'm here. They're used to listening to me."

"Oh? Did you train the captain?"

"Yes, I did. The general made sure he went through all the same training as any other soldier. After Jitlaniri, they tried to promote him, but he refused it. I heard he's declined at least one promotion since."

She put the canteen in the water again and tried to sound casual. "Jitlaniri?"

Ges cackled. "You don't know about Jitlaniri?"

"I know Jitlaniri is a mountain town near the Chornivian and Dattuck borders."

"I guess I'm not surprised." He took the full canteen, dropped a pinch of powder into it, capped it, and handed her another. "The Chorniv and Dattuck came together against the city. Some say ten thousand strong against a town half as big, and a quarter of those Rys. They captured the commander, and he surrendered, but the captain and his company fled into the mountains. During the night, they caught a Dattuck scouting party. They snuck into the camp dressed as Dattuckers, freed the commander, and escaped. They made sure the Chornivians saw them, and that a few Chornivians, including an officer, died on the way out. The alliance between the two armies fell apart. I hear they killed more of their own than our boys did the day before."

She touched her lips with two fingers. *There's more than one kind of magic.*

＝（●）＝

Doctor Metris and ten Rys hurried over. "We were told to report to you."

Ges handed Zheann another canteen as she said, "The captain wants to make several hundred torches. Your first task is to hex the trees or the pitch to shorten the time that will take. Second, hex the torches, so they light when someone approaches or holds them."

A Rys woman with a burn scar across one cheek blushed. "I remember doing that as kids. You know, to scare people. Having a torch light when someone comes close won't be a problem. I suppose you'll want them to extinguish once the people are past."

Ges gazed into the distance. "Yep."

How am I going to do this? With a sigh, Zheann rose. "Do any of you know how to hex a pine to get the pitch to flow more quickly?"

The woman shook her head. The doctor and a man with brassy hair looked at each other. The second man said, "Is that like getting metal to flow?"

"It's easier. I can't use magic right now—"

"And we shouldn't use it near her," the doctor added.

She shrugged. "My father used to collect resin to sell at our shop. He used a hex that made it flow without burning the wood. Let me teach you all." She looked at the man who'd mentioned metal. "If it's the hex you use, you can lead the crew and help them work out any difficulties in the process." She worked through the hex with them several times. *If pitch flows through wood, and metal flows through... what does metal flow through? It doesn't matter. The hex should work the same. What else flows through? Blood through bodies. No, the Med are already too good at that one. Water flows through lots of things. That's one to keep in mind. Ash through the air. Maybe useful. Does light flow through the dark?* She knit her brows. *Sound through the air.* They unknit and rose.

The doctor canted his head. "What are you thinking?"

"Do any of you know how to throw things using magic?"

The doctor and the man with brassy hair nodded.

"See if you can combine the flowing hex and the throwing hex and use it to make the captain's whistle go all the way to the mountains."

The brassy-haired Rys' eyes brightened. "I think I can do that."

"Good, the captain headed that way." She pointed. "You'll have to explain the whistle hex idea. I just thought of it." The Rys hurried off, and she returned to filling canteens. *That went better than I expected. Maybe if I'd payed more attention to the games the other kids played, I would have known how to play those tricks, too. I'll bet Papa knew. Now, water flowing through what? Hurrying? Slowing? Stopping.*

A single whistled note came from the direction she'd sent the Rys. A second, louder chirrup followed.

Come on.

The third grew louder still. The soldiers standing near her looked around.

Four piercing notes rang out. She stuck her fingers in her ears and closed her eyes as three more followed. They echoed from the mountain. Ges nudged her with a huge grin in his eyes. "He told them to send Rys. If they didn't hear him, they're deaf."

And if they did hear him, they're deaf.

Ges patted her on the shoulder hard enough she had to take two steps to keep from falling. "Good thinking."

She rubbed her shoulder. "Thank you." She returned to filling canteens. *Papa made pitch stop flowing by reversing the hex that made it viscous. Viscosity. What can I do with that with water?*

Someone west of them whistled. Zheann stood. "Ges, what's going on? What does that mean?" A second and third whistle repeated the message.

"Look!" Ges pointed west.

Far above them and looking impossibly far away, a tiny light shone. As she watched, a second light appeared below and to the right. Someone cheered. Others joined in.

Ges clapped his hands. "All right, boys and girls, stop gawking and get to work. There are two mountains to be defeated, and one just showed a chink in its armor. So, quit your lollygagging. What d'ye think you are, a bunch of reh—" He looked at Zheann and blushed, "baby birdies in a nest, waiting for your Mama to feed you? Fly, you fools!"

Zheann ducked her head and choked on her laughter. *Being polite? Don't strain yourself.*

⋙ ◉ ⋘

Zheann pushed a cork into a canteen, collected a second and stood. One light was lower. Her cheeks ached. She schooled her smile, only to find her mouth in rebellion. *It can't be Mama or*

— 241 —

Mistress Jenem, but whoever is sending them must recognize the problem. How many are they sending? They have work they have to do in the mountains. A dozen? A dozen would be good.

"Looks like they're making progress. How long do you figure before they get here?"

She started, and turned to object when Foden answered, "A third." He squinted westward. "Maybe a little more."

Oh, not talking to me.

"Right." Ges' whistle began and ended on the same note. "One third!" he shouted. Others repeated the order along the line. The soldiers cutting wood handed or tossed their axes to new soldiers. Men shouted as if they had money on which one would finish first. Soldiers and Rys tossed and stacked wood with the same enthusiasm. Even the line moving the pitch in buckets hurried to position them along the woodpiles. Another group led horses to the wagons and hitched them.

Like angry bees. Zheann moved onto the road, searching the blackness below the higher light.

"Use your eyes, Athenque-spawn!"

Ges pulled Zheann from the path of a soldier with what looked like a tree trunk on his shoulder and fury in his eyes. "Some of my boys are a little lacking in manners." He snatched the canteens from her hands, whistled, and tossed them. A breath later, he caught two more and handed them to her. His eyes laughed. "It's encouraged. It's a little hard to ask them to kill someone while they're being polite. Looks like our friends are below the tree line. It will be closer to the half, maybe two-thirds before they arrive. They'll make better time once they're lower, and you can watch them then." He walked with her to a cook-fire. "Get something to eat, then get packed. Captain Moln will want to be on our way before they get here."

"How many do you think they'll send?"

He studied the darkness. "It depends on how much they've gotten done. Anda is the scout leader, Erevo's the construction leader. Erevo doesn't like interruptions or interferences, and we're a big one. They can't know who whistled, beyond the fact that it was someone who knows the whistles there's a Rys involved." He looked at her from the corner of his eye.

She'd filled more canteens while keeping an eye on the food line, and when the Med line dwindled, she joined two Rys. The Med who handed her a plate filled with steaming fish, bog berries, and flat bread was more coated in ash than anyone she'd seen. She looked at the cooking food, and at her plate. *There's a shield over the cook fire. Good, I don't have to eat ash again.* She held the plate beneath her cloak as she found a place near other Rys to stand and eat. Rumaging through her pockets, she drew out a small pouch and held it to her nose. When the cook bent over the fire to turn the fish, she returned it to her pocket. *Manners,* she scolded her mourning tongue.

Four Med collected their plates and sat on the logs at the fire. Two watched her, their dark eyes reflecting the firelight. "Does she look injured to you?" one asked the others.

"Nope. She looks like someone trying to play the captain for a fool."

"I would never do that." Zheann turned to leave. The other Rys had melted into the darkness. *I was wrong. The Med know the magic to make a Rys invisible. All it takes is an accusation.*

"Or maybe helping her husband commit treason. Either way, she hasn't been making herself useful."

"Who gave you permission to leave?" a third voice asked. "We were having a friendly conversation."

What does it matter? As soon as they don't need us, they'll remember they forgot to exterminate us. I am my father's daughter. She met a dark gaze. "You have an interesting definition of friendly."

"Garesherick Moln is our captain."

"Then perhaps you should think more highly of his judgment." She shoved a large piece of fish into her mouth.

The one who had been silent stood, his hand on his Billy club.

When the first Med hissed, "He's coming," the one with the truncheon sat again, shoved half his flat bread into his mouth, and chewed.

Zheann swallowed. "Oh good, then you can express your concerns to him." *Oh good, then you'll have to defer my execution.*

The captain helped himself to a mounded plate. "Is there a problem?" He shoved an overflowing fork full of food into his mouth.

Zheann took a bite of her fish and shook her head.

"No, sir." The soldier with the truncheon said around the mouthful of bread.

I hope my grin reaches my eyes the way Ges' reaches his. "They were telling me how much they admire your wisdom and leadership."

His eyes narrowed. After a breath, he pointed west. "The light has reappeared. You, men, get ready to move out. Keep it orderly." He turned away. "Zheann..."

"Coming." She poured the bog berries into the flat bread and put the plate in a stack. She waved at the cook. "It was good. Thank you." *That wouldn't have convinced one of my students.* She hurried after the captain. What had been one light had divided into six. It was much lower. Her cheeks ached again.

"From now on, make sure you're with a Med you know you can trust."

"You've already made it clear what you think of my judgment of character."

He rounded on her. "Then let me make this easy for you to

understand. Stay near me, Foden, Ges, the general, Prince Kathoa or Prince Esherick. Yes, I know you haven't met the princes. You will soon enough."

"And how do I do that while doing everything else?" As they walked away from the firelight, darkness loomed over her. She recoiled, gasping as she lost her balance.

"Watch!" The captain grabbed her arm, keeping her from falling. "Have you told Doctor Metris about that?"

The men at the fire glared at her.

She pulled her trembling arm free. "No. He can't do anything about it." She lowered her voice. "I can't seem to stop sensing danger-in-the-dark." *What happened in that room? How long before I panic unless I'm sitting in a room with no shadows and no windows?*

"I've been thinking about that. Doctor Metris says the attack damaged your connection to magic. That means either someone attacked you with magic, or you did something harmful with it. It must be something you Rys aren't used to. That means either the Dragons attacked you, or something about what Estaen has taught you is harmful. He may not have realized the damage he convinced you to do to yourself." He looked down at her and grimaced. "You're right. The dragons make more sense." He stopped and turned toward her. "Do you remember the day my father stopped at your shop to get some ginger?"

She winced. "Yes."

"That was the first time I ever killed anyone. It seemed like I had nightmares about it forever. The first time I was seriously injured, I considered building a cottage in Kotich. I nearly got myself killed trying to protect myself from injury instead of trying to win. Sometimes it takes memories longer to heal than it does bodies." Another explosion roared past them and echoed from the mountains. The captain squinted east into the gloom. "Where's the water? It keeps making noise, but no water."

"Every time we hear an explosion, and water doesn't follow it,

I hope I've been wrong. If the kingdom doesn't flood, you can go home." She walked west again.

"Until we defeat the dragons, you are staying with us."

"Captain, they can hear my thoughts."

"I haven't forgotten. That could be useful if you could eavesdrop on their thoughts or make sure they hear what we want. Right now, you have knowledge about magic no one else does. We can't risk losing it."

You don't understand. "It's knowledge I can't teach if I can't work magic myself."

"We don't know how long you won't be able to hex, but you've already proved that wrong. Children need demonstrations. Adults who already understand the basics can work from instructions. Just tell them you're injured. They should understand and want to learn from you. Who else would have thought of mixing hexes for flowing and throwing?"

"I'm still amazed that it worked." She took several slow breaths, forcing back the desire to argue. They arrived at the western end of the line of fires. "You may be right, Captain."

"I want to sit in on the classes."

"What? Why?"

"The more I learn about magic, the more I'll know how to fight the dragons. It will also help me figure out how to use Rys in battle. The general has long said Rys are useful, but I think we need to use you more strategically."

Teach him about magic? Wait until Fiwal and Leed realize what they've started. "We're people, Captain, not weapons." When he continued to look at the road, she added, "but you're right. We must change the way we see each other. I never thought of trying to teach a Med about magic, except how to use what I've sold to them. To fight the dragons, we will have to think strategically, magically, and creatively."

"Once this is over, I'm planning to suggest to the general to convince the king to choose some Rys advisers. You won't get to be queen like Fiwal wants, but you should plan to be a busy woman."

Herb seller, teacher of practical magic to the Rys and theoretical magic to the Med, adviser to the king, and student of the Athenque? You seem to have lots of plans for me, Captain. It's a long way from living in exile and hoping no one figures out I'm the wife of a traitor. It may be better than being a slave to the Athenque, but what about what I want? Why doesn't anyone seem to care about what I want? What do I want? I want this to be over. I want things to ...well, not to return to the way they were...I want better. I want peace.

Eight horses separated from the light above them as another explosion boomed in the east and echoed in the west. The Captain frowned. "When they get here, keep in mind, they may have Erevo's authority, but you have mine as long as you behave yourself. I have the general's, and he has the king's."

Chapter Twenty-Two

Igsole, 27 Troleng 153, West of Jitherick

"Zheann, what are you doing here?" Ronsath dismounted and hugged her. "We came because we thought your torches were spent. Erevo sent us because he believed there weren't any Rys in this group. Why didn't you...?"

Zheann fought back tears. "I can't do magic. I can't remember how it happened, but Doctor Metris thinks someone magically attacked me. We think it might have happened while I was using Far Sight. What did the general tell you before sending you away? And why did you come instead of staying in the mountains with Dren?"

The captain pulled Zheann away. "Mistress Ronsath, we have a deadline and too few Rys working to help us reach it. You can exchange status reports later."

Ronsath inclined her head. "Yes, Captain."

The five other Rys and two Med soldiers dismounted. They walked to where Doctor Metris and the others sat on the ground, wrapping bark around rough-hewn sticks, and murmuring their hexes. The image of black and white birds with iridescent blue wings and tails flashed through Zheann's imagination. *They sound like Eunaela's magpies. Ten magpies, good luck. Do we sound like a bunch of birds muttering mindless noises to Estaen?* She resisted the impulse to shudder.

Once introductions were made, one newcomer examined the pile of wood and buckets of pitch. "Top off the buckets with water. Heat it until the pitch dissolves. Also, you can use grasses for the wicking."

The woman with the burn scar peered at them. "Will it matter if the ash is in it? We tried to keep it out, but it's everywhere."

The man shrugged. "We'll have to see. If we're lucky, it will only make them smoke or sputter, but I think we can filter it out if we need to. We've had a little longer than you do work out the problems."

Ronsath waved at the glaring captain and put her arm around her daughter's shoulders and they walked to her horse. She took her pack from behind the saddle. "Whatever attacked you must have done so after you checked on us. How do you feel?"

"It feels like someone cut off my fingers. I can't sense or do magic and other people using magic around me gives me headaches. Doctor Metris gave me medication for them. Unfortunately, it has to overcome the headache it gives me before it can overcome the headaches the other magic causes."

Ronsath gave one of her *that's not funny* smirks. "What *can* you tell me about what happened?"

"Not much. I was alone in the room where you slept, and I made a list." She handed it to her. "They found me unconscious, I woke a day and a half later in a wagon, and I'm afraid of something in the dark."

Ronsath held the paper toward the light. She frowned. "Leed and Fiwal aren't dead?"

Zheann sighed. "No, the last I knew, they were with three dragons. Fiwal doesn't seem too pleased with how things turned out. Leed is as angry as ever. One dragon claims to be Queen Donezan."

"Does she?"

"It's possible. According to Estaen, Athenque can't die."

"And Estaen knows this..."

Zheann's face grew warmer. "Because he's an Athenque, too. Apparently, Donezan and the others rebelled against their king and came to our world. Donezan admitted as much.""

Her mother mouthed a silent "Ah." She read the list again. "Since you crossed them off, you must have Far Sighted them, too. The attack seems to have come after that. Estaen and the Athenque aren't crossed off."

"Estaen disappeared when the dragons escaped. I don't think it's a list of people or groups I Far Sighted. I doubt I could Far See the Athenque. They're magical, not physical."

"And you know that because..."

Her cheeks warmed. "Estaen said so."

"You seem to trust Estaen."

"He saved my life. He taught me how to do magic without words."

Ronsath's ash-covered eyebrows rose. "So, let me guess. We're not only the Med's archenemy, doomed for extermination for Fiwal and Leed's crimes. We are also the only hope for their salvation?"

Zheann grinned. "Not only those. We're also pawns in a war between two groups of magical beings."

"You are your father's daughter."

⚬⫷⦿⫸⚬

Several Rys returned with armfuls of grasses, and the others went to work. The woman with the burn scar walked over. "The captain wants torches to light when someone approaches them. I've been thinking. When we did it as kids, they flared quickly to scare people."

"I remember doing that," Ronsath said.

"Mama?"

Her surprise must have been evident because Ronsath grinned at her. "That's not quite what we want here. Let's go try a few experiments." She led the woman over to some bushes.

The captain watched them go. "How soon will they be ready?"

"Soon. They can work the magic on as many as ten torches at a time. After that, you can light them in a fire." She waved a hand toward Ronsath and the other Rys. "The ones they're working on will follow the same pattern."

"Is there any reason Med can't do what they're doing now?"

"Only Med reasons."

"It's all in your approach." He glared at her and turned toward the Rys on the ground. "Doctor, I'm going to give you some help." He whistled. Soldiers quickly surrounded the work area. "Watch how they dip the wicking and wrap the torches. The man who correctly wraps the most gets an extra week's wages." The soldiers watched the Rys with the intensity of a falcon watching a mouse. When they finished their demonstration, the captain whistled, and the men jostled and shoved one another as they scrambled for supplies.

The ache in Zheann's head grew worse. She took a sip from her flask and walked to the next fire. *Mama said I checked on her. It makes sense.*

"You're either thinking or trying to use magic," the captain said.

"I'm trying to figure out what happened at the palace. Mama said I used Far Sight to check on her."

"You also crossed off Leed and Fiwal. Could they or the dragons have attacked you?"

"Why would they have waited until after I crossed them off? I doubt I would have checked on Leed and Fiwal. They were with the dragons, and they committed treason." *I did, too.*

"Unless you crossed them off before you checked on them or crossed them off for some other reason."

A Med handed torches to the captain, Zheann, and a handful of others at the fire. She touched the flames with hers and sighed silently as the darkness around her fled.

⚬

The captain lit his torch. "Zheann, get ready to leave. Ronsath, stay with the Rys here. If the dragons find you, they'll use you to control Zheann. The general may not have told you, but we sent you away to keep you safe from the dragons."

"It was the only reason we left."

"Your being here defeats the purpose. Right now, we need her focused on keeping the ocean from rushing through the pass."

Ronsath nodded. "Erevo told us about that when he caught up with us."

Zheann thought of the notes she'd handed the captain. Her eyes filled with tears and she turned to him. "Do you realize stopping the ocean from coming through the passes is as impossible as stopping the mountain from exploding?"

"Isn't the whole point of magic to do the impossible? If we're going to die, we may as well die trying to live. Sitting around, waiting, would be boring. If we succeed, our children will have a chance to grow up fighting with one another."

"You say that like you think it's a good thing." *He's as bad as his father. They won't listen.*

"It's better than the alternative." He smirked. "I'm a soldier. It's what I know. It's all our people know. We can work on doing a better job of it after we survive this crisis. It's not only our lives you're going to save. There are cities beyond the mountains. Half the kingdom lies through that pass."

Ronsath's touch warmed Zheann's arm but Ronsath addressed the captain. "Add to your list of crises the question of how we'll survive if this darkness doesn't end soon. No light, no plants, no food. If we don't solve that problem, those who die in the flood will be the lucky ones."

The captain swore. "You work on that problem while Zheann works on hers."

Zheann looked from Ronsath to Captain Moln. *Dren starve? After all this?* Her knees hit the ground, cracking her teeth together and setting off a dull pain in her skull. Her body tried to tell her these things, but her mind focused on the image of Dren, starving. *It's a good thing Fiwal and Leed didn't die. They need to see what they've done. They deserve to perish with the rest of us and watch their children suffer. I'll see to it they do.*

"Get on your feet, Zheann. It's time to head for the pass."

"You heard Mama. Why bother? It's kinder if we all die beneath the waves." Her voice sounded tiny, and far away.

"Yes, I heard her. I also gave her the job of solving the food problem."

Ronsath put a hand on Zheann's shoulder. "Captain, may I ask at what point you will recognize there is no hope?"

Zheann looked at him as he looked westward with hard eyes. After several deep breaths, he looked at them again, and when he spoke, his voice was little more than a murmur. "I will cease to hope the day Zheann dies."

"That's not fair." She pushed to her feet, holding Ronsath's shoulder to keep her balance. She opened her mouth, but no ideas for further complaint emerged.

His eyes smoldered. "Nothing has been fair since Queen Donezan walked into the lives of Rysa and Medenva. Will it be fair to the Rys if they die because you surrendered while there was still a heart beating in your chest? Will it be fair to Dren? Focus, Zheann."

Zheann focused on her mare's ears, sensing the captain's presence beside her and group of Med and horses behind her. When they rode into the foothills, another explosion roared and echoed around them. "Where is the pass?"

"That's the good news. It looks like the camp is about where the pass begins. The waves will lose some strength getting to it. It continues some above that, about half as high as the peaks. So, if we're lucky, the water won't even reach the pass."

"Our luck hasn't been good."

"This from the woman whose life was saved by an — two Athenques and who may have survived an attack by another."

Who married one murderer and is a cousin to the other. Whom the dragons consider a traitor. And who is being asked to do the impossible when she can't work the magic to light a torch. "And the bad news?"

"The pass is gentle and wide."

"Great," she said. In the torchlight, rocks lined the road, ranging from gravel to boulders larger than the captain's horse. *Go through the motions, so he can't blame you when you fail.* "Captain, see if some of your men can move the largest stones into a line across the entrance to the pass. Leave room for the carts but position other rocks at the road we can use to plug the hole. That will be our first line. Have them do the same thing every fifty paces going through the pass. If they can't use rocks, tell them to use logs, but use boulders first. Have them move the camp as high as they can. Living like mountain goats is better than washing away or being crushed."

"Fifty Med paces or fifty Rys paces?" The captain's face gave no hint of humor.

"Let me talk to Jenem about it. It depends on how tall the dams are and whether the magic will hold and topple or collapse. We don't want one dam destroying the next as it fails."

Chapter Twenty-Three

Divhad, 30 Troleng 153, Mountain Pass

As Zheann and the captain rode into the mountains, they passed groups of men and horses dragging trees and moving large boulders on log rollers. One Med gestured and shouted, "Work base straight ahead, camp up and to the left. The mistress is up there, too."

Ye fen dernai haloim! How are we going to build dams that can block this? The mountains rising above her to the north disappeared into the ash and darkness. The mountains to the south were mere shadows. "Once I talk to Jenem, I'll have a better idea what to do."

"Go talk to her now. I'll join you after I've heard the reports." The captain called to one of his men to take the horses, dismounted and helped her from her horse. The work camp looked like a disturbed ant's nest.

She hurried to the camp farther up the mountain. *Please, let me be wrong. How can the water reach all the way here? If I am wrong, people will be unforgiving. They will be anyway. If I'm right, how can we stop it? Why didn't I fight harder to bring the dragons? I'd even welcome Estaen's dernai if he offered to help. Of course, he wouldn't, and the general wouldn't accept help on the dernai's terms.*

Three buildings were dark, but light shone through the door and windows of a fourth. "Mistress Jenem?"

A candle appeared at the door of a cabin to the left. "Over here."

She followed Jenem into the cabin. Dren slept on the last low bed against the right wall. More beds lined the left wall. Jenem used her candle to light several others on a table in the center of the room. Her eyes twinkled. "I hope I don't look like you. I have never seen anything quite like this."

"I'm afraid it's going to get a lot worse." Zheann leaned on the table and slowly sank into a chair. She summarized her trip, ending, "Something attacked me after I checked on you. I can't do magic."

Jenem's eyes softened. She circled the table. "Injury or magic?"

"They found me unconscious and I stayed that way for at least a day. Doctor Metris thinks it's an injury. It doesn't hurt, much. I've tried to work magic, but nothing happens."

Jenem put her hands on either side of Zheann's head and murmured magic. After four breaths, Zheann twisted out of her grasp. "Stop!"

"I'm sorry."

"Mama?" Dren pulled at the cloth on the lower half of her face as she sat up.

"It's not your fault." Zheann hurried over and sat on the bed next to her. "I'm here. You have to leave this on." She tapped the cloth and hugged her daughter, listening as Dren told the story of her adventures in a mix of words and jabber.

She interrupted her story and pushed away. "Mama tinks."

"Yes, I do."

"Need a baff."

"Do I? I thought you might want to smell as bad as I do. Now, are you hungry? I am. You stay here with Mistress Jenem while I find something for us to eat." Zheann put her notes on the table. "When I come back, we can figure out solutions to this mess. You can read my notes while I'm gone. I'm afraid they won't be much help."

"You'll find food in the building with the lights," Jenem said. "I know some of what happened. Kwin used Far Sight to reach me, too. We have corresponded. They are fleeing inland. He found some old records that describe the world bleeding fire. Once they translate them, he'll let us read them. He told me you have a present for me I should open right away."

"Oh!" Zheann pulled two packages from her pack and handed them to the old woman. "One came from your cache from the jideker. The other, from Kwin."

Jenem unrolled both packages. Her eyes teared when she saw belongings she'd left in the cache. She looked from the small bundles of rocks and containers of water and snow, to the other package, to Zheann, and back. "Samples?"

Zheann straightened. "Next time you correspond with him, thank him." She examined a black stone. "He was cleverer than I. If he had given the package to me, I would have opened it in front of the dragons. They might have taken them, so we couldn't figure out how the Kotich trapped them. That will help once we survive the mountain's explosion." She tapped her notes. "Feel free to add to and correct any of my ideas. Want anything to eat?"

"Tea."

As soon as Zheann was outside, she leaned against the cabin and closed her eyes. *What do I do? Keep them here or send them away to be safe? Do I need Mistress Jenem's help or could Erevo give the answers we need? Why didn't they go further west? That's easy. They don't understand the danger, and they want to be helpful.* She took a swallow of medicine. The dull ache throbbed and relaxed. *They're here now. Erevo might know more than Mistress Jenem, but ... I don't know him. I don't want to share my ideas and have him laugh. I can discuss them with her and then send them on their way into the mountains somewhere safe.*

She jogged to the well-lighted building. Halfway there, the scent of roasted boar set her mouth to watering. She focused on the welcoming square of light, hurrying to its safety. She stepped to the side and slowed her breathing as she waited for her eyes to adjust. Finding an empty tray, she joined the line of others as they helped themselves to soup, boar, roasted vegetables, bread, and tea.

She stopped before she got to the door. *There's something in the dark.* Her feet refused to move. *It wants to kill you. Don't be ridiculous, Zheann. You're safe. Ye fen dernai efoim.*

The captain, Foden, and several Med strode through the door. When he saw her, the captain's gaze narrowed. "Mistress Zheann? We're going to get some food. Which cabin are you in? I'll join you."

So soon? We're not ready. "The second one to the left. Come when you're done eating."

"Do you need help with that tray?

He knows. Her face warmed. "Uh, no. Thank you." She rebalanced the tray and continued toward the door.

"Foden, get a torch and light her way, so she doesn't trip over a twig and waste the food."

Foden glowered and took the tray from her. "You get the torch."

They hurried into the darkness. "The captain told you?"

"I'm supposed to keep an eye on you." He sounded disgusted. She imagined his sneer under the cloth that circled his head.

"Is it as bad as it looks?" he said

"Not always. I'm sorry to have taken you away from your dinner."

"You didn't." He clomped into the cabin and put the tray on the table. "Figure out some answers." He hurried out the door.

She put a cup of tea on the table for Mistress Jenem and untied the cloths around Dren's face and her own. "The captain will join us as soon as he's eaten." She handed Dren a thick piece of bread and dipped another piece in the soup and held it to her nose. Her stomach begged for the food, but her nose expressed disapproval. *Will we ever have herbs again? If Mama is right, we'll starve to death.* "Here, Dren, you eat this. I'm not as hungry as I thought." She held the bread out, and Dren took it, blue eyes cheery.

Jenem frowned. "I see you've spoken with Ronsath." She pushed the bowl of soup toward her. "I've been thinking about her concerns about sunlight. We can overcome that. Starving yourself won't help Dren in any case. She needs her Mama to be strong and courageous."

She's an elemental. Tears welled. "Mistress Jenem."

"Sit and eat." The old woman tapped her finger on the table to punctuate the command. "I'll talk."

Zheann sat and shoved a spoon of soup into her mouth.

Jenem put her tea next to the packets of ash. "Your theory is sound. If the mountain explodes, it will push water and rock away. The lowlands of the eastern half of the kingdom will flood, at least temporarily. Erevo and I have agreed that damming the passes is the most obvious choice."

"Do you believe it will work?"

Aqua eyes twinkled at her. "It would probably have been easier to stop the mountain from exploding."

Zheann clenched her fists to keep from crying. "Several Athenque said it was impossible."

"Then this is the next best idea. We're already in the mountains if the dams don't work, and from what Erevo says, the general has ordered evacuations. We have to try. The only alternative at this point is cowardice and irresponsibility.

"Erevo prefers the idea of one large dam. If it doesn't hold, we have no recourse. At least two dams seem necessary, one at the east end of the pass and one where it turns south. The problem is that the pass is also the best escape route for those fleeing to the west. Which will allow the most people to pass? A few larger, or several smaller? Which can we close quickly, one or two massive walls, or a dozen? The other complication, of course, is how much of the dam will be physical, and how much magical. I doubt we have the time or resources to make physical dams. If we do make them, we'll need magical dams until we complete the physical ones."

Zheann swallowed soup. *Try.* "Mistress Jenem, the biggest problem is that I'm not sure it will even work. Is the land west of the mountains high enough to keep the water from flowing in from the north, south, or west? Maybe we should let the water go and live in the mountains."

"You should have paid more attention in Master Turisba's class. Yes, the western half is higher and has more mountains."

"I understood it to mean that you had to go up, through the mountains, to get there, and when you got to the other side, you were as low again." Her face flushed. "It didn't seem to matter much."

"If we can block the passes, we will have done all we can, and I have hope it will be enough." Jenem raised a finger. "Now, changing viscosities presents some interesting possibilities and challenges." She sipped her tea. Where gray ash didn't cover her hands, rough red blotches did. She gestured toward the tray. "Keep eating before it gets cold. There is no sense wasting it."

Zheann chewed on some boar. Her hands looked as bad. *The ash? How do we keep it out of the buildings? Simple shields will work, but how do we power them?*

Jenem tapped the papers. "The biggest problem is with the scope of the magic. For example, how much ice will it take to block the pass? If we don't change enough, will the water break it? Will the water melt it and put us back where we started? How do we control how much water we turn to ice? Might we accidentally turn all water into ice? Would we turn the Medenva kingdom into the Great Ice Land? How many people would the cold kill?"

Did the shamans kill the Kotich when they trapped the dragons? Nu didn't mention it.

"No matter what we do to the water, it leads to the same questions. How much is enough? What happens if we do too much?" Jenem slapped the table, looked at her hand and shook it gently. "We are woefully uneducated. Attempting anything too big may be as catastrophic as the mountain exploding, or worse. As daunting as damming the pass may be, it is the simplest, safest choice proposed. The drawback to any plan is the uncertainty. I cannot imagine enough water flowing over the land to cover the mountains, but we have no way of knowing how high to build the dams."

Dren patted Zheann's leg. "Mama, pease?"

Zheann gave her a piece of boar watching as the girl sat on the floor and munched. *So, dams.*

"Now, as much as Ronsath's food problem is a real problem, there's something to consider first: the black rock. It is ash. I've seen areas where forests have been burned. New plants grow out of the ashes. It feeds them."

"Estaen said something about the black rock being dried world blood." *Could using it for fertilizer help counter the lack of light?*

Jenem tipped her head to the side. "A poetic description. If the sky is raining powdered world blood, might not the fiery world blood also reach us?"

"You know something about the places where the earth bleeds?" Her heart constricted. "I hadn't thought of that. We can't hope to protect ourselves from it."

Jenem's thin, wrinkled face softened. "That may or may not be true. Magic can be potent if you know how to use it."

"Now you sound like Estaen and the captain. Every time someone tells the captain something's impossible, he tells me to do it. The night after we met him, Estaen helped build a shelter using mostly magic. He taught me to do magic without words."

"A useful ability. How are you doing with it?" Jenem's smile broadened.

"Can you?"

"Sometimes, with simple hexes. It's not something I want the Med to know, and I don't work on it much."

Zheann frowned. "The captain and Foden know. They helped me practice, but I know what you mean. Estaen told me to consider the nature of magic. I keep coming to that. Is the reason I can't hex because I have missed something about its nature? What if that's why we fail?"

———

Jenem looked toward the door, and Zheann turned.

The captain ducked as he stepped through it. He took off his cloak and draped it across a table. "The others are arriving. According to the sentries, the wagons will arrive soon. The third wave shouldn't be far behind. In a few thirds, we'll have things underway. Some men will have to keep working on the camp. Most can work on the dams. How do you want them constructed?"

Jenem lowered her tea. "You'll want to check with Erevo. He may know the practical aspects of some of this better than we do. We're considering theories. I suggest you use an arrowhead shape with the tip pointing east, like the bow of a boat. That will turn the water to the side. The resulting turbulence may disrupt the westward current. Make sure the tip and both edges where the dam meets the mountain walls are the largest boulders you can use."

Zheann put her hand on Dren's head. "Dren, don't stare."

The captain stuck out his tongue.

Dren giggled and took a piece of bread from the tray.

Zheann rolled her eyes. "Mistress, can we construct the dams so they crumble instead of falling like a tree?"

She pursed her lips. "I should think so. Especially if they are more magical than material."

Try. Be courageous and responsible. Zheann turned to the captain. "We're debating the number of dams to build. Erevo wants one big one, and Jenem thinks two or three. The problem with those is that it will be difficult to allow people to get through the pass and difficult to maintain. We don't have the time or material to make a material dam. We may not have the magic to support a magical dam. I need to talk to Erevo about it. If we could make something like the water wheels I saw in Jifreb, we could use the water to power the dams."

Jenem shuffled to the paper that detailed the wheels. "Flood waters tend to carry silt, rocks, trees and even boulders. They will destroy the wheels."

Zheann slumped. *Nothing works. How are we going to do this?*

Jenem patted her hand. "Mountains are windy and have streams. We can try to use those to power some magic. Even if it doesn't power the dams, not having to power everything else may help. Magic works like a lever. The amount of force needed depends on the length of the lever and where you place the fulcrum. We need a long lever and a sturdy fulcrum."

Jenem took another sip of tea. "Let's start with several dams. Ten if we can, with the next to last at the point where the pass turns south. That way people can continue to flee through the pass for as long as possible. Erevo's Rys may even know how to draw power from the earth itself. If we get all ten completed, we can fill between them. The eastern dams should slow the water. Building them may give us better ideas."

"You said Erevo only wants to build one dam."

Zheann's face pulled into a grin she imagined to be like one of her father's. "Tell him he is building one. It's just in layers and lots bigger than he thought. You outrank him. He can't argue unless he has an even better idea." *Let Erevo tell you it's impossible. Maybe you'll listen to him.*

Jenem gathered the vials, packets, and stones, rolling them in their packages. "Before you go, Captain, thanks to Kwin, we may have a way to figure out how the Kotich trapped the dragons.

"That's the best news I've heard all day. As soon as we defeat the sea, you can tell me about it."

She held the bundle out. "For now, take these samples. Keep them among your things and at a distance from anyone or anything magical. They may be a key to stopping the dragons, but if they can stop a dragon, imagine what they would do to a Rys. Zheann has been carrying them. It might explain why Zheann cannot do magic and not some unremembered attack. If so, we should also be concerned about the ash falling around us. I have not sensed or heard of anyone else having difficulty with magic. But if the Kotich hex permeated the mountain, and it explodes, our magic may be inhibited. If we are lucky, if the ash is causing her troubles, it is only because the injury makes her more sensitive."

Chapter Twenty-Four

Myot, 34 Troleng 153, Mountain Camp

What am I doing here? Jenem, or Erevo, or the captain, or the general, or the king should be here. I'm not a leader. I'm a mother and a teacher. I don't even believe this will work. Zheann scanned the room. Jenem sat along the side of a middle table. Five Med sat at the farthest tables, talking among themselves and glowering at everything. Erevo sat with them but stared at the door. She sighed. *Keep up appearances.*

A few Rys sat around the tables across the room, including a tanned man with the same unfortunate apricot hair as the palace steward. *That has to be Torweno.* She walked past a tub in the center of the room, glancing at the small box in the water. She continued around the table and took a seat next to Jenem. She put her hand on Jenem's shoulder and braced herself. *Alright, Zheann, you're a teacher, call these reluctant students to order. Get them focused so they can convince the Med it won't work. If I had magic, I could act like a Med.* She grimaced. *That makes no sense, but there's more than one kind of magic, and magic isn't rational. Maybe acting like a Med will help or acting like Papa. Would Papa still have hope?*

"I will cease to hope the day Zheann dies," the captain had said.

Estaen's voice whispered. "There is reason to hope but not to hope for that on which you have set your heart."

On what have I set my heart? The answer stung. *On someone else fixing things.*

Jenem murmured a few words. Noise and water exploded from the tub followed by a series of pings that decreased in volume and pitch over the course of several breaths. All the Med and half the Rys in the room threw themselves to the floor, ducked behind overturned beds and tables and swore. Water covered half the floor and a quarter of the people.

Erevo rose from his crouch. "Mistress Zheann!"

She smiled. "That was a tiny demonstration of a much larger problem that we need to solve. Everyone take a seat. The next explosion you hear may send a great deal more water over a much larger area."

Ges grinned at her fiercely as he and a few Med sat. A few more than half the Rys sat at the tables or on the beds.

Zheann looked at Jenem. The old woman held a cup to her nose, hiding a smile as she sipped her tea. She nodded.

Zheann nodded back and looked at her class. "You may know these things already, but there's no time for useless speculation or evasion. My husband and my cousin released Athenque from a mountain off the Great Ice Land coast. In doing so, they damaged the mountain. The explosions we've heard come from there. It's going to explode, and when it does, the ice that covered the mountain, and the sea between it and us will flood the lowlands. We don't know for sure how far the water will come, but it is possible it will come this far, and our families' survival is our responsibility."

More than half the Rys were listening. Less than half the Med even bothered to pretend. She softened her voice, keeping each word clear. "If *you* fail, both the Med and the Rys lose. That is how serious the problem is. Each of you has skills that can help us stop the water here. Anyone who chooses not to help may return east with your families."

The remaining Rys and all but four Med sat. A Med woman with her hands on her slim hips raised one hand, palm up. "Go on." A Med at one of the tables mumbled something and coughed a laugh.

Torweno raised a hand. "Where are the dragons?"

At least he raised his hand. "We are watching for them, but the mountain is our priority. We will build a series of dams. That way if one fails the others may not. Mistress Jenem has suggested an arrowhead or ship's prow formation. If they fail, we want them to crumble, not topple. Neither Mistress Jenem nor I are builders. Ges and Erevo will organize you into three teams. Each team will develop a more detailed plan for your dam and present it for approval in a sixth. Ges?"

A Medenvaris man stood up. "Wait. Do you appreciate how large the pass is?"

"I do. I had hoped it was narrower. It will require both Med and Rys audacity, and it must happen as quickly as possible because we don't know when the mountain will explode. We will return in a sixth with Captain Moln. Ges? Erevo?"

—«◊»—

Zheann and Jenem walked to the dining hall and sat at a small table away from any Med. Zheann closed her eyes and let the minty bouquet of her herb tea percolate through her soul. She turned her face toward the lights and closed her eyes. *Oh, to stay here forever. It almost makes me feel alive. Almost.*

Her conscience grumbled at her. *You're doing it again.*

With a sigh, she said, "That could have gone better. Thank you for the explosion. It got their attention nicely."

Jenem leaned toward her as a Med walked by, lifting her tray over the teacher's halo of white hair as Jenem sipped her tea. "You're welcome. It could have gone much worse. Keep an eye on Torweno. He has always been more like Leed than like his father. He did better with the more concrete things than with theory."

"He won't sabotage the dams, will he?"

"I don't think so. He might run away to join the dragons. Keep an eye on him and expect to be challenged. Now, have you tried magic recently?"

"In the last hundred breaths? No. I've been preoccupied with trying to get Med and Rys to work together in a foolish attempt to save the kingdom, so the Med can return to their planned slaughter."

"I think they are past that insanity at this point. You seem to be holding onto it more than they are. For all their faults, and they have many, their grudges tend to be short-term and sporadic violence followed by long-term nagging. And speaking of nagging...magic?" She moved her hand in a circle.

Zheann rolled her eyes as she sighed and put her cup on the table. She stared at it, reciting the magic in her mind, willing it to move. Next, she murmured the magic. When she repeated the hex, the cup slid the width of two fingers. Her head ached. Her heart capered.

Two tables away, a Med slammed his hand on a table with a loud bang. Beyond him, the cook snaked his way around the counter. When Jenem looked at him, he glowered but returned to his post. She turned to Zheann. "How does your head feel?"

"No worse than before I did it, but I did it!" *Liar!* "Do you think it was because I had the samples with me?"

"That, or you are simply recovering from the injury Doctor Metris described. Has he checked on you recently?"

"No, and if he did, he'd scold me for that." She clicked her mug against Jenem's before draining it. "Now, let's go find the captain so we can review the plans." *It's still impossible, but if I can do magic...*

Chapter Twenty-Five

Myot, 34 Troleng 153, Mountain Camp

The ash and darkness that filled Zheann's waking hours joined the dragons, water, and fire in her dreams. They left her both exhausted and restless as she dragged herself out of bed, rubbing her neck to ease the pain. She took a large sip from her flask and tried to blink the grit from her eyes. Dren sat in Ronsath's lap, playing with her doll and chatting. Zheann's eyes teared. *How soon will they have to leave me? The captain is right. We must find a way. I must make one, because I can't fail Dren.*

"... if a dam breaks, water entering the space between the dams will freeze?" Jenem gazed at Torweno and two other Rys men at a table. "Would that limit the hex sufficiently?"

But I'm not ready to help save the kingdom. Tea. She left them to their discussions, pulled her scarf over her mouth and nose and stepped into the darkness seeking its gift of anonymity.

Instead of going to the commissary with its comforting light, she sat in the ash, considered the dark sky, and waited for her head to stop aching. As the medicine did its job, she mouthed magic. A pebble at her feet rolled a few fingers' breadths. The pain increased but she continued. It moved toward her. She picked it up. *Native stone not earth blood.* She put it in the ash and pushed it again, watching a word form: *E... f... o... i....* The little stone stopped against the toe of an ashy over-sized boot.

"Athenque-spawn!"

Her head snapped up.

A tall Med stood before her; his face hidden in his cowl. Four Med stood behind him, all wearing the same black cloaks. *Wonderful, a mud with an audience.* Beyond them, no one paid any attention. A half a dozen soldiers walked by without looking her way. *Correction, an influential mud with an audience. Where is the captain? Where is Foden or Ges? Where's a prince when you need one?*

She rose. "Yes, sir?"

He pointed to the cabin. "Get your people out of the cabin."

"Captain Moln..." Pain exploded in her jaw and cheek, and in her opposite shoulder as she hit a rock. She stifled a cry, then bit back angry words with no meaning she knew could harm. The taste of copper filled her mouth, and she spat blood. She tried to push herself to her feet and fell again, rolling to hold her throbbing shoulder.

The Med bent close, grabbed a handful of cloak and yanked her to her feet. "Do as you're told."

Even with his mouth covered, she imagined his sneer. His eyes invited her to hesitate, even for a breath. She staggered, caught herself, and trudged toward the door, wiping at her tears. The Med followed her. When she hesitated at the steps, his hand hit her shoulders, staggering her again.

<hr />

Don't let Dren see. Don't let me frighten her. Ye fen dernai efoim.

Ronsath carried Dren to the corner and busied her with a piece of glowing resin. Jenem and the three men were on their feet. She passed the table. "The Med need the cabin." Her voice sounded flat. Dead. She tucked the handful of Dren's possessions into her pack. *All she has left. How long before they take it away?*

Mistress Jenem nodded at Torweno as she folded the papers on which they'd been working. "Please go find Captain Moln."

Zheann collected her belongings before the men walked through the door. *Life reduced to so little that I can put them away in less time than it takes someone to cross a cabin. Will they decide even that is recompense? What use would it be to them? Just something else they can take.* She coughed to hide her sob.

The Med stomped into the cabin with his entourage. He pushed back his hood to reveal abundant ashy, black hair. He pointed at Jenem. "You. Get us some food that doesn't taste like charcoal or smell like sulfur. You two, find us some hot water. We are cold, tired, hungry, and want to wash this filth off. It's going to take a lot of water. Leave your things where they are and do as I told you."

He turned to one of his men. "Go find the Molns. This softness with traitors must stop."

Another Med removed his hood, revealing hair no less ashy or black. "Your father turned everything over to the general. Esherick trusts the general's son the same way, and everyone knows some witch enthralls him."

"Enthralls them all." A third man sat at the table and with one sweep of his arm, knocked the dishes and remaining papers to the floor.

The leader turned toward the room." I don't suppose we can expect comfortable beds. If Esherick doesn't see the wisdom of ordering their extermination, a riot or two will wake him up." He turned toward Jenem again. "What are you still doing here? I told you, leave that garbage there and go get us some food and water." He threw belongings from one bed into the fire.

Jenem raised her chin and murmured one word. The fire went

out, leaving neither smoke nor coals. She faced the angry Med. "Gladly, and you can explain to your king and your people that when it came to a choice between your comfort and their lives, you chose the hot meal." She strode toward the door, but a black-haired retainer stepped between it and her. "Sir," she said, "your lackey prevents me from fulfilling your commands."

The Med raised his fist. As he swung it toward Jenem, his feet left the floor. He screamed as he flew through the doorway.

Pain rolled like thunder through Zheann's head. Outside, people were shouting. She met her mother's gaze. "Take Dren and go." Her voice sounded like a low purr to her.

Ronsath picked up the child, but before she and Jenem reached the door, two remaining Med pulled out truncheons. One raised his toward Ronsath.

The fourth Med took a step toward their leader. "Her mouth didn't move, Ben. There must be more outside, hexing Med." The apprehension in his eyes reflected in Ben's.

"Let them go. Touch them, and I will kill you." Her voice went from a purr to a growl, and the last four words came slowly, with clarity and emphasis. She became two people, one shrinking to the floor and dying, the other with the power to take the lives of any who threatened those she loved. *This is what I need to be against the water and the dragons. Too bad I won't live long enough.*

Ronsath turned toward her. "Zheann, come with us."

"Mama, go."

Jenem took Ronsath's arm and they hurried into the darkness with the screaming Dren. Zheann watched them without seeing them. A Med laughed.

The ash-covered giant ambled to her, his eyes wild. He pulled the cloth from his mouth. His lips pulled back, baring white teeth. "I am going to enjoy killing you and ridding the Med of your disease."

His rancid breath, mixed with sweat, and the ubiquitous sulfur-stench enveloped her in a miasma worse than any in the bogs. She turned her face away. "Look at me when I'm talking to you!" His fist hit her chest. Her shoulders hit the bed frame. A hand yanked her to her feet again. A fist swung toward her. She cringed, and it hit her left shoulder, knocking her across the bed. She landed on her head and right arm on rough wood planks.

"Get up." He raised his truncheon.

She pulled her legs off the bed, let them fall to the floor, pulling her knees toward her chest and crossing her arms to hold both shoulders. She closed her eyes and murmured magic. The bed creaked. She sensed the Med looming over her.

He swore in tones that sounded more surprised than hurt. "You think a hex will save you, half-breed? I'll —"

Boots pounded across the wood floor. Something thumped. The Med howled and cursed. More boots clomped toward her.

"Treason!"

She opened her eyes. Foden and another soldier dragged the cursing Med away from her.

"I'll see you all hang! She's a Rys. She's got you hexed. I'll give your women to my men..."

A new voice said, "Shut up, Benvor." More scuffling was followed by what sounded like something being dragged.

She closed her eyes tighter.

"Kathoa! She hexed —"

"Take him out and tie him to a tree. If he gives you any more trouble, include that tree in the first dam."

Benvor? He's one of the princes. Why are we helping these monsters?

"We're doing what is right," her mother's voice answered in her memory.

Are we, Mama?

She heard the captain's shout. "Go find Doctor Metris." She opened her eyes as he reached toward her. He grimaced and shook his hand. "Zheann, whatever you're doing, stop. It's safe now."

"It will never be safe." She waved her hand obediently.

He helped her onto the bed. "Where's the flask the doctor gave you?"

"My left pocket."

He pulled it from her cloak and held it to her mouth. She took a swallow of it and coughed. Pain flared in her chest, but the edges of it softened under the medication's effects.

A soldier stood next to the captain. *He looks like the madman. A prince. The madman called him Kathoa.*

"This is Mistress Zheann," the captain said. "She may not look like much..."

"Looks can be deceiving." The soldier gave her a pained smile. "My name is Kathoa. It seems you got your magic back. I'm sorry that bit of refuse bothered you."

Another prince. Zheann blinked. "He was threatening Mistress Jenem, Mama, and Dren. So what? I hexed a Med. They hang witches for less than that."

"If he's alive when this is over, Ben will issue you a formal apology. I'll see to it either Esherick or I issue a formal pardon. For now, an informal pardon will have to do." He raised his voice. "No reparations against her, against her family, or against the Rys will be tolerated until or unless Esherick, the general, or I command it. Anyone disobeying me will join Benvor." He turned as he spoke, glaring at everyone there, ending facing one of Benvor's men. "Do you hear me?"

The lackey nodded but looked at Zheann with open hatred.

"Good, then get out of this cabin and you and the rest of Benvor's friends can spend the night in the pass. Report to Erevo and ask for tasks to keep you out of trouble."

As the lackey wrapped his face, raised his hood, and slunk away, Kathoa clapped his hands and rubbed them together. "Good. And make sure you make that especially clear to my half-witted half-brother." He regarded her again. "Captain, post a pair of guards with specific orders to bludgeon and arrest any idiot who decides to waste our time by making us come back here." He gave her a smile that mixed good nature with chagrin. "For what it's worth, I wish you'd have thrown Benvor, too, but through a couple trees. Even more, I wish I'd been here to see it." He glared around the room. "None of you heard me say that. Take care of things here, Captain." He swept from the cabin.

Chapter Twenty-Six

Myot 34 Troleng 153, Mountain Camp

"I'm sorry, Zheann. We got distracted. From now on, you will have two guards, as Prince Kathoa ordered." The Captain sat on the bed beside her. It creaked under his weight.

Even rolling her eyes hurt. "Would your guards have stopped a prince? Could they have stopped him and his friends from acting the same way they, themselves, have acted all their lives?"

Guilt and anger warred in his gaze.

She glared at him. "Six soldiers walked by when he first assaulted me. They walked away. Will your men do anything but walk away if he comes back?" *And what am I going to do about it, except act the same way we've acted since Taelferga surrendered?*

"If you can identify them, I will make an example of them."

If I can..."She shook her head. "Six Med soldiers wearing black cloaks, with scarves around their faces and their hoods raised to keep the ash out."

After several breaths, he looked away from her. "Were they headed toward the commissary, or away?"

"Toward." The pain eased, but she found herself clenching her teeth in a rictus grin behind her scarf. "If we survive this, he'll claim he's the one who got my magic back for me and saved us all. Will your people think him a hero or a villain?"

"Most people see him as an arrogant fool and have for a long time. The family has more than its share. Several of his younger brothers will inherit the throne before he does. As for what the Med will think, that will depend on what you do with your magic. I've already heard gossip that you didn't mutter. That will make them nervous. Try to be careful, will you?"

Try to be careful, when every mud I see thinks he has the right to treat me however he pleases, and I have no rights at all?

⸻

Doctor Metris hurried into the cabin, removed his cloak, and tossed it on the first bed. He unwound the scarf from around his face and let it fall next to the cloak. He gazed at them with furrowed brows and spoke with authority, his thin hand sweeping toward the door. "If you folks will give us a little privacy." He crossed the cabin and knelt next to Zheann as the Med filed into the gloom.

Captain Moln gave her one last glower as he strode out.

What does that mean?

As soon as he was outside, he whistled a series of notes that seemed to go on for several breaths.

What did that mean?

The doctor peered at her. "So, what did they do to you?"

She unfastened the cloth around her nose and mouth, revealing a bruise along her jaw. Slowly, she unbuttoned her shirt and tried in vain to blink the tears into submission as he helped her work the material off her arms.

"Barbarians." His eyes sparked with undisguised hatred.

The door is open. Did anyone hear? "Doctor, be careful. Prince Kathoa may agree with you, and right now the captain may, too, but it's one thing for a Med to call a mud a mud, especially when he's the Med's brother, and another for a Rys to do so."

He spoke through gritted teeth. "Look at yourself, do you think any aren't mud?" More loudly, he said, "Where is the flask I gave you?"

"Yes, I do, and I already had some. It helped."

He rummaged through his pack, drawing out a jar. He applied salve to her shoulders, chest, back, and jaw with a light touch and murmurs. Where his fingers touched warmed and the pain eased.

He handed her the salve. "Keep using it four times a day. Do you need me to repeat the activator?"

"No, thank you."

He glanced toward the door and lowered his voice again. "I heard you threw a prince through the door. How does your head feel?"

"It still hurts. He wasn't a prince, only a prince's lackey."

"Well, you know how rumors tend to grow. Attack one and you've attacked them all, no matter how much he deserved it, and they all do."

She scolded in a voice little louder than a whisper. "Doctor, mind your tongue before you lose it, or more."

"Don't worry about me. I'm the only doctor here. They need me more than they need you. No more magic. Give yourself a day or two to heal. Get some rest." He turned away but looked at her. "Someone said you threw the mud without speaking your hex."

"The mountain won't care if you're the only doctor here. We don't have a day or two for me to heal."

"You aren't the only Rys around who can work magic."

She glared. "You're right, I'm not, but I don't hear you coming up with solutions to our problems. If you see Jenem or Ronsath on your way out, ask them to come in. We have work to do."

He stood, looking at her while she buttoned her shirt. He appeared ready to say something, then changed his mind and strolled toward the door. As he donned his cloak and scarf, he looked at her. "Try to stay out of trouble for a few hours, will you? I'd like to get some sleep."

You're as bad as the Med. How am I the cause of your sleep problems? "If I'm not to use magic, how do I activate the salve?" She gave him what she hoped was one of her father's smiles.

"Ask your mother. I'm sure she knows how."

Chapter Twenty-Seven

Divhad, 2 Enoate 153, Mountain Camp

Two days later, Foden walked through the cabin door with Ges at his heels. He looked haggard, but there was a vibrancy to him she hadn't seen since they were on Awasain Jeingsi. "Collect your things. You're moving. They're building compounds and barracks west along the mountains and south of here. Ronsath, you and Dren will join the captain's family and the royal family there. Lady Tiena Moln will look after you. Ges will take you to them. Mistresses, you will go to the overlook. The general and Esherick arrived two thirds ago, and they're waiting for you."

Ah, the masters' masters have arrived. Zheann handed Dren's things to Ronsath. She picked up Dren. "You are going with Grandmama again. Can you be a good girl for me?"

Dren looked at Zheann, then turned and leaned toward Ronsath with a wide grin. Zheann chuckled and pulled her close, kissing her cheek and hugged her. Dren squirmed and held her arms out to Ronsath again. When Zheann put her on the floor, she hurried over and climbed onto Ronsath's bed.

I've left her with Mama too often. Does she resent it? Does Mama? Does she feel like I'm abandoning her? She collected several pouches and the medicines the doctor had given her and put them in her pockets. She tucked the papers they'd been discussing in her pack with the books she'd taken from the jideker in Jifreb.

Zheann's heart writhed again as Ronsath carried Dren out the door. *She's lost her Papa, and her Mama is too busy trying to save everyone to go with her. Does she notice? Does she care? Oh, Little Dren. I'm sorry.*

"Mistresses?"

Zheann and Jenem followed Foden to an area that workers had widened. The general and the prince stood on a boardwalk built out from the trail. Ash coated their cloaks and piled in rings around their feet. Workers had cut a cave into the mountainside and lined the wall with cots. Foden put their bags on the second and fourth cots before striding to his place at the general's shoulder.

He's like a Rys to them. Does he ever resent it as much as we do? Zheann stepped onto the boardwalk, picking a spot behind the prince's other shoulder. Far below them, a river of torches stretched to the east. Some appeared stationary. Many more flowed toward them. *So many. That's good, but what are we going to do with them? What would the view have been like before the ash and darkness? Could we have seen the sea?*

The general continued staring east. "There are reports of a dragon with a group of Rys east of Jitherick. What are our plans if they attack?"

You should have thought about that before you refused to surrender. Jenem touched her arm. She stepped back and drew the older woman beside her.

The captain winced. "We have focused on the pass."

He's a Rys to his father?

The general put a hand on a post. "But now the dams are almost complete. It's time to secure the area."

"Gentlemen." At the reproof in Jenem's tone, all four Med turned toward her. She gave them a tiny smile. "We can have no idea what the dragons can or will do. Nor can we know what effect our magic may have on them. Zheann tells me an Athenque told her they cannot be killed, and I am inclined to believe him. If the Kotich could have killed them instead of trapping them, we would be in Jitherick sitting by our fires drinking tea. We have no way of knowing what magic will work against the dragons. Some magic shields from the physical, and shields against at least some magic. Perhaps we can protect the dams if we have warning. We can't protect the plains, and we must keep in mind that our shields may be useless against the dragons. I have an idea which may help, but it will take time to develop. Or we can surrender, gain their aid and betray them with the convenience of knowing where they are."

How readily we discuss treason. We are our mother's daughters.

"We will not surrender," Esherick said, his voice gritty and low.

The captain stepped back. "They have no reason to attack until after the mountain explodes. Why kill people when you can sit by and watch them die? We don't know how the dragons will attack if they attack."

Zheann put a hand on the railing. "Look at them. How long will it take to get them past even the first dam? What about the people we can't see yet?"

The general grunted. "It will take too long. No matter how much time we have before the mountain explodes, we will lose more than we save. This can't end well. We will watch our people die. When it's over, we face both the dragons and starvation through the winter."

"We're going to have to watch our people die." Her mind emptied, and the general's words echoed. She walked toward the pass, pulling her cloak against her ribs. *Ye fen dernai efoim. I can't do this.*

"Beyond winter, if the sky stays dark," Jenem said.

"Mistress Zheann," the general called.

She stopped. "I'm sorry, I can't stand by and watch them die." *It's my fault.* Another explosion rumbled. "I'll do what I must, but I can't talk about watching people die like one discusses what's for dinner."

Prince Esherick turned toward her. "Mistress Zheann, none of us want to watch our people die. The general is being realistic."

A metal band crossed his forehead. *He looks more like Kathoa than Benvor does. Did they crown him king already?*

"As for this," he gestured at his forehead. "The people who are going to survive will need stability and visible leadership. We share that responsibility."

Her cheeks grew hot. *Was my surprise that obvious? There is something in the dark... magic!*

"Whether we like it or not," he said.

She saw movement, but before she could focus on it, the general took a step back. The shaft of an arrow protruded through his cloak, angled toward the valley, blood flowing along its length.

"General!" The captain held him in a bear hug from behind and dragged him toward the cave.

Foden hauled Esherick back and shoved him past his commanders. "Inside! Now! Zheann, shield the king!"

"Jenem?"

The teacher murmured.

Zheann looked toward the pass and worked Far Sight. She stood next to a fire. A bow rested against a rock. She turned around. Across the pass and up, the lights outside the cave shone dimly through the ash. *Did the Rys assassin use Far Sight? Was that the magic I sensed? Did he choose his target more carefully this time or didn't it matter? Could anyone make that shot without magic? With the ash and darkness? Could Fiwal? Leed? Kaff or Luhaxa? How many traitors are there among the Rys?* An image of her father lying in bed, holding her hand flashed through her mind. He had come home with a nagging cough, and nothing Mama or the doctor did had helped. She returned to the observation deck as Foden raced toward the path, the arrow fletching in his hand.

King Esherick moved to follow his soldier but stopped abruptly. He put his hand against something and pushed. "Zheann!"

"Not Zheann." Jenem walked toward him. "Your majesty, you have no right to endanger yourself."

"I'll have you gutted."

Jenem's eyes opened wide. "Which of your brothers inherits the throne if you are killed?" She sat on a cot. "Will he do a better job as king after your first act as king is to throw your life away? I am sorry, your Majesty. I believe you will do a better job than your brothers. I do not want you to waste your potential for nothing, nor do I want to take responsibility for your death."

The red of Esherick's face deepened. He stood, breathing deeply several times before he walked to the cot next to hers and sat.

As they argued, Zheann found her pack and put it on the bed. She drew her flask of pain medicine and the bottle of salve from it and took them to the captain. "See if you can get him to drink a little of this and work the salve into the wound."

The captain held the flask dribbling amber-colored liquid between bloody lips. The general swallowed. More blood bubbled as he struggled to breathe. He tried to grasp the arrow's shaft.

"No, General." The captain held the general's hands. "I will do what needs to be done. I am honored to be your son. I will lead as you have taught me." The older man bared bloody teeth and closed his eyes. After a few breaths, he lifted his fists and dropped them on the cot with a thud. Garbled words came through clenched teeth.

At the sound of someone running on the path, the captain turned. His dark eyes held neither the glint of hope nor the plea for help she expected. They held resignation, rage, and tears. A few escaped unnoticed as they flowed through ash on his face.

———— ·《●》· ————

Doctor Metris slowed to a walk as he arrived. He glared at

Zheann as he passed. A moment later, he knelt across the cot from the captain. With a knife, he peeled away layers of clothing soaked with bright red blood. He murmured as he examined the wound.

Zheann turned away, tears stinging her eyes and teeth clenched. *Intruder.*

Esherick pushed himself off the cot. "Close the dams. We're getting distracted. All our work won't matter if the dams aren't closed before the water arrives."

Torches flowed from the east like a lazy river. "Not yet." *Don't ask me to do that. I can't.*

Foden jogged to where they stood. He frowned at Esherick before turning to the captain. "We found an abandoned bow and quiver of arrows across the pass, almost to the other side. The fletching matched the style." He looked toward the general. "On the way back, we identified the owner."

The captain stood. "How? Whose are they?"

Foden looked at the ground. "The ...owner claimed them, said they'd disappeared earlier."

"Whose?"

"Prince Benvor's."

The captain swore.

"Prince Benvor couldn't have done it," Zheann heard herself say. "In the dark, at that distance, someone had to have used magic." *Did the assassin know about what Benvor did to me, or what Kathoa said to him? Why else would he use Benvor's weapons?* She closed her eyes. *At this point, the only people who don't know about what happened are the people who have been here for less than a third.*

Beyond him, the captain grimaced. "Do it, Zheann. Tell me when you're ready and I'll give the signal."

Doctor Metris looked up, his face twisted in dismay. "You can't strand all those people..."

Esherick stepped toward Zheann. "There is an assassin in our midst. If he kills you and Jenem, who will close the dams? Close them."

"The assassin wants to kill Med. Even if he doesn't, there are lots of other Rys who can close them. The magic is simple."

The doctor rubbed his face with both hands and returned to his patient. After a moment, he dropped the bloody arrow. His murmuring sounded like he was gritting his teeth.

"We put the torches out there to tell us when the water is coming. We have time." She looked at her hands clasped in front of her, pleading. She lowered them to her sides, clenching them into fists instead.

Doctor Metris rose. "I'm sorry."

The captain looked east. There was nothing to see but gloom and darkness, but he didn't seem to notice.

The doctor rubbed something on his hands and murmured. He took his bag and stalked past her. He looked sick, but anger stormed in his pale blue eyes.

Esherick loomed before her. "Your heart will break no matter when you close them. Close them now, Mistress Zheann. Do as you're told."

For all his talk, he's no different. Not this time. "Give me your word as king there will be no Med justice. No riots. No reprisals. I want it signed in your blood if that's what it takes, and I want you to build trails over the mountains around the dams."

"There is already a trail along the mountains across the pass. Men are working on one that goes around the other side of this mountain." Esherick studied the captain. "Captain Foden and General Moln will make it clear to my army. I will tolerate no riots and no reprisals. They have permission to kill any Med who disobeys that order except the general."

Captain Moln turned.

Zheann watched something rise inside him like a massive wall.

Through gritted teeth, he said, "No."

"Who would you suggest? I didn't want to be king this way either, *Little General,* but none of us has a choice. We don't have time to find someone who knows as much about what's going on, or who the army respects as much as they do you."

Little by little, the wall of his will crumbled. He closed his eyes in surrender.

Both have lost their fathers in the past month, at the hands of Rys. Both their worlds are shattering, but the general was wrong. He didn't have to watch, or listen to, our people die. He was spared that, as he would have been spared being the one who condemned them. That was always to be part of my shameful place in history.

He nodded once and stood with head bowed.

He's broken. As broken as I am, but differently, for a different reason. I keep breaking. There can't be anything left to break, but I keep breaking. All I wanted to do is save my people.

Jenem walked to her side. She put a hand on Zheann's shoulder. "He's right. There will not be a right time. It is better we do what we can to save some than to save none because we cannot save all."

Lightning flashed, followed by a long rumble of thunder that ended with a crack. Zheann flinched. Her throat ached, and her voice seemed as dry as the ash blowing on the breeze around them. "Give the signal to prepare."

The general gazed at her for several breaths. He worked his mouth before his whistle rang out. It echoed from the mountains around them, and from the lips of soldiers. Zheann worked the magic to raise a shield to keep people from rushing the dams. The first screams tore through her heart like knives with jagged edges. Tears left more tracks in the dust on her cheeks. More whistles shrilled above the screams. Zheann linked arms with Jenem, and together they murmured the magic that added the grinding of rock against rock to the cacophony.

Chapter Twenty-Eight

Divhad, 2 Enoate 153, Mountain Camp

"Zheann!" Several voices called after her as she ran from the cave. If the camp had seemed like an ants' nest before, it was now a hornets' nest. Three Med streamed around her, missing her by finger-breadths as they ran. Watching them, she came to an abrupt stop against another person. She grabbed the Rys man's arms to steady herself. He pulled her hands away and stumbled on as if they had not collided.

She kept moving as a plaintive voice called, "Valenra? Has anyone seen Valenra?"

Another answered, "Henkim..."

She pulled her hood forward. When she got to an area with no cabins, she kept walking. Torches outlined areas along the path where people congregated. *We have a trail that bypasses the dam. It will be harder, but they are not trapped. There's no way to save them all. I knew that. Why do I feel like a murderer?*

A hand grabbed her arm. "Lusa?"

She gasped as she turned to look into green eyes that would be beautiful if broken hope hadn't filled them.

"I'm sorry," the woman said in tones that made the words magical.

What can I say to her? She put an arm around the woman's

shoulders. "Let me look for her." She murmured the hex for Far Sight and found a dark figure lying on the ground at her feet. She knelt. *Are you alive?*

As if in answer, the figure rolled over.

Alive! Now, where are we? To her right, pinpricks of campfires marked the mountainside. *In the pass.*

Desperate green eyes stared at her.

Zheann put a hand on her shoulder. "Lusa's alive, asleep in the pass somewhere. I couldn't tell exactly where. Find her quickly and move into the mountains." Her head snapped as the woman yanked her forward, wrapped her arms around Zheann and sobbed.

"Thank you." she repeated several times. She released Zheann, pushing past her as she hurried down the trail.

Zheann followed her until the torchlight ended and her feet refused to continue. She put her hand into her pocket and touched two balls of twine. *The captain — general has my flask.* Ahead, campfires dotted the trail leading to the pass floor. She searched them until she found one at which the people looked small and hurried to it. Someone moved over. When she sat, he handed her a cup. Empty-eyed faces stared across the fire.

She let the scent of herbs soothe her, and the taste bathed her with comfort and warmth. *If light and sanity can infuse hot water, this mug of tea is light and sanity. It's only the magic of memory, but I'll take it.* The next person nudged her, and she took another small sip before handing it on. *When I used Far Sight before, it took me to where the assassin had been. I want to go where he is.* She shrank into her cloak hood, stared into the fire, and worked Far Sight.

⫘⫘●⫘⫘

A hand touched her shoulder, a voice whispered near her ear.

"Zheann, don't say anything, please. Come with me. We need to talk."

She scrambled to her feet to face bright blue eyes peering from a grubby face. He pulled his scarf down. She knew the eyes, but they stared out of a face that looked childlike. He put a finger to his amused smile and walked away.

How dare you? Throw him against the mountain first. Silence him before he does something more to hurt someone. She followed until he stepped into the shadows beside a building.

He took her hand, pulled her close and pressed his lips against hers hungrily.

She melted into the embrace, desperate for the comfort of his touch. He smelled of sulfur and sweat. She tensed as she pushed herself away from him, back into the feeble light. *Don't bother whining about the dark. You have more important matters to attend to, like deciding whether to silence him or kill him.* "Fiwal, what are you doing here? How did you find me?"

He grinned, the picture of nonchalance. "It wasn't hard to find you. I waited near the Med commanders until you showed up. It wasn't hard to get away from Donezan, either. Once you left, she didn't seem to care much what Leed and I did. What did you do that impressed her?"

"I have no idea. Maybe I was the only Rys woman there." *Weren't you the one who thought me impressive enough to be queen? Or did you only think I was malleable enough to be your queen?*

He scowled and looked away. "I wish I'd never heard about the dragons. From the day we set out to find them, everything has gone wrong."

"You mean the day you and Leed killed the king."

"No, Zheann, that's what you don't understand. We didn't. Or, I didn't. I didn't know anything about it. We went to find the dragons. I wanted them to free the Rys and make you queen." His eyes rolled.

"And, yes... I wanted to be a hero. Leed talked me into using a stimulant so we'd get there faster, and he killed some Med soldiers. He tried to kill more soldiers on the mountain. Then you were there, and you attacked us, and the dragons took you, and everything went wrong."

So, it's all my fault? It's always someone else's fault. "I heard you laugh."

"I was stimulated. They were Med."

He looks so earnest and desperate. Can he be so stupid? "That made it all right? They are people, Fiwal."

"It was the magic. I wasn't thinking straight. They are our enemies. We had victory in our hands, and then it all fell apart." He looked toward the fires and turned back to her; his face eager again. "Anyway, none of that matters now. I know I made a mistake, and I want to make amends. We need to stop the dragons."

"From what?" Her stomach tightened. *Something else?*

"Taking over. You heard Donezan."

"Yes, I did. Did you hear any specific plans after we left?"

He brightened. "Yes. Leed told her he has allies in Jitherick and a in few villages to the east. They were going to collect his troops, then they were going to fly into the mountains to wait for the water. He said our allies in Jitherick would go with the people of Jitherick. They'll be ready when the time comes to overthrow the king. I didn't know we had any allies in Jitherick except my family, and I haven't seen them."

The eyes and enthusiasm I thought I loved are there. Which of us is the bigger fool?

"Zheann?"

"Fiwal, someone brutally killed the king. You said you didn't know about it, but they used night berries. Who else had them but us? You knew about the allies in Jitdornoi. They talked about you after they tried to kill me. According to them, you married an idiot with no idea what you were doing. They were right."

"What? No, I didn't tell them that. I wanted to tell you. Leed said not to, that you wouldn't approve."

"You mentioned the dragons to me once, the day I met you. You could have mentioned them any number of times before Leed told you not to. You seem to have discussed them with him more than once."

"My family told me not to talk to you or your parents about the dragons. You weren't ready yet. You weren't rebels, but I always hoped someday you'd understand. I told you they lived in the Great Ice Land, but we didn't know where. Then, Leed found a story about the Kotich trapping the dragons in ice. He finally believed. We had to try to free them. You understand, don't you?"

"You released the dragons. You damaged the mountain, and when it explodes, it will destroy our homeland."

He shook his head. "No. I told you. I made a mistake."

"And less than a third ago, someone used magic to kill General Moln."

His eyes opened wide. "I didn't—"

"You keep saying, 'I didn't,' but you're always right there. I can't tell whether you're guilty or foolish. If they catch you, they won't listen to your constant claims of innocence. If you want to live long enough to make things right, hide in the mountains. Figure out how to prove you didn't to Med who have already killed other Rys because someone did, and to the families of the dead Rys."

Another explosion cracked and echoed through the pass. Taking a step back, he grabbed her arm. "Zheann, come with me."

"Are you crazy? They don't even know you're here. You can sneak away. They'll come looking for me. Go, Fiwal. Be safe somewhere, and when this is over, we can figure out what to do."

"I wanted you to be proud of me."

"You chose the wrong way." She walked away. *Do not look back. Don't even try to figure out if you believe him. Or love him. Keep walking.*

She passed the campfire where she'd been sitting. Someone had taken her place. *There went my chance for sanity. Something else for which Fiwal owes me.* She passed two more fires tended by silent watchers before smiling to herself. *I guess that was childish. If I lose my sanity, it's thanks to something in the dark that wants to kill me. Do I look as ... bludgeoned as they do?*

Papa's voice whispered by a hearth fire in her mind. "Little Hedgehog, how long is forever?"

She'd snorted. "Longer than anyone can say."

He'd grinned. "Do you know why magic works?"

"Why, Papa?"

"It works because you believe it will work forever. There's another kind of magic that works when you don't believe it will work forever."

"Papa, that makes no sense," she'd said, and his face had lit with one of his silly Papa smiles. *Ah, Papa, but it does, and you waited forever for it to do so. These people need some of your special magic, Papa. The kind that makes us laugh and think. We need it to last the forever we're waiting until the mountain either explodes or doesn't.*

After she walked past two more fires, a yawn escaped her. The muscles in her neck and shoulders relaxed as if someone had removed a plug in her spine, allowing the stress to flow out. A breath later, she caught herself humming.

A group at a distant campfire sang her song.

How?

As others joined, one voice soared above the rest. When the chorus died away, someone shouted, "Jalira's Rise!"

A woman with silvery white hair stood, and opened the new tune with sweet, capering high notes. After several breaths, the tones became words. The faces visible in the gloom transformed from haunted to—

Content? Eunaela! Zheann hugged herself. *She made it! Does she have the books? I'm not sure it matters if we have her. This is just what we needed... what I needed.* She worked her way around the fires until she stood in the shadows near the singer. She paused, noting a dull ache in her head. *There's magic in her song. Well, they say there's more than one kind of magic. I need hers. We all do.* She let the music flow through her.

"Is there a song you'd like to hear, Mistress Zheann?"

"No! Yes. Anything. Something about life and hope. Do you have to sing well to work your magic?"

"It helps. Do your customers prefer their magic to taste good or foul?"

Zheann canted her head to the side. "I see your point. Yours is like bog berries in cream with honey."

Her laugh was low and gentle. "Music touches the magic within." She broke into a rambunctious song and within moments, those who had earlier stared empty-eyed danced and laughed.

With her on our side, we may do this. She heard herself laugh.

She sang a slow song next. As its last notes floated away, a whistle rang out from above them and east.

Zheann's heart sank. *No, no, no*, but more whistles followed.

A huge grin spread across Eunaela's face, and she clapped as she continued the whistler's tune.

The cap—general? He knows music? More music than I do, it seems.

When the song ended, Eunaela waved to her audience and sat. She patted the log next to her. "Come, sit with me, Zheann. I hoped I'd find you soon."

Zheann's heart overflowed at the invitation. She hurried to sit; afraid someone might take her spot "How are you? How are Danden and Naori?"

"Those little imps are well. I've been keeping them in the caravan since the ash started falling, and I am grateful. If you hadn't warned me to come west when you did, I might not have come west at all. I owe you my life and a collection of excellent books. If the news about the mountain exploding is true, I wish I would have taken more books." She gave a little smile. "It seems the possibility of everyone dying has distracted the Med from the idea of all the Rys dying. Did you find the dragons?"

Zheann rolled her eyes. "Leed and Fiwal's releasing them is what damaged the mountain. One is Donezan."

"Really? I'd like to meet her." The singer's voice was loud in her surprise. She lowered it again. "Or would I?"

"Yes, and no. Better not. You seem quite familiar with dragons."

"I am a lover of stories, and there are a few good ones about Athenque. If we get through this, I'll share them with you."

"I'd like that. Mistress Jenem is right; we're woefully uneducated."

The singer hummed an agreement. "I'd like to talk to you about that, too. Someday, perhaps soon, I'll get too old to travel. There's a great deal I could teach."

"Bayista's Song!"

Eunaela waved toward the voice. "But those are stories for a less troubled time. Would you like me to research anything?"

"The obvious. Do you think you could sing a lullaby to a mountain? Or an ocean?"

"Of course, but I doubt it would do any good. They can't hear."

Zheann chuckled. "Neither can candles but we speak our magic to them all the time, and they light."

Her violet eyes narrowed.

"Bayista's Song!"

"I'm going to have to think about that. I doubt I can sing an injured mountain to sleep. Instead, I'll stay awake with it, thinking about candles." Her smile lit her face. "Excuse me, *Bayista's Song* has been requested, twice." She rose, grasping the opening of her cloak and swinging it in an expansive flourish as she launched into the rollicking ballad.

Zheann listened to her song before returning east through the camp. Ashfall hid campfires, but she listened as voices sang another ballad about a young man of dubious sense who bluffs his way through every predicament. *That sounds like Papa.* After a moment, a whistle from above her accompanied Eunaela again. *The general? How does her singing effect the Med? They don't have magic. Or do they not have Athenque magic? Either it's an example of a different kind of magic, or it may be that Eunaela's doesn't only touch magic. She said she's a soul singer. Can you have a soul without having magic? Have we been thinking about that wrong all these years?*

She paused and stared at a fire. *Are we thinking about this all wrong? Should we be working on magic to command the water the way we do flames? What we need may be a lullaby for the mountain or the sea."* She clenched and flexed her hands as she walked. *That makes no sense, but when has any of what Estaen has taught me about magic made sense? The pass is not the problem. The dams are not the solution. The mountain is the problem. The water is the problem. We've been thinking about the physical challenge, not the magical. How foolish. I'll have to talk to Jenem. Maybe—*

The explosion knocked her to the convulsing ground, sending puffs of ash into the air around her. Its rumble and the echoes from the mountains surrounded her with noise that seemed like it would never end. She covered her ears as she staggered to her feet. A hand gripped her arm roughly. She screamed and tried to pull away.

"Stop it, Zheann!" Foden pulled her toward the path. When she stumbled, he pulled her onto his shoulder and jogged.

As the explosion's rumble gave way, screams and whistles took its place. Several sharp notes blasted next to her ear, and she jounced harder. At the cave, he dropped her feet first in the light of a torch. She took several steps to catch her balance. A second, louder explosion drowned out all other noises and threw her to the quaking ground. *Were we wrong? Will the explosion destroy the world?* As the pandemonium died away, she hurried to join the others at the platform's edge, looking east. The lines of refugees that had been snaking their way along the mountain trails disintegrated. Torches moved in all directions in wobbling circles. She shuddered with the sudden realization of quiet.

"Is that it? That has to be it." The general's look slowly became a glower. He came to life, punctuating a series of whistles with curses.

Esherick rose to the balls of his feet. "Where's the water? Does anyone see the water?"

The ground shuddered. The general dragged Esherick from the platform onto firm rock. "Zheann?"

Zheann put an arm around Jenem's shoulders, but the older woman stared eastward. Zheann stared, too. With her free hand, she wiped a trickle of sweat that rolled from her forehead to the tip of her nose. Her stomach knotted. Muscles in her legs tightened as if preparing to run. *Run! Run where? How do you outrun a flood? How do you race what you cannot see? A magical lullaby for the mountain? For the ocean? It's too late.*

⸻ «◦» ⸻

Below the platform, a few torches were close enough for Zheann to see their holders. *Run! Run this way, into the mountains. Climb higher.* Her gaze returned to the darkness while her fingers pushed her cloak over her shoulders.

Jenem pointed. "Look, an..." She leaned against the railing and caught at the hood of her cloak as a gust of wind blew it back. "I thought I saw more torches...but they're gone again."

Zheann's cloak billowed and she pulled it close. *There's something in the dark, and it will kill you if it can.*

This time, I suspect you're right. Why is the wind so warm? Is it because the mountain exploded, or because the world is bleeding fire?

Esherick shook his head. "Looks like lightning. Can the ocean bring a storm with it?"

After a few breaths, another tiny spark flared and disappeared, this time far above the ground. Lightning moved across the landscape but not the sky. The torches farthest east disappeared.

Jenem's eyes widened. "Do you feel the heat? I don't know where the water is, but what approaches feels like dark fire. The *torches* might have been trees catching flame as the heat reached them."

"How could the fire reach us before the water?" Sweat trickled along her spine. *The problem is not the pass, or the dams. The problem is the mountain and the ocean and the heat."*

The general's eyes widened. "Can you hex shields for us?"

"We won't have time." Zheann took off her cloak, squinting as blowing ash stung her skin. "Mistress, can we draw energy from the heat?"

Jenem looked into the darkness. "Power traps?"

"Big ones. What can we use?"

"Anything, I think. Metal would be ideal, but wood or rocks will work. How do we get them out there?" The Med drew their swords and tossed them at her feet.

Zheann rubbed her hands together. "You make the traps. I'll get them out there."

"General, can we use your father's sword?"

Jenem!

General Moln hesitated for a breath. He pulled it from its sheath and put it with the others. "He'd be happy to continue to fight."

They placed the swords in a line on the ground and Jenem murmured magic. She touched a sword with a torch. Its light disappeared. When she pulled the torch away, it stayed dark. "Zheann, start with these. We need more, metal or wood."

Foden pulled an arrow from his quiver. "Does size matter?"

"Not as much as you'd think."

He whistled a complex series of notes.

As Med ran toward the observation area, Zheann grasped the first sword. Its weight pulled her off balance. *How do they wear these things, let alone fight with them?* She braced herself. The sword flew from her hands far into the darkness, unaffected by the buffeting wind. *This will take too long.*

General Moln waved the soldiers over, shouting as he nocked arrow after arrow and released them into the gloom. "As soon as Mistress Jenem hexes your arrows, shoot them east as far as you can. When you finish, get everyone out of the pass and into the mountains."

Four swords sailed into the gloom as Foden and two soldiers knelt with three soldiers behind them. When they emptied their quivers, another group took their place.

Several soldiers dropped armloads of rough-cut staves and torches. "We'll bring more as soon as we can cut them."

The heat and wind continued to build. Something roared. *A dragon? How long can we stay here? This is taking too long.*

"Keep throwing," Jenem told her.

Lightning flashed below, and above them to the east. She wiped her forehead on her sleeve. Grit dug into her forehead. *The ash!* "Jenem, hex the ash!"

The old woman's eyes widened and narrowed, and she murmured her hex again.

I can throw four swords at once. I can throw ash. It's magically no different from a ball of twine. A giant onion. And I don't have to worry about missing my target. I can use the wind to throw the ash. Magic must do what it's sent to do... what I send it to do. She bared her teeth in a grin and glared into the wind. *Make the ash fall to the ground.* The sting of ash against her skin stopped. A breath later, it started again. *Fall* she commanded again. *Across the hills and lowlands, fall, and keep falling.* Staring into the darkness, she shouted, "Open the traps."

Jenem raised her hand above her head, closing and twisting it. She turned toward Zheann, wide-eyed. She turned east.

⸺⊶⊷⸺

In a flash of lightning, a blue dragon flew before a roiling gray cloud. Lightning shone through and outlined its outstretched, iridescent wings, flashing from his wings to the cloud and from the cloud to both the dragon and the ground. Without seeming to move, he wheeled east into the gray wall.

"Is it working?" someone shouted.

Zheann shouted back. "I think so. We're not dead."

They watched the cloud rise, illuminated by lightning strikes. It billowed, falling and pooling among the foothills. What the cloud touched burst into flame before the billowing grayness swallowed it. Lightning flashed again all along the leading edge. Instead of billowing toward them as it had, it crashed to the ground like a waterfall. The hot wind from the east stopped and, in its place, a chilly wind blew from the west. Zheann found her cloak, shook the ash out of it and fastened it in place.

Lightning struck again. Gray covered the ground amid a forest of blacked tree stumps. *It's all dead.*

Along the trails, torches moved drunkenly. Someone nearby uttered a long string of curses. *Several somebodies.* The lines ended where the paths met the plains. The few flames lighting the area showed twisted or burned bodies.

Jenem grimaced and twisted her hand. "See if you can pull the power traps back."

Zheann held out her hand. She pulled at what she hoped was a power trap. She pulled a second time. The general grabbed her arm and pulled her off her feet as two swords and a pole clattered to the ground where she'd been standing. All three shone in the torchlight. They were burnished gray.

"Uh...thank you."

The general's dark eyes twinkled. "You can't catch twine. Remember that."

She pulled the remaining traps more carefully and stepped away.

Jenem examined a pole. "They are safe to touch," she said as she caressed it. "You can take your swords back. Don't try to remove the ash. You might release the energy we've stored in them. We'll find a way to bleed it off later. Let us know if you feel anything unusual. We can bundle the poles together and keep them with us, too. They could prove useful."

As Zheann pulled another pole back, Esherick said, "So what about the water? Is it coming, or is that it?"

"We have to assume it's coming." Zheann caught a pole and grinned at the general.

"That's one."

As she pulled on the last power trap, screams rose behind her. In the dim torch glow, the dragon's leathery blue-white skin shone as it flew through the pass. Zheann flung herself to the ground. Something heavy landed on her, pressing the air from her lungs. She squirmed her head free as the dragon paused, flapping its wings, and circled, heading over her again. In its talons was a pair of poles. Foden scrambled to his feet, freeing her, and brandishing an ash-covered sword. A barrage of arrows flew at the dragon.

Donezan didn't appear to notice. "I saved your lives. Your pathetic magic didn't protect you. I did."

Jenem murmured raised her hand and twisted it closed.

Donezan dropped the poles with an infuriated shriek. She shuddered as she banked north.

Jenem's eyes widened. After a moment, she frowned and opened her hand again. "That was disappointing."

General Moln watched Donezan disappear into the darkness. "I thought you said Athenque are magical beings. Why didn't your traps trap her?"

Zheann pulled the poles from the pass. "The Athenque may be too powerful or have too much control over their magic. Maybe she didn't touch them for long enough. Or, maybe the traps were already too full." She turned to Jenem. "Did I miss a possible explanation?"

"I can think of none. I am encouraged she responded the way she did, instead of wheeling around and attacking."

Zheann turned in a slow circle, stopping when she faced east. *Now there's something else in the dark that wants to kill me.*

Chapter Twenty-Nine

Divhad 2 Enoate 153, Mountain Camp

J enem woke Zheann with a gentle touch on her shoulder. "It's
time for your watch."

*For an old woman who has spent four thirds watching through the
ashy darkness for the world's end, she looks ... calm.* She rolled onto an
elbow and squinted toward the cave's entrance. "Anything?"

"If there had been, I wouldn't have needed to wake you. There is
food and tea on the table." She sat on another cot and unpinned the
braid she wore pinned to the back of her head. Pulling it over her
shoulder, she settled in to rest.

Zheann rubbed at her eyes and pushed her braid off her shoulder.
As she walked to the table piled high with food, she untied her scarf and
surveyed the cave. The new king twitched in his sleep. The new general
stood talking with Foden, the new captain. *Odd that they don't have
regular soldiers keeping watch, but would I leave the job to any other Rys? I
guess not. The old general's body is gone.* Her heart ached as she crossed to
the table and took tea, cheese, and an apple. She carried the food out to
the platform. *Everything tastes like ash. Do I have any comfort weed?*

Foden followed her and stood staring into the darkness as he
chewed. Only a few torches moved along the mountainside or in the
pass. Hushed sounds came from the camp below them.

Is everyone listening? Or are they hiding? It'd be nice if Eunaela would sing again, but we need to hear the water, and to sleep. "Did you find out who killed the general?" She nibbled on a piece of cheese.

Foden glanced at the cave. "No. The guards don't remember seeing any specific Rys near Benvor's things."

Be careful. "Leed and Fiwal had allies in Jitdornoi. It makes sense they might have allies in Jitherick or somewhere else."

"Have anyone in mind? And would you tell me if you did?"

"I have no idea, but I would tell you. General Moln was working to save lives. He didn't deserve to be killed, at least not then."

Foden glanced toward the cave. "General Moln was a great commander. I moved to Jitherick to learn from him. I wish I'd told him that."

After chewing on a piece of bread, he looked away for a moment. When he looked back, his face was expressionless. "So, you're sure Fiwal didn't do it? Did he say so?"

"What?"

His eyes filled with mockery. "How do you think I found you after the explosion? We learned our lesson about keeping an eye on you. We arrested him before you found the singer."

Zheann peered into the gloom. *He's right. I knew. I had too many other things on my mind, like killing thousands of people.* "I doubt he knew the general was dead until I accused him. He told me he thought Leed had allies in Jitherick. He said he didn't do it, that he hasn't done anything. He claimed he didn't know who the allies were because all he wanted was to go find the dragons."

He crossed his arms. "And you were fool enough to believe him."

"He is a fool enough to believe what he said to be true. It's easy to focus on what one wants and not notice inconvenient details." Her heart lurched, but she remained calm. *We're talking about the man I thought I loved, the father of my daughter. Why don't I feel something more? Why can't I seem to care? Why am I more upset about not being upset than I am about Foden's arresting my husband?* "I doubt he did it. I doubt he's any better with a bow than I am. We didn't have one."

"He could have used magic to guide the arrow."

"Then why would he need the bow at all?"

Foden turned her toward him. "You're still in love with him."

"What does love have to do with it?"

"It makes people stupid."

"Don't you love your women?"

"No." He looked into the darkness. "General Moln loved his wife. The general loves his wife. I haven't found a woman worth leaving the rest for. Don't start giving me advice, because you didn't do so well." He glared at her.

Let it pass. "You're right. I hope you find her, and that you have the courage when you do to be stupid." She sighed. "Yes, he, or any elemental, could have used magic to throw the arrow and then left the bow to make it look like a Med did it."

Foden grunted.

That didn't go well. "I still don't think Fiwal killed him."

His shoulders sagged. "If not him, then who?"

"It would have had to have been someone who seemed to belong where he was. Otherwise, people would have noticed."

"Unless he made himself invisible."

"The arrow couldn't have been, or he wouldn't have been able to sight along it. Do you think people would not have noticed a floating arrow?"

"So, invisible because people expected to see him, another Rys refugee among thousands. In the chaos, no one seemed to notice a Rys carrying a Med war bow."

She caught his glance as he turned it away from her and considered the darkness between the first two dams. "He had to have known about what Benvor did. Otherwise, it's too big a coincidence that someone grabbed Benvor's bow. Whoever took it had to have planned to use it to implicate Benvor in some crime, but how could he know the general would be there?"

"The opportunity presented itself."

"Foden…"

"Listen!" He whistled two notes.

————))(((◦))((————

Foden's whistle relayed through the camp as the general strode to their sides. "Where is it?"

The whole camp came to life with shouts and the banging of equipment and boots. Below, torches streamed toward the mountains. *What were they doing in the pass? Didn't they clear it?*

Foden stepped back and pointed east as King Esherick joined them. "Water."

The king put a hand on Foden's shoulder as if to gain height and see better. "Get light out there."

Zheann turned toward the cave as Jenem emerged from it, holding a torch and a power-trap together and murmured, fusing them. She held it out to Zheann. "Light this one and throw it as far and as high as you can."

Zheann took the staff and gazed in grim satisfaction as fire blazed around the torch.

The general smirked at her. "Make sure it lands torch up."

She glared. "Did you have a specific spot in mind?" The staff flew from her hand, rising in a high arc. *It's not enough light. More light.* It gave them a glimpse of something black and winked out. She snatched the second staff from Jenem's hands. "Better get two more, in case."

She stared at the torch. "Close your eyes." She closed her own. *More light. Daylight.* Brilliant light shone through her eyelids.

The king cursed.

Teach you not to listen when I tell you to do something. She returned her attention to the torch. *Fly high, stay high. Do not fall.* After she sent the miniature sun flying out over the foothills, she shielded her eyes with her hand.

The hills looked as they had before, blacked trunks of trees surrounded by dark gray snow. Further east, where the torchlight was dimmer, the lowlands looked black."

The general whistled three times, long and piercing, and others relayed the message through the camp. He continued to stare at the scene below the torch. His jaw tightened. "Foden, take the king higher into the mountains."

Esherick pushed Foden away. "I'm staying here. I'm not going to stand on the top of a mountain and watch my family, friends, and people die."

What does he see? Zheann looked at Jenem, who looked at her in horror. She turned to the east again. *What do they see?* The black extended north and south to the horizon curving away a little in at the southern end. In places, it appeared to shine. She gasped as her mind finally made sense of what she saw. *It's moving. The black is the water.* Tears spilled. *I hoped I was wrong.*

"It looks almost serene," Jenem said. "Like a broad river flowing."

The general continued to watch. "Too bad we're in its way."

The shiny darkness devoured the distance between them. As it approached through the foothills, it grew like bread rising on a mantle, as if the hills had not existed. *It's moving fast, but it seems almost lazy. And quiet. I thought it would roar like thunder. Its hold is magical, mesmerizing. Will it flow over the mountains?*

Use magic with it as you did with the torch. The key is to stop the water. On an impulse, she held out her hands. *Stop. Be at peace. Come no further. Do not enter the pass. Obey me!*

The ocean hit the first dam. For three breaths the barrier squealed as its parts strained. With a resounding crack, the dam failed, and the water kept flowing.

Chapter Thirty

Divhad, 2 Enoate 153, Mountain Camp

It hit the mountain and splashed onto the platform, knocking them off their feet. Foden wrapped his arms around her. She coughed as she struggled. "Let go!" She got to her knees in time to watch the water slam into the second dam. Keens echoed through the pass as the water rose along the face of the dam.

With a thundering crash, the second dam collapsed. Jenem appeared beside her, her mouth moving but the words drowned by the cracks of collapsing dams. It crashed through the pass, carrying carts and equipment, trees, and even boulders. Together, they hexed the third dam, visible because someone had mounted torches on it.

She turned to where the waves pounded against the mountains and swept into the pass. The scream came again from further west. *Third or fourth? Did I miss one?* The screaming ended in another crash of wood, boulders, and water into the pass.

She threw her magic into the next dam as the water hit it. The scream rose again as wave battled hex. *Ye fen dernai haloim! The problem is not the dams, or the water. The problem is with the magic. The problem is with me. How many more before the pass turns south? Will that help? Magic must do what I send it to do. But I'm sending it to do the wrong thing to the wrong thing.* She held her hands out toward the water. *Yes, I know, water can't see. It can't hear, either.* She pictured the ocean when she'd first seen it aboard *The Chaser*, with gentle waves. *That's what I want. Stop. Be gentle.* She let her hands fall to her sides as the dam collapsed.

Water thundered into the next section. *Listen, it's quieter.* Zheann opened her eyes and watched the water calm.

"You did it!" Esherick picked her up, swinging her in a circle as a cheer rose from along the mountainside. On her third revolution, the king stopped and swore. Another wave surged into the torchlight. It flowed over the platform and swept them off their feet, filling her mouth as she tried to scream. She floated past the end of the platform. A hand grabbed her wrist and pulled. A second hand tightened around her arm. The water's drag decreased and Esherick pulled her closer. Arm in arm they staggered to the mountainside and followed it to the cave.

She coughed and spat salty, gritty water. From the west came the scream and crash of water destroying another dam. *Peace. Be still.* She coughed several times as the noise diminished again. She wheeled about. *Which way is east?* "Get me a torch!" She coughed again.

"Where are they?" The king cursed and grumbled.

No time! Light! A dim glow suffused the cave area.

Esherick grabbed several torches, shoving the first into her hands. Blood from an abrasion trickled down his cheek in rivulets.

She took the torch to the ledge. The platform and its railing hung in tatters. *How did we survive?* She threw the wood toward the east and lit it. *Bright. Let us see.* The light flared over a pacific black ocean,

Esherick ran toward the camp, whistling.

Afraid to leave the ledge or stop watching the sea for waves, she called to them repeatedly with a growing sense of futility. In the darkness of her sorrow, she heard Donezan's quiet chuckle.

Afterword

Zheann's story, like so many stories, was a confluence of ideas. When my father needed more help than I could give him while working, I quit my job to be his caregiver. I decided that the time had come for me to become the writer I'd dreamed of being more than thirty years ago and joined Jerry Jenkins' Writer's Guild. The book I'd been writing wasn't working, so I put it on a shelf and searched for something new.

For some reason, I got Martin Luther King, Jr's <u>Where Do We Go from Here?</u> and Shelby Steel's <u>White Guilt.</u> In one of those books, there is a quote that I can no longer find. It set off a spark and gave me a theme. About the same time, I saw a National Geographic map of what they thought Doggerland looked like and explained how they believe it flooded. The tsunami reminded me of another tsunami that circled the world twice after the eruption of Krakatoa, as described in <u>Krakatoa: The Day the World Exploded</u> by Simon Winchester, and Awasain Jeingsi rose off the coast of the Great Ice Land.

Around the same time, I re-read Ursula LeGuin's <u>Wizard of Earth-Sea</u>, and felt strongly that the story needed to be told from one character's perspective. It's only as I write this that I realize it may have helped inspire the title. I started out wanting Zheann to be a magical "soccer mom." That didn't quite work out, but an elementary school teacher seemed close enough. When she, the captain and Foden reached the mountain, the story was too short. About that time, a question crept into my thoughts. What would a magical being be like? That question, C. S. Lewis' The Great Divorce, Guilo, from Frank Peretti's This Present Darkness, and possibly Tom Baker's Doctor Who inspired Estaen, who later told me he would not do what I had planned for him to do.

The dragons were a reluctant but obvious choice. Originally, there was to be only one, but I found myself with five. Donezan was inspired by White Witch from C. S. Lewis' Narnia books. Suddenly, I had parallels between the Athenque and the dragons, the Rys and the Med, and the first three chapters of Genesis.

Put simply, Earth Fire was like trying to wrestle with an octopus. It is and is not the story I envisioned. We have both grown in its writing.

Appendices

Appendix A: Characters

Amdiri	
Leed	Zheann's cousin.
Poyen	Zheann's father.
Rinsha	Leed's wife.
Ronsath	Zheann's mother.
Anda	Rys Scout Leader.
Bin/Binra	see Foden, Binra.
Crammer	Med soldier.
Danden	Male Mynah Bird owned by Eunaela Muthea.
Dolika, Metris	Rys doctor from Jitherick.
Donezan	Athenque/Dragon who married Rysa.
Dorlew	Med, Captain of *The Chaser*.
Ebbiui	Kotich shaman from Nu's story of the trapping of the dragons.
Erevo	Med in charge of construction.
Estaen	Athenque named by Zheann.
Foden, Binra	Garesherick Moln's best friend and lieutenant. Med.
Gare/Gares	See Moln, Garesherick.

Gaumio, Artgesy	Med Drill Sergeant.
Genter	Athenque/Dragon.
Ges	Gaumio, Artgesy.
Henkim	Someone being sought in the camps.
Herick	Med rebel to whom King Taelferga surrendered. First king of the Med Kingdom.
Higor	Kotich employee at the shop in Guelph.
Hikiel	See Owem, Hikiel.
Horse	Athenque Zheann first meets as a great dark gray horse.
Jeron, Kwin	Rys. Former student and "epistolary lover" of Jenem. Lives in Kotich and accompanies Zheann to Awasain Jeingsi.
Kaff	Leader of the rebel Rys in Jitdornoi.
Keherth	Author of <u>Ageless Queen</u> and <u>After the Queen</u>.
Kwin	See Jeron, Kwin.
Kwusejeinsye	From Nu's story of the trapping of the dragons. "One Who Accepts the Curse." Name given by Solviya to a non-Kotich who showed up to help the Kotich trap the dragons.
Leed	See Amdiri, Leed.
Libvas	Med captain from Jifreb. AKA: Scar.
Lil	Friend or relative of Kaff who died from Geperra poisoning.
Little General	See Moln, Garesherick.
Little Hedgehog	See Sevem, Zheann.
Lord Roll-in-the-Dirt	Med who accuses Zheann of hexing him.
Luhaxa	Female Rys rebel at Jitdornoi.
Lusa	Someone being sought in the camp.

Medenva	Brother of Rysa. He was rejected by Donezan. Ancestor of the Med people.
Medenva	
Benvor	Half-brother of Esherick and Kathoa.
Esherick	Son of Eswok and Kenora, Prince and king of Med kingdom.
Eswok	King of the Med Kingdom. Husband of Kenora and others. Father of Esherick, Kathoa, Benvor, Trisheri and others.
Kathoa	Son of Eswok and Kenora, brother of Esherick.
Kenora	#1 wife of Eswok, Queen of Med Kingdom.
Metris	See Dolika, Metris.
Moln	
Garesherick	AKA Gare, Gares, Little General, Captain, General) Son of Lamal and Halonca Moln. Captain and later General. Named for his Grandfather.
Halonca	Mother of Garesherick and Hewi Moln, wife of Lamal.
Lamal	Father of Garesherick and Hewi Moln, husband of Halonca. General and advisor to Eswok Medenva and his sons
Mothea, Eunaela	Rys minstrel and soul singer.
Murgka	Athenque/Dragon.
Nuagte	AKA: Nu. Kotich shaman and teacher who goes with Zheann to Awasain Jeingsi.
Nuthov	Overlord of the Kotich tribes in Nu's story of the trapping of the dragons.
Ocojee	Kotich shaman from Nu's story of the trapping of the dragons.

Orn	Village Rys kid.
Owem, Hikiel	Rys, chef at the palace.
Palol	
Etsitty	Son of Naris Palol, apprentice palace steward.
Naris	Rys, Palace Steward. Father of Etsitty and Torweno.
Torweno	Son of Naris. Blacksmith's apprentice.
Parklaw, Estaen	Rys poet for whom Zheann names Estaen.
Rysa	Brother of Medenva. He married Donezan.
Sael, Tahke	Rys carpenter whose shop was next door to Leed's shop.
Scar	See Libvas.
Sendre	Rys family mentioned in chapter 2. One or more of them were Captain Moln's first Rys victims.
Sevem	
Dren	Daughter of Fiwal and Zheann.
Fiwal	Zheann's husband.
Zheann	Main Character, wife of Fiwal, mother of Dren, daughter of Poyen and Ronsath Amdiri, teacher of herbal magic at the jideker in Jitherick, and owner of an herb shop.
Sharn	Athenque/Dragon.
Skwoln	Kotich shaman from Nu's story of trapping the dragons.
Solviya	Kotich shaman from Nu's story of trapping the dragons.
Taelfa	King of the Rys who officially enslaved the Med.

Taelferga	Grandson of Taelfa. King of the Rys who officially freed the Med.
Tanroi	Med friend of Benvor's.
Ti'ilar	Someone Estaen handed back to his mother broken and bloodied by his own hand.
Tinjier	Rys aboard *The Chaser*.
Turisba, Dovo	Med Headmaster at the jideker in Jitherick.
Valenra	Someone being sought in the camp.
Venkis	Athenque/Dragon.
Yenai	Rys cook at the Palace.
Waro, Imeni	Eunaela Mothea's daughter.
Zheann	See Sevem, Zheann
Zunal, Jenem	Rys teacher at the jideker in Jitherick.

Pronunciation Aids:
G	Hard (Get).
J	Soft (Jab).
Z	has the s in measure.

Appendix B: Dates and Times

Tecur has ten months with six-day weeks.

- Days: Divhad, Solim, Tarewo, Igsole, Myot, Uxio.
- Months: Stabut, Ghanys, Grekund, Iazin, Rilowis, Tevarn, Amdoa, Redarm, Troleng, Enoate.

The story beings on Troleng 18. Troleng is also the month in which the Harvest Festival and the anniversary of Taelferga's surrender to Herick.

Days are broken into nine parts: Midnight, Before Sunrise, Sunrise or Sun Ascending, Before High Sun, High Sun, After High Sun, Sun Descending, Sundown/Sunset, Evening or Night or Before Midnight. A third is approximately an hour. A sixth is a half-hour, and a ninth is about 10 minutes.

Appendix C: Places

Jit, Ji, Jut	City, place, or home.
Awasain Jeingsi	Mountain off the coast of the Great Ice Land where the dragons were trapped.
Chornivia	Kingdom south east of the Med Kingdom.
Coilea	Nation north west of the Med Kingdom.
Dattuck	Nation south of the Med kingdom
Great Ice Land	The land of the Kotich
Jideker	"Place or Home of Memories." Use for both schools and libraries
Jifreb	Sea Port north east of Jitherick.
Jitamyas	Village between Jitherick and Jifreb
Jitdornoi	Village between Jitamyas and Jifreb.
Jitherick	City of Herick, capital of the Med Kingdom

Appendix D: Herbs

Herbs and plants play a significant role in the story, and some of them are familiar.

Barberry	Fruit, bark, and roots used to treat gastrointestinal difficulties, to boost the immune system, purify the blood and to treat malaria. The fruit is also used to make jam, jellies, and wine.
Bitters	Not a specific herb, but herbs that make

	food move through the digestive system more easily – laxative.
Bog Berriess	Berries that grow in bogs, like Cranberries.
Buckthorns	Purgative herb.
Camphors	Anti-inflammatory, antifungal, antibacterial.
Carminatives	Not a specific herb but herbs that reduce flatulence (gas.)
Elder Flowers	Purgative herb.
Farams	Herb.
Fennels	Anise.
Fire Thorns	Plant Fiwal and Leed sought in Jifreb. Breaks up ice.
Geperras	Poison that "turns people's arms and legs into ladies' ribbons" and causes both nausea and diarrhea.
Goldenseal	Purgative Herb.
Hiaba	Herb known for its fragrance.
Ice Flower	Plant Fiwal and Leed sought in Jifreb, probably used to break up or melt ice
Lemon Balm	Herb that has lemony scent but spreads aggressively.
Lirgen	Evergreen tree.
Mandrake	Purgative herb.
Mibehen	Stimulant.
Mustard	Herb with a variety of medical uses.
Night Berries	A very tart blue or purple berry that sometimes upsets the stomach and is therefore used as a purgative. Grows in bogs.
Ohema	Herb that inflames the throat and mouth, making it painful to speak or swallow.
Peppermint	Herb used for flavor and to calm stomach issues.

Poke Root	Purgative herb.
Quansk	Hallucinogenic herb.
Rue	Anti-inflammatory herb sometimes used to treat diarrhea.
Senna	Purgative herb.
Simma	Stimulant
Soap Wort	Purgative Herb
Tireshet	Herb that Leed and Fiwal were seeking at Jifreb, probably used to break up or melt ice
Yasaga	Herb that Leed and Fiwal were seeking at Jifreb, probably used to break up or melt ice
Unnamed	The herb used to cause the blisters that killed the Med soldiers. May have been something like Giant Hog Weed

About the Author

Allyn Ransom is a collector of trivia and information, public speaker, poet, author of a family history spanning (according to tradition) all of human history (it's a long story,) and an amateur photographer.

While in college, she read an overview that described the heroic fantasy as a story in which a hero returns to the place where the story began, having changed in ways that the place did not. In the course of her life, she has returned to her home, to two different employers, two church denominations, and, for the past four years, she's traveled in circles between homes in Pennsylvania and Florida in a domestic heroic quest to care for her father. When she decided to return to her dream of writing, it seemed only natural that she return to the genre that spawned the dream.

She has been a library clerk, an administrative assistant, a teacher, a public speaker, a genealogist, a glorified stock clerk, and a purveyor of pretty stones (of the sort one wears,) and a private caregiver. Of her writing, she says that her goal is to write good stories that explore themes and contemporary issues apart from their emotional and personal baggage.